Chihuahua Press
Provincetown MA

First Published in the United States of America
by Chihuahua Press 2025

This is a work of fiction. All of the characters, organizations, and events portrayed in this novel are either products of the author's imagination or are used fictitiously.

An Imperfect Life

KAREN JASPER

CHIHUAHUA PRESS

PROVINCETOWN, MA

Dedication

The story of Christine Macabee isn't my
family's story, but all the love certainly is.

To my own beloved family,

Janet

Jess

Mike

Ryan

Drew

Logan

&

Reese

I can't imagine my life without you.

Acknowledgements

So many people contributed to this book in so many ways, but special thanks to:

Janet Beattie: my partner in life and love. I can't count how many times Janet read and reread the many iterations of this book;

Jessica Cochrane: my daughter. If I were to bundle everything I have ever learned about unconditional love, loyalty, and sacrifice, that bundle would have her name on it, in capital letters;

Laura Horah: proofreader extraordinaire, who shared her time and expertise far beyond what I expected;

Jessica Larson: cover designer, whose clever idea to highlight 'easter egg' clues on the front cover was exceeded only by her patience with my daily changes and rewrites;

Bill Michalski: who after a long absence, magically reappeared to design and format the interior pages;

Mairead Reddy: my friend, sage, and graphic designer, always willing to lend me an ear, hand, an idea, or a fix-it;

I'd be remiss not to thank two social media groups whose members are still answering my non-stop questions about writing, resources, and publishing tips. Thank you to the Women Writers, Editors, Agents Group; and the Self-Publishing Support Group.

And finally, thank you to you, dear reader, for supporting my work and cheering me on. You're wind for my sails. ♥

STRONG ARMS
2012
By Christine Macabee

I will catch you in the free fall
Should life become a grinding haul.
I will help you to your chair
Where you can play some solitaire.
I will stand in front of words and trains
Anytime they cause you pain.
And anything that blocks your step
I will beat back to safety's depth.
You've done all this for me
With simple generosity.
You complement all that I lack:
I just hope I give it back!

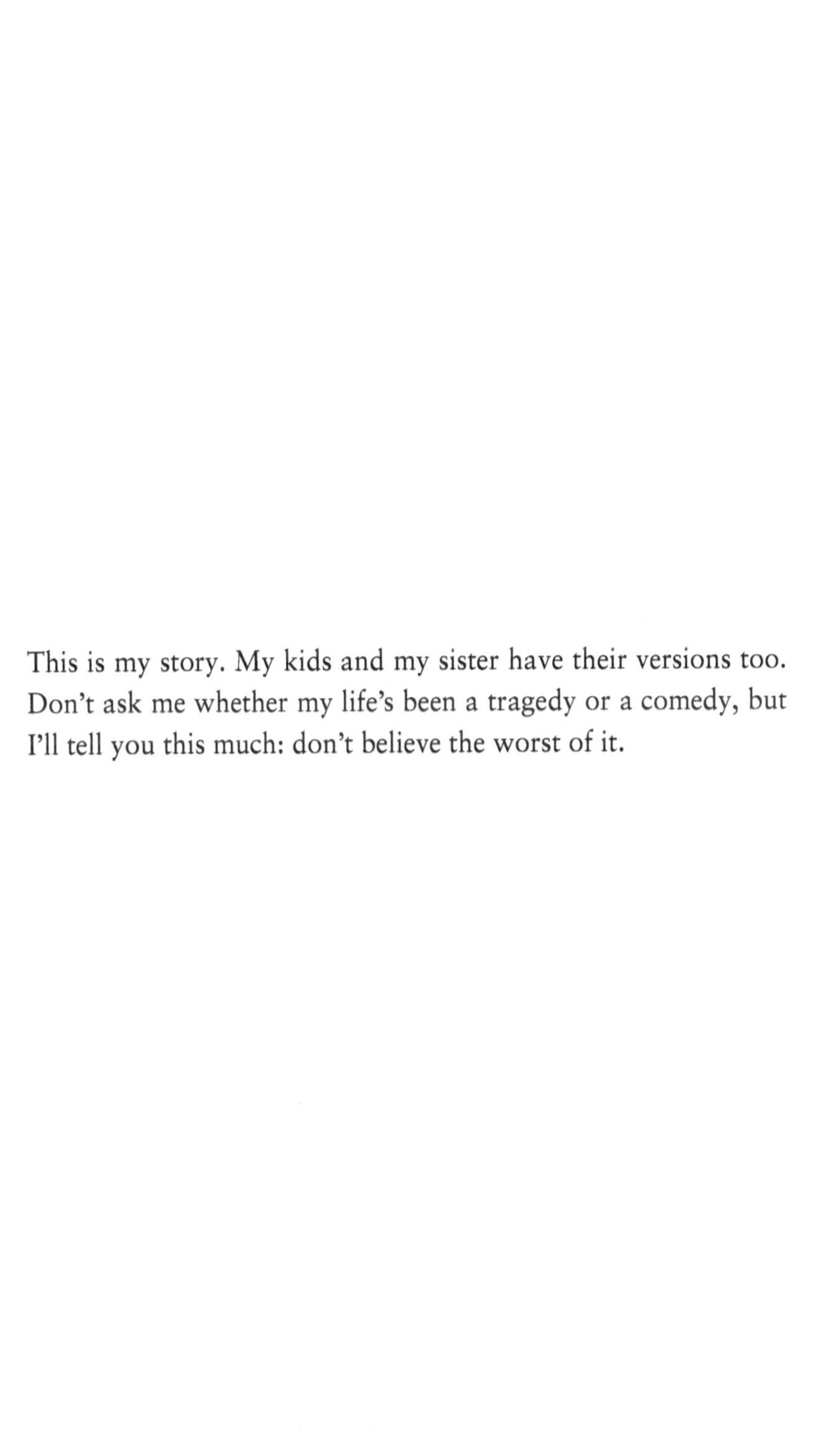

This is my story. My kids and my sister have their versions too. Don't ask me whether my life's been a tragedy or a comedy, but I'll tell you this much: don't believe the worst of it.

PART 1

The Early Years

1

Christine
1960

On a gray damp morning when both our parents were consumed by either alcohol or anger, my sister Louise dragged her suitcase down the back stairway and left me for good. We'd both been up since five, barely speaking but not out of each other's sight. I helped her lug that musty suitcase to the kitchen and out the back door.

Daddy was long gone and Mommy was still asleep when the giant black car pulled into the driveway. No one got out, but the engine kept running. Louise looked at me in the saddest way I'd ever seen. And truly, I don't think there was a worse moment for me in all my childhood. She put her hands on my shoulders and awkwardly pulled me to her. She smelled of that weird Shalimar perfume.

"Pip, it's going to be alright. You'll see."

I couldn't speak. Louise wiped my face with both her hands.

"I want you to stand at this window and wave to me until you can't see the car anymore," she said.

I nodded. And I sobbed. Louise wrapped her arms around me again. She kissed the top of my head, something she had never done before. "Stay out of their way," she cautioned. "I put a five-dollar bill under your pillow. That should keep you in school lunches until I come back, and then I'll give you more."

I grasped onto a ray of hope. "When? When will you come back?"

"I'm pretty sure in three weeks. Christine, remember: I'm marrying God, but they told me I can still be your sister too. Don't forget that."

I watched Louise drag that suitcase to the driveway. She looked back at me once, waved, and disappeared into the back seat of that giant car. A man came across from the driver's side, closed the passenger door, and put the suitcase in the trunk. I stood at the window as she asked, and I waved as I watched her go to the life she needed. My eyes tried to hold that black car back, but it got smaller and smaller until it was gone from my sight.

2

Four years older than me, my sister Louise needled her way into my affairs from the very beginning. Even in sixth grade, she was tall and proper, and every day she balanced books on her head for good posture, determined to control what she could. When she turned sixteen, she wore her hair up in a bun, explaining her old lady look by referencing some hair stylist in *Seventeen Magazine*. In my eyes, Louise was grown-up her whole life. If she was ever a little kid, I didn't know it.

I don't know how she turned out holier-than-thou, but by the summer I turned twelve, Louise had become a bona fide Catholic groupie. She went to Christian Doctrine classes every Thursday after school, she never missed Sunday Mass, and she said the rosary in our shared bedroom every night, in secret like a refugee.

Our parents believed in very little beyond the daily Eucharist of my father's beer and my mother's gin. God was an enemy in our house, but Louise knew better. She was in tenth grade when she came home with a pair of rosary beads given to her by Patti Mancelli, a classmate who also taught her the words to the prayer, 'Our Father.'

"Look what I have," she showed me, carefully pulling the rosaries from a small black velvet pouch and holding them in the palms of both hands. "These are special, Christine. They've been blessed by God the Father."

I could tell Louise felt something powerful from them. She hung the beads gently on her bedpost.

"They'll keep us both safe," she assured me.

But that very night, our own father burst into our bedroom. Who knows how, but he honed in on the rosary beads and had a fit.

"No way!" he thundered. "Get those goddamn beads out of here, now." And for good measure, despite Louise's shock and wellspring of tears, he added, "There is no goddamn God, and even if there was, he sure as hell hasn't done a goddamn good thing in this house."

Louise was flabbergasted. "Throw them away, now!" he commanded. As if apologizing for what she was about to do, she cupped her fingers around the rosaries and walked to the little white wicker wastebasket between our beds. She leaned over and placed them inside. Daddy scowled until she stood up again, then he stormed out without saying another word.

"Oh, my God," Louise whispered. "Patti told me to take extra care of the rosary beads, to never let them get tangled, and not to ever lose them or throw them away. She said it would be a cardinal sin if I wasn't careful and that God would be very upset with me."

She waited until it was dark and thought I was asleep. I heard her pull the rosaries from the waste basket, return them to their black velvet pouch, and tuck them between her mattress and box spring. Every night for the next two years, she welcomed the blessing of one Father and risked the wrath of another, caressing those beads in her hands, under her pillow, muffling a strand of 'Hail Mary' prayers into her top sheet. Then, she quietly slid out of bed and returned the rosaries back under the mattress.

We never knew why my father hated God so much. During one of her infrequent visits, Grandma Alice mentioned a car accident that killed my father's baby brother and left him in a foster home for two years. Louise concluded that would be a good reason for an uninformed person to stop believing. But I don't think my father ever believed. He just hated everything.

My mother was ninety-nine percent oblivious a hundred percent of the time, and even though Daddy resented Louise and me, sometimes he also felt responsible for us. He was gruff and bitter, but every so often a softer quality snuck out, unlike our mother, who vacillated between drunken stupor and tear-filled guilt. You could almost touch Daddy's disdain for Mommy's weakness. He left the house every morning by 5:30 a.m., even on weekends, and most of the time he didn't come home before seven at night. He'd say a quick hello to Louise and me, ask if Mommy had eaten anything, and head upstairs, holing up in the bathroom, sometimes for an hour. When he finally came out, he'd sit with Mommy in the living room for a few minutes and yell at Louise to make her some toast. When the grandmother clock pinged at eight-thirty, he walked us upstairs, opened our bedroom door, clicked his teeth the way a cattle herder does, and commanded Louise and me to bed. We didn't dare object.

But every so often he leaned down and ran the back of his finger across my face.

"Sleep tight, kiddo," he'd grumble.

Daddy's reaction to the rosary beads strengthened Louise's interest in convent life. I think that one event also extinguished any remaining loyalty she may have had toward our parents.

"It's bad enough they don't go to church," Louise told me, "but to curse God—that's as bad as it gets. I refuse to be condemned to hell or even purgatory just because our parents are sinners."

Louise began attending weekly Mass with Patti Mancelli's family, and she arranged to be baptized and confirmed, thanks to Sister Mary Agnes, a local nun who must have decided to save Louise.

"How come you never take me to Mass with you?" I asked.

"I can't," Louise answered. "There's only room in Patti's car for me, and besides, God knows all about you. He takes care of both of us."

That was fine with me. After the rosary bead explosion, I had no interest in church because I was too afraid of my father's reaction. Besides, at the tender age of almost twelve, I didn't need God because I had Louise. And, I also had Sabrina.

3

1952

Don't worry. I'm here too.

I was in first grade when my imaginary friend Sabrina first appeared. Louise hadn't arrived home from school yet, when my mother had clutched the kitchen tablecloth to keep herself from falling, and everything on it crashed to the floor, including a glass vase that had belonged to my Grandma Alice. Before I could clean up the mess, my father came home and saw the vase smashed in pieces. His bitterness exploded into rage.

"Damn you," he hissed. He grabbed my mother's wrists, pushed her backwards, and she fell onto the blue leather armchair he'd also inherited from his mother. If she had fallen three inches to the left or the right, I think she would have cracked her head open.

Daddy glared. "I'm so sick of you." His whole body shook and he let loose a string of "Goddamns" and even the F word before he snatched his keys from the hook on the wall and slammed the kitchen door so hard the curtain fell off and crumpled in a heap on the floor. He was back in fifteen minutes, breathing heavily, wringing his hands all around his head, and jiggling from one foot to the other.

"You can't be trusted," he said, fuming. My mother looked confused, trying to understand him. "I'm sick of cleaning up after you." He shook his head back and forth and ignored me. I didn't dare make an extra move or even look at him. I just swept up the broken glass as quietly as I could.

When a sliver of glass sliced my right thumb, I pressed my bloody finger in a dish towel, ran upstairs, and hid in my bedroom, pleading over and over, *Please come home, Louise, please, please come home now.* I could hear them downstairs.

"I've had it, Margaret. Every goddamn day I come home and wonder what damage you've done. If it's not broken glass, it's puke in the bathroom."

"I'm sick, Thomas," Mommy slurred. "You should be nicer to me. Christine's nicer to me than you are."

I'd heard this back and forth so many times. I tried to distract my fear by humming the melody of "Wheels on the Bus." That normally helped me stay calm, but this time, I heard a voice.

T-T-T-They get mad at me too. Does it scare you when they get mad? It scares me.

I was totally startled. It was like listening to a littler version of myself, but not exactly. There was a maturity in how precisely the words were pronounced. *But don't worry,* the voice added, a little more confident. *I know where we can go when they yell too loud.*

"Where?" I asked. It was crazy that I responded.

Either under the bed or way back in the closet, way in the corner. This was definitely a child speaking. *And if Daddy comes looking for us, you can stay there and I'll pretend to be you.*

"How would you do that?"

I know how, she said.

"Who are you?"

I'm Sabrina. I'm your friend.

I came to learn that Sabrina was my age, looked just like me, liked everything I liked, and she stepped in and took my place when I got slapped or pushed for moving too slowly or for trying to help my mother reach the bathroom in time. One time she took my place and pulled Mommy off Louise when even my smart, brave sister was afraid. Right away I knew it wasn't fair that Sabrina took all the blows, and I worried about that part. Also, I was old enough that I knew this wasn't normal. I knew that Sabrina couldn't possibly be real, but I was desperate.

"Maybe we should share the bad stuff," I whispered to her one night after I'd been whacked in the face. It was dark and I was huddled in bed. Louise had brought me some ice wrapped in a dish towel.

Sabrina whispered back, *No, it's okay. I can take care of us, Chrissy. It didn't hurt. Don't worry.*

"Don't be saying that stuff," Louise warned me when I told her about Sabrina. "You could end up in a mental hospital if you talk to imaginary people."

After that I was careful to never mention Sabrina to Louise or to anyone else, and I was careful when and how Sabrina stepped in for me. Sometimes I insisted that she back down and keep quiet. She tried to comply, but whenever I walked past the playground on my way home from school, she couldn't contain her excitement. I knew she was peeking out through my eyes, hoping for a quick stop on the swings or a jettison down the circular slide. I never minded—we both deserved some fun.

So, between Sabrina and Louise stepping in, and me knowing when to get out of the way, my childhood worked out pretty well—except for my eleventh birthday.

My teacher surprised me with cupcakes for the whole class, and all the kids sang "Happy Birthday" to me. Probably because

I was on cloud nine when I got home, I asked my mother if she could braid my hair. Her eyes widened and she sat up straight.

"Are you kidding me?" she screamed. "You should be helping me, not the other way around. All you kids do is take." She was furious.

"You're grounded!" Before I could say a word, she screamed again. "Get in the coat closet and close the door. You stay there until I let you out." This was something new and it was scary.

A minute later, she opened the door just wide enough to throw an empty coffee can at me. "If you have to pee, use the goddamn coffee can."

We're okay, Chrissy. Don't be scared. This time Sabrina's assurance didn't help. It was pitch black in that closet and the coats smelled like mothballs. Fortunately, my banishment was over almost before it began.

"Help!" Mommy screamed. "I need the bathroom. Now!"

I pushed open the closet door and ran to her. I held her up with my arm around her waist until she reached the toilet. Then I waited and helped her back to the winged-back chair she just about lived in.

Sabrina was disgusted. *This was the worst. I'll lock her in a closet someday,* she said, *and the next time, we should call the police.*

When Sabrina made threats like that, I promised her playground time. One time I gave her my entire set of marbles to keep her quiet. I couldn't figure her out. Was it possible that she was real? Were there two of me? Most of the time she was feistier than I ever dared to be, and sometimes she was dangerously more impulsive. I worried about that. Sabrina took the blows and protected me, but sometimes she got so mad I had to protect her, too. I can't even count the number of times I kept things from escalating. One or two of my mother's slaps or screams were always better than a full-fledged knock-around. Usually Sabrina agreed with me, but if I had left it up to her, there would have been times we didn't back down.

It's funny describing her, because beneath the feisty part, Sabrina was as scared as me. But she ended up with my hardest memories. Maybe I wouldn't be so strong and optimistic if Sabrina hadn't protected me.

I realize that this little girl stuff makes me sound like a certified nutcase. But what I knew from the first time Sabrina spoke to me was that I deserved a normal life. I deserved to be happy, to grow up safe, to get married and have kids and be the best mother. I was lucky that I had protection from Sabrina, and later on, from poetry. And after that, from my fantasy husband, John Denver.

Unfortunately, none of these things helped fill my hungry belly. That part was left to Louise and me.

4

Being hungry was no fun, but being embarrassed was worse.

"What's in your lunchbox today?" Ann Capocchio asked me every day. She always showed me hers: a peanut butter sandwich, a brownie wrapped in a Mickey Mouse Club napkin, baby carrots, and cheese whiz with crackers.

This was not my kindergarten lunchbox. Not even close.

"I have a Milky Way." I tried to sound cheerful. This was my mother's favorite candy bar and the one thing she kept stocked.

Ann knew I had no real lunch, so I think showing me hers was second best to sharing her bounty with me. The teacher gave everyone their own carton of milk, but I made sure she didn't know that all I had was the candy bar. My parents would have exploded if my school ever called them about my lunch.

About two weeks after the start of school Louise, as usual, came up with a plan.

"You know that jar of peanut butter we hide in the shed? Let's hide some crackers, too, and some days we can make you a cracker sandwich. And if we can't do that, you can stop at Mr. LaRosa's store and ask him for some bread. He's nice that way."

My hunger wasn't just about food: I wanted my mother to care about me. Just once, I wanted to come first. It was safe for my five-year-old self to walk the three blocks home from school. But when I got home, every day I had to push aside mounds of half-eaten food and dirty dishes just so I could put my lunchbox, worksheets and teacher notices on the kitchen counter. I always looked around and imagined something different, as if I might reshape my childhood from sheer will. I wanted my mother to look at my papers, to be excited for me. But except for Tuesdays, when she somehow managed to take a cab to have her hair and nails done, every day was the same. She sat in the living room, her body sunken in her chair, her legs flopped apart and her head limp on her chest. Sometimes her mouth was wide open and I hated that. Her arms hung over the arm cushions, and her fancy fingernails dangled down like sharp pencils just above the Victorian rug. She barely looked up at me, and sometimes she'd grunt and weakly lift her hand.

"Hiya," she'd mumble. "Get me some toast, will you? And clean up this mess."

Most days she had thrown up on the rug. I hurried to clean it before Louise showed up, and both of us made sure there were no messes anywhere before Daddy got home. He went ballistic when Mommy messed things up. Sometimes he screamed so loud that Louise and I would hide in the garage, even in the cold rain.

When I got older, it made me sad to remember my mother in such a bad way, because even Louise said there were a few good times in our house. Maybe once a year, when her parents, my Grandma Moo Moo and Grampy, came from Las Vegas to visit, Mommy took a shower and got dressed, and one time she actually cooked fried chicken and made mashed potatoes. And once she sang "Goodnight Irene" to me, almost better than Ronnie Gilbert. Another time she asked Daddy to bring home a butter-cream frosted chocolate cake from the Waltham Supermarket bakery for Louise's birthday.

My best memory of all was my mother sitting in her chair, braiding my too-frizzy red hair. She did this twice, and her fingers were soft and she was extra careful not to hurt me. It felt wonderful.

"Love you Chrissy," she whispered one time. She was slurring like crazy but I knew this was important.

"I love you too, Mommy."

"Oh good," she said. "Because Mommy needs you, baby."

That moment was as real as the neglect. But how does a kid handle good memories when they're so tangled up in bad ones? How does not really having a mother affect a kid? Without Louise and Sabrina, there was no way I would have ended up okay. I was lucky. And, just before my twelfth birthday, another huge safety net fell into my lap.

5

1959

I was not the kind of kid who went to summer camp. I was skinny and poor, and my crumbled clothes and wild red hair—inherited from Grandma Moo Moo and periodically cut by my father in one minute flat—made me look like an orphan. But at twelve years old, while Louise turned to God, I miraculously found Dr. Seuss and Robert Frost.

A year earlier, my sixth-grade teacher Mrs. Erickson had taught my class how to write an ionic pentameter poem, with four lines and two rhymes. She gave us the choice of four subjects to write about: nature, friends, summer, or birthdays. My choice was easy, as I knew nothing about nature and my summers and birthdays were totally iffy. So that left friends.

Ann Capocchio was still showing me her jam-packed lunch box and making not-so-subtle comparisons to my scarcities, but I considered her my best friend. I don't remember exactly what I wrote, something about friends who don't bend and help you mend in the end. Maybe because nobody else rhymed, Mrs. Erickson chose my poem to hang on the wall outside our class-room. She put a giant pink construction paper arrow above it with a sign that said *Poem of the Month, by Christine M.*

I still remember that giant arrow pointing to my four-line poem. It was the first time I knew what it felt like to be special, to feel worthy and good enough. Mrs. Erickson's acknowledgement got things rolling for me. I was ready the next year when I, a nondescript scrawny seventh-grader, got chosen for a free week at Camp Meadowbrook.

My teacher Mrs. Nelson handed me a sealed envelope with the South Junior High School insignia on it. Whatever it might say, I knew right away there would be a problem at home. I tucked the envelope in my underpants and waited for Louise to come home. Then I waited until she went upstairs to change her clothes. It was a big deal for us to have clean school clothes period, so every day Louise folded up one of her two respectable school outfits— either her white blouse and black skirt or her blue sweater and brown pleated skirt—and carefully put them back in her dresser. When I heard the bureau drawer close, I tiptoed past my mother and up the stairs to our bedroom, where I handed Louise the letter. She looked at me suspiciously and opened the envelope. I watched her read it to herself and shake her head.

"Tell me, Louise," I said. "What is it?"

In a low voice, she read it out loud:

Dear Mr. and Mrs. Martin:

Your daughter Christine has been nominated for a Young Scholar award at our school. Students who demonstrate exemplary conduct and high scholastic potential are selected on the basis of achievement and need. I am pleased to inform you that Christine has been awarded a one-week, fully paid scholarship at Meadowbrook Summer Camp for the summer season this year. The camp runs from Monday through Friday, 9 a.m. to 4 p.m., during the second week in July and includes one sleepover. Transportation is not provided, but if your family meets our financial needs criteria, she will qualify for a city bus voucher.

Activities include daily swimming lessons, supervised boating on Lake Cochituate, and in Christine's case, based on her preference, writing and poetry classes. In order to obtain your permission for this program, please complete the enclosed application and return it to me no later than April 15.

Sincerely,
Mrs. Andrea Nelson
Seventh-Grade Teacher

Louise put the letter down on her bed before she looked up at me. She looked very sad. "Christine, this is great. It shows how smart you are." She stopped. "But you can't do it."

"Why not, Louise?" My chest tightened.

"Because Mom and Dad would never drive you to camp and they would never agree to financial aid."

"What? Why?! That's not fair!" I was mad.

Louise spoke calmly, "Well, you can show Mom this letter if you want to see for yourself."

"Louise, I'm twelve. Is this going to be my life? It's bad enough at home, but I can't even do something good at school?"

"Let me think about it, Pip." Louise called me Pip when she tried to sound extra kind.

Three days later, my almost sixteen-year-old sister handed me back the letter, my mother's forged signature scribbled large on the authorization form.

"Shhh," Louise said. "It's all set. You're going."

"But how?"

"I asked Sister Mary Agnes and she'll drive you back and forth. She already cleared it with Mom."

"How, Louise?"

Louise had her determined, sneaky look on her face. "Sister showed up at the beauty parlor yesterday, and she was so enthusiastic and loud about it, Mom didn't dare say no."

"So why did you sign the form instead of Mom?"

Louise chuckled. "Christine, let's not push your luck. You're going, and there's no reason to add another step to it."

6

That week at summer camp, poetry crawled into my backpack and never left.

Camp Meadowbrook was divided into pods based on interests: Archie's Athletes, Wanda's Writers, Danny's Dancers, Manny's Musicals, and Sally's Scientists. Once a day everyone had swim and boat time on a lake, and on the last night, we had an amazing sleepover in the giant dining hall. We sat around a campfire and listened to ghost stories and guitar music. All week, we ate meals together: scrambled eggs and bacon for breakfast, and for lunch or dinner, hot dogs, corn on the cob with butter, macaroni salad, pickles, cookies and cupcakes. It was pure heaven.

The best part of all was the three solid hours I spent in the Wanda's Writers class with Mr. Brennan, every day for a whole week. There were eight of us—fifth to eighth graders, all eager to play with words. I still remember when Mr. Brennan read Robert Frost out loud:

"Two roads diverged in a wood and I—
I took the one less traveled by,
And that has made all the difference."

The words were so simple, but the message hit me like a ton of bricks. Heck, if I practiced, maybe I could write poems like that. And even more important, I understood what Robert Frost meant, because I was also on a road less traveled—not because of any courageous choice, but because I had to be.

I wrote a poem about courage and read it out loud on the last day of camp:

> Come on Christine, you can do it
> You should act as if you knew it
> And when you're wrong and grind to a halt
> Even then, it's not your fault.
> Give things a try, learn as you go
> Study hard and you will know
> Your life will shine and will be bright
> So don't feel bad, it will be alright.

All the kids and Mr. Brennan clapped. Afterwards I tucked the poem in my underpants for the drive home. I didn't have parents who took care of me, but I wasn't alone either. Louise had God the Father and now I had her, Sabrina, and Robert Frost. I had *choices*, just like the two roads.

Me, a little girl who could help herself with words and ideas: that says something hopeful, don't you think? Somehow, even through the worst of it, I grew up with hope, and after that week at Meadowbrook, I knew my hope would really make all the difference.

7

My excitement didn't last. Louise waited until we had changed from our school clothes and Mommy was passed out in her chair.

"I need to talk to you, Christine."

Right away, I knew this was serious. I could tell because Louise sounded more concerned than bossy. I had no idea what she might say, because after my week at Meadowbrook, I was in good shape.

"Okay, talk," I said flippantly. "What's it about?"

"It's about Sabrina."

"What about Sabrina?" This was the first time ever that Louise had voluntarily mentioned her.

"I went to the library and looked up people who have imaginary friends." She paused to see my reaction so far, which was more confused than curious. "I found this psychology book and I learned a lot, Christine. The book said that a person who makes up someone who's not real does that because they need someone else to handle their pain."

"That makes sense," I said. "That's what Sabrina's done for me. But what pain are you talking about? We're both in pretty good shape, aren't we?" I asked.

Louise was quick to answer. "In your case, the pain of having a mother and father who drink. And especially having a mother who yells and sometimes hits you."

"But what's wrong with Sabrina taking my place when that happens, except, of course, it's not fair to her either."

"That answer is exactly my point," Louise said. "She's not real and you make her sound real. The book called this dissociation. I looked up that word and it means stepping out of your body and not being in reality. It's serious."

"But how can it be serious if it helps me?"

Louise had a ready answer. "People have to see a psychiatrist when they start talking to people who aren't there." She looked at me straight on. "Do you know Sabrina isn't real?"

"Of course I do!" I answered. "Louise, when we were little, we both had our Ginny dolls, and you talked to yours like she was real. I remember you asked her if she wanted candy, and you tucked her in your bed with you at night. How is Sabrina different?"

"The difference is whether you actually KNOW that Sabrina can't do a darn thing to protect you, because she doesn't exist."

"Poems don't exist either, but they protect me too."

Louise looked stumped. She must have decided it was time to get to the point. "Look Christine, do you think you should see a psychiatrist? I can't have my sister living in a make-believe world just because our real world is bad."

"Louise, Sabrina doesn't even show up very much anymore. I know what's real and what isn't. I'm just a normal kid trying to make the best of bad parents. But I'll tell you, the day Mommy pushed me into the closet and slammed the door on me, it helped me to think that Sabrina was there with me, because then I didn't feel alone. Plus, I always call for you first, but sometimes you're not around. I think you should be happy that I've had someone, real or not, to help me out."

Louise looked oddly relieved. She checked in one more time.

"So, you know she's not real?"

"Of course I know. But she's still my friend. Sort of."

"You can't mention Sabrina to anyone but me."

"You've told me that before. Actually, you've told me never to mention her to anyone, including you. But okay, if anything weird happens, I'll tell you."

"Fine," Louise said. "And now that you're older, you might think about keeping a lucky charm in your pocket. You can rub it for good luck when you're in a jam."

"You're kidding me! For real, you have a lucky charm?"

Louise grinned. "Yup. That and my rosary beads."

8

1960

It was true that Sabrina rarely showed up anymore. And things really began to change when I hit puberty. Sabrina started having panic attacks, and sometimes she couldn't stop crying, no matter what. More than once, when my shoulders shook like an unhinged washing machine, I knew that it was Sabrina's doing because I tried to never cry.

Since my week at Meadowbrook, when things got really bad at home, I stayed in my bedroom and read poems. I also got better at taking quick care of my mother's demands so she wasn't as mean. I was almost thirteen, old enough not be pushed around so easily. But one day, when my mother threw a vase in my direction and I barely made it upstairs in one piece, Sabrina reappeared.

I'm still here, Chrissy.

Louise kept telling me I was too old and it was too weird to talk to Sabrina. I knew she was right, but I wasn't sure how to handle it. Sabrina had done so much for me. I didn't want to hurt her. Plus, where would she go?

"It's okay, Sabrina. Now that I'm older, I can handle her."

I know, you don't need me so much. You're older and smarter. And you have Louise. And you have poems.

I felt bad. "We can still go to the playground," I said. But we both knew better. I was growing up. I could take care of myself. Every so often I heard her little voice say *Yay! Good job!* and cheer me on, or *Be careful.* But as of my thirteenth birthday, I had confidence. I had poems. And I had Louise.

Until I didn't.

9

Louise joined the convent three days after her high school graduation. It was a total shock to everyone except Sister Mary Agnes.

We were at Burger King sharing French fries when she told me the details. First, she showed me a ring on her finger. She said it was from 'The Lord.' Then she licked the straw from our chocolate milkshake and cleared her throat.

"Pip, Sister Mary Agnes is helping me to join the Sisters of Mercy."

I knew I should be happy for her. "That's great, Louise. But what is it? Is it a special club?"

"No," Louise said. "It's a convent." She cleared her throat again. "I have to live there."

"Live there? Not home? Not with me?" My whole body tightened. Things would change; I could tell right away.

According to Louise, I was old enough to get myself out of my parents' way. But the thought of losing my sister was paralyzing. I stopped eating and I cried for a week. At first Louise ignored my swollen eyes, but finally, she huffed into our bedroom, pulled out the wooden pirate's chest she kept under her bed, and took a two-dollar bill from it.

"Come on, Pip, we're going to Burger King and we're going to figure this out."

I never minded the walk up Moody Street and onto Main. It was always cause for celebration, except for the time my creepy fourth-grade classmate Johnnie Hardwick tried to pull my pants down.

"Listen Pip, I have to join the convent. God has called me. People don't have a choice in things like this; you just have to do it. I could go to hell if I don't."

I was crying before she finished her sentence.

"Cut that out," Louise said. "This means you and I will have a special way for God to protect us, not just now but forever. And I've asked Patti to keep an eye on you."

I rolled my eyes: Patti was too preoccupied with her boyfriend Buddy the drummer to keep an eye on anything else, and certainly not on me.

"Plus," Louise continued, "they said I could come home at least one weekend a month. I told them about you and they said that qualifies as community work. And besides, it takes two full years before I'll be an official sister. By then you won't need me as much."

I looked for some doubt on my sister's face and in the way she waved her hands around when she talked to me, but all I saw was determination. I was going to lose her. It was the biggest crisis of my life. I dropped my French fry and sat there in Burger King and cried.

"Stop! This is not just any convent," Louise snapped. "The Sisters of Mercy are different. For one thing, most normal nuns stay inside and they don't leave, but the Sisters of Mercy walk around and visit poor people in their homes and sick people in hospitals. I'll have to pray a lot, but I won't be stuck inside. I can have a life outside, Christine, and you'll be in it."

This new information sounded a little better, but not by much. I tried to take it in, but all that mattered was Louise was leaving me.

"Can we still come to Burger King sometimes?"

Louise sighed. "I honestly don't know if I'll be allowed to go to Burger King. I'll ask, okay?" My deflation was so apparent. "And if not," she said, "we'll go somewhere else."

"Where?" I needed a picture I could look to.

"The park. Or maybe you could come and visit me where I live."

That grabbed my attention. "That sounds good. Could I live with you, Louise?"

This one true question was now laid bare. Louise knew there was no good answer.

"Christine," she said. "You can't, but you'll be okay. Don't worry about that stuff now. Besides, nothing happens until I take my vows."

"How long does that take? And can I live with you after that?"

Louise pivoted. "The vows take time. There's three of them: first poverty, then chastity, and then obedience." She chuckled. "The obedience one worries me!"

Myself, the word "chastity" worried me. I didn't understand what it meant, but I remembered it had something to do with sex—not that I understood sex either.

"What does chastity mean?"

"It means I won't have any other important relationship except my life with God. No boyfriends, no husbands. Just God."

This was even worse than I thought. By now terror found its way to my arms and legs and I started shaking. Even Louise knew that part was too much. She corrected herself.

"Except for you, Christine. They told me I will always be able to love my sister. Just because I'm going to marry God doesn't mean I have to leave you."

"Promise?" I begged. I was desperate. "Louise, maybe I could join the convent too?"

"No way," she answered. "You're too young; you have to finish school, plus I don't think marrying God is the right thing for you. If it was, you wouldn't need that Sabrina. You have her, Christine. I have God." She paused. "But I promise, I won't ever leave you."

"I don't have Sabrina anymore," I said. "I just have poems now."

"Well, okay," Louise said. "That counts."

My world crumpled in that Burger King. Whatever life I would have ahead, I was sure it would be small and lonely. Sabrina was pretty much gone, but now, a thousand times worse, my sister would be gone too.

I thought Louise might cry too. She had to save herself, that's all. I didn't know until years later that she hoped the Sisters of Mercy might also save me.

10

Dear Christine, well, I'm here. I'm in a second-floor apartment in Hartford, Connecticut with three other girls. There are two more girls and a very strict sister who live on the first floor and we all eat meals together. I share a bedroom with a girl named Deloris and she keeps her night light on all night, and she talks to herself. I told her she's keeping me up, and she said she'll try to talk lower, but there's nothing she can do about the light because she says she needs it to fall asleep. I'm supposed to get along with everyone so I can't really complain, but I have to figure out some way to get that light off.

I reminded the head sister that I need to go home at least once a month to make sure you're doing okay and she said that is fine. They also said I can take you to Burger King! So I'll see you soon. How are things at home? I hope you have enough food. The sisters are taking up a money collection to make sure I can give you enough every month. So don't worry!

Your loving sister, Louise

Louise's vow of poverty meant she would be dependent on the nuns for whatever she needed. The brochure she gave me said that whatever money the sisters earned went into a common fund to help people in need. That must have been where I came in, because Louise managed to give me at least five dollars and sometimes even a little more every month. I couldn't bring food home because my father would have a conniption, but if I left for school even five minutes early, I could stop at LaRosa's and pick up something good for my lunchbox. Usually I bought two slices of American cheese, two slices of turkey, and grapes or an apple. I also kept an eye on the jar of peanut butter in the shed so I never went completely hungry. This part of Louise's marriage with God benefited me, and I made sure my new and improved lunches found their way to Ann Capocchio's eyes.

Other than that, life was not good without Louise. She wrote to me every week, telling me she was learning to imitate Jesus. I didn't like that: I wanted her to keep being herself. In her first month working for God, she was assigned to a food pantry, and after that she started tutoring first graders at an elementary school. I laughed at that because besides me, Louise had no patience with kids. I knew she wouldn't be like God with those kids.

Louise did her best to come home one weekend a month. We still went to Burger King, but it wasn't the same. Daddy expected us to catch up on cleaning, washing, and trash pile-ups. Louise didn't exactly complain, but she wasn't happy like she used to be. Sometimes when I wanted to talk to her, she was too tired, and other times she just stared into space.

"Louise, you have to talk to me. Why are you being so mean?"

"I'm not mean, Christine. I have a lot on my mind. This novitiate phase, I'll have to pray more, be nicer to people, and get ready for my marriage with God. It's a lot of pressure, and then Daddy lays all these chores on us."

This marriage to God always scared the bejesus out of me. "What if you don't want to marry God? Is there any way you could marry me instead?"

I knew this was a ridiculous suggestion, but I was desperate.

Louise rolled her eyes. "You know sisters don't marry each other! We'd get arrested. But I have to marry God, that's a requirement. It's the being so nice to everyone that's the hardest. Some of the girls drive me crazy. That Deloris still sneaks her night light on as soon as she thinks I'm asleep. It's a lot of pressure."

"You can scream at me, Louise."

My offer seemed to stir something in her because she sat beside me on the bed and put her hand on my knee. "Pip, I feel terrible knowing you're here without me. It's worse when I come home and see the situation for myself. But you have to take care of yourself; God wants you to do that."

"He's never said that to me," I replied. "I don't mind if he wants to talk to me but he never does."

"He talks, Christine. But maybe he thinks it's better if you hear it from me."

11

1961

When Louise finished her novitiate year, she'd be ready to make those big three vows and then God could send her anywhere, not just in Connecticut or the United States, but even to another country. By the time she was eighteen and I was fourteen, my sister could be gone for good. It was bad enough to have a nun for a sister, but to maybe see her all of once a year, if that—the thought was enough to ruin my entire life.

The Sisters of Mercy may have been perfect for Louise, but she only lasted a year. She wouldn't tell me what really happened, but apparently the Head Mother Superior decided Louise was not cut out for an apostolic life. When given the option of being expelled or voluntarily leaving, Louise chose the latter, but not before she found a purple magic marker and wrote her name with a halo over it in one of the bathroom stalls.

Lugging her suitcase and wearing a guilty grin, Louise came home as sanctimonious as ever, ready to resume Sunday Mass with Patti Mancelli.

"Are you mad at God for being back home?" I asked.

"Never," Louise answered. "God always does the right thing, even when something seems confusing." She grinned. "Besides, here I am. Aren't you glad?"

I was in ninth grade and weighing whether to let Anthony Guidano touch my breasts. Our mother had miraculously stopped drinking six weeks before Louise's return home, but I heard my father say that the damage to her memory and liver was permanent. Plus, it was obvious. Mommy was present, but she was also blank. She spent a lot of time in bed, and when she was up, she had to balance herself on the furniture or the kitchen counter so she wouldn't fall. She still took a cab to the beauty parlor every Tuesday, and once or twice she made herself scrambled eggs, but other than that, she was more a zombie than a mother.

Anyway, with Louise back, things were easier for me—except my freewheeling privacy came to a halt. She kept track of my homework and curfews, and she obnoxiously read my diary about Anthony and my breasts.

"Absolutely NOT!" she screamed out of the blue one afternoon when my mother was still at the beauty parlor. Standing outside our bedroom door huffing and puffing, she demanded that I get myself upstairs immediately. She shook my diary above her head.

"Listen to me, Pip. Not at thirteen, not at sixteen. Your body is a vessel of God. You have to keep it chaste until you get married."

I was so startled that I overlooked the fact that she had no right to go through my things.

"What are you talking about? And what does 'chaste' mean?"

"It means nobody touches your privates!"

I tried to redirect her. "What about kissing?" This was actually a timely question because Anthony had kissed me with his tongue and I liked it. "Are you sure you know about this, Louise? Anthony told me if I let him touch my boobs, I will feel it down here and it will be great." I pointed.

"NO, NO, NO!" Louise screamed. "You'll go to hell!"

She nagged and lectured me non-stop for the next week but the hell part was enough all by itself. I told Anthony I had to be chaste and he broke up with me almost immediately. After that I kissed and humped my way through my teenage years but no boy got further than that until Norman Sheffield, and that one time was so fast and weird it's still a blur.

Because of my sister's fractured but still functional pipeline to the Lord and her ability to scare me, I maintained my sanctity and virginity as insurance that there would be no place in hell for me. Sometimes Louise told me not to be so sure, but I knew better. After all, how many people had a sister who talked directly to the Lord?

12

1963

By tenth grade I was capable of handling myself without parents and pretty much without Louise. She worked full time as a secretary at the Waltham City Hall and neither of us showed up at home until five o'clock, when we were sure Daddy wasn't there. Mr. LaRosa still slipped me day-old bread and an occasional candy bar, but at almost sixteen, I was old enough to work summers. Between Louise and me, food was no longer a problem. Daddy was rarely home and we stayed out of Mommy's way. She'd stopped drinking, but more often than not, she was still in her bathrobe when we got home, and sometimes I don't think she ate anything the whole day until one of us brought her some supper. Louise and I knew how to cook macaroni and scrambled eggs, so one of those choices was our evening meal about five days a week. All in all, life was pretty okay. I was smart in school, and boys had more interest in me than I had in them, which suited me just fine.

Almost through my sophomore year, I walked out of school like always and Louise was waiting for me. I knew right away something was wrong.

"Mom's gone, Pip," she said.

"She left?"

 No, Christine, she *died*."

I didn't know how to take this in. "She died?"

"She fell down the stairs and hit her head."

"Was she drinking?"

"No, I don't think so. I think she fell by accident, but her brain was probably already soft from all those years, so when she banged it, it must have killed her."

"Where's Daddy?"

"At the bar."

"Wow."

Wow. That's all I could say. I didn't cry. I spent the next two days thinking that the sadness was going to hit me all at once. I'd spent my whole life wondering if my mother loved me, and now she was dead.

"Louise, I am going to be a good mother someday."

"Yeah, well, just make sure it's someday and not now, Christine."

"What do we have to do?"

We were at Burger King, half orphans for almost eight hours.

"Sacred Heart is taking care of the funeral. It's not up to us, we're still kids, you especially. I think we just have to be sad and wear dresses. Grampy and Grandma Moo Moo are coming from Las Vegas and we have to be nice to them."

"Are they nice?" I asked. I'd only met them twice, and both times they pretty much ignored me.

"Not really," Louise said. "But you have to act a certain way at funerals."

I just nodded.

Louise's matter-of-fact advice carried us nicely through the wake. About two dozen people showed up at the Joyce Funeral Home, and they signed their names in a satin white book. Everyone said they were sorry for our loss and Louise and I just said thank you. About half the time Daddy stood beside us with his hands stuffed in the pockets of his brand-new black suit. The rest of the time he smoked cigarettes outside or sat alone in the back of the room. He looked uncomfortable and shrugged his shoulders when anyone approached him. Grampy and Moo Moo stayed in the front receiving line with Louise and me but they were weird: Grampy kept telling people how to win at the slot machines, and Moo Moo cried a phony cry and blew her nose into a wrinkled cloth handkerchief.

We were all back at the Joyce Funeral Home the next morning.

"Go give your mother a kiss," Moo Moo told Louise.

Daddy intervened. "Don't touch her!" he barked, "Just say goodbye and make the sign of the cross."

Louise and I knelt at the casket together and we did neither.

For the two nights of the wake and funeral, Grampy and Moo Moo stayed at our house but Daddy barely spoke to them. Louise said she heard them talking about an insurance policy, and Daddy raised his voice and apparently pounded his fist on the table. At the church service they sat in the front row of the benches with us, and when Moo Moo cried, I cried too. Louise looked at me with a slanted eye that told me I was calling up fake tears. But for that instant I actually wasn't.

Mommy was buried at the Calvary cemetery. Nine people came to the graveside, Louise and me, Daddy, Grampy and Moo Moo, Mommy's hairdresser, two people from Alcoholics Anonymous, and a neighbor from across the street. A priest held a Bible in front of him and said a prayer, and he invited everyone to take a flower as a souvenir.

Two days later, Louise went back to work, I went back to school, my father went back to the bar and his side-dish, Mary Lou McCarthy, and my grandparents went back to Las Vegas. Only our mother stayed put, no longer in this world. I prayed that she would find eternal life like the priest had said, and I prayed that if she had more kids in her eternal life, they wouldn't have to ever know the part of her that drank.

13

Seven months after Mommy died, Louise once was again waiting for me when school got out. This time I already knew why.

Just after lunch, news spread that President Kennedy had been shot and killed in a motorcade in Dallas. I was in the principal's office getting a pass for a field trip when I heard my housemaster talking to the principal. They both looked like someone in their family had died. President Kennedy was handsome, with a beautiful, elegant wife and two cute kids, so this was a big deal, even to the whole school. Someone shot the president of the United States while he was waving to the crowd, sitting beside his beautiful wife Jackie, in an open convertible.

Louise was white as a ghost. I hadn't taken two steps out the door before she was tugging at my coat. "You heard, right?"

I nodded. "What happens to the country, Louise?"

"The vice president takes over," she replied. "But it's a national tragedy. And he was Catholic, you know. The first Catholic president." Louise was crying real tears. "Listen," she said, "I think we should go to church and pray."

Louise had never asked me to pray with her before. We walked three blocks to Saint Mary's and once inside, we sat up front, second bench from the altar. There were about fifty other people already scattered around.

"How do I pray? And what should I pray for?" I whispered.

"Just put your hands together and say a general prayer to God. Pray that the murderer gets arrested and that the president's family doesn't suffer. This is a lot worse than Mommy dying, Christine."

A day later, Louise was working weekends at the Waltham Spa and I was sitting at her counter enjoying my two scoops of butter-crunch ice cream when a man named Jack Ruby shot the president's murderer, Lee Harvey Oswald, in the stomach and he died right on national television. A customer came in and told everybody.

"This whole thing is the worst thing that's happened in our lifetime, Pip." Louise made the sign of the cross.

"This is really worse than Mommy dying?"

"Really worse," Louise replied with surety in her voice. "Much worse. This is the leader of the free world." She paused. "And besides, something's very weird. How could one man kill the president from a sixth-floor window and then the man who kills him gets shot right on television? Something's fishy about that."

Every year from then on, when November twenty-second rolled around, Louise's fishy conspiracy theory reappeared. "Another year of the unsolved mystery of who killed President Kennedy and why," she'd say. Even years later, when we were adults having Chateau pizza with my eight-year-old son Cole, she was still questioning what really happened.

"You still think it was a plot?" I asked.

"Darn right I do. Maybe by the Republicans. They paid Oswald to kill President Kennedy and then they paid Jack Ruby to kill Oswald so he couldn't talk."

"But this is America, Louise. Our government doesn't kill people, certainly not the president."

"Don't be too sure," Louise cautioned. "Trust in God but tie up your camel."

"What? Where do you come up with these sayings? What the heck does that even mean?"

My Catholic follow-the-rules sister snapped out her answer. "It means you never know, so be prepared."

14

1965

If things had been different Louise and I might have gone to college. But as it was, after her failed attempt with the Sisters of Mercy, Louise had finagled a scholarship to Katherine Gibbs Secretarial School for a six-month executive secretary program. She began her job at the Waltham City Hall, working in the tax department, and, after two years on the job, her no-nonsense, just-the-facts approach to almost everything probably drove her co-workers crazy. Myself, three days after my high school graduation, I began steam-blowing one-hundred-degree hot water from the insides of four-inch-long and three-inch-wide copper cylinders called bellows. I applied for the factory job and I started work the next day.

"You sit in this chair and we bring the bellows to you in boxes of five hundred," the boss Mr. Irving told me. "Then you hold each bellow over this heat stick and it dries the water out of each one, and then you stack the dry ones in this other box."

Easy enough, I thought. I liked the idea of counting how many I could do in the eight- hour shift.

I sat in one spot all day trying to be fast without burning my fingers. Louise kept saying my job was a dead end, but I liked it.

The assembly department was housed in a dingy brick building, in the middle of an asphalt parking lot in front of a Raytheon building that towered over it, about a half mile from my childhood mess of a house. The factory itself was as big as an airplane hangar and the cement floor was a killer. Nothing had been upgraded since the Standard-Thomson plant moved to Waltham in 1947, the year I was born.

Almost every day Louise complained about me working there. "That job is ridiculous, Christine. You should come to City Hall and work as a receptionist. You like meeting people."

I ignored her. "I like the plant, Louise. But guess what? Today the Board of Health ordered a shut down until management gets rid of the mice in the locker rooms. We cheered out loud when we heard the news and we didn't stop cheering until Mr. Irving threatened to dock our pay." Louise looked disgusted. "Then the pest company showed up an hour later," I added, "before closing time, so nobody got in trouble."

All the girls in assembly except me sat at a long wooden table and talked non-stop while they crimped and soldered small thermostat parts that would later be installed into new cars. Even though my station was thirty feet away, I was included in the ruckus of everyone yelling back and forth. We were so loud that sometimes the packing department manager complained.

"Christine, did you see Dean Martin drunk on TV?"

"Hey, girls, what time is Alma's baby shower?"

"Slow down with those bellows, Christine. You're giving the rest of us a bad name!"

No matter how careful I was, at least once a week I burned my fingers. Every time, Mr. Irving cautioned me that it was my fault. He was all business. Most of the two hundred-plus union employees made fun of him, and not just because he wore the same faded-green polyester suit every day. You couldn't ask him for time off if it wasn't on the schedule at least two months in advance, and the most we ever got for Christmas was a sixteen-pound frozen turkey, even when the plant was in high production. All we knew about Mr. Irving was that he didn't live in Waltham, he had an accountant daughter who worked for Polaroid, and he was a total creature of habit. Every morning, he stood beside the punch-in time clock and barked at us, "Keep moving girls, keep moving." The next time we would see him, he entered the lunch room at precisely twelve noon every day and sat alone at a table near the door. Lunch was always the same for him: a tuna fish sandwich and a small bag of potato chips. He made a precise half circle spread of chips in front of him, and he never looked up.

"Do you think he's a good guy outside of work?" I asked Alma.

"Nah," she said. "He has no personality. Besides, he's cheap."

"Do you think he's lonely?"

"He has a daughter," Alma said. "He's lucky for that: daughters take care of their parents."

I thought about that. Would there be a time when Louise and I would take care of Daddy? I couldn't imagine it.

15

I had worked at Standard-Thomson for barely two months when I married Norman Sheffield, because I was sure I was pregnant. Sometimes he smelled like mothballs and his wavy black hair was always greasy, like a bad version of Elvis. But on our fourth date, after three stupid whiskey sours and fifteen minutes of making out in the back of his car, he pulled out his dink and pushed himself against me. I was nervous and inexperienced, and before I even understood what was happening, Norman released this sticky mess onto the crotch of my jeans. I didn't dare tell Louise until my period was three weeks late, and by then Norman was bugging me to get married.

"He ejaculated?" Louise shrilled. "What were you thinking?!"

"It happened so fast," I said. "But it's my fault, I know that. He said we should get married."

"You can't be serious," Louise screamed right into my face. Steam could have come out of her ears; she was so agitated.

"First of all, you don't know if you're pregnant until you see a doctor. And from what you're telling me, it doesn't sound like his sperm could have even gotten through. Sperms don't jump through fabric, Pip. And even if you are pregnant—God help us—you can't marry him. He's a creep."

"Louise, it's my fault."

"Oh, stop that, Pip. Some things just happen. But you can't marry him, Christine. Don't do it."

But I did.

My father signed the papers and a justice of the peace married Norman and me at the Waltham City Hall. Louise begrudgingly stood up for me and shot disapproving looks right up until the marriage was official. I moved into Norman's bedroom at his parents' house, and three days later he came with me for my first ob-gyn appointment. Louise was upset that I didn't ask her instead, but this was my mess to handle.

In those days you dressed up for church, bus rides, and doctor's appointments, so I wore a starched short-sleeve, collared white blouse, a cheap two-inch-thick black belt with a gold buckle, and an off-white billowed skirt. Norman and I sat in the waiting room and he flipped through the pages of *National Geographic* while I just sat there. When he finally looked at me, he had a weird expression.

"Your seat," he pointed, "Is that blood?"

I looked down. Yes, blood. Lots of it. It had soaked around the sides of my skirt and I could feel squishiness underneath me.

"Norman," I said, "get the receptionist."

"Why?" he asked. It was such a stupid question.

"Norman, go—just go get her. Hurry up."

A woman in her fifties with gray hair twirled in a bun looked up from her typewriter and approached me with clear irritation and an unsympathetic face, until she looked down and saw the blood. I don't know if her reaction was about the office furniture or my own pathetic circumstance, but she snapped to attention.

"What do you need, young lady?"

"A towel, ma'am? Something I can wrap around myself so I can get to the bathroom?"

"I'll get you sheets," she said. She came back with an extra-large sheet and an extra-large johnny. I waddled to the ladies' room and cleaned up as best I could. When I got back to the waiting room, she had covered my bloody chair and put a huge 'Do Not Sit' sign on it. She shooed me in to see the doctor and it took him all of two minutes to say I was not pregnant and this was not a miscarriage. This was just my period.

Norman shuffled beside me as I took short duck-like steps to the parking garage. I was all wrapped up in clean sheets, praying they were thick enough to spare me further embarrassment. My clueless husband pulled out a stack of paper bags from the trunk of his precious Chevy Malibu and spread them across the passenger front seat. Sitting on top of those crumpled grocery bags and looking like *The Return of the Mummy*, I faced two facts head on: *I wasn't pregnant, and Louise was right.*

When we got back to the house, I took a shower and went to bed. Norman shook me awake at four-thirty to join them for supper at Joe's Spaghetti House. Conjuring the image of blood red tomato sauce with my own predicament, I faced the full range of Norman's stupidity and by association, my own. That wasn't the last straw, but it was pretty close. The very, very last straw came two weeks later, when he told me in his fake sing-song voice that his mother had invited us to keep living with her, not just until we found our own place, but for the next year or even two.

"I can save up for my motorcycle," Norman said, so pleased with himself, and as an afterthought, "And guess what else? We could probably afford a week on the Cape."

Norman's mother was still choosing his clothes and still doing his laundry. She cooked our meals and kissed him goodnight *on the lips*. Plus, he was boring. No longer pregnant, the next day, a Saturday, I feigned a headache and waited until Norman and his mother left for grocery shopping. I called Louise, who was still working her part-time job running the soda fountain at the Waltham Spa.

"Louise, when are you done? Can you come get me? I need to move home."

I left Norman a 'Goodbye—I'm sorry' note and tossed my belongings into the back seat of Louise's car. She didn't say a word until we were two blocks from home.

"That'll teach you not to listen to me. He's a mama's boy with jeans that keep falling off his puny hips, and no way could he support you. You'd be working the rest of your life."

"The real problem is he's a dud," I sighed.

"That's my point," Louise said.

It was pouring when the Falcon turned into our driveway. We sat in the car for five minutes, waiting for a break. There's something about gray days that always got me thinking. This time I knew I must be a royal mess if living with my father again, who was now pretty much a total drunk himself, was an improvement. As it was, Louise had already been plotting her move to somewhere other than home. Now, I knew she'd stay there with me. I was glad and I knew Louise was glad. I was safer with her around.

"Louise, can I get out of this marriage?" I asked.

She nodded. "It's called an annulment. Probably. You weren't even married a month, after all. I'll ask the attorney at City Hall what you need to do."

I didn't hear from Norman again, but he signed the papers and our marriage was canceled like it never happened. A few months later, his mother confronted Louise and me at the Watertown Mall, in front of the Doggie Do Pet Store. She flat out told me I had ruined her son's purity. I listened to her politely, but when she turned and walked away, for the first time ever in my life, I gleefully raised my middle finger.

The last I heard Norman was herding cattle in Montana. Can you imagine a grown man shouting cowboy *'yippies'* and twirling a lasso?

PART 2

Jimmy

16

1966

Four months later, I met Jimmy Macabee. I wasn't sure he was smart and I wasn't going to get stuck with another dud. But my friend Marcie talked me into going with her to watch Killer Kowalski defend his wrestling title, and afterwards we went out for pizza with her boyfriend Mack and his friend, Jimmy. Three times that night Jimmy winked at me, and then he asked for my phone number. The following Sunday morning the doorbell rang and Louise found a wicker basket at our back door. It was filled with homemade buttermilk biscuits tucked into a vintage dish towel. On top was a card with my name on it and a picture of a gorilla saying *'Wanna Wrestle?'* The card was signed *'What are you doing Saturday night, from Jimmy Macabee.'*

I later learned that Jimmy's sister came up with the idea and baked the biscuits for him, but still, I was impressed. One date led to another and after a couple of months, I was Jimmy Macabee's girl. He was my first real boyfriend, and he was clean and neat, like a shorter version of Johnny Cash, except he had a slight beer belly overlapping his belt, and a buzzed haircut. Jimmy's grin was his best accessory: when he smiled, he looked like a leprechaun. He could light up a room, and the more he drank, the more fun he was. He wasn't a brain surgeon, but he was street smart. He worked full-time as a car mechanic and he could fix anything, not just cars.

We were married on the fourth of July, a tribute to Jimmy's patriotism and an accommodation to my desire not to use my vacation days for our wedding.

"No honeymoon?" Marcie asked me.

"No," I answered, "I'm saving my time for a vacation later. Why waste the chance to celebrate when you can use a holiday instead?"

The church was next door to the Taylor Street Autobody shop, where Jimmy worked. He bought himself a three-piece brown striped suit for the occasion, and I wore my prom dress, a leftover from my one-time-only date with Vernon McNally, a strange boy with thick glasses, who asked me to be his prom date three months in advance, and then pretty much ignored me, even on prom night.

We limited the guest list to Louise, our parents, Jimmy's brother and sister, and three friends each, all of whom were in the wedding party. Two years older than me and an Army veteran, Jimmy arranged for free use of the activity room in the basement of the Veterans of Foreign Wars building. I cooked most of the food with Louise's iffy help, and Jimmy's mother made the cake, three layers with vanilla icing and to my great dismay, a Red Sox logo above the cursively curly *'Congratulations Jimmy & Christine. Go Red Sox!'*

We splurged on a waitress named Marabella and paid her two dollars an hour to walk around serving tiny meatballs and vegetables with dip, and then to set up the large pans of lasagna, toss Wishbone Italian dressing into the salad, and make a tower of bite-sized chocolate mint brownies surrounded by orange nasturtiums. Her final task was to clean up afterwards.

"I may be cheap," I told Louise and Jimmy, "but I'm sure as hell not washing dishes at my own wedding."

During our first dance, Louise placed a six-by-eight-inch handwritten sign and a medium sized metal bowl in front of the lasagna, the sign saying, "Tips both welcomed and needed. Please be generous."

In place of a honeymoon, Jimmy and I had sex two times a day for a full week. He kept telling me that I had turned his life around, which made me laugh because I pretty much agreed with him. He was never a troublemaker; he had never been arrested or anything like that, but when he drank, you never knew what he might do. Once he passed out smack in the middle of the fancy water fountain at the Mount Auburn Cemetery. And another time, he totaled a perfectly nice car when he fell asleep at the wheel. His ridiculous excuse was eating a half dozen jelly donuts at three a.m.

"The sugar made me dizzy," he earnestly explained.

On our third night as husband and wife, Jimmy and I moved in with Louise, who at twenty-two, had rented a two-bedroom apartment on Crescent Street. She wasn't crazy about Jimmy, but there was no conflict during our eight-month stay with her, until I announced we were buying a house. I thought Louise would blow a gasket.

"You can't afford a house," she hissed. "Are you both nuts?"

After that she became more vocal. "He drinks too much," she said.

"Everybody drinks," I shot back.

"Mark my word," she said.

Jimmy knew better than to get into any kind of hullabaloo with my sister, but I was happy to take her on. "Louise, why can't you just believe that we know what we're doing?" And for good measure, "Are you sure you're not mad because we're not inviting you to live with us?"

"Hell no," she shot back. "Live with you two? Why would I want to do that?"

"Then be happy for us."

"I'll be happy for you on your way to the poor house," she said.

"Louise," I told her, "if you keep it up you will not set foot in my kitchen."

17

Jimmy and I took out a twenty-two-thousand-dollar mortgage and moved into our six-room Cape Cod style house at 150 Grove Street, two miles from Louise, five blocks from work, and seven blocks from Daddy. By now Mary Lou the Hoo was living with him and they both drank heavily. Louise and I avoided going anywhere near either of them. Even driving past the house made my heart beat too fast.

My house, however, was a dream come true. It was brand new, right across from a playground, in a good neighborhood mostly inhabited by lower-to-middle class families like us, and in the city of my childhood. Most of our neighbors worked in factories or at entry-level jobs, like me.

Sleeping in my new house that first night was the happiest I had ever felt. I worked the seven a.m. to three p.m. shift at Standard-Thomson, and almost every day after work Louise and I organized and cleaned and decorated. We hung pictures and scrubbed floors and bought country curtains and red potholders, and even Louise squealed when we found the perfect black and white cotton rug for in front of the kitchen sink.

Way back in kindergarten, I had kitchen dreams. Mommy and Daddy put no effort into anything in our run-down house. Louise and I never dared to invite our friends home, not just because we worried that Mommy might scream or fall over in front of them, but because there was dirt everywhere you looked, especially in the kitchen and the living room. Once a week I swept the kitchen floor and Louise washed down the counters but we never walked barefoot anywhere, except in our bedroom. I promised myself that when I grew up, I'd have a shiny kitchen, a refrigerator full of food, blue Formica countertops with those wavy metal chrome edges, and a black and white tiled floor. I imagined every detail in my mind, even how the dishes would stack in the cabinets. One time I described my kitchen to Louise and told her how we'd wash the floor every week and watch the little bubbles float up from the kitchen sink when we washed the dishes.

"Who says I'll be cleaning your kitchen?" she shot back. "I'll have my own kitchen."

"Then I'll help you," I said.

Louise was ready to fire back at me again, but for once she thought the better of it.

"Okay, Pip, I guess that can work."

Unlike Louise who still could barely fry an egg, I taught myself to cook. Jimmy loved my fried chicken with dumplings and gravy, and it was a cinch to make hot dogs and beans and a tomato and lettuce salad slathered with Wishbone dressing. I loved how happy all this made him. Once we had kids, I started making spaghetti and meatballs every Thursday night and every Sunday I made a pot roast or roast beef with mashed potatoes and gravy and fresh green beans. Louise had God the Father and I had my poems, but I felt complete once I added my home cooking to the mix. I could have forgiven my mother's drunkenness if only she had cooked for us.

Every day I ran my fingers all along the three-inch wavy silver smooth chrome edges of my counters. Louise didn't share my excitement.

"You have too many appliances on those counters," she barked. "There's hardly any room."

I just smiled. "Louise, complain all you want. I've waited a lifetime for those appliances, and if you can stop grumbling for even five minutes, I'll make you dinner."

"Fine," she said. "But don't forget I hate mushy mashed potatoes. Don't overcook the potatoes."

I threw a green bean at her. "Okay, Louise. Let's hope my fingers aren't so burned from blowing out those damn bellows. You might not know it, but it takes dexterity to peel potatoes."

18

Four months after we moved into my dream house, Jimmy got in a fist fight with a co-worker and lost his job. I was three months pregnant with our first born Claudia, and our mortgage payment of one hundred and fifty-three dollars a month seemed within reach until it wasn't. I earned eighty-nine dollars a week at Standard-Thomson and we had no savings.

I was outside, watering flowers, when I heard Louise's familiar shrill.

"Yoo hoo, Christine."

She had a bag of groceries in each arm. I knew they were groceries because a bunch of green carrot tops flopped over one of the bags.

"I thought I'd do a little shopping for you," she said.

I stood up and wiped my hands on my apron. "Who told you?"

"Jimmy."

I started crying. Louise had none of it. "Cut that out, Christine. We have problems to solve."

I followed her inside and watched her unpack the grocery bags: two loaves of Wonder bread, six cans of chicken noodle soup, three cans of tuna fish, five pounds of potatoes, carrots, celery, lettuce, Jimmy's favorite lemon cake, a gallon of milk, Coke, baloney, three pounds of hamburger, a chuck roast, and white American cheese. Inside one of the bags was a cashier's check for three hundred dollars. I couldn't believe it. I tried to hug Louise and she shooed me away.

"Don't ask," she said. "I'll just say while you and Jimmy whoop it up at the VFW on Sunday afternoons, I dutifully sell Avon products at church." She nodded firmly. "I knew it would come in handy someday."

19

Until Claudia arrived, Jimmy and I had dinner with Marcie and Mack at the Chateau Italian Restaurant every Friday night. We never changed our order: free and fresh white Italian bread with sesame seeds on the crust, slathered with butter; then toasted raviolis; and then a large cheese pizza with half green peppers and mushrooms. Jimmy and Mack each had four or five beers to my one and Marcie's two. By the time the pizza arrived, Jimmy's tongue and humor was definitely loose. I held the car keys and drove us home, but I never worried about his drinking until he lost his job. Almost overnight three or four beers a night turned into double that, and he began adding whiskey shots behind my back. When I took out the trash, I saw the empty bottles. I didn't press him on it: I figured this was his way of handling temporary stress. But when he went back to work, he didn't stop.

I felt an edge about Jimmy's drinking—but he was still so sweet. He teased me when I overcooked his damn beloved beets or shrunk his undershirts in the wash, and after supper, sometimes right in the middle of the tv show, *Hollywood Squares*, we made love on the couch. He was tender and he took his time. When I told him I was pregnant, he was super excited and super solicitous, forbidding me from taking the laundry to the cellar unless he was there to help, and guiding me to the couch as soon as I finished the supper dishes.

"We have to take care of that little bundle you're carrying," he said.

I gave birth to a baby girl at the Waltham Hospital at seven p.m. on Tuesday, January 17, 1968. Thankfully, Jimmy had finally returned to work, so when I called him at four o'clock to tell him my contractions had begun, he said he had a Chevy engine to finish up, and asked if Louise could take me to the hospital and he'd meet us there. In those days it wasn't unusual for a husband to sit out the actual childbirth, and I wanted Louise with me anyhow, so that was fine. But when he didn't show up by seven-thirty, Louise called the bartender at Callahan's Pub and he put Jimmy on the phone. In a commanding voice, Louise demanded that he come to the hospital, and he arrived an hour and a half later, unsteady and drunk. There was no way I let him hold our baby daughter that night and truly, he didn't care.

Things got worse. Claudia and I went home three days later and Louise stayed with us for the next two weeks. Jimmy was distant from the second I carried Claudia into the house. His sense of humor was replaced with complaints; he was too tired, it was too hot, I was too demanding.

"I didn't expect to be ignored," he sulked.

"What did you expect?" I shot back. "We have a little baby here who needs her mother and you're whining about *Hollywood Squares* and sex on the couch?"

"I didn't friggin' expect her to cry all night. How do you think I can work if I don't sleep?"

"She has colic, Jimmy. I'm the one getting up with her. Wear earplugs, for God's sake. I don't ask you to help with anything. The least you can do is be nice."

Soon enough, Jimmy was stopping at Callahan's every night after work and getting home later and later, shaky and exhausted. I hit the roof, but honestly, he didn't seem strong enough to pull himself together. Thank God for Louise. She arrived at my house every afternoon at four-fifteen, right after her shift at the City Hall. We ate supper together and she never left before eight-thirty, once Claudia was finally asleep. I knew Louise was disgusted with Jimmy but we didn't talk about it. He didn't stop drinking, and maybe he couldn't. Things got worse by the day. Either he was slamming doors or coming home and passing out. When Louise finally confronted me, I begged her not to say anything, not just to Jimmy but to me too. I couldn't bear to hear how bad it was. Claudia and I began sleeping in the second bedroom while King Jimmy and his earplugs sprawled out in our marriage bed. He was so ornery that I took to warming the baby's bottle at five o'clock each morning, before he got up, and I fed her in the living room, feeling some combination of tenderness for my baby and disgust for my husband. I let out a giant sigh of relief once I heard the kitchen door close and I could properly start my day.

Despite Louise's warnings, I was so enamored with my new baby and my house and my kitchen that I didn't do what I should have. Instead, I stupidly waited for Jimmy to come around while the months passed. You'd think I would have straightened this out before we had more children. But miraculously, when Claudia was eight months old and finally slept through the night, Jimmy stopped drinking. He went to Alcoholics Anonymous, got himself a sponsor, and held and cooed with his baby daughter. And he apologized.

"Christine, I thought I was ready for a baby, but I guess I wasn't. When I lost my job, I knew I was supposed to take care of us and I couldn't. So, with you pregnant, I panicked. And then the night Claudia was born, even though I had a new job, I went to the bar and I just kept drinking. I was ashamed, but I was mad too. This wasn't how I saw our life. Drinking calms me down. But I'm sorry. I'll make it up to you."

I was twenty-one years old and I knew enough about alcoholism to fill a book. But I didn't make the connection. Me of all people: how could I not know about the pull of alcohol?

"I forgive you, Jimmy," I said, and I meant it. "But you have to make amends with Louise. To her you're a bum." Before he could respond I added, "I cannot have you and my sister at odds with each other. You messed this up and you need to fix it."

Jimmy sent Louise twelve long stemmed red roses with a note, *To my sister-in-law Louise, I'm sorry and I've stopped drinking. For the sake of my marriage, I need you to forgive me. Thank you. Jimmy.*

Louise ignored Jimmy for the next three weeks. "There'll be no dispensation from me until that man is sober for sixty days." And for good measure, she added, "And even then, I don't trust him. He doesn't like kids."

"Louise, that's ridiculous. Of course he likes kids. Even AA says it's a day at a time. I will not have friction in my family. You have to move on; do it for me."

Louise reluctantly responded with a handwritten note which she sent by certified mail:

Dear Jimmy,
My sister deserves a good husband and a good father for her baby. She already has a good sister and a good little daughter. I hope you straighten out. I forgive you (for now.) Sincerely, Your sister-in-law Louise

Jimmy stayed sober for sixteen months. We had lovely days; sometimes he was still on edge, but for the most part he worked and I gardened, and together we watched Claudia learn to smile and walk and talk. I cooked supper every night in my fancy kitchen, we watched *Hollywood Squares,* and things were calm. Even Louise was impressed.

The serenity ended just before Emily was born. The same pattern began again: a couple of beers after work, missed suppers, and each day Jimmy became more absent and more distant. He stopped drinking again, off and on, but after a few weeks he'd be back at Callahan's, and Louise was back helping me. This time, he drank straight through Emily's arrival and toddlerhood and right up until Cole was born two years later. I finally stopped expecting anything different from him because not expecting made things easier. Anyone who's lived with an alcoholic knows how crazy and unpredictable it all gets. Even when I confronted Jimmy and begged him to stop, or I tried guilting him, he just kept drinking. How in holy hell had I let this happen, to me of all people? I finally gave up.

But not Louise. She kept track of Jimmy's failures as closely as the accounting sheets she prepared at City Hall.

"You have to go to Al-Anon," she told me. "It's for the families."

"I don't have time to go to Al-Anon," I fired back.

"I'll babysit. You have to go. He'll drag you down the way Mommy and Daddy did us. And the kids..."

I don't think I was ever as angry at my sister as I felt at that moment. "Shut up, Louise! You have no right to say that. My kids have a *mother.* That's totally different than our situation. I protect them and I always will. It's not the same and you know it."

Probably for the one and only time in her life, Louise backed off. "You want me to just ignore it, Christine?"

"Yes," I said, "Yes. I need you to ignore it. Don't make it harder for me."

Louise shook her head. "Okay, Pip. You win. You know I'm here."

"Okay, Louise. Thank you."

I knew she was right and I knew Al-Anon would confirm what I wouldn't face. But I needed time. I needed to get a grip. And I needed to make sure my precious babies suffered no harm from a father who drank, and a mother who pushed that reality aside.

20

1972

Cole was born when Claudia was four and Emily was two, and the very day Louise and I brought him home from the hospital, Jimmy announced he'd stopped drinking. To make good on that, he went to AA and came home with a sponsor and a new attitude.

"I'm going to be there for you and the kids, Christine," he told me. "You make supper, I'll bring home my paycheck, I'll stay sober, and I'll pick up pizzas every Friday night. I know I've messed things up pretty bad. But I'll make it up to you and the kids." He nodded. "Deal?"

How I wish my mother or father had made this offer to Louise and me, even once. Maybe the fact that they didn't and Jimmy did influenced how quickly I responded.

"Okay, Jimmy, deal."

My God, he tried. He was home by six o'clock every night and after supper he cleared the table and scraped off the dishes while I got the kids ready for bed. He even planted shrubs and a peach tree in our yard his first sober spring. He stopped seeing his high school buddies at Callahan's. And while I fed and put baby Cole to bed each night, he lay on the couch, still watching the

Squares, but now he snuggled with Claudia and Emily until their bedtime at seven-thirty.

He made it eight months.

"Here we go again," Louise said. "Good God Jesus."

It was worse this time. With the chaos of three kids under five, life with Jimmy was like stepping on hard boiled eggs with the shells still on them. Even when some of the inside was okay, there were too many cracks and broken pieces to salvage anything good from any of it. I never knew if he'd be jolly and joking, asleep midway through supper, or even home for supper, or slamming doors because the noise got to him. When he pulled himself together and tried to stay sober, he struggled, and of course that made everything even harder. The on-again off-again confused the kids and left me in a state of fuming impatience. I did not intend to marry a weak man, but that's what I did.

This time, with Cole not even a year old, Jimmy's drinking drained away any patience I had left. Louise was ready to pounce. She finally spoke up. "You have to do something, Christine. He's a terrible influence."

The next time Jimmy staggered into the kitchen, it was ten o'clock on a Friday night and one look at him confirmed what I already knew. I shot him an evil look, walked to the linen closet and threw a clean sheet and pillowcase at him. "You're not sleeping with me tonight. And tomorrow we'll see if you should even be living in this house. I won't allow this anymore, Jimmy. You can stew on that fact."

He said nothing. I stormed upstairs and left him holding on to the kitchen counter.

The next day I burst into tears when Louise called me.

"Oh, that son-of-a-bitch," she said. "I knew it. I knew it, Christine. Thank God you've finally come to your senses."

Jimmy was repentant. He tried to stop drinking yet again, I'll give him that. He begged me to be patient. I was twenty-five years old with three young children and a drunk of a husband. Louise was no help. "Get rid of him, Christine. Wait too long and he'll burn the house down."

<h1 style="text-align:center">21</h1>

From the first moment I heard him sing "Leaving on a Jet Plane," the singer-songwriter John Denver filled in the spaces that Jimmy couldn't. It wasn't just because of his wholesomeness, although I swooned over his granny glasses, cereal bowl haircut, and toothy grin that just about took up his whole face. John Denver sang songs that time-traveled me to the fresh air of the Rocky Mountains and to the open-air flights of majestic eagles. The simple rhymes in his songs were perfect:

> Springtime is rolling 'round slowly,
> Gray skies are bringing me down,
> Can't remember when I've ever been so lonely,
> I've forgotten what it's like to be home...

I joined his fan club in 1968 and for a time I was his New England coordinator. It was a position in name only; there were no responsibilities that came with it, but I had bragging rights.

John Denver became my imaginary fantasy husband. I was determined to meet him in person.

"I want to see if his hands are soft," I told Louise. When I asked her to go to his spring concert in Boston with me, she hemmed and hawed, but I knew she'd come. She helped me hatch a sneaky plan: I'd call my U.S. Senator and ask if he could arrange a backstage meeting on behalf of my very ill sister, poor sickly

Louise. For months, I went to bed dreaming of meeting John back-stage. But my plan failed before it even began, because Jimmy's drinking reached a crisis point. He was stopped for driving under the influence, put on probation again at work for arguing with a customer, and he was slamming doors at home more often than he opened them. I didn't have time to daydream or plot to see my make-believe husband: I had to deal with my real one.

I called Father O'Malley at Sacred Heart Church and asked to meet with him at the rectory.

"Can we talk on the phone?" he asked.

"I'd rather come in, Father."

I felt his reluctance. He was almost rude. "I'm very busy," he said.

"I'm very confused," I replied. "I need help."

This was the first time I sought counsel beyond my sister. At two-thirty on a Saturday in May, when I could have been plant-ing sunflower seeds and planning magical gardens with the kids, Father John O'Malley listened to me for fifteen minutes, nodded his head several times, and handed me one Kleenex after another. Then he leaned forward, his face maybe two feet from mine.

"Mrs. Macabee, you made a vow to your husband, in sick-ness and in health. You cast him aside and he'll probably end up in an alley somewhere. When a man is weak, he needs a strong woman. Surely you can find it in your heart to keep your family together and help him."

"But Father, our children..."

"Does he hurt them?"

"Well, no, not really, but seeing him like this can't be healthy for them."

"Ah, but Mrs. Macabee," he just about smirked, "God knows a broken family is worse."

I returned home that afternoon steeled to make the best of a bad situation. First, I called Louise. "Look," I told her, "Father O'Malley says I need to make this work. I need you to accept that and not give me grief about it. I'll handle Jimmy, that's all I can do, okay?"

I could tell Louise was surprised. I half expected her to tell me to ignore the priest, but I think she was too tangled up in holy ambivalence and her allegiance to the Catholic Church. In the weeks that followed, it took everything she had to honor my plea, but she did. No matter how bad things got with Jimmy's drinking, she kept her opinions to herself. It helped that she was a devout Catholic, but I knew she lost a lot of respect for Father O'Malley because of his terrible advice.

22

With Louise's nagging pushed aside, the next week I asked our thirteen-year-old neighbor, an honor student with a high responsibility gene, to babysit the kids. I needed to talk to Jimmy in private. I found him stretched out on the couch, watching a rerun of *Bonanza.*

"Jimmy," I said, "I need to see you."

"Now?" He grumbled, but he knew I meant business.

"Yes, now."

He pulled himself up and walked with me to the kitchen just as the babysitter knocked on the door. "We'll be less than an hour, honey," I told her.

Jimmy and I drove to the Dairy Queen on Main Street, like we used to do before the kids. He must have known this was serious because he didn't question me. In the middle of our hot fudge sundaes, I told him how it was going to be.

"Jimmy, Father O'Malley says I should let you stay in the house and I should try to help you. If you want me to go to AA with you, I will. I can't make you stop drinking, but if you're ever sincere in wanting help, I'll be there. If not, and you keep drinking, I'll cover for you with the kids as long as you don't lay your disappointment about your miserable life on them. But if you ever lay a finger on any one of them, or you scream at them to be quiet when they're just making the noise that kids make, I swear you'll be out of the house faster than you know what hit you."

Jimmy said nothing. He tightened his grip on the plastic spoon he was holding and swirled his ice cream in one direction and then the other. He didn't look at me straight on. I expected him to scowl but he didn't. "Say something, Jimmy. I'm not having this conversation with myself."

Finally, he looked up. He looked empty and pathetic. "Okay, Christine."

That was it. I swear, we didn't discuss his drinking again for the next eight years. I look back and think *No way: eight years?* We slept in the same bed and every so often he rolled on top of me and I let him release himself, but it was never the way a loving husband and wife would be. In my mind Jimmy got smaller and smaller with each day, each month, each year. Every so often he showed up for one of the kids' school events, and when Cole turned nine, he let him drive his precious Ford truck back and forth in the driveway, but with disastrous results. That's another story.

The day I lugged Father O'Malley's stupid advice home with me, I vowed to become both mother and father to the kids. I got books on parenting from the library, and I read about the traits and qualities that fathers give their children. I attended concerts and sports games, I learned how to throw a baseball, and I built up enough strength in my five-foot-five body so that, even back then, I could carry a toddler Cole around on my shoulders. One thing I'll say for Jimmy: he showed up for work and he handed over his paycheck. I made him bag lunches every day and I gave him ten dollars a week, which of course he spent on booze, except on Christmas, when, with great fanfare, he'd bring home a half dozen giant caramel apples, all rolled in crushed peppermint, and on Valentine's Day, when he sent me roses. But otherwise, Jimmy was a shadow in our household.

Thank God I had Louise, my poems, and, of course, my John Denver.

23

1977-1982

When Cole started kindergarten, I went back to my old job. Mr. Irving let me have nine a.m. to three p.m. mothers' hours, so I was home until the kids left for school, and just about home when they came flying in the kitchen door with their backpacks and papers. I still chauffeured them all over town, and I had supper on the table every night at six. I made no allowances for missed supper time. Some of the coaches and teachers didn't like it when they missed practices or special events so they could eat with their family, but I didn't budge. Sometimes the kids rebelled, but mostly they accepted this was just the way it was. I figured my insistence was a glue for all of us; we ate together and we stuck together. Jimmy was rarely around, and between Louise and me, we had everything pretty well covered.

The biggest chunk of the family's afternoon and weekend time got poured into sports. Claudia and Emily intermittently played school basketball, and at one point Cole was tied up in baseball, basketball, and for a short time, to my dismay, football. He was apparently a natural athlete. The kids and I attended all of his games, and I had to admit I loved watching him play. When he was nine, his baseball coach asked me for a meeting.

"Your son has an extraordinary talent, Mrs. Macabee. His assistant coach and I both feel with the right opportunities, he could develop into a professional baseball player."

"Isn't he kind of young for you to know that?"

"Yes, and no," he chuckled. "He's a natural. We'd like to see him play on the statewide junior league team this summer, and maybe advance to state class A in the fall."

"But he's so young. Isn't class A for older kids?"

"Normally, but we think Cole can compete."

I wasn't sure where he was heading. "What would you need from me, Mr. Murray?"

"We would need your permission to enroll Cole on a traveling team."

"How often would he miss supper?" I asked.

The coach looked surprised. "Unfortunately, pretty often," he said. "Most of the games start around four, and more than half of them are an hour or more away from Waltham."

"I'm sorry, my children don't miss supper. We eat as a family."

He looked surprised again. "I understand, Mrs. Macabee. But you have to understand too. It's a great opportunity for Cole."

I let Cole make the decision. I know he factored in my rules about supper. I wanted him to excel in sports if that's what he wanted, and I might have given in, but on his own he decided to include our suppers in his summer plans. He was happy to enjoy himself playing with his friends, swimming at the Penny Pool, just doing normal kid stuff.

Still, the emphasis on sports became bigger and bigger in our household. Even Claudia and Emily were into it. Their collective excitement watching the 1981 Super Bowl surprised me: even thirteen-year-old Claudia huddled on our couch with Cole and her first unofficial boyfriend, watching the Oakland Raiders and the Philadelphia Eagles compete. I dutifully served them nachos and mini hot dogs and sodas during the game, but I kept thinking, *all this excitement over football?* I just didn't understand it. And I kept thinking, *How can I push their excitement for poems?*

It bothered me that athletes were so important, and I didn't like the emphasis on winning. Not everybody was good at throwing or kicking or catching or hitting a ball and besides, how was that more important than art or music or writing? Poetry had saved me. I wanted my kids to know that power. Louise thought I was talking Greek.

"How does football help society?" I asked her. She looked at me like I lived on a different planet.

"What's the problem?" she said, "It's fun to watch, and it builds teamwork. The kids could do worse, Christine."

"But sports can't be everything."

"But why criticize? And who says it's everything?"

"But it kind of is, Louise. I don't want Cole growing up believing that. Or the girls either. Competition's bad if you end up feeling good about yourself just because you're better than someone else. What about the kids who can solve a math problem but can't kick a ball? What message does that give? And should a football player be more important than a teacher or a scientist? Or a poet?"

Louise looked right through me. "Christine, sports figures are heroes. There's nothing wrong with that. Kids need heroes. Besides, how is that different than you and your John Denver? I don't hear you objecting to all the crazy people who think he's the second coming."

Ah my John Denver. "It's not the same, Louise. I pretend he's everything a husband should be and it helps me ignore Jimmy. That's all. It's not like I live and breathe him. Besides, I'm telling the kids they need to be good at three things, not just one. Sports only counts for one. John Denver, he sings, he writes, he protects the environment. That's three things."

Louise was having none of it. "If you want the kids to be involved in something other than sports, come up with something else. But for the love of God, will you lighten up about supper? How do you expect Cole to be a good team player if he can't show up for practice?"

I still didn't budge right away, but I did lighten up a little. And as for Louise's challenge, it took me three weeks to settle on my master plan, and once I did, there was no stopping me.

24

While the kids were learning how to breakdance, I announced the date and time of what I called "The First Annual Macabee Potluck Poetry Slam." If poems weren't the main draw, I knew food would be. To entice my athletic son, I wrote to the New England Patriots' quarterback Steve Grogan and asked him to sponsor the event. And I asked him to come. Barely a week had passed before Cole came flying into the kitchen, waving an envelope with the Patriots' insignia on it.

"Steve Grogan, Mom! It must be from Steve Grogan!" He ripped open the envelope and unfolded a typewritten letter with a fancy Patriots' logo at the top.

Dear Mrs. Macabee:

Thank you for inviting me to your Poetry Contest. Due to a prior commitment, I won't be able to attend, but I applaud your effort and wish you a successful event. My personal favorite poem is 'The Fish' by Elizabeth Bishop. Please feel free to share it on my behalf.

Sincerely,
Steve Grogan,
New England Patriots

"That's unbelievable!" Cole just about screamed, shaking the letter in mid-air over his head.

We were both tickled. My poetry slam was officially on.

25

Claudia made the flyers, we slipped them in the neighbors' mail-boxes, and I mailed some to friends and friends of friends. The First Annual Macabee Potluck Poetry Slam officially began at six o'clock on a Saturday night, at my dining room table, with nineteen adults and twelve children.

Two weeks earlier, to prepare for speaking in front of an audience, I let everyone stay up past midnight to watch Johnny Carson and *The Tonight Show*. I figured who better than Johnny to show how to entertain an audience. We ate popcorn in our pajamas and Louise slept over. Luck would have it that Jimmy Stewart was Johnny's guest that night and by some unbelievable coincidence, he recited a poem about his dead dog Beau. Johnny Carson, Emily, and I cried.

I insisted that Jimmy stay home for my big event. I didn't want the embarrassment of making excuses for him. The whole night he sat in his mother's blue leather chair, tucked into a corner of the dining room. He watched and listened and every so often he smiled, but he didn't say a word. Guests arrived and munched on the finger food I'd assembled—nachos, chicken wings, deviled eggs, and plenty of chips and dips. All the kids sat around the dining room table and everyone else circled their chairs around the kids.

I banged a spoon on a glass and introduced the event.

"Hello everyone. We have seven aspiring poets who will recite poems tonight. Everyone who participates gets a free ice cream cone from Cabot's in Newton. The grand winner will be determined by a show of hands and besides the ice cream, wins two tickets to the Embassy movie theatre, plus a free bag of popcorn."

The first presenter was ten-year-old Billy Alexander, who lived down the street from us. Billy's mother, a doctor, and his father, a lawyer, lived in a modest six-room ranch unbefitting their professional status. Their only son Billy reflected that simplicity: like my kids, he wore clothes from discount stores and he carried not an ounce of superiority in his four-foot-two lanky frame.

"I like funny poems," he began, "so I chose "Daddy Fell into the Pond," by someone named Alfred Noyes."

Alfred Noyes? I knew him: he wrote "The Highway Man," one of my favorite poems with one of my favorite opening lines:

"The wind was a torrent of darkness among the gusty trees.

The moon was a ghostly galleon tossed upon cloudy seas..."

"I hope you like this," Billy said, as he stood up, took a step backwards, and extended both arms, palms up in front of him like a politician.

"...Everyone grumbled. The sky was grey.
We had nothing to do and nothing to say.
We were nearing the end of a dismal day,
And then there seemed to be nothing beyond,
Then Daddy fell into the pond!"

When he finished, Billy reacted to his applause with a toothless smile and a thumbs-up from his parents. He was the first to clap for the next presenter, five-year-old Alicia Alpert, who couldn't remember more than the first line of "Twinkle Twinkle

Little Star." Once it was clear she could go no further, we all clapped anyway, and she curtsied unapologetically.

And so it went. When it was Cole's turn, he stood up with surprising ease and pressed the start button on his handheld tape recorder. He slapped his hip and he and the Animals began singing together:

> "There is a house in New Orleans
> They call the Rising Sun
> And it's been the ruin of many a poor boy
> And God, I know I'm one…"

Cole looked around, grinned, and sang the lyrics with a low, sultry voice I'd never heard from him before. Everyone but Claudia and Jimmy followed and clapped along, and when he finished, the room exploded with applause and laughter. None of us had ever heard him sing, let alone croon and rhythmically move his body like that. He took his seat, obviously pleased. I was sure this was a big win for him, and I had a feeling this was the moment he got hooked on performing.

Claudia followed with Edgar Allen Poe's "The Raven." She had clearly practiced her recitation and began forcefully, emphasizing and enunciating every word:

> "Once upon a midnight dreary, while I pondered, weak and weary,
> Over many a quaint and curious volume of forgotten lore,
> While I nodded, nearly napping, suddenly there came a tapping,
> As of someone gently rapping, rapping at my chamber door."

By the time she reached the final verse, Claudia had exclaimed 'Nevermore' eleven times and had held everyone in rapt attention. Her arms and hands had moved all over the place, her speech was rapid, and each word dripped with drama. She took a bow and pretended to blush. Even though Cole had successfully worked the crowd, I could tell by her expression that she expected to win the grand prize.

My Emily was the last presenter of the night. She cleared her throat and looked at the handwritten paper she held in front of her.

"Last month," she began, "Mom let us stay up to watch Johnny Carson. This guy read a poem about his dog and that's the poem I am going to read. It's called "Beau" by Jimmy Stewart. My teacher helped me find the words in the library. It's long but it's worth it."

Claudia glared. She had coached Emily to recite "Trees" by Joyce Kilmer, a safe and boring poem. The poem about Beau was anything but.

> "…He never came to me when I would call
> Unless I had a tennis ball,
> Or he felt like it,
> But mostly he didn't come at all
> He would wake up at night
> And he would have this fear
> Of the dark, of life, of lots of things,
> And he'd be glad to have me near.
> And now he's dead."

Emily gained steam as the obvious tragic ending became clear, and several of the kids cried. Even my neighbor Marla Sacks sniffled into her embroidered handkerchief.

Everyone but competitive Claudia clapped as Emily stood and bowed.

When all the readings were finished, if I had any regret at all, which I didn't, it was only that my John Denver wasn't represented. I had tried to bribe Cole to recite "Rocky Mountain High," but it was just as well he didn't because even Jimmy applauded his rendition of "The House of the Rising Sun." His father's approval was a small victory that I prayed meant something to my son, and for once I was thankful for Jimmy.

When it came time to announce the grand prize winner, instead of a show of hands, I passed out index cards and asked everyone to write down their choices. When Louise tallied them up, Emily outnumbered Cole by two votes. With the winner decided, and Claudia deciding to stop sulking, Louise and I brought out four cheese pizzas, my giant chicken and potato casserole, and Mrs. Alexander's chocolate pudding pie with graham cracker crust. Everyone ate and giggled and talked non-stop, except Jimmy. He left when the first guests did. Louise and I waited until all the kids were asleep before we pulled out the bottle of scotch hidden in the coat closet, and we celebrated with two generous shots each. I was thrilled with how the night had gone, but the benefits from The First Annual Macabee Potluck Poetry Slam didn't last long. Three weeks later Jimmy slammed Cole against the wall.

26

Cole forgot to put the trash cans back in the garage, and when Jimmy backed his truck into them, they clanged and rolled all over the driveway. His anger was always immediate, triggered by any number of Cole's infractions: he was slow to take out the trash, he forgot to put things away, he rolled his eyes when his father snarled at him. At ten years old, Cole's carelessness was often at fault, but Jimmy's temper fueled by booze was the bigger problem. This wasn't the first time he went after Cole, but it was the most serious.

I took care of this incident plenty fast: after I pulled Jimmy off, I threatened him, and then I insisted that Cole recognize that his father's response was a hundred percent wrong. I wanted my son to understand that the fault was the alcohol and I told him the same thing again three months later, when Jimmy pulled him off the couch by his hair. Cole had again left the trash cans in the middle of the driveway. Jimmy had slammed the truck in park, stormed into the house, and went after Cole, screaming in his face. I heard the commotion from the kitchen and I was in the living room in five seconds flat. I punched Jimmy off my son and shoved him backwards so hard he was lucky he landed halfway on the soft arm of the couch instead of flat on the hardwood floor.

Cole stood dazed, trying not to cry. I walked to the wall phone and dialed the police. "Officer, this is Mrs. Christine Macabee of 150 Grove Street. I'm calling to report that my husband James Macabee just assaulted our ten-year-old son. I don't want you to come this time but I want it recorded because the next time I will want him arrested and out of the house."

I hung up the phone and walked back to Jimmy. I glared into his drunken face, "Did you hear that, Mister?"

He looked down and said nothing.

"Touch one hair on the head of any of the kids ever again and you're out of here."

My face was as red as a tomato. I screamed, "I mean it, Jimmy, oh my God, I mean it. Never ever again. Do you hear me?"

Cole didn't move. He watched his father nod.

"Come with me, son." I reached for Cole's hand but he pulled it away, like an electric shock had just zapped him. "Come with me, Cole." I must have said that a dozen times.

"I have homework, Mom," he said, and he disappeared to his bedroom.

An hour later Cole, now in his pajamas, walked into the kitchen. Jimmy was long gone and I was washing dishes. He put his arms around me from behind, pushed his face into my back and just clung. He was crying, a rare reaction for him. Even when Emily whacked him in the head full force with a baseball bat, he didn't cry.

"Mom, it was my fault."

I was prepared. "No Cole, it was *not* your fault. Your fault was not putting the trash cans away. You'll make plenty more mistakes like that in your life, because everyone does. It's important to learn from our mistakes. But no one, and I mean no one, has the right to come after you for a mistake. No one has the right to lay a hand on your body and no one has the right to blame you for their own shortcomings. Your father has to either curb his temper or his drinking. That's his choice. Do you understand?"

He nodded.

Once again, I knew I should tell Jimmy to move out, but I couldn't bring myself to do it. I kept hearing Father O'Malley's words: *families stay together*. I was also worried about money. I couldn't imagine Jimmy living separately from us, and I wasn't sure I could count on him financially. And finally, I made such a big deal drumming the importance of loyalty and devotion: what would it mean to the kids if I kicked their father to the curb?

That night, for the first time ever, I actually prayed. I prayed that Cole understood what I had told him; that he knew not to take the blame for someone else; and I prayed that he had an outlet inside him, like Sabrina had been for me. For weeks after that ugly incident with Jimmy, I kept reading about father substitutes and I kept thinking about what to do. Once again, in my silly way, I turned to poems.

27

1983

I bought a burlap bag and filled it with dozens of doodads, similar to Jack-in-the-Box prizes. I kept the bag near the dining room table and opened it every time one of the kids recited a poem at supper. I established a limit of one kid, one poem a day, but over time poetry became as much of a staple in our house as my fried chicken. I did this mostly for Cole but it benefited all of us. Cole quickly offered up two or three poems a week, so many that I went out of my way to fill the burlap bag with his favorite three-inch plastic GI Joes and other boy-like army and dragon figures. Louise had her prayers, I had John Denver, now Cole had burlap doodads.

Jimmy had no part. Since my warning, he kept his temper under wraps but he was like wallpaper in our household. The kids seemed okay: I had no worries about my bookworm Emily, but I kept my eyes on my pent-up Cole and my hormone-active Claudia. Jimmy stopped going after Cole; mostly they ignored each other, and Cole seemed back to his carefree self. But Claudia was another story. I suspected she was thinking about having sex with her boyfriend and that suspicion grew when I heard her on the phone with him: *No, I know, but I'm not sure, I don't think so, probably not, I'm not sure, well, of course I know it will be great*. To me this was teenage code for actual temptation. I made a plan to corner her after supper: I'd pretend I knew more than my guesstimates. I waited for her to come home from school but Jimmy came home first: he walked in the door at five, at least two hours earlier than normal. I took one look at him and knew what happened.

"I didn't get the promotion," he said. "They gave it to Benny."

"The new guy?" Even I was shocked at that.

"Yeah, the boss told me it was because of my temper and the argument I got into last month in front of a customer."

"You were drinking on the job that day, Jimmy. That's a deal breaker right there."

My husband looked so discouraged I almost wanted to comfort him. But I couldn't. His drinking caused us so much grief. The time before this one, when Jimmy was up for a promotion to shop supervisor, he got in a shouting match with Manny, the parts manager. He ended up on probation for three weeks. The boss took him back because Jimmy was an experienced mechanic, but here he was now, rejected and humiliated all over again and I had no ability to help him. Our marriage was a disappointment all around: we were a shell of man and wife. This time, passed over for a job he knew like the back of his hand, and passed over for a kid not even twenty-one years old, blocked from a raise we sure could have used: this time I'd had it. I was surprised at what came out of my mouth.

"Jimmy, I give up. You should give up too if you're going to drink your life away. I can't live like this anymore. It's not fair to me and the kids. We can't count on you and you give me nothing but trouble." I hesitated, but not for long. "I want you to move out, Jimmy. Go live with your brother." There was no stopping me. "I grew up with it, Jimmy. I can't take it. It upsets me in bad ways and that's not good for me or the kids. Or for you. The kids are older now and it's not fair to them. You have to leave. I mean tomorrow. I mean tomorrow this time."

Jimmy looked down at the floor for what seemed like forever. He gripped his work cap with both hands and for a second it looked like he'd lost his balance. But even seeing him flinch, I didn't back down. My clarity was probably fueled by my concern for Claudia and a fear that her father was the cause of her hormones. And of course, there was Jimmy's hostility toward Cole. I just waited. When he finally looked at me, he was crying. He fell toward me and also to my surprise, I instinctively put my arms around him. His whole body shook.

"Oh Jimmy…this is so sad."

"Okay," he whimpered, "I'll stop. I've messed up everything."

"Stop?"

"Tonight. I'll go to AA tonight."

Life has certain defining moments that arrive from nowhere and insist that you notice. This was one of those moments: Jimmy and I had been through this scene dozens of times and this time I was so clear that Jimmy had to leave, that we were done. But the words that came from my mouth didn't say that. "Okay, Jimmy."

I knew this wasn't just about losing his family. Like most alcoholics, Jimmy was at the precipice of losing everything; maybe even his will to live. "Go to AA tonight," I told him, "and tomorrow tell your boss you're a new man. Tell him you'll be ready for the next promotion."

Jimmy pushed his face further into my shoulder. I hadn't held him like this in years. "I'll do that," he said.

I pushed him away from me and insisted on eye contact. "But Jimmy, I'll know if you drink. Believe me, I'll know. And if you do, you have to move out."

"I know," he said. We both knew this time I would hold him at his word.

28

Jimmy went to AA that night and came home still promising. He woke me up before dawn and whispered "I love you" the way he had many years ago. I felt him hard against me and we made love for the first time in probably a year. He lay on top of me and trembled, and in that moment, hope returned to my body like a blood transfusion running through it. There was no explanation for why I would trust him or hope this time would be different. The only thing I could think of was that we had reached the end of the line. He was about to lose everything and I was about to banish him. The next morning, he asked if I could have supper a half hour later than normal so he could go to an AA meeting right after work.

"I'll go to the five o'clock meeting," he said, "and then head home."

"Fine," I told him. "I'll make your beets."

It was pouring when Jimmy left for work. He looked so silly with his floppy yellow fishermen's rain hat crooked on his head and my black and white polka dot umbrella tucked under his arm. When he got to his truck he turned around, raised his thumb high in the air, and blew me a kiss. He called out to me and mouthed "Thanks," and he waved. I waved back from the dining room window. I watched him dive headfirst into his truck even though he was already drenched. Just the way he moved in those seconds, I saw that Jimmy was a man freed from burden. His truck zipped up the driveway, he waved again, blew the horn twice, and took a sharp right, heading toward Bright Street. I watched until he was out of sight, and to my great surprise I said out loud: *I'll be damned.* The day was miserably wet and gray with a forecast of rain that was supposed to last until midnight, but miserably wet and gray was not what I felt. I felt hope and that hope was the color of lemons.

I worked my shift humming "Annie's Song" and "Oh Calypso!" Alma asked me why I looked so smug and I just smiled. Was I getting my husband back, the old Jimmy? I had a crazy feeling he'd come through this time; maybe because he was so scared. I told myself I might even be willing to make love with him twice a week. I decided I wouldn't say anything to Louise until Jimmy was sober for one solid month because I knew she'd harass me. I could just hear her: *"Dream on, Christine!"* I wanted to give Jimmy this chance and she would never understand. I didn't understand either: it was as though I had some mind conversion and common sense had nothing to do with it.

After work I stopped at the Star Market and picked up everything I needed to make Jimmy's favorite: my chicken pot pie and his roasted beets. It was still raining so I covered my head with a paper bag. I looked like the scarecrow in *The Wizard of Oz.*

When I got home Cole was rushing out. "Heading to practice, Mom. See you at six."

"Practice in the rain?"

"Yup, the coach says, 'That's life.' "

I shook my head. "Don't bring that mud home. You have an extra half hour. Your father's home for supper tonight."

Cole looked at me funny. "How come?"

"Things might be looking up, son."

"Sure, Mom, fine."

I remember thinking, from his passive reaction, such a toll we've all paid.

29

I made the pie crust and the beets were boiling and my day was still lemon yellow when the phone rang a little after five. Right away I heard the formality of an unfamiliar male voice.

"Mrs. Macabee?" This was a serious tone, not rude but not friendly either. I nodded and said yes at the same time.

"Ma'am, this is Lieutenant Madden of the Newton Police Department. There's been an accident, ma'am, involving your husband, James."

"What...?" My right hand gripped the receiver and my left hand stirred the beets. I braced the phone between my chin and right shoulder. "What happened?"

"Ma'am, one of our officers is about to arrive at your house."

At my house? "Officer, please." I knew this was not normal. I lowered my voice and begged. "I have children. You have to tell me."

He spoke reluctantly. "There's been an accident on 128 at exit 19."

"Oh God," I said. I felt blood rush to my face. *He's been arrested. Damn him, I thought, not one damn day.*

Instinctively I asked, "Did he hurt someone?"

"Ma'am, Officer Sterling is on his way. He will escort you to the hospital."

A second fact quickly surfaced. "Lieutenant, is my husband hurt?"

He was silent. "Lieutenant," my voice was now a whispered panic, "you have to tell me. I have children. What's happened?"

The officer spoke evenly and his tone became softer. "Your husband apparently stopped his vehicle to help a young woman with a flat tire in the breakdown lane near the exit on 128. As you know, it's been raining heavily. He was changing the tire and the jack let loose. He was struck in the head." The officer stopped and waited.

"Go on," I said.

"Officer Sterling can provide details, ma'am."

"Don't do this to me, officer. You have to tell me right now. Where is my husband?"

There was silence for a long time but I waited and said nothing. Finally, he spoke again. "The EMTs were not able to revive him, ma'am. I'm sorry."

I whispered, "You mean he's DEAD?" I turned the beets to low and balanced myself on my Formica counter.

"I'm very sorry, ma'am."

"Are you positive?"

"Yes, ma'am. We have confirmation from the hospital."

"What hospital?"

"Newton-Wellesley."

"Okay, I need fifteen minutes. I need to see him, officer."

"Yes ma'am. Officer Sterling will escort you."

"No. I'll take myself. No police coming to my house. Tell the hospital that I need to see my husband, will you tell them that? That they have to wait for me?"

"Yes, ma'am. I will do that."

I changed out of my housedress into black slacks and a white silk blouse. Louise arrived eight minutes later, out of breath and storming through the kitchen door, dressed in her tattered blue flowered flannel nightgown with a thrown-together purple scarf around her pinned up hair.

"The one time I decided to..." She stopped. She looked at my face and froze. She lowered her voice. "Oh my God, Christine. Are you sure?"

I shook my head. "No, actually I'm not. I have to see for myself. But why would a police officer tell me that if he wasn't sure?"

Louise nodded. She looked around. The oven was on and Jimmy's beets were still boiling on low on the stove. "What should I do?"

"Finish cooking the beets. Let them cook for another ten minutes and rinse them with cold water. Cut up the chicken and potatoes and vegetables and put everything in the pie crust and put the oven at three fifty. Or don't—I can bring home pizza. Claudia's at a friend's, Emily's at band, Cole's at baseball practice. They could be home any minute. Don't tell them anything, Louise. Make something up. I'll be back as soon as I can."

She nodded.

"Louise, I want you here if I have to tell them."

"Of course." Louise said in her most dignified voice, the one she used at church meetings.

30

I swung the car in reverse, gunned it backwards up the driveway, and floored it forward for a left turn onto Grove Street. Two cars blocked me from turning left on Willow and only when I shook my fist at them did I comprehend why I was rushing. I arrived at the Newton-Wellesley Hospital in seventeen minutes and parked outside the emergency room entrance. Two ambulance drivers were having a smoke in front of me and I resented that. I grabbed my purse, straightened my hair, and stepped out into the dreary rain, taking wide, strong steps through the hospital's double doors. The lobby was so bright I put my hand above my eyes and approached the nursing station. *I look like Tonto*, I told myself. I approached a young woman who was chewing gum at the reception desk. Her hair was pulled back in a ponytail and her perfect fingernails were too long for someone whose job involved typing.

"I'm here about James Macabee." There was no need to say more than that. She had difficulty looking at me but her voice was kind. This was not standard emergency room fare. The feeling I felt from her was a combination of pity and formality.

"Let me get Dr. West for you, ma'am. Why don't you have a seat? He'll come out to talk to you."

"Thank you." I wasn't sure if I said this out loud. I sat down in one of those orange plastic swirl chairs; I counted eight of them all riveted together in one row. The fake leather black pocketbook Louise gave me at Christmas hung from my right wrist and I clutched two fresh Kleenexes in my left hand, which was moving aimlessly until I realized how strange that looked. I willed it to rest in my lap. I sat straight up and stared ahead, focusing on nothing. My feet were perfectly aligned and I didn't move. Louise's nuns would have been pleased with my posture. I didn't dare make eye contact with any of the five or six people also waiting. One man held his left hand in a bloody bandage and beside him a teenage girl with blue spiked hair leaned over a little boy who looked about four, lying limply on her lap.

When a tall, thin man in blue scrubs walked toward me, I knew it was Doctor West. We nodded to one another and he asked if I was Mrs. Macabee.

"Yes," I nodded again. When I stood up, he rested his hand on the small of my back and I followed him through swinging doors labeled 'Hospital Personnel Only.' We said nothing until we reached the nursing station, then he turned to face me and pointed in the direction of a long row of small cubbies, about eight in all, some open and empty, and some covered by floor-length curtains. He pointed to the last cubby on the left. That curtain was closed.

"Mrs. Macabee, what have the police told you?"

My energy was too low to waste a word on small talk. "They said my husband is dead. I'm hoping you tell me something different." I looked at him earnestly. My tears were slow to form but it was obvious they were close.

Doctor West nodded. "I'm sorry," he said. "The force of the trauma was severe." He knew to keep it short. He was young and most likely he'd performed this role before, this harbinger of horrible news, but I could tell by his face that he hated this part. I tried to prepare myself and I was glad to be with a doctor who had enough compassion that it bothered him to deliver this kind of news. He put his hand on my back again and cleared his throat.

"Your husband sustained a severe closed head injury. The police report said he was apparently changing a flat tire and the car jack failed and the body of the vehicle fell onto him. He was unresponsive at the scene with no vital signs. He was pronounced deceased at four fifty-five p.m." He looked to me for clues about how much more to say.

4:55? But what about AA?

From the look on his face, Dr. West didn't expect my next question. "Did you do an alcohol count?"

"Yes," he said. He paused to be sure I wanted to know.

"And...?"

"Point eight." He watched my expression. *Yes, the doctor nodded, the alcohol count was over the limit. Yes, he agreed, that was probably a factor.* He waited for me to say more, but instead I opened the gold clasp on my pocketbook and pulled out the fancy handkerchief Claudia had given me last Christmas. I blew my nose, wiped my eyes, forced my chin up, pushed my head back, and looked at him head on.

"Thank you, Doctor. I'd like to see my husband now."

Dr. West guided me forward thirty, maybe forty steps, stopped, and slowly pulled the curtain back. In the tiny space, about ten by fourteen feet in all, the first thing I saw, tucked in the far right corner, was a royal blue leather chair, eerily similar to the one from my childhood. I felt a wash of confusion from that, but only for a second, before the medical equipment took over, and then the gurney. I knew the rounded mound on that gurney, covered by a starched white sheet, was Jimmy. Dr. West stood in place as I approached. I put my hand on the sheet and felt Jimmy's chest.

The doctor looked at me, calculated if I was ready, and in one smooth movement he pulled the sheet back to expose Jimmy's face and upper torso. My husband looked so slight. *Had I not noticed that before now?* His chest fell into itself, sunken and deflated and his face was covered with purple and blue bruises, especially on his right side. But worst of all was the swelling and the discoloring all along Jimmy's right eye and nose and cheek bone. He looked so beaten up my heart broke for him. I brought my hand to my mouth and I whimpered. Dr. West put his arm around me.

31

Whatever I felt—shock, grief, disbelief—gave way to anger on my drive home. Even in my diminished state I made no effort to ignore the alcohol count: *Damn it, Jimmy, damn you. You did this, Jimmy. You pulled me in again for one last time. Thanks a lot, Jimmy.*

I wanted to run away, but instead I kept thinking, *What should I tell the kids? How can I tell them?* That was the paramount thing on my mind: Jimmy's actual death—what it would mean to me, to all of us—would come later. I was upset and angry but along with every other feeling a person could have in such a circumstance, I was also weirdly relieved. Not even one day after he promised, Jimmy's drunken carelessness had killed him. Hearing that alcohol content was the final, final straw for me. Jimmy had a sickness that he couldn't control and I couldn't control and I had to face the fact that no amount of prayer or promise could change that, in life or death.

My fingers clenched the steering wheel, and I kept my forehead and jaw tight to push back tears. Over and over I repeated, *focus, Christine, focus.* I stopped and picked up two dozen readymade square pizza slices. The kids needed comfort food and I doubted Louise had managed to finish the chicken pot pie. It had stopped raining and I looked up to a breakthrough almost-blue sky. *No* tears, I told myself. *How I handle this matters. The kids will remember how I tell them, how I sound.*

I pulled into the driveway and Louise met me at the kitchen door, looking grim. She'd had no time to change her clothes or straighten her hair in her traditional old lady-top-of-the-head bun so she looked oddly disheveled. I nodded and she understood. *He won't be around tonight. He'll be invisible and inaccessible and I have three children to explain this to.*

The table was set and the kids were waiting. Cole stood and came at me, not six inches from my face. "What's going on, Mom? Where did you go and why is Aunt Louise here?" Emily and Claudia didn't move. Louise puttered with the pizza box.

"Okay, kids, okay. Let's get the food on the table and we'll talk."

Louise had managed to remove the white meat, legs, and wings from the chicken and she brought it on a serving plate and placed it beside the pizza box. Claudia handed out pizza slices and Louise passed the chicken.

"The beets…" Louise muttered, "I didn't know what to do with them."

"No beets tonight," I said. There was no way we were going to deal with Jimmy's beets tonight.

"Get your drinks, kids."

Emily and Claudia hadn't said a word. I couldn't read Claudia; she seemed mostly impatient. I noticed she had a hickey on her neck and it killed me not to call her out on it. But this wasn't the time to do that.

Cole was stone-faced. The tick-tick-tick of our grandmother clock sounded so urgent I wanted to throw it across the room. I took a deep breath.

"Kids, your father had an accident. A bad accident."

I gripped the table with both hands. This must be what white knuckling meant.

"Daddy was helping someone change a flat tire in the rain and there was an accident." I held on to the table like I might fall but my posture gave nothing away. I wanted to be calm and factual and in control of my next sentence but it was hard to push the words out.

Louise piped in. "A car fell on your father," she said.

There was no sound except the ticking clock. I forced myself to finish Louise's sentence.

"And he died."

32

The grandmother clock was counting out the minutes of Jimmy's death. Emily sobbed. She was the first to speak. "Oh God," she said.

I kept my head up and my chin straight. These kids counted on me and I wanted my steadiness to be strong as steel. Sitting across from me, Claudia locked her eyes on mine.

"Mom, are you serious?"

I nodded. "It was an accident on Route 128."

Cole shook his head, looked down at his hands and said nothing. He had a look I didn't recognize, almost like embarrassment.

Louise picked at her fingers.

I checked Cole's expression again; his face was blank and he didn't move. I made a mental note to especially watch and worry about him. Maybe all Jimmy's meanness would bring up feelings the other kids wouldn't have.

Still crying, my thirteen-year-old Emily wiggled onto my lap and I stroked her hair from behind.

"Listen kids," I said, "listen to me. We'll find ways to remember Daddy. But we're going to get through this. We're all going to keep doing our normal things and we're going to have our regular meals and we're going to help each other. It's normal to cry or feel confused or scared, but we are not going to fall apart and we are not going to let this change our family." And knowing I should stress loyalty, I added, "Your father will stay in our hearts."

My mind raced through what this all meant. It's not like Jimmy was part of our day-to-day. But you only get one father. Louise and I hardly ever saw our own father but he was still our father.

I was about to say something about grief when we were startled by a sudden knock on the door. It was Marla Sacks, our neighbor across the street. She and her husband had a yard that looked like the city dump: old tires and car parts scattered all over the front lawn. They yelled at their two kids too much and too loud but it was also true the kids were terrors. Marla had a lock on being the neighborhood gossip but she meant well.

I opened the door only a quarter way. That made it clear I wasn't inviting her in.

"Marla, this is not a good time."

"Just a quick question," she began but when she took a quick scan of the scene in front of her she caught on. "Christine, what's wrong?"

I lowered my voice so the kids wouldn't hear me. "Jimmy had an accident this afternoon. He died."

"Oh my God!" she screamed. Her animation jolted everyone.

"Oh, Christine honey, I'm so sorry." And as an afterthought, "Is there anything I can do?"

"No, thank you Marla, not now." I moved to close the door.

"Well," she said, raising her hand to keep the door open, "I came because I wanted to ask if Jimmy could help Joe move some scrap metal." She meant no rudeness and she continued, "We wanted to borrow his truck..."

"No, Marla. Not today."

"Oh, okay, of course not. I'll come back later. I'll make some pies for you. I'm so sorry, Christine." She slunk away reluctantly. I knew she would gladly forfeit the loan of Jimmy's truck for the details of his death, but I just shut the door and returned to the table.

Emily was now semi-composed. "Did he have pain?"

This was a transition point and I welcomed it. "No pain," I said emphatically. "The doctor said Daddy died right away. There was absolutely no pain. The last thing he did was try to help someone, and he was on his way home for supper tonight."

There was no way I would ever say otherwise to my kids.

Cole shook his head. "But how...what about...?" He stopped and started again.

"What, Cole?"

He looked perplexed. "What about the bills, Mom?"

I shoved away this question with a flick of my hand. "Don't you worry about that, son. That's a grown-up question and Aunt Louise and I will handle that just fine." I looked at my sister and she nodded. She would be a full-force in my life again; my domineering holier-than-thou sister who I had to admit seamlessly handled the mechanics of life.

"Rest assured, children," Louise said. "That will not be one of our worries."

33

The next morning, Louise came back from sunrise Mass with a box of donuts. "It's easier to grieve with donuts," she announced.

I wasn't ready for levity, but she was right.

We were all at the table. "Kids," I began, "when you see Daddy, he'll be in a casket. He'll look like he's asleep."

I wanted them to be prepared at their first funeral. "A lot of people will come to pay their respects. You just have to thank them for coming. The wake gets over at seven, so afterwards, we can go to Pizza Hut. Then the next morning when we come back to the funeral home..."

"Stop, enough information," Louise interrupted. "Let's just stop at the Pizza Hut part for now. Donuts this morning, pizza tonight."

The kids nodded. Enough was enough.

Mr. Joyce Junior, barely twenty-five with a crewcut and a tailored three-piece suit as black as night, sat at my dining room table and told Louise and me what to expect. I balked at the idea that Jimmy's one and only suit would be buried with him, but he convinced me that looking good in the casket right to the end was important.

"We could skip the pants," he conceded, "because the casket is arranged so only Mr. Macabee's top half is visible."

For a brief moment the image of Jimmy in his boxer shorts was laughable, but wasteful or not, I decided it was not acceptable.

Jimmy's brother wanted him to hold their mother's rosary beads and that was fine, but Jimmy's hands had grease lines permanently embedded in them from years of working on car engines.

"Mr. Joyce, can you clean my husband's hands?"

"Certainly."

"What about his face?"

"None of the bruises will show, and we'll do our best to minimize the effects of the accident. I think you'll be very pleased with Mr. Macabee's appearance."

Well, I wasn't pleased. It didn't look like Jimmy: his face was still swollen and his lips were red with lipstick and his skin was pulled so tight he looked fake. As soon as I saw him, I tried to erase how he looked from my mind.

There was a constant line of well-wishers: relatives, neighbors, co-workers, high school friends, churchgoers, and a few local people who didn't know Jimmy but made a habit of attending Waltham's wakes and funerals. Manny and Joe from the auto shop had guilt all over their faces, Jimmy's AA sponsor, Brian, kept apologizing, and our neighbors, the Alexanders, who knew about Jimmy's drinking problem, simply cried, and I cried when they did.

The kids and I and Louise headed for Pizza Hut that night in pretty good shape.

"It felt like we were movie stars," Claudia said.

"Daddy knew more people than I thought," Emily said.

"It was okay," Cole said.

"He looked sober," Louise said.

34

At the funeral the differences in my kids were on full display. Eleven-year-old Cole, tall, trim, with his blond hair and blue eyes and perfect teeth, looked handsome and wholesome. He stood anchored, someone who could be counted on. Fifteen-year-old Claudia, with large gold hoop earrings and dressed in an all-black pants suit, looked more sexy than reverent. She could have been a night club soloist. Jimmy would have blown a gasket. Emily was barely thirteen, still a little girl in her sky blue, silky, knee-length dress with pale white flowers on it. We'd used an electric roller on her hair, so her curls fell just above her shoulders like Chinese lanterns, and I let her put on my pale pink lipstick. Myself, I wore a black, knee-length dress with a black scarf, black nylons and black flats. We were dressed and ready when Louise waltzed through the door with more donuts.

"This morning everyone gets two donuts each," she said. "Special occasion. Help yourself."

"No crumbs on your dress clothes please," I added.

I cried when the church organist played "Danny Boy." Even Louise wiped away a few tears. Claudia's black mascara ran down her face. Cole looked straight ahead with a locked jaw that made him look like an honor guard. Emily cried non-stop. Louise whispered something to her, opened her oversized shoulder bag, and motioned to Emily to feel around inside. She emerged with two strips of red licorice. Louise nodded. Emily gave one strip to Cole and they both quietly nibbled.

Afterwards, in the church parking lot, I chastised my sister. "Licorice in church? What were you thinking?"

Louise huffed back. "I told Emily it was holy licorice blessed by the cardinal himself and that it turned regular tears into healing tears."

"Louise," I said, "that is so ridiculous."

Later that night, when we were all back home and sitting around the table eating leftover fried chicken, Emily pulled out a new package of red licorice.

"Have some," she motioned to us all, "It's holy. You'll be glad you did."

35

The weeks that followed were a blur of calls to insurance companies and neighbors at the door with casseroles. To my surprise Jimmy had a death rider on our mortgage: the house would be paid for free and clear. And when Louise shuffled through the papers he kept in his nightstand, she found a twenty-thousand-dollar life insurance policy. That meant the kids could all go to college and there would be close to enough to handle day-to-day without involving Louise in our finances. Plus Mr. Irving at Standard-Thomson told me I could have my full-time job back whenever I was ready.

"Do you still want the bellows?" he asked.

"Of course."

"Grief hasn't changed your self-abuse," he said.

I laughed for the first time in what seemed like years.

Six weeks after Jimmy died, I went back to work, still on the first shift, but now full-time. This meant the kids got themselves off to school, but I was back home early enough each afternoon to keep an eye on everyone, especially Claudia, who apparently thought kissing boys was the eighth wonder of the world. I still hadn't dealt with her hickey on the day Jimmy died, but I was more vigilant.

For the first month post-Jimmy, Louise moved in with us. Her fussiness and bossiness drove the kids crazy but I was grateful, just like when we were little. All my life, what would have happened to me without my sister? I didn't normally compliment her, but one night after the kids were in bed, I asked her how she managed to turn out okay despite our childhoods. At least I'd had her; when she was little, she just had herself.

"Oh no," she corrected me, "I'm sure I benefited from the foster family I lived with until I was almost three. I don't remember much about that, except the woman sang to me a lot, and she smelled like baby powder."

This news shocked me. "What? You weren't with Mommy and Daddy?"

"No, the state took me away. I don't know who reported them; I always wondered if it was Grandma Alice. But guess what, Christine? It probably saved my life. I read an article that the first two years of a baby's life are the most important because that's when you learn if you're safe or not. That foster family must have taken good care of me."

"What about me, then?" I asked.

"You had me."

"Louise, you were four years old when I was born."

"Almost five."

"And you took care of me at five years old?"

"I did. I changed your diapers and I gave you your bottles. The milk was always cold because I couldn't use the stove but when you cried, I either gave you a bottle or put you in my lap and rubbed your face."

"Wow. How come you never told me?"

"Told you what?"

"About the foster family. And that you did that for me?"

"I never thought to tell you, that's all."

"Did you ever thank the foster family?"

"No, the Department of Social Services doesn't tell who it was and by now they've probably forgotten me or died. But you know what, Christine? The day I got sent back home the woman gave me a Raggedy Ann doll to take with me and I slept with her every night like she was my sister. Until you came along and then I had a real sister."

"Louise, this makes me cry."

Louise hmphed. "Not me. It makes me lucky."

And with that, Louise, my big sister winked, puckered her lips and landed a kiss on the top of my head.

PART 3

Teens

36

Jimmy hadn't kept up his life insurance payments. The twenty-thousand dollars I counted on wasn't coming, and my hope for summer camp for the kids ended before it began. The money and camp would have been nice, but it wasn't what mattered most. I was determined that the kids and I would take care of one another and I drilled that message to them every chance I got. But barely a month after Jimmy died, I got a call from Cole's school.

"Mrs. Macabee?" The voice on the other end of the phone was rushed. I didn't like that from the start.

"Yes, it is. Who is this?"

"This is Mrs. Wiley, your son Cole's guidance counselor at JFK. I'm afraid we may have a problem. I'm calling because Mrs. Wright sent him to the office for drawing inappropriate pictures in class. And when she confronted him about it, he was rude to her."

"Rude? That doesn't sound like Cole. What kind of inappropriate pictures?"

"The one I have in front of me shows a coffin with a huge sword through the top of it and birds flying all around it."

"Mrs. Wiley, I don't know you and it sounds like you may not know my son. His father died recently. That drawing doesn't sound awful, given the circumstance. He probably needs the school to cut him some slack."

"I'm sorry, Mrs. Macabee. We are all very sorry for your loss. But it's unacceptable for Cole to talk to his teacher like he did. And these drawings—we're worried about him too."

"What did he say to Mrs. Wright?" I kept my tone civil.

"He told her she was making a big deal out of nothing. He was rude." Mrs. Wiley paused. "We have to consider that insubordination, Mrs. Macabee. That's cause for suspension. We need you to address this so it doesn't go any further."

Mrs. Wiley's voice was so formal and tight it was a good thing we weren't in the same room, but I knew better than to argue. Schools are factories of conformity, after all.

"I'll talk to Cole," I said. "It won't happen again."

That afternoon, Cole looked at me sheepishly the moment he opened the kitchen door. He waited a minute for my reaction and when there was none, he put his backpack on the table and pushed his hands in his jean pockets.

"I know the witch called you, Mom."

"Which witch?"

Cole grinned. "Mrs. Wiley, the counselor. Mrs. Wright sent me there because she was concerned about me. That's what she told me."

"Is there reason for concern, Cole?"

I nudged him toward a chair at the dining room table and I pushed my chair beside him until we were shoulder-to-shoulder. I waited because I was pretty sure what would happen next and I was right. His tears came slowly, small little fissures, and his head fell on my shoulder. I wrapped my arms around him.

"What is it, son?"

"I know we're in trouble, Mom."

My head snapped back. "No, we're not."

"I heard you and Aunt Louise talking about Dad's life insurance. And what if you die too? We're still kids." More tears.

"Cole, there's no way I'm dying. None. Zip. Zero. Look at me. I love you kids and I love life. I'm healthy as a horse. You've held these tears in too long, that's all. They were bound to come out."

"You can't promise."

"I can."

Of course this was an assurance no human being could honestly make, and Cole knew it too, but he needed to hear it.

"Cole, honey, it's important to talk about your feelings. If you keep fear inside you, it grows into pictures of coffins and swords and mean birds."

Cole smiled. "She told you."

"Yes, and she said there were more but she didn't tell me about any others."

"Well, one was a man floating face down in a river."

"Daddy?"

"I guess so, but Mom, I'm sorry: I really don't miss him. I didn't want him to die, but it's better without him." He hesitated and swallowed. "Do you think I had anything to do with his accident?"

"Oh my God, no. Why would you think that?"

Cole wiped his face. "He hated me, Mom."

"Cole, listen to me—he didn't hate you. We all suffered from your father's drinking. When you drink like that, you lose your kindness for other people. You got the worst of it because you're a boy. I tried to protect you but it's my fault you had to put up with it. Of course it was scary when Daddy was drunk and mean. But I was never scared because I knew he was more bark than bite, and I knew I could protect us all. I should have known you wouldn't know that."

Cole looked down on his hands. They were fidgeting in his lap and a distraction from looking at me straight on. "Is it awful not to miss him, Mom?" He cleared his throat again. "And why was he coming home for supper that night? He was never home for supper."

The confusion in his voice just about killed me. "He was coming home because he promised me he stopped drinking and we'd all have a fresh start. But he didn't keep that promise. And he did something reckless, drinking and driving and then changing that tire in the rain."

I knew there was more to be said. I knew my son needed honesty. "I don't miss him either, honey." I said this so nonchalantly I think it surprised both of us. And I added, "Cole, your father chose to drink. He chose drinking over his family. That's a tragedy, but it's not your fault or anyone else's fault."

I wrapped my arms around my son and held onto him for a long time. I couldn't protect him from what had already been stamped into his life, but I'd be damned if he didn't know that his mother would never be far away.

37

1985

Cole was an athlete and Emily was a bookworm and I had no real worries about either of them. But Claudia was a different story. Even though she was smart and confident, and sweet and dependable, her involvement with boys troubled me, and once she started high school my concerns hit high gear. Boys pursued her: she had no shortage of flirtations, blind dates, second dates, long dates, even a marriage proposal from a weird kid who worked the nightshift at the Pancake House. Most of the time she was nonchalant about the boys she dated, but she also made excuses for most of them. They could be late picking her up or troublemakers in school; it didn't seem to matter to her. She let things like that slide. I was increasingly concerned that she didn't know how to judge the *character* of the boys who pursued her.

The day before her senior prom I overheard Claudia and Emily talking.

"Doesn't it bother you that he hasn't checked in with you yet?" Emily asked her sister.

Claudia answered right away. "No, and I have no idea what you're talking about, Emily. First of all, you don't really date so how would you know anything? And second of all, he's not going to stand me up for our prom. Nobody would be that bad."

I don't know how Emily reacted to that, but after a quick silence, Claudia spoke again.

"Listen, I don't mind waiting and putting a boy first, even if I might get mad sometimes. Even Mom says that's a good thing, to be patient and kind. I'm not worried about when Jeremy will call me. But I don't take any crap, either. Any boy who's too selfish, or mean to me, I'd definitely dump him."

Claudia was partially right: I did stress the importance of putting other people first. I considered that as a glue for our family and a good rule in life. But listening to her explanation, it didn't sound right. Also, she seemed especially susceptible to the physical part of teenage dating. I won't say the sexual part because as far as I know there was more excitement than arousal. But when she turned seventeen, I let her go on the pill. There was no way I was going to risk Claudia getting pregnant and messing up college and her life. Louise was mortified.

"You might as well pay for a motel room, Christine. You are wrong, wrong, wrong."

I didn't agree one bit. Not to say I ignored the problem: I made a point of being in the kitchen Friday and Saturday nights when Claudia came home from the Knights of Columbus dance or from a date. She probably wondered why I was baking bread or making beef stew or cleaning the kitchen counters at midnight, but it worked for me. She had a midnight curfew and not a minute later. One night she waltzed in twenty minutes late and looked guilty as hell. I saw a damn hickey on her neck. I thought fast and spoke slow.

"You're late."

"I know, Mom. I'm so sorry. Jeremy ran out of gas and his brother had to bring us some."

I nodded. "Did you have a fun time?"

"Yes."

"How was the movie?"

"Good."

"Let's sit down."

"Why? Am I in trouble? I'm not usually late, Mom."

"Claudia, I would call that hickey on your neck trouble."

Punishing Claudia for the hickey was the easy part: I grounded her for a full week, but I knew a hickey lecture would fly right over her head, so instead, I talked about the sanctity of real love, and how important it was to physically wait for that.

"I'm worried about your decisions with boys. You don't know enough yet, Claudia, about holding out until you meet your soulmate."

Claudia looked slightly amused and mildly curious. "But how does anyone know who that is? I can't imagine Daddy was your soulmate."

I didn't lie. "No, honey, I guess he wasn't. And look what happened. You'll know when you meet the right person. But you have to be older, at least twenty-one to even know. Please wait, Claudia, I beg you to wait. Don't give your body away like it's some prize at a carnival. You have to control your urges. Those birth control pills are just an insurance policy. I'm trusting you to not need them."

She didn't try to con me. She listened, but I couldn't be sure she understood the importance of what I told her. For the next five years, until she was out of college, I suspected Claudia used that insurance policy on a regular basis. Some people operate from a physical plane and I think she was one of those people. There was only so much I could control. And once she became a full-fledged adult, and especially during her years-long affair with the married man, I prayed Claudia knew the difference between love and passion. She saw her father and me in a passionless marriage, that's for sure. Years later, when she was all tangled up and heartbroken, every so often I wondered if that married man might have been her soulmate. I didn't know, because I couldn't bear to meet him.

38

1987

I hated when anyone asked me about life without Jimmy. If I told the truth, which I never did, our family felt so much easier without him. There must be a special place in heaven for people who love and live with alcoholics, with all the unpredictability, broken promises, self-loathing, and constant turmoil that comes with it. After Jimmy died, for the first time in my entire life, I was free of all that. I kept a close leash on the kids, we ate meals together, Louise and I and the kids rented a cabin at Canopy Lake for a week every summer, and as a family we kept reading and rewarding poems. But when my kids were old enough to fix their own sandwiches and hang out unsupervised, I was free to be a little footloose and fancy free with Louise.

I don't remember how we began our gallivants, but they became staples of my social life. Louise picked me up promptly every Saturday at 9:30 a.m., impatiently honking the horn of her 1980 limited edition black convertible Thunderbird she named Prissy. She mostly drove Prissy from May through October, claiming that April weather was too slippery and November and winter weather was also too slippery, but for the short rides to breakfast and then to the mall, Prissy did just fine. The two of us rode her like a champion stallion. First, we headed to The Iron Skillet Cafe, arriving at 9:47 a.m. almost to the second. Linda May Elliott, who graduated from Waltham High with Louise, grinned and pointed us to our corner table by the double-casement windows, our regular spot overlooking the parking lot. Linda May brought out a plastic gold carafe of hot coffee and two small metal pitchers of half-and-half. Louise ordered the Texas special, two eggs sunny-side up, three strips of bacon, and home fries on the grill with green peppers and onions, and I ordered a side of fresh fruit, a large bowl of oatmeal with extra brown sugar, Canadian bacon, and whole wheat toast with strawberry jam. I always laughed at the obvious differences in our food choices, but when we clinked our coffee cups together, our differences melted away.

"Helen Tomassi is having a face lift!" Louise announced. "It's costing her six hundred dollars and you know damn well you can't change a pig into a parakeet. The poor woman."

"Who told you?"

"Marie Bunifucco. She told me for spite because she'd do it too if she had the money. Another case of trying to change a pig into a parakeet."

"Louise, I think that's a weight loss example."

"Well, what would you say then, Miss know-it-all?"

"I would say you can't teach a fish to fly."

We were still laughing when Linda May delivered breakfast. We poured ourselves more coffee.

"So how did Cole do in the trials?"

"He made varsity," I said, nodding for emphasis. "He'll be the captain of his baseball team by the time he's a junior. The coach told me he's a natural athlete and he's popular so the players listen to him, but the best part is he's not conceited. I don't know where that kid gets his confidence. And you know, Louise, he's the first one to help me with the house. He cleans the yard, he sweeps, he puts the groceries away. Sometimes he cooks with me. And he likes poems! He's the whole package."

Louise tilted her head. "He obviously has genes from our side of the family."

"Aww, don't go bashing Jimmy again. He was smart, Louise. The booze just got to him."

"I'll say," Louise said flatly. "You chose a doozy, Christine."

I pushed back. "And you chose God and God divorced you before a year was up."

"Christine, the Lord needed me elsewhere." Louise fluttered her eyes.

"Bull. That's not why you got booted from the convent. What exactly did you do, Louise? All these years, you've never told me what happened."

"Maybe I'll tell you in another ten years."

"No, tell me now. Please. I'll pay for breakfast."

Louise sat back as if we were in for a long story. "Looking back, I may have been wrong. But it was so frivolous at the time even the junior Mother Superior thought I should have been given a second chance."

"A second chance?"

"Okay, a third chance. Or was it a fourth chance? Any hoo, Sister Theresa was so strict, she made us wear our bras to bed. We thought that was crazy because really, it was." Louise began laughing before she even had a reason to. She composed herself and continued, "Remember the itching powder I bought for Cynthia Franklin's pajama party?"

I shook my head.

"No? Well, don't ask me why but I took it with me to the convent. Then one night Sister Theresa left her bra in the group bathroom: it was just flopping around on the bathroom door knob. I knew it was hers because it was a 42-triple-D. We joked that she needed lifts in the back of her shoes just to keep her from falling forward flat on her face."

I shook my head. "This story sounds ballsy already."

Louise grinned. "I sprinkled half the powder in both bra cups and I rubbed it in really good and then I shook the excess over the trash can so she wouldn't know. I told all the girls, of course, except my roommate and that girl from New Hampshire. What was her name? She was such a mouse. We kidded that she was already married to the Holy Ghost." Louise chuckled. "Any hoo, the next morning at Mass, Sister Theresa was on the altar assisting Father Davidio. At first, she started to squirm. She tried to ignore it. But by the time Father read the gospel she was grabbing her boobs like crazy. She pressed and rubbed and twisted them up and down and from side to side. We tried to keep straight faces; we tried, but we couldn't. We were laughing even before she ran off the altar screaming, "Help, help, it's spiders! Spiders!"

Louise and I laughed so hard we just about spit up our food.

"Don't ask me the rest, Christine. It's too painful to relive the injustice that befell me because of that one innocent lapse of judgement."

"But what happened to Sister Theresa?"

"The emergency room."

We roared.

After breakfast, depending on the weather, Louise and I did one of two things. When it was cold or rainy, we went to the library and read magazines—*Life, Vogue, Mademoiselle*, and our favorite, *Cosmopolitan*. But if it was sunny, we headed for our bench in the middle of the Waltham Common. Louise knitted and I mostly watched birds. We also talked non-stop. *Did Emily get her period? Is the plant closing early on Christmas Eve? Would you let anyone touch your toes for a pedicure?*

Sometimes we walked around the square block perimeter of the Common, and sometimes we pulled out my copy of last week's *Sunday Globe* and read the arts and movie section out loud. But mostly, we sat and kibitzed, like always.

"We had it rough as kids, Louise."

"You worse than me, Christine. But look how we turned out. We're still standing and nobody knocks us around. And you even managed to have nice kids." She paused. "I just hope Claudia keeps her pants up."

"Don't start, Louise." And when I added, "Zip it," we laughed so hard I almost peed.

We were ready to eat again by noon time, rotating where we went and never repeating the same place within a twelve-week cycle. Our favorite was the tried-and-true Chateau Restaurant on School Street, followed by Grassfields on Lexington Street and the Chinese Buffet in back of the Stop and Shop Market. We also had all of Moody Street and all of the Watertown Mall to choose from, and that meant the Twin City Steak House, Applebee's, and the mall food court with choices of pizza, Chinese, Italian and Philadelphia cheesesteaks, all rolled into one. We especially liked the mall because afterwards we slid right into the Ann and Hope department store and shopped the afternoon away. We bought cosmetics, greeting cards, licorice, underwear, occasionally a sweater or nightgown for ourselves, and always necessities and presents for the kids.

For a self-professed cheapskate, Louise was generous with her money. She'd saved a bundle during her decades working at City Hall, and that didn't include her pension. She hated to see me struggle, so she bought most of the clothes for the kids. This was a blessing and a curse, because sometimes Louise arbitrarily picked out their clothes and Claudia especially hated her taste.

"I refuse to dress like Barbie!" she whined. When it reached the point where Louise was returning just about everything she bought for the girls, we reached a necessary compromise: I would accompany Louise on all shopping trips not supervised by Claudia or Emily themselves. But aside from their rejections of Louise's taste in clothes, the kids had every reason to look forward to Saturday afternoons because around three, Louise and I arrived back home with plenty of shopping bags. There was usually one top-secret bag—early birthday or Christmas presents—but for the most part, our purchases were a free-for-all. We spread the contents across the dining room table and the Macabee version of a weekly treasure hunt began. Clothing was easily decided by sex and size but the other purchases became a guessing game. I'd hold up a tube of hot pink lipstick or a miniature hot car and ask, "Who gets this?" More than once, Louise warned me that I was asking for trouble because the kids often fought about who got what, *It's for me, No, it's for me!* but I continued this practice until Emily got married.

"It's a good way for them to learn that you can't have every-thing you want and if that's a problem, you have to figure out a way to share." That was my explanation, and for the most part, it worked.

Louise stayed on for homemade pizza on Saturday nights. All of us worked an assembly line along the kitchen counter: I rolled out the dough, Louise spread the tomato sauce, Cole sprin-kled the mozzarella cheese, Emily added the pepperoni, or sau-sage or both, and Claudia made the salad. Midway through sup-per, I always asked if anyone had a poem to share. Some nights there were none and some nights there were several. Extra points were given if the author of the poem was sitting at the table.

On the fourth Saturday of every month, I brought out the burlap bag with an extra twist: a two-dollar gift certificate to

Brigham's Ice Cream Parlor for the Poem of the Month, which I alone decided. I also kept coming at the kids with my own arsenal of poems. I read at least two. If they gave me a hard time, I threatened them with John Denver songs.

"Another nice Saturday," Louise confirmed, her phony brown vinyl pocketbook tucked under her boobs.

"Yes," I said. "We know how to make good times happen."

"Oh, by the way, Christine—" she began.

"Don't say it, Louise. Whatever it is, I don't need to hear it at the end of a nice day." I looked at her firmly. "No advice, remember?"

She huffed. "Someday you'll be sorry for not listening to me. So far you have a zero- batting record for husbands and thank God you're an all-star when it comes to children. But…"

"No buts!" I raised both hands palm up in front of her face, then pushed them apart, I leaned forward and planted a wet kiss on my sister's lips.

"See you tomorrow," I said. "Don't forget to bring dessert."

While Louise revved up Prissy, I sat in my living room and sunk into the couch, letting gravity claim my arms and legs. I tucked Jimmy's favorite pillow behind my back and made the sign of the cross. I heard the bath water run upstairs, watched Cole pull a calculator from the desk, and reminded Claudia that her curfew was midnight sharp and hickeys carried huge penalties.

Everything was pretty perfect for a long time. I kept a close eye on Claudia, Emily was a happy bookworm, and Cole showed no signs of discontent. I understood that he expressed himself differently than his sisters did, so I wasn't concerned that he didn't talk much about his feelings. I figured he was just being a boy.

39

1990

"Did you hear?" Cole's high school buddy ran up to him in between classes. He was so eager to share the news.

"Hear what?"

"Mr. Avecedo. He's gay!"

"He likes boys?" Cole tried to hide how shocked he was.

"Yes, he likes boys. And he's in big trouble."

In his whole life, my teenage son knew only two kids who were different. One was Manny Ricardo who had six toes on his left foot, and the other was Paul Moscano, a dark-skinned kid from the only mixed-race family in town. So, when Cole told me his eleventh-grade history teacher had been outed at a gay pride march in New York City, I could tell that his view of normalcy was turned upside down. Somebody had sent the school principal a photo of Mr. Avecedo wearing tight shorts and a muscle shirt, holding a rainbow flag on Fifth Avenue, and sporting a rainbow bandana around his head. The school committee arranged an emergency meeting and he wasn't exactly fired, but the next day he was pulled off coaching the girls' basketball team. Most of the kids and some of the teachers thought it was ridiculous to stop him from tossing balls to hormone-filled teenage girls. But not everyone felt okay about a gay teacher at school. He taught until the end of the year and he didn't return in September. Cole's biology teacher told him that he and the school had come to a "mutual understanding."

When this happened to Mr. Avecedo, I think it triggered something inside Cole, and he began to think more seriously about himself. Jimmy made things so difficult for him. His father criticized everything, even that his hands were too soft. My son looked and acted like every other boy his age, but in some vague way, I think Jimmy knew and I think Cole knew too, that he wasn't exactly a 'normal' boy.

Cole dated girls all through high school but something was always missing. My son was a gentleman: he assured me that he never traded stories with the guys about who scored, and he thought bragging about it was lame. But the incident with Mr. Avecedo seemed to stir up a confusion I guess he always felt, but as far as I could tell, he stayed naive about any preference for boys until his first year in college. He sheepishly told me about an incident during his freshman year, one night after a Friday night beer binge at the Old Town Bar in East Providence. He'd had too much to drink, passed out in his dorm room, and when he woke up, his roommate—an equally athletic kid from New Jersey— was in bed with him. He said that after that night, he still dated girls, but it wasn't the same.

If Cole fought with himself about being gay, he finally came clean during his sophomore year at Brown, seven years after Jimmy died, when he brought Shawn Mullins home with him for Christmas. I knew this was an important step, and I was glad he didn't have to face his father's judgements. I don't know if he could have handled that. I knew Louise would hit the roof, but not forever. All in all, I was relieved and hopeful that Cole was finding himself. This was long before the explosion of AIDS changed everything.

40

Christmas was a big deal in our family. Claudia and I cooked and baked for weeks before our celebration officially began on Christmas Eve. Cole told us that his friend Shawn's parents were in Switzerland and he had no family and no place to go for the holidays. I instantly welcomed him, because a new guest meant a new dynamic and new conversations, and I loved all of that.

"Do you like poetry, Shawn?" I asked ten minutes after he and Cole arrived.

"Not really, Mrs. Macabee," he said, "but I've learned some poems from Cole and I like everything he writes or reads to me."

"Well, you'll be hearing "A Child's Christmas in Wales" tonight," I told him. "And afterwards we'll each open a present. I noticed there's a few packages for you under the tree. And tomorrow you and our twenty-five-pound turkey will hear some of our favorite poems of 1990." I smiled. "We are a poetry family. Even the visiting dogs like poetry."

Later, while Shawn showered and I fussed with the buffet table, Cole snuggled into me from behind and wrapped his arms around my waist.

"I'm glad to be home."

My wheels were turning even before I turned to face him. I could tell that he knew my expression meant something.

"Honey," I said slowly, "can I ask you something?"

"I think so."

"Is Shawn gay?"

Cole reacted with a noticeable jolt, like a burglar alarm had gone off. I didn't let on that I noticed.

"What makes you ask that, Mom?"

"He looks gay. Most men don't wear pink shirts. And he moves his hands in a certain way."

"What if he is, Mom?" This would be the first time we talked about this subject directly.

I lowered my brow, pulled my chin back, and tightened my mouth, as if to say, *Are you freaking kidding?* "Cole Macabee, you know I don't care one bit." I stared hard at him. "But is there something you want to get off your chest?"

"Maybe," he said.

I lowered my voice to almost a whisper, "Cole, you do this however and whenever you want. None of us cares except maybe Aunt Louise and heck, I enjoy seeing her riled up. All that matters is that you're happy and that you choose good people who are good to you. Your family loves you, period."

Dozens of people showed up on Christmas Eve for our family's good cheer and jammed-packed holiday buffet. Cole's high school baseball coach came, all the neighbors brought liquor, and Claudia brought a date, a tall, thin guy with a mustache who immediately creeped Louise and me out because he couldn't keep his hands off her.

At midnight, after the last guests left, Claudia and Cole got ready to recite "A Child's Christmas in Wales." This was a tradition we had for just about forever.

"Okay, kids," I announced, "Grab some of Claudia's cookies and make yourself comfortable. The night's still young!"

Our tradition had two parts: first we recited the poem and then we each opened one present from under the tree. Cole always picked one of Claudia's gifts because it was usually something that glowed, glittered, or made sounds—one year a pulsating night-light, once a talking robot, last year a watch with a rim that turned neon colors. This time it was one of those glitter balls you hung in the ceiling and it twirled a disco light all around the room. He grinned at Shawn and made a dance move.

It was a grand night. All the kids sat on the floor, and we all laughed for no reason. Even Louise, teetering on and off the couch and unsteady from several of Marla and Mr. Sacks' gin and tonics, laughed three octaves louder than her normal dignified self.

After everyone else headed to bed, Cole, Shawn and I stayed up for another half hour. We had fixed up a comfy space in the guestroom for Shawn, and it was rewarding to hear how relaxed he felt.

"You have a great family, Mrs. Macabee," he said. "You're like a perfect mother."

I laughed. "Thank you, Shawn. I can be tough, but I try to be deliberate about when."

He hesitated. "I hope this is okay to ask you: Is Cole's Aunt Louise okay with me being here?"

"What makes you ask that?"

"She looked uncomfortable with me, like she didn't know what to expect. And then she pulled me aside to tell me pink was her favorite color. Out of the blue. I didn't know what to say. It made me wonder if she might wonder if I was gay, or if she might be a lesbian?"

I nearly fell over. "Shawn, nobody here cares if you're gay. And no, Aunt Louise is not a lesbian," I said emphatically. "She's a guilty Catholic."

Everyone except Claudia was downstairs by seven o'clock the next morning. I made the coffee and laid out our traditional Christmas spread: an extra-large bowl of fresh strawberries, a tray of sliced honeydew melon, two New England Coffee Cakes cut into large pieces, and plenty of bacon. I woke up Claudia at 7:30 and fifteen minutes later, with our breakfast plates still balancing on our laps, we began opening presents. I was so happy there were small gifts for Shawn: a poster of the Citgo sign in Kenmore Square from Claudia, an Austrian beer mug from Cole, and two dozen homemade chocolate chip cookies from me. By now I was pretty sure Shawn didn't have a family like ours. I was proud of my kids and glad to include him.

It took almost two hours to get through the unwrapping. Just before we sat down for our turkey dinner, Cole and I were in my beloved kitchen, fixing the turkey sides. Shawn was on a walk with Emily, while Claudia and Louise lounged on the couch.

"Hey Mom," Cole said, "There's this poem by Oscar Wilde, it's called "The Ballad of Reading Gaol." He wrote it in 1895 while he was in a hard labor prison for being gay. I want you to read it."

I wiped my hands on my apron. "I gladly will, honey. Or you and Shawn could read it to me before you head back to school?"

Right away, I could tell that Cole wasn't ready for a public airing about being gay. Plus, I think hearing Shawn's and his name together was a jolt. I tried to correct myself, "Oh. I mean, well, what do I mean? Aren't you and Shawn...?"

He just nodded and then he smiled. I poured us each a glass of zinfandel wine, an indulgence I permitted the kids on holidays.

"Mom, thanks for making this easy for me."

"That flattery will get you everywhere, Cole Macabee. But the best part about me is that I'm your mother."

We clinked our glasses together. To this day I remember the sound they made because at that very moment, I believe my son knew it was okay to be who he was.

"I never wanted Dad to know," he said.

"That's fine," I responded, "But it was always his problem, not yours."

"And what about Aunt Louise?" he asked.

"It's up to you, Cole. She'll probably make a big Catholic hullabaloo about it, but it'll blow over. Because she loves you. And because there'd be hell to pay if she ever made you feel bad."

"Here's to another Christmas in the Macabee family," I announced at the end of the day, just before we all headed back to our other lives. I spread my arms upward and began singing John Denver's song, "Annie":

"You fill up my senses
Like a night in a forest..."

I was interrupted by Louise's impatient voice, "Oh, for God's sake, Christine!"

I laughed. "Merry Christmas, everyone!" I raised a glass of water above my head. "I'm so glad we're all together. Life is good."

Again came Louise's shrill voice, "Christine, don't be too sure about me; by next Christmas I could have eloped with a younger man."

Cole hesitated for the briefest moment, and with a grin on his face, he looked at Shawn.

"Me too," he said.

41

1991

Cole was asleep and still living in his college dorm when Aunt Louise called him. He barely managed to mumble a hello into the phone but it didn't matter: she started talking immediately.

"Cole!" she commanded, "It's me. It's ten o'clock. Why aren't you out of bed?"

He shook himself awake. "I'm up."

"Oh good," Aunt Louise sounded oddly sing-songy and definitely phony. "Your mother says I could end up in purgatory if I don't accept your circumstance. Can you believe she said that to my face?"

Louise held the master deed on judgements. Cole knew she would disapprove that he was gay on religious grounds alone, but to her credit she hadn't said a word about his Christmas confession until this groggy morning months later.

"I'm calling to make amends. Wake up, Cole! I can tell you're half asleep! I don't have all day." And then, again before he could say a word, she added, "I'm thinking about when you took me bowling for my birthday. How much fun we had. We should do it again."

This was her version of out-of-the-blue free association, but he knew where she was headed. It didn't matter that she couldn't see him nod because she had no need for a response. She just wanted him to know that nothing would change. The past was safe in the present. The bowling escapade took place on Louise's forty-seventh birthday, not long after our Christmas celebration. Louise told me all about it.

Cole's present to her was the two of them bowling and then ice cream sundaes at Happy Meadows in Lexington. This was a very generous present on Cole's part. He gave up prime week-end time and risked major embarrassment at the Lucky Strike Bowling alley, because whenever Louise threw a bowling ball, she slammed it down so hard the alley made a cracking sound.

"I only bowl every couple of years," she'd cackled. "That and the roller coaster at Revere Beach. I still go on that every five years. But I'm already three years behind." Louise loved the sound of her own jokes. But on this morning, her call to Cole had a specific purpose. She began gradually, or so she thought.

"Anyway Cole, do you remember when I pointed out that feminine-looking man on the alley next to us, and I asked you if anyone could be more homosexual?"

He remembered. He told me afterwards that Aunt Louise's hand had reached her mouth in two seconds flat. "Oops," she'd said. "That was too blunt. Let me change that and just say that his plaid pants are a bit unusual."

At the time, Cole had just shrugged his shoulders. But now, he added, "Aunt Louise, it's okay. I don't take your homophobia personally. But you should know that most people who are gay or lesbian are born that way. You should know that."

"Well, Cole," she replied. "I really don't. I cannot imagine what one man would see in another. Where are the curves, Cole? The lipstick and the girl parts? How can boys act like girls?"

"Aunt Louise, it's not about boys acting like girls. I don't act like a girl, right?"

"No, you mostly don't," she conceded. "Except when you wear those pink shorts."

"You told my friend Shawn that pink was your favorite color."

Aunt Louise cackled again. "I said that to make him comfortable. Everyone knows blue is my favorite color."

Cole had shaken his head and shrugged. "Auntie, being attracted to someone of the same sex is either something you're born with, or it becomes a choice and it's just who you are. Not all gay men are the same. Some are feminine, some are masculine; heck, some are so big and hairy they're called 'bears.'"

I wish I had been there to see Louise's reaction. "Oh, dear God, Cole," she said. But Cole had no time to respond. The bowling manager was approaching them.

"Ma'am," he said in a very serious voice, "I'm afraid I'll have to ask you to leave if you keep slamming the balls on the alley."

"Christine, that man ruined my score," Louise later told me over ice cream sundaes at Cabot's. "He threw off my timing. I could have broken my previous record."

"You could have broken his alley," I said.

"That's ridiculous," Louise countered. "Since when does a bowling alley break?"

So there they were, my son Cole and my sister Louise, now on the telephone, months later, too early in the day, and Cole knew that his Aunt Louise was dancing all around his sexual preference.

"So, you're calling me because…?"

"Your mother keeps nagging me. I'm calling to come see you at school. Unless you'd prefer to go bowling again?"

"Um, no, no," he said. "But yes, sure. Come with Mom and we'll go out to lunch. But you can't drill me with questions about being gay. Sometimes it's hostile enough out here."

He probably should have withheld that last comment: It was no surprise that he predictably visualized what Louise would say next.

"Cole," she said, "that is precisely a reason I think you shouldn't be gay."

He probably wanted to strangle her. Instead, he politely but firmly answered back. "Aunt Louise, it's who *I AM*. What don't you understand about that?"

Louise tried to de-escalate. "I would like to understand what you get in exchange for taking such risks."

Detente. Coming from a homophobe, that was a fair question, if only because it at least had some curiosity and honesty to it.

"Come, Auntie. You and Mom."

"Okay, Cole, I just have one small favor to ask you."

"What?"

"Don't wear pink." She quickly added, "And not just because it's girly. Don't tell your friend, but it's actually my least favorite color."

42

1992

In his senior year of high school, my athletic son had been offered three college scholarships and a minor league baseball contract. Louise and I assumed he'd jump at baseball with the Iowa Cubs, but instead he chose college at Brown University in Providence, Rhode Island. He majored in journalism so he could be a TV sportscaster. I made him promise to always love the Red Sox, but it was his dream to work in the New York City market and that meant covering the hated Yankees. All through his college years I kept up my nags about the Red Sox and about poetry—the latter especially because Cole needed an outlet for his feelings. Sometimes he agreed and sometimes he didn't.

"Boys do things differently, Mom. I work my stress out physically."

"That's good too, Cole, but don't ever forget the power of the poem."

He always grinned at me. "Yes, Mother," he said. "Of course. That too."

I was so proud of him, but of course my worry-free days didn't last. In 1985, when the sexy-hunk actor Rock Hudson died of

AIDS, I had no idea what it really meant. But by the time there were enough AIDS-related deaths of gay men in the United States that the Centers for Disease Control was predicting up to two hundred thousand new cases over the next two years, and news of an AIDS epidemic was showing up on the nightly news, my concern for Cole had taken on a new life. Could AIDS actually happen to my son? Not even the death of an eighteen-year-old "normal" boy named Ryan White had stopped people from labeling AIDS a gay disease and a gay curse and God-fearing Christian judgments became commonplace. People reacted in all kinds of ways, most of them unkind, ranging from denial to fear to who-cares.

Every time Cole came home, I hugged him and checked if he had lost weight. But Louise kept nagging me to do more. At her urging, I finally sent Claudia to evaluate what I wasn't able to do myself. Normally, I felt I could say anything on any subject to my kids. But I was too uninformed, and probably too nervous to know what to do, so I sent Claudia.

"Honey, I need you to check on your brother."

"How?" Claudia rolled her eyes but she knew I was serious.

"Keep in closer than normal touch with him. Go see him. Don't pretend you don't notice if something looks off. And tell me everything."

43

Claudia

I rocked back and forth on the balls of my feet, waiting for my brother to buzz me in. I knew my mother had reason to worry because I worried too.

A senior at Brown, Cole lived off campus on the third floor of a triple-decker, in an apartment with its original oak floors and oak trim around the doors and windows. In the midst of my nervous shuffle, the lobby door swung open and there he stood. My first thought seeing my brother was *I don't know how he does it—he'd look good in a mud wrestling match*. His blond hair was combed to perfection, curled just below his ears in his cultured preppy way. He peered at me and feigned surprise. *That suspicious grin he has,* I told my mother afterwards. *Mom, he was wearing an L.L. Bean blue flannel shirt with jeans creased in the front that he must have actually ironed. The only way I would ever look that good is if I was about to head out for the night. But Cole always looks good: is it a gay thing?*

"Come in, sis, come in," he said. I followed him up three flights of stairs and through his hall into his living room. He pointed to a spread of warm brie cheese surrounded by sesame crackers surrounded by a wider circle of green grapes, all arranged on a platter on the coffee table. In one motion he jumped onto the couch and folded his legs underneath him.

"So why are you here?" he asked, "What's your motive?"

I knew better than to fudge an answer. "Mom."

"And?"

"She asked me to come."

"And?"

"She's worried."

"And?" This time I heard a slight catch in Cole's throat.

"And she's worried."

"About what?"

"About AIDS."

"What about AIDS?"

"Cole, cut it out. Will you talk to me?"

His body fell back into the couch cushion. I sat across from him in a beat-up rocking chair. "Okay, sis. What are you fishing for?"

"We don't care that you're gay, Cole. You know that. And who the hell am I to talk? My sex life could be a feature in *Cosmopolitan*. But this is different. They say it's a death sentence." I regretted saying that immediately. By any measure, it was not a helpful statement.

"My life is not just about sex, Claudia." Cole rightly corrected me. There was a crispness to his voice, as if he had repeated this exact sentence many times before. He popped a grape into his mouth and took a deep breath. *I felt bad for him, Mom.*

"Look Claudia, I won't kid you. It's all horrible. You wouldn't believe how many guys are sick, and eight guys I know have died in the last three months. I don't talk about it at home because it's too hard. It's an escape for me when I come home."

"Do you have it, Cole?"

"Do I have what, Claudia, AIDS?"

"Yes."

"No, but I can't predict what's ahead." Cole paused. "I don't know what you know or don't know. There is so much misinformation. Someone I was with last year was just diagnosed as HIV-positive, so it's certainly possible I'm infected." He paused again. "I won't kid you, Claudia: it's a bad scene, terrifying really. It's hard to look ahead; my career in sports and thinking about Mom and all of us if we had to go through that."

This was not the reaction I expected. I thought he'd be irreverent or irritated and maybe even pissed. Instead, he was upset, blinking his eyes, kind of rapid fire.

"Mom asked me to come, Cole, but this isn't something you need to keep from us, and certainly not from me. I'm terrified too. But what now? You can't sleep around."

Mom, I said it and wished immediately I hadn't. It was so disrespectful. As if I even know what he's doing.

There was a controlled anger in Cole's response. I think he held back what he really wanted to say. "See, that's part of the problem right there. Everyone makes it about sleeping around, like it's the scarlet letter. It's not like that. I'll be tested every six months. I use condoms. I help my friends who are not so lucky." He stared hard at me. "I've joined a men's group at the student health center. There are fifteen of us. We support one another." He shook his head. "Two guys died last month..." His voice trailed off with so much sadness.

"Oh Jesus, Cole." I moved to the couch and wrapped my arm around his shoulder.

Mom, I told him, 'Cole,' my voice as soft as I could make it, 'we're here for you. Whatever you need. We're afraid for you.' I said it exactly like you told me to, Mom. I told him you made me practice that last sentence and we both laughed about it. He's okay. He told me, 'Claudia, I have a year left of school and I'm signed up to do an internship at the Providence Journal. I've never really slept around, anyway.'

"Who knows you're gay, Cole?"

"Oh, all my buddies here. I'm not ashamed of it, but I have obvious concerns about gay bashing in my chosen career."

"How are you treated?"

"Medically?"

"No, socially."

"It depends. The people who know me and care about me still know me and care about me. Some people who suspect I might be gay avoid me. That would include the mailman and my dentist and some of my professors. They can't totally avoid me but when I see they're uncomfortable I know enough not to offer a handshake or to take a step toward them. You wouldn't believe how many guys have families who've disowned them. Like they're freaking dying and they can't go home."

"That will never be us, Cole."

"I know." He shrugged. "But in sports I'm toast if I'm out as a gay man. I'm lucky I look like a normal jock. Am I supposed to give up my goals because I'm gay? The artist Robert Maplethorpe died from AIDS, Ms. Kitty from Gunsmoke after that. And this kid Ryan White. But somehow, it's all seen as a promiscuous gay men's disease caused by sleeping around. Never mind that a fucking monkey from Africa probably brought the virus over here."

"Mom wants me to tell you to keep reading and writing poetry."

"Ha!" Cole laughed, "The Macabee answer to everything. And speaking of poetry, how is Mom doing with her fantasy husband? I heard there's news." Cole smirked.

"Oh my God, Cole. She's coordinating his New England fan club. Wait until you see what she did in her bedroom. She has this huge poster of him over her bureau. With his goofy breakfast bowl haircut."

Cole smiled. "I'll be home next weekend, Claudia."

"Oh good," I responded. "I'll tell Mom you're doing fine. That's what I should tell her, right?"

"Yes, exactly," he nodded. "Leave it at that."

"Oh, by the way," I said. "I have news. I met a guy."

"Another one?" Cole teased. "Who's this one?"

"An attorney who likes to shop."

"That checks off a few boxes."

"Yup," I smiled, "It does. His name is Fabian Fontaine, which is a hoot, since people say you look like Fabian the actor. If he makes it past the fourth date, I'll bring him by."

Cole laughed. "I won't hold my breath."

I laughed too, thinking of the dozens of men I'd dated and discarded.

I left my brother with a growing uncertainty. Surely Cole wouldn't get AIDS. Surely, he wouldn't die.

PART 4

Love

44

1997
Christine

Life had given me plenty of reasons to worry, but my fantasy husband wasn't one of them until, in the late afternoon of October twelfth, John Denver crashed his plane into Monterey Bay. My scream was so loud, Louise rushed to the kitchen, expecting to find a natural disaster. Instead, I was holding the phone above my head and shouting to the heavens. Even Marla Sacks said she heard me from across the street.

"He's dead!" I shrieked. "He died!"

"Who? Who?" Louise shouted back.

"John! He died today."

"John? John who?"

"Louise, don't toy with me. I know you've never liked him."

"Never liked him? John? Christine, who is John?"

"John DENVER, Louise."

"John Denver?"

"Yes John Denver, My John Denver."

"Son of a holy beatch, Christine. You scared the holy hell out of me." Then, as an afterthought, Louise added, "I have only a measured amount of sympathy." She looked at my shocked expression and she softened. "Okay, what happened?"

"A plane crash. He was flying his new plane and it crashed in Pacific Grove, California. Not even an hour ago. That's all I know, Louise. And to think we never made it to his concert."

"Well, you know I was just going because you were paying for my ticket."

"Don't get snotty while I'm grieving, Louise. This is an unspeakable loss for me."

And indeed it was. John Denver died a holy mess, a horrible and shocking end for my troubadour. His new two-seater, fiberglass plane plunged straight down into the water and both he and the plane broke into pieces on impact.

I needed a proper goodbye. Over the years Louise and the kids barely tolerated my obsession with him but since he was now dead, I insisted that everyone forego one Sunday afternoon and join me in a celebration of his life. Cole backed out because his television job required him to cover the World Series and Red Sox trades, and Claudia backed out because she was in charge of a friend's baby shower. That left Emily and Louise. To put it mildly, they were reluctant participants.

Sweet Emily, grouchy Louise and nosey Marla Sacks watched silently while I lit a candle and passed out a copy of his actual memorial service and the lyrics to my favorite John Denver song, "Perhaps Love."

Emily picked up the handout, "What are we supposed to do with this, Mom?"

"We're doing a sing-along."

Louise groaned. "Not in this lifetime, Christine."

"Louise, John Denver wrote about hope, love, and the human spirit. And taking good care of mountains and eagles. I'd just like us to honor him and pray for his children and his wife Annie. We won't pray for his second wife, Cassandra."

Louise rolled her eyes but I ignored her. "Maybe you'd like to hear about the plane crash."

"Spare us the details," Louise huffed. "Imagine if the priest had given us a blow by blow of Loretta Levine's car crash."

It was obvious that the sing-along was a bad idea. But that didn't stop me. "At least send a prayer to John's family, but remember, not to his most recent wife. She's a bee-atch. And it's okay if you just move your lips with the song. Or close your eyes."

Marla spoke softer than usual, "Of course, honey, we'll sing."

I looked at Louise. "I'm telling you all right now," I said, "when I die, even if I'm a hundred years old, I want this song at the church. This and "Red Rubber Ball" by Bobby Vee."

"It's called Rubber Ball," she corrected me. "There's no 'Red' in the title."

I stared her down. "Shush, Louise. It's "Red Rubber Ball" to me."

I insisted we hold hands. Louise heaved again but she cooperated. I turned on the recorder, closed my eyes, and Marla, who was not capable of carrying a tune, sang along with me. Emily told me afterwards that Louise rolled her eyes the whole time, but this tribute did me a world of good. John Denver saved my sanity while Jimmy drank.

When I brought my chicken and broccoli casserole to the table, a few of my tears fell into the platter. "Help yourself, everyone," I said. "And don't worry that I cried in the casserole. Tears have nutrients."

45

2001
Claudia

Cole made it through college and the attorney Fabian Fontaine didn't make the cut. Nor did any of the other guys who came and went after him.

I was three days past my thirty-third birthday when I met William Brimfield in a laundromat. I'd just signed a two-year lease on an elegant Victorian building on Memorial Drive in Cambridge, a one-bedroom, one-bath apartment overlooking the Charles River and barely seven blocks from my sister Emily. I could walk to Harvard Square and on ambitious days, all the way to the Museum of Science or Quincy Market. I had no complaints: my job at ABT Research was stimulating and lucrative, I'd turned down three marriage proposals, and I had no shortage of men or friends.

Lamenting that the hookup of my washer/dryer was in the heartless hands of an irresponsible plumber who charged time and a half for Saturday service and then failed to show up, I begrudgingly lugged my lingerie and favorite sweats to the Soapy Suds Clean-O-Mat, located on the corner of Mount Auburn Street and Putnam Avenue. As I publicly banged my fists on the unco-operative change machine, mumbling a quiet 'fuck' in my most irritated voice, a man approached me with an amused grin. His chin was perfect and his nose was perfect, but his most perfect feature was his eyes; green, intense, and a bit dreamy. I locked in on him, and even years later, in the dark rooms of a Marriott Courtyard or a Holiday Inn Express, when his breathing slowed and he lay limp on top of me, his eyes would always be as I first remembered them.

"Can I help you with that machine?" the man asked.

I looked up: he was a half foot taller than me, and I grinned back.

"I'm not a laundry type of girl," I said coyly. "I'm here because a plumber didn't show up this morning and my...well, never mind why." This was the beginning of my typical schtick with men, balancing myself on the edge of provocation and infor-mation and short-circuiting both in my abrupt silly way.

"That's interesting," the man said. "I'm not a laundry type of guy, but my plumber didn't show up either and I have a sick baby girl at home who threw up over everything, her bed, the kitchen tablecloth, the dishtowels, the couch, everything." He grinned again, "I can give you some of my quarters."

I smiled. "Sir, I cannot allow myself to be indebted to a stranger in a laundromat. My mother taught me that in second grade."

"I could charge you the price of your company until the wash cycle ends," the man responded. "Or I could help you bang your way through this change machine you're swearing at."

A normal wash, rinse and dry cycle is approximately ninety minutes max. During that time, this man I would come to know as Wills, with his soft chin and dreamy eyes, sat next to me in one of those orange plastic scoop chairs. We twisted our bodies side-ways so we three-quarter faced one another, and I told him how and why I had moved to Cambridge and he told me how and why his wife convinced him to move to Arlington, and we offered up sympathies for having to endure the laundromat on a Saturday morning. Then fate decided to stir things up.

"How many kids do you have?" I asked.

"Three," he answered. "Zoie is seven, Ryan is five, and the baby, Petunia, is almost one."

"Petunia," I tossed my head back, "That's a sweet name."

"My wife insisted," he responded. "It came to her in a dream. She said a robin told her if we had a girl and we named her Petunia, she would sing her way through life and accomplish great things."

"Interesting. How long have you been married?" I asked.

"Nine years." For a nanosecond he looked away. When he looked back, I saw him quickly scan my fitted jeans and black ankle boots and my deep purple blouse with its subtle black dots (And in case anyone might miss the fact that I was feisty and fashionable, accessorized with a dark blue scarf dotted every few inches with little pink pigs.)

"Nice scarf," he said. He avoided my eyes. "What about you? Are you married?"

"Not even," I answered. "I'm ambivalently single." I smiled and added, "I have mixed feelings about marriage in general. And you? Are you happily married?" I blurted this last part out without thinking. I corrected myself before he could answer, but not before his head snapped back ever so slightly, followed by a momentary twitch in his left eye.

"Oh jeez," I said, "I'm sorry. What a jerk I can be. That's not a laundry question," I said sheepishly. "I asked because I'm not married and I never know whether I want to be."

Without speaking, he looked back at me. Normally I would have squirmed and broken the silence with my quick wit and impressive vocabulary, but instead I just stared back.

Finally, he cleared his throat. "Hey, is this weird? I'd love to see you again."

I'd heard this line before, multiple times, in bars, on subways, and in other places where handsome men, lonely men, and married men for some reason found me approachable and safe and—I knew not to kid myself—a probable good fuck. Sometimes I said yes: those times when I equally sized up the guy as approachable, safe, and sexy. But lately I had absolutely sworn off married men. They were too needy, too complicated, too messy.

I looked at him directly. "How come?"

"I don't know," he answered. "I can tell you I've never said this before."

"In a laundromat?" I laughed.

"No, not in a laundromat, not anywhere."

Presumably as a goodwill gesture, he reached out his hand and I let him fold it into mine. It was a handshake but more than that because he didn't let go. He stared at me and I stared back. *Think, think, think*, I told myself. *Married, three kids, decent: all the worst signs.*

He spoke again, "May I call you? Maybe for coffee or lunch?"

I waited a moment and then pulled my hand away. I opened my purse and found the Waterman pen Cole gave me when I got promoted to lead researcher. I ripped a page from my Moleskine, neatly wrote out my full name and phone number, and handed it to him. I didn't make eye contact and I barely moved at all.

"Claudia Macabee," he said. "My name is William Brimfield. My friends call me Wills."

"Nice to meet you, Mr. Wills." My lower body spiked.

"Claudia," he said again. "I'll ring you up, Claudia Macabee. Thank you."

46

Wills called at 7:15 on a Monday night, two weeks and two days after we met at Soapy Suds. I was sitting on my couch watching the nightly news, with a plate of pork fried rice balancing on my lap.

"Hello," I said, anticipating an irritating sales call. The voice on the other end was masculine and light.

"Miss Macabee, this is William Brimfield. I believe we have the Soapy Suds Clean-O-Mat in common, and I was wondering if you would be so kind to meet me for lunch at your convenience."

"Ah, you, hello," I replied. "I didn't expect to hear from you."

It was true. I had thought about this man afterwards but he was married and I knew better. I figured he knew better too. I was almost relieved he hadn't called.

"Well," he said. "I'd love to see you. Catch up on dryer softeners, you know. And maybe clams on the half shell."

"Oh, both my specialties!" I chuckled. "Those and deviled eggs. My mother taught me more than necessary about deviled eggs."

Don't do it, I told myself, *you don't date married men anymore*. But logic did not make it to my tongue. I hesitated but not for long. "Sure," I said. "Okay, sure."

He laughed. He sounded pleased. "I know so little about you. Where do you work? What do you do for work?"

"I work at One Center Plaza in Boston; the half circle building across from City Hall Plaza. I do research and I write the internal communications for my company. Sometimes the job's good, sometimes it's boring, and sometimes it's bad, like layoffs bad."

"What's sometimes good?" Wills asked.

"Sometimes good is everybody gets a ten percent bonus this year."

"I help companies figure out things like that," Wills said.

"Oh yeah? How so?"

"I'm a financial analyst. Mostly employee compensation and corporate planning."

"That sounds like a lucrative career, Mr. Brimfield."

"Not necessarily with three kids and two car payments," he laughed. "But I have no complaints."

This string of conversation done, the next few seconds were awkward. I spoke first. "Are you sure you want to do this?"

"Meet you for lunch? Most definitely."

A Boston landmark since 1827, Durgin-Park has a tradition of brash no-nonsense waitresses happy to sass, and they don't mind if you sass back. The restaurant sprawls across an ancient second floor of an old building with creaky plank floors and the kitchen serves portions of prime rib bigger than the average dinner plate. A campy holdover from days past and located smack in the middle of the Quincy Market, Durgin-Park was still a popular tourist attraction and perfect for a long lunch.

Wills was waiting at the Clinton Street entrance, dressed in a camel hair knee-length tweed overcoat over a Brooks Brothers gray pinstriped suit, a starched button-down white shirt and a deep purple silk tie. *Classy,* I thought as I approached him. I saw his grin ten feet away. When I got close enough, he tossed his head back and opened his arms to greet me. I let him bear hug me, I smelled his after shave, and I felt the softness of his face. He held on to me for several seconds longer than appropriate.

"How nice to see you again," he said. "You dress up good." *That grin.*

"You too," I said. *God, he's gorgeous.*

We sat across from one another at a giant-sized family style table.

"What'll ya have?" the waitress barked.

Wills looked at me. "Wine okay?" he asked.

I shrugged. "Sure."

"A bottle of Beringer chardonnay?" he asked again, looking at me, and I nodded. "And two orders of clams on the half shell?" He checked with me for the third time and I nodded again. "A bottle, Mr. Brimfield? We are planning to go back to work, aren't we?"

"Unfortunately, yes," he said. "I have to. Do you?"

"Yes," I lied. I had cleared my afternoon.

He might have caught on. "Next time let's have lunch and then walk through the Common and end up on Newbury Street."

By any standard, this was an odd statement. He spoke as if we already had a history. As we raised our wine glasses and toasted, he reached for my free hand and squeezed it before letting go.

"I know this is weird," he said.

"I'm not worried about weird," I replied. "I'm worried about reckless."

Wills nodded. "I thought about not calling you. But I was so glad when I did."

We made small talk: school, family, favorite cities, obnoxious co-workers. There was no awkwardness in the way we laughed and engaged with one another. We shared bites of our meals: fried scallops for him and baked stuffed cod for me. We agreed on chocolate graham cracker pie for dessert and shared that too.

"You're wonderful, Claudia," Wills said. There was sadness in his tone. "I couldn't stop thinking about you. Now I can't take my eyes off you; the way you laugh and the way you hold that fork in between the wrong fingers."

I laughed. Such a wacky come on. "My mother tried to correct that particular habit for years, but my hand had other ideas. And it is my hand, after all." I laughed again. "Where are you from, Wills?"

"California."

"What part?"

"Marin County, just outside of San Francisco."

"Where did you go to college?"

"Harvard."

"Ooh," I said. "Smart."

He smiled. "I got a four-year scholarship because of wrestling."

"My mother would like you. She married my father because they both liked wrestling."

"I doubt it was that simple," Wills said.

"Actually, it might have been," I replied. "My father was an auto mechanic, and a tool and die specialist, whatever that is. He died when I was fifteen. My mother works in a factory but she's a poet at heart." I hesitated. "My father was too simple for her. Plus, he drank."

"Ouch," Wills said. "My father drank too. That's craziness that gets hardwired into you."

"I guess," I said, "but my mother did a good job raising us."

"Not mine," Wills said. "But I know what a great mother looks like. I'm in awe of how great at it my wife is."

I felt a twinge. *This man is honest*, I thought, *and I would have to accept that about him.*

He continued. "My mother finally divorced my father because of his drinking, and it was better from there."

"How old were you?"

Wills thought a minute. "Twelve. We moved around a lot, California, Seattle, Tucson: anywhere his job assigned him. And boy, did my parents fight. Nothing physical but they screamed at each other like other people talk about the weather. So, when my mother decided she had enough, she moved my brother and me back to San Francisco and thank God, life calmed down."

"I understand that. My mother stayed. She covered for my father. Most of the time he wasn't really around, even when he was."

"It's a hard thing to grow up with alcoholism," Wills said. "You learn to behave in certain ways, to keep things from getting out of hand, and you learn to keep your home life a secret. At least I did."

I nodded. "My mother had a master plan to make sure we knew how to handle life. She set up contests; she'd ask us at supper, *What's the best thing to do if someone steals your lunch?* Or, *You're walking home and your best friend tells you her uncle hit her. What should you do?* Or, *You desperately want a two-wheel bike and you need twenty-five dollars, but you've only saved eight.* And not just that. She insisted we learn to love poetry; more poems than I can even remember. Over and over, she told us, and she still does, that a good poem can solve anything. Somehow, we side-stepped my father."

"Hmmm," Wills smiled. "And now?"

I smiled too. "Now that I'm an adult, her solutions aren't as foolproof as I was led to believe. But I do think she was on to something, because all three of us are pretty okay. Even though we're screwed up in different ways, and who isn't, my family has roots, and I have to admit, sometimes a good poem really can help."

Wills seemed intrigued. "I like that. I'll remember that. My wife and I follow the 'Wings and Roots' approach to raising our kids."

I felt a tenderness toward him. "I'll bet you're a good father. But you travel for work, yes? Is it hard for you and your family when you're away?"

"Yes, and no," Wills answered. "My wife's an attorney, and she keeps everything organized. I'm never away more than a week a month. I call home every night and every morning. My son loves to talk to me on the phone. He's five and he asks me one question after another. Last week, he asked me to describe what I saw walking from the hotel to work. He said, 'Tell me what you see at each step, Daddy. Are there buildings? Trees? How tall are they? Does anyone say hello to you, Daddy? Do you say hello back?' Then he asks me what color my job is. What color! Can you believe that?"

"What did you tell him?"

"I didn't know what to say. I told him jobs aren't colors so then he asked me, 'Then what shape is your job?'" Wills chuckled. "It got me thinking. I deal with people, numbers and computers all day, and maybe I should start thinking in terms of colors and shapes. It might spice things up."

"So what did you say to him?"

"I told him that Daddy helps people decide how to spend their money. I could hear a light bulb go off on his end of the phone. 'So your job must be green, Daddy,' he told me. 'And it must be round, like nickels.'"

We both laughed. Then, for no discernible reason, we stopped. Wills leaned forward and reached his hand across the table. I followed suit until our fingers interlocked.

"Wills," I said, "I don't think this is a good idea."

He looked confused. "Claudia, I've tried to shake you out of my head. I'm so excited to see you again. Like I told you before, this is not something I've ever done. I want you to know that—not ever. I...I just want to spend time with you, to know you."

"It's not just spending time, Wills," I said.

"No, it isn't," he agreed.

"It's not like we can just be friends. I can hear my mother, Wills. And I can tell you she would not approve."

He cleared his throat. "Do you believe in love at first sight?"

I tilted my head. "I don't know. Maybe. Probably."

"Claudia, I can't explain how connected I feel to you."

My ambivalence was obvious, but I cut to the chase. "What do you expect me to say? You're married and you have children, a nice wife, and a good career, and what could that possibly mean for either of us? Even in the best circumstance, we end up pining for one another, or you leave your wife and miss your kids. There's no happy ending here, Wills. Surely you know that."

He winced. "Isn't there some way we can make this okay; could we try? The thought of not seeing you again; it's just awful."

I pulled my hand away. I needed time to think. I knew this was wrong and I knew he was right. "I don't know." He waited. "Okay," I told him. "Let's try another lunch. Or maybe dinner. Let's wait a few weeks. Maybe we can just enjoy each other. But please don't push this, Wills, please. I'm not good at heartbreak. I'm..."

"What?"

"I'm better knowing where I stand. And I'm better with friendships."

It was Wills' turn to cut to the chase. "Claudia, I don't know if I can do that. I have a problem. I don't want to kiss my friends."

47

Emily

Cole was on television and Claudia was falling in love. And then there was me.

I was so different than my extroverted siblings, and sometimes I wondered why. I had a feeling my father had something to do with it. I remember being five, maybe six, hiding from him.

"Mommy, why does Daddy get mad?" I probably asked my mother that question dozens of times in one form or another, and every time she answered in pretty much the same way.

"Daddy isn't mad at you, honey."

"Who is he mad at?"

"He's mad at himself."

"Sometimes he yells too loud."

"Honey, your daddy has a problem, but he's not mad at us. We hope one day he won't yell anymore and he'll be happy. But for now, when he forgets to use his words or his inside voice, he needs to go outside or we'll stay out of his way until he's okay again. He's not upset because of anything we've done."

That's probably how I learned to stay in the background. The background was my safe place. My father didn't exactly scare me, but I knew better than to step in the middle of his grouchiness. I remember snuggling inside my mother's apron until the coast was clear.

I was also a fragile kid. I wasn't physically frail but I cried on a dime. There was no way I could keep up with Claudia's confidence, even at an early age, and when we got older her sex appeal with boys made me feel even geekier than I obviously was. I found my own niche by being smart. I was an honor student all through high school and after college, I landed a good job at an ad agency. I traveled to national accounts a few times a month, mostly to Kansas City. I was proud of myself: I owned a two-bedroom condo in Cambridge, just a few blocks from my sister, I excelled at work, and I went home for dinner with my mother every Sunday afternoon. I was a hundred percent independent and a hundred percent happy.

I was still a teenager when Mom offhandedly pegged me as her child most likely to stay single, like my Aunt Louise. She was only kidding, but she had that right. I had no interest. Except for my brother, I found boys immature and boring. I liked books a lot more than dates. And no way did I want to date just because it was the thing to do. This part was easy because no one ever asked me out. So, while Claudia was making out under the athletic bleachers, I was a happy homebody reading *Pride and Prejudice*. All through high school and college, I had only one boyfriend, and even that was iffy. After four months of dating and a few times of heavy petting, he broke up with me during lunch. No reason, just a quick 'I'm sorry' and 'Good luck ahead.' I dated a little after that, but by the time I hit my thirties, there were no prospects in sight, and that was fine with me. I was in no way ready when Mr. Brett Butler wedged his way into my perfect life.

48

"May I sit here?" the man asked me, motioning with his head that my carry-on luggage was occupying an empty seat. I nodded but didn't smile. There were other seats available and there was no need for him to bother me. I kept reading *People Magazine*, a guilty pleasure I only enjoyed when traveling, lapping up the details of Meg Ryan's divorce from Dennis Quaid and Bette Midler's new tour. He put his briefcase down and turned to me. "I'm going to get coffee," he said. "Can I get you something?"

"No thank you."

"Would you mind keeping an eye on my briefcase?"

Ballsy, I thought. But I'm polite. "Sure."

I looked up at him. He wore a light brown corduroy sports jacket with dark brown fitted slacks and a light blue cotton shirt with a button-down collar and no tie. His shoes were L.L. Bean moccasin slippers, to his credit, at least not those horrible tassel dress shoes that so many men wore as a fashion statement. He had a youthful smile, a grin almost. Extending his hand to me in a polite confident way, he was friendly personified. But I nodded instead of returning his handshake: that felt too personal.

I watched this guy walk up the terminal ramp, the back of his hair resting slightly on his shirt collar in a way that reminded me of the Beatles' Paul McCartney. He was slightly bowlegged; his knees buckled with a hitch that could have been a swagger, and I didn't like swagger in men. In my limited experience, that preceded arrogance. *What's with him?* I wondered.

He returned with two cups of coffee and two Boston creme donuts. "I thought you might like to munch after all," he grinned.

I shook my head. "No donuts for me," I said. "But thanks for the coffee."

"Okay," he smiled, "two donuts for me."

This exchange was totally out of my comfort zone. No guy had ever approached me with this kind of interest, and I was too reserved to flirt back. I looked at him again. Blue eyes, a neatly trimmed mustache and beard, cut close to his face. A slightly out of whack nose which he later told me came from an ice hockey collision in eighth grade. Baby soft skin, white straight teeth, a genuine smile. I looked at his hands. Definitely a professional man; no callouses or roughness. A college ring.

He sat down and crossed one leg over the other. Relaxed. Not concerned about looking feminine. "Where are you headed?" he asked.

"Boston."

"Oh, me too. The 7:05?"

Oops. Nope. Already too personal. "I'm taking a flight later tonight. I'm meeting someone for dinner."

I watched him take a huge bite of the first donut. Glazed chocolate bits stuck to his beard. It made me laugh and I handed him a napkin.

"You and those Boston creme donuts. Here," I motioned. "For your face."

He grinned sheepishly and extended his hand again. This time I shook back.

"My name is Brett Butler. Not from *Gone with the Wind*. The Butlers from Framingham, Mass." He grinned again. "This person that you're meeting: is it a guy?"

"Yes, that's one way to describe a boss."

"When my boss wants to meet me for dinner, I run the other way."

"Oh, not me," I replied. "Mine covers for me when I sneak out of work to shop for shoes."

He smiled. He looked at my feet. "Steve Maddens. Fashionable, well-made and comfortable."

Red flag! What a strange thing to say. Such a dorky pick-up line. "You're into shoes?"

Brett Butler threw his head back and laughed. "It's not that bad. I used to sell them. At the Framingham Mall." Sensing that I'd already made a wrong conclusion, he added, "In college. My part-time job."

Mr. Brett Butler was a talker. In the span of twenty minutes, he told me all about his family: his working-class machinist father and his third-grade teacher mother, his two sisters, one who ran a Cambridge bakery and the other who occasionally sewed clothes for the singer Diana Ross. He was an assistant manager at Market Basket, a New England-based grocery chain where, after thirty years, the family owners were still feuding for control. He was the youngest in his family and he chuckled telling me about his two older sisters dressing him up and bullying him around in third grade, when the blue nail polish they put on his fingers got him beat up.

"No tolerance for sissies in third grade," he said. "I got a black eye and they got grounded. What about you?" he asked. "What do you do?"

"For work? I'm in advertising. And I'm taking courses in fashion design."

I hadn't told anyone about my plan to pursue fashion, not even Claudia. I'd made that decision a few months earlier, because I had no idea how to put colors and fabrics and style together. I was aware that I looked like a fish out of water at work, and I felt awkward. Plus, Claudia regularly let me know that my clothes choices were wrong.

Brett Butler leaned forward. "I can tell you're talented, just by your shoes." That smile again. "Listen, I hope this is okay. I don't see a ring on your finger. Do you think your boss would mind if I asked for your phone number? Or your email address? Or am I being too pushy?"

I ignored that last question, and I kept my voice steady. "My boss wouldn't mind, but I might."

"Would you?" He asked this politely.

"I'm not sure. If you're married or into drugs or alcohol or if you live with your parents, the answer is I definitely mind."

He tilted his head back and chuckled. "No to all of that. I'm single and normal. I'm just Brett Butler from Framingham, and by the way, who are you?"

"I'm Emily Macabee from it's too-soon-to tell."

"The Macabees from Scotland?"

"No, the Macabees from Ireland."

He nodded. "So, Emily Macabee, I live in Framingham and you live somewhere north or south or east or west of Logan Airport and I'm here in Kansas City for a domestic wine conference. I do the ordering at my store. Yesterday I got approached by a wine wholesaler for a management job that would have me moving from New England. That could be a problem for a fledgling relationship. But it's been my experience that nothing is insurmountable. Usually."

"Relationship?" This was too much. I made my displeasure obvious. "Mr. Butler, are you crazy? My history with men is not good and I'm guessing with strange men in airports, even worse. And, in any case, who thinks about a relationship in the first thirty minutes of meeting someone? I'll take a pass, but thank you anyway."

He smiled again. "Some people can see the future," he grinned. My put-off didn't seem to register. "What time is your flight? Is it the 7:05? Can I buy you a drink? Or meet you in Boston for dinner sometime?"

"I have dinner plans and I'm flying home later tonight, Mr. Butler. Did you even hear what I said?"

"Yes, but I'm no stranger once you get to know me. I'm a good guy, Emily."

He looked like a puppy, eager and innocent. He sucked me in. "Okay, maybe lunch in Boston sometime. I'm not promising."

He nodded. "Lunch works. In a nice public place, maybe with your girlfriends at a nearby table?"

I grinned. That could be true.

"I understand. I have sisters. And a mother." He reached inside his sports coat and took out two business cards. He wrote his home and work numbers and his email address on one and gave me both. I wrote the same information on the other card and handed it back to him.

When I arrived home five hours later, an email was waiting for me.

My distinct pleasure to make your acquaintance, Ms. Emily Macabee. How about Saturday, January 23 for dinner at Anthony's Pier 4?

Fondly, Mr. Brett Butler

It was ridiculous. Within days, we were talking twice a day on the phone and sending each other comical emails.

I finally agreed to meet him at Pizzeria Uno on Route 9 in Framingham.

"One thing first," I typed to him the night before. "Tell me again, reassure me, promise me that you are not married and do not drink or take drugs to excess." I wanted to add a smiley face but decided against it. Too fluffy.

His reply came ten seconds later: "Nope on all counts. And I don't live with my mother. I'm just a single guy living my life, who recently turned down a job in Kansas City, and you never know, I might be ready to fall in love with you."

He ended with a smiley face.

49

Brett managed to charm my whole family. Underneath his charm was a commonsense reliability that caught us all off guard. I began believing I could count on him, and he made sure I knew that. Six weeks after our first date, when he met my mother, he walked into her kitchen and went for the gold.

"Mrs. Macabee," he fawned, "your kitchen is so sweet. I love your black and white checkered curtains and the rug matches perfectly. When I'm lucky enough to have a family someday, I'd like a kitchen like this."

My mother melted. "Why thank you, Brett." She looked at me with a preliminary stamp of approval. "Would you like a glass of wine? Is red okay? Please, make yourself comfortable."

Later, when Brett and I were in the car headed back to my condo, I teased him with snarky disbelief. "You suck-up," I said. "You knew darn well how my mother feels about her kitchen because I told you!"

He grinned. "Yup, but everything thing I said was true. The only part I left out was the part that I hoped my family would include you."

Other than the fact that I know I'm a good person, I couldn't understand what Brett saw in me. I had no real flaws but I wore drab and unflattering V-neck sweaters and slacks and jeans that almost always looked a size too big. I went to my senior prom only because Cole fixed me up with a guy he worked with at the Star Market. Other than that, I didn't have a single date until my sophomore year in college. And before I met Brett, my only real adult relationship was with an architect I dated for four months.

Brett was charming. He played on a softball team with a group of twelve guys who called themselves the "BA's" which stood for 'Bad Asses.' He told my Aunt Louise it stood for Bad Apples and he freely offered my family his wacky humor and an outstretched helping hand. He was hinting at commitment on our second date. It took me some effort to slow things down.

One night I let him read what I'd written a decade ago for a sociology class assignment:

I'm a nerd who's not bothered by that fact. I want my place in the world to be as a strong, independent woman, like my mother. I believe that my intelligence and willingness to work hard will ensure my financial independence and professional respect and that means a lot to me. I'm open to marriage but I'm not desperate.

Brett just smiled. "I know destiny when I see it, Em, We're a match."

"But I don't move that fast."

"That's okay," he assured me. "Destiny's in no rush."

At that moment we had no idea what explosion destiny soon had in store.

50

2001

"Emily, the World Trade Center!" Claudia was screaming into the phone "Are you watching?!"

I had walked into total chaos at work. Everyone in my office was already in a state of panic, calling home, glued to the news, in shock, crying, and holding on to one another. My sister could hardly catch her breath. "Oh my God, Emily. A plane from Boston was hijacked and just crashed into the World Trade Center! Near where Cole is!"

"Yes, yes, I know. The TV's on in the lunchroom. Is it terrorists? What's happening? What about Cole? Do you know if he's all right? How far is the FOX building from the World Trade Center? Did you call Mom?"

"I don't know anything," Claudia struggled to talk. "I don't know anything because I can't reach him, Em. The phone lines are all tied up. They're closing my building. It's a state of emergency. Listen, I'm leaving now and I'm coming to pick you up. Watch for my car. We'll go right to Mom's. Call her and tell her we're on our way. Oh my God."

It was all horrific.

Claudia and I got to Mom's at 9:10 a.m. and Brett arrived fifteen minutes later. She and Aunt Louise were hysterical, falling into our arms and saying Cole's name over and over. Aunt Louise had rosary beads wrapped around both hands.

"I can't get through to him," Mom cried. "I need to know he's all right. What if the station sent him there to cover the crashes?"

My brother was a prime-time sports reporter for FOX News in New York City. Mom's fear was real.

The plane from Boston crashed between the 93rd and 99th floors of the North Tower at 8:46 a.m., and seventeen minutes later a second Boston flight crashed between the 77th and 85th floors of the South Tower. In both buildings, the elevators had jammed and the stairways were filled with smoke and fire, trapping hundreds of people inside. The four of us watched the television as terrified souls jumped out windows, one after another, from seventy to almost a hundred stories high. In split seconds, they must have known they had no other choice: staying inside meant they'd be burned alive by the raging heat and fire that was all around them.

Just before ten o'clock, the South Tower of the World Trade Center had collapsed like an accordion, smashing to the ground and leaving gray choking dust that covered a half mile of city blocks and everyone in its path. Thirty minutes later the North Tower collapsed in the same way. We watched the buildings fall like a scene in a slow-motion science fiction movie. The white ash from human bones and buildings and important papers covered the faces and clothing of scores of people who ran for their lives. The panicked sound of Aunt Louise's muffled prayers and the clinky movement of her rosary beads made our panic even worse. We were terrified my brother had been near those buildings.

Cole finally called Mom from Manhattan, forty-five minutes later. She couldn't stop crying, so Claudia took the phone from her and tried to sound calm. By then a third plane had crashed into the Pentagon and a fourth plane had crashed in a field in Pennsylvania.

Cole was out of breath and Claudia could barely hear him because there was so much chaotic background noise. "It's okay, tell Mom, I'm safe, it's okay. I can't talk long. Don't worry if you don't hear from me. I'll call again as soon as I can. It's an attack on the country. I'm safe, honest. Who's with you?"

Claudia tried to control her voice. "We're all together at the house. Emily and Aunt Louise and Brett too."

Cole rushed his words. "Wait to hear from me, Claudia. All of you, stay inside. The two planes from Boston: they think the hijackers slept in Newton last night, that's just five miles from you. Stay inside. Listen to what the president and the news tells you to do. I'll call as soon as I can. I have to go. I'm safe. Don't worry about me. Take care of each other. I love you."

And with that, my family, with Brett and without my brother, huddled together for hours, watching the aftermath as hundreds and thousands of family members and friends began plastering photographs of their loved ones all around the crash site. They were praying for miracles, even when it became clear they would never again hear from the people trapped in the two towers. There would be no bodies. There was only dust.

Two thousand nine hundred and ninety-six people died that day, the victims of the worst terrorist attack on American soil.

In the days that followed, everything changed. The airports added security guards and searched every passenger for weapons, for boxcutters, even for bombs potentially hidden in shoes. Mid-Eastern people and mosques became targets of hostility and violence. The United States no longer felt safe. For my family and my friends, because we lived around Boston, almost all of us knew someone who'd been personally affected. Claudia's secretary lost her brother, Brett's bakery manager lost his cousin, my neighbor lost her sister and brother-in-law and their two-year-old little daughter. For weeks, you couldn't go anywhere without seeing homemade shrines to loved ones and without understanding the overwhelming sadness that blanketed everything.

I was so grateful my family was safe. It wasn't lost on me that my brother played a role in reporting this American tragedy; my sister was knee-deep in an affair; and I was being wooed by a very decent man who I now believed was the real deal. My family had been spared, but horror had encircled us and it was close to home. We were lucky to be alive. And most of all, we were lucky to have each other. Somehow this tragedy left my heart and head more open to Brett, and I knew I could trust him. I let myself fall in love with him.

51

2002

Four months after 9/11, Brett asked me to marry him at his go-to, special occasion restaurant, Anthony's Pier 4. He was bragging about the intricacies of selling shoes when a skinny waiter with a Charlie Chaplin mustache approached us, a metal breadbox strapped over his shoulder. He used metal tongs to open the breadbox and proceeded to place two hot popovers on our appetizer plates. The butter was still sizzling when Brett reached into his shirt pocket and grinned like a Cheshire cat.

"Butter your popover, and then open this," he said. He pushed the little aqua Tiffany box toward me. I dropped my knife.

"Open it," Brett said.

I gasped. A pear-shaped diamond ring shot rainbow prisms all across the white linen tablecloth. Not to be outdone by the glitter, Brett pushed back his chair and knelt down on one knee in front of me. "Will you marry me, Emily Macabee?"

"Oh my God, Brett! You're serious? Now?"

"Will you?"

I was floored. Nearby diners cheered. This was a set-up. After he'd planned this elaborate moment, witnessed by tables of strangers all around us, I certainly couldn't embarrass him. "Oh jeez. Yes," I said. "Yes, Mr. Butler, I will."

Mom applied for a home equity loan to pay for the wedding. She informed us of this with deep pride in her voice.

"No, Mom," I told her. "You can't afford it and we can. Pay for my shower at the Chateau and that's enough. I want pink roses and blue hydrangeas on each table. Pay for my shower and help me plan the wedding."

"No way, the bride's family pays," my mother said.

Brett piped in. "Christine, we'll love all the help you can give us. But let me foot the wedding. Please do this one thing for me. Help Emily plan the invitations and the menu and all the decorations. We need that kind of help the most."

Mom shook her head. "You're a charmer, Brett. But no."

Brett pushed back. "I already have the money, Christine. I've been saving for my wedding since high school. Honest."

To my surprise, Brett won that argument. After watching Mom and Aunt Louise go head- to-head for years over disagreements large and small, this was one of the first times I saw my mother give in.

Brett and his family were Catholic, so he and I completed the Pre-Cana marriage counseling the church required, and we made arrangements for a Catholic Mass wedding at the Sacred Heart church in Waltham. My very Catholic Aunt Louise was thrilled about this, but she quickly made her displeasure known to Mom because Brett and I were now living together before marriage. Mom told me about the whole conversation.

"They're having sex, Christine," Aunt Louise complained to her.

"So, what's your point?" my mother asked.

"What's my point? They're sleeping together. And from your reaction it's obviously your fault."

"I'm not going there with you, Louise. It's none of my business and it's definitely none of yours. Em is an adult and she's happy, that's all I care about. And besides, you don't know if they're having sex, and don't you dare ask them."

The following week, an unsigned Catholic Mass card arrived in my mailbox. A congratulations card and note from my mother came a week later.

Dear Emily,

Since I'm positive it was Aunt Louise who sent you that Mass Card, I thought I would follow it with card of my own. I couldn't be happier for you and Brett. I know you're marrying a good man. You're the first in our family to enter holy matrimony and I want to be sure you understand something. I loved your father when I married him. He was a good man too, but he had the disease of alcoholism and it interfered with him being a good husband and a good father. In the beginning, we loved one another as much as you and Brett love one another. So I have two pieces of advice for you both: Don't ever let drinking get out of control, and the kitchen is the heart of a home.

Love always,
Mom

52

2003

Brett and I asked Aunt Louise to read the gospel at our wedding Mass, and for the occasion we presented her with a wrist orchid just like Mom's. With a hundred and twenty guests spread out in the pews at Sacred Heart, Aunt Louise zigzagged to the altar wearing her signature black polyester pantsuit with an orange and green scarf around her neck and her oversized fake leather black pocketbook clutched close to her hip. She adjusted the podium microphone and opened the Bible in front of her. She cleared her throat, straightened her posture to form a perfect line, and began: "A reading from the Holy Gospel according to Matthew 5:1-12a:

"When Jesus saw the crowds, he went up the mountain,
and after he had sat down, his disciples came to him.
He began to teach them, saying:
"Blessed are the poor in spirit,
for theirs is the Kingdom of heaven..."

Aunt Louise stopped abruptly and turned beet red, interrupted by a gurgle that quickly became a whine and then a growl. In a flash, her six-pound King Charles Spaniel, Sophia Loren, had jumped from her pocketbook onto the altar floor and spun around directly facing Father O'Neil. Sophia sniffed the shocked priest's robe once, squatted, and peed on his shoe. Looking like a penguin on speed in his tuxedo, Brett rushed over and picked up Sophia while her perfect arc of urine continued to tinkle out. He did his best to aim it into the flower arrangement of lilies to the left of the altar. Holding Sophia at arm's length, Brett and I locked eyes and cracked up. Father O'Neil laughed too and within seconds, everyone but Aunt Louise and my mother were in hysterics. Mortified, Aunt Louise scooped her little rat dog from Brett and stuffed her back in her bag. She looked around for guidance.

"Proceed," Father O'Neil nodded, which she did with impeccable pronunciation, given the circumstance. I felt my mother's steam from thirty feet away.

The reception was held at the Sheraton Hotel in Boston. Brett and I paid for everything and Mom was calmed by the fact that she and I planned the entire reception, from flowers to food to music to drinks. Just before Brett and I made our entrance into the grand ballroom, he handed me an envelope. "Open it quick, Em."

Inside was a card with his homemade drawing of a blue house with a front porch and a white picket fence. I unfolded a cashier's check for twenty thousand dollars, signed by Brett.

"It's our down payment," he beamed. "We can start looking."

"What?!"

He beamed again, "Em, I've been saving for this day even before I began touching people's feet in college." We both laughed. "I've waited all this time for you." He took the card and check back from me and tucked it inside his tux jacket. "Best we don't lose this."

We swung our arms together like little kids and walked into a room of boisterous cheers and clinks. When the commotion settled down, I spotted Aunt Louise standing by herself and looking distraught. Before Brett and I headed to the bridal table, we walked over to her and I extended my arms. Aunt Louise hesitated for a second or two before she let me hug her.

"It's all okay, Aunt Louise. You made it memorable."

"Your mother wants to kill me."

"She'll get over it," I laughed. "How many times has my mother said that about you?"

"She shot me daggers, Emily."

"I'll tell her to relax, Aunt Louise. It's my wedding and we're a happy family. But I'm curious: what made you bring Sophia to the church?"

Aunt Louise let out a deep sigh. "My dog sitter got cited for trying to poison her neighbor's rooster. The damn thing was waking her up every morning at four thirty." She looked at me with a most serious expression. "I was in a fix, Em. I couldn't leave Sophia home all day and I couldn't miss your wedding, so I spread her cookies and some leftover chicken at the bottom of my pocketbook and tucked her in. I figured she'd nibble herself to sleep. The damn dog had to pee." She stopped for a brief moment before asking, "Did she pee on the holy robe, Emily?"

"No, she missed. Just his shoe. And maybe a sock. Father O'Neil was fine with it, honest."

Aunt Louise's confidence returned like a rocket. Her face lit up.

"Well okay then, let's be sure to save all the scraps of filet mignon. And Sophia likes cake too."

53

Claudia

In a million years I never expected Emily to win the marriage lottery. Growing up she was so reserved around new people that sometimes I had to beg my friends to include her. While Cole and I were outgoing and popular, Emily was quiet and scholarly. Right up until the moment she brought Brett home for dinner, I was pretty sure she'd be following Aunt Louise into old maidenhood. How Emily ended up with a man who talked a mile a minute and could be counted on in the stickiest situations, I'll never know.

And somehow, Emily, who cried the hardest and the longest at Daddy's funeral, seemed to have escaped the effects of his drinking. I tried to understand how that could have happened, and the only thing I could come up with was that her modest expectations protected her.

"I used to cry that I didn't have as many friends as you and no boys ever noticed me," she once told me. "But I knew I was loved and I figured if Mom and Aunt Louise managed to have a good life, I could too."

The day of her wedding, Emily told me that she hoped I would find a guy as wonderful as Brett. I winced and she noticed.

"It will work out," she said softly. I wanted to tell her it already had, because she had found a good guy, and so had I.

Two years into my affair with Wills, I was still crazy about him. I had accompanied him on a couple of his yearly conferences, and I began to plan my vacation time around his work trips. We were cautious and professional, and at the end of the day, once back at the hotel, we'd part ways in the lobby and head to Wills' room separately. Moments later, we were scissored together, unable to take our hands off one another.

Although Wills was careful to select events where his colleagues wouldn't recognize me, I started wearing costumes so we could both feel freer. I chose my appearances based on the clientele. My stash included all kinds of glasses and three distinctive wigs: blonde, auburn, and jet black. In Cleveland at his software seminar for school principals and administrators, I wore a knee-length sky blue dress with black flats and a purple paisley wrap-around scarf.

"Hello, nice to meet you, I'm a third-grade teacher," I whispered to him at the buffet line. "I know all about school principals. I used to date one." I flashed a devilish smile.

Another time I became an avant-garde journalist with black patent leather boots that reached my knees, a tight black sweater and tight black skirt, black rimmed glasses, my own hair pulled back, and I finished off my look with large hoop earrings.

"I've been propositioned in this outfit three times so far," I quietly chuckled over lunch, "and the day's not half over. Maybe I should change professions; I could never wear this to my office."

"No," Wills whispered back, "But you could wear it to my office, if only I had a lock on the door."

"Oh no," I grinned, "I already have my wardrobe planned for that visit. And may I add you will also need window shades. And padded walls."

54

Wills and I met at my apartment every Tuesday night and I cooked dinner for us. Afterwards we made love for at least an hour before he was due home. The rest of our time together was hit and miss. Sometimes we had a few hours on a Saturday afternoon. There was never enough time together, but we made it work.

This time, on a mild evening in early spring, Wills was late. When he finally arrived, I'd already put the scallops Florentine back in the refrigerator and I was in no mood for excuses. He came with a bouquet of roses from Cumberland Farms and guilt written all over his face.

"I wait enough already, Wills. It's rude when I'm cooking dinner and you show up two hours late."

He pulled me to him and pressed his body into mine. "Honey, I'm so sorry. Natalie took a spill and we weren't sure whether or not she needed to go to the emergency room. I couldn't leave and I couldn't call."

There were always reasons: Petunia had thrown up, the neighbor's cat was up a tree, Natalie made plans and hadn't told him. Most often I accepted that this was part of the deal, but my patience thinned when it came to my cooking. My mother brought me up believing that meals were sacraments and even though there might be exceptions, they should be rare.

"Sometimes it's important, Wills, that I don't have to wait. And do we have time to even eat now?" My posture was slumped and tight, no easy aberration for a woman who took a one-semester modeling course at Emerson College.

Wills kept his arms around me. "Yes, let's eat," he said softly. "We have time." I rarely inquired about the reasons Wills might be delayed. But lying in my bed after a passionate forty-five min-utes of making love, I asked. "So what happened to Natalie?" And then, more soberly, "And is she alright?"

"She had an accident."

"What?"

He seemed evasive.

"What, you don't want to tell me?"

"She fell off the bed," Wills said.

"Wait, stop, maybe I don't want to know this."

"No, no, I was in the other room." He thought a moment, then continued. "She has a vaginal prolapse. Do you know what that is?"

I nodded. "And..."

"Well, she has this three-inch round rubber pessary thing and it's crazy to put in and take out. She has to reach inside with her fingers and find this little hole to grab onto to pull it out. She has to lie on the bed with her legs straight up in the air and this time she lost her balance."

"Oh, dear God, Wills. She fell off the bed?"

He grinned. "It was a sight. We laughed about it once we knew she was all right. But she banged up her back and her leg and it look an hour of ice before she could stand up straight again." He stopped, waiting for me to acknowledge his predica-ment. "I couldn't leave until we knew she was all right."

"What a scene that must have been," I said.

"She shoos me out of the room when she takes it out or puts it in. Which is fine with me." Wills laughed and I laughed too. It was always obvious that he loved her, but he never talked about their intimacy, and I never wanted to know. I assumed they made love but infrequently, judging by his hunger when he made love with me. And besides, I was much more interested in his family life: what the kids were up to, where they went for summer vacations, who cooked on what nights.

"I wish there was a way I could know your family, Wills," I said. "I know that must sound pathetic, but it's hard not knowing your children, and sometimes even Natalie. Do you think we would like each other?"

"I do," he answered. "If things were different..." His voice trailed off. He tightened and stretched his body on top of me again, pushing himself into my hips and thighs. He loved when I opened to him. He told me he loved hearing me breathe and my soft moans when he entered me. At first, he moved slowly and then more forcefully, in and out, in and out, until we were both ready. He also told me that making love with me was the only time he'd ever had a mutual orgasm with a woman. One night at his weekly poker game the subject came up and by Wills' account, not one of his buddies had achieved that. And sometimes we had multiple orgasms: for him, even three times before he finally ejaculated.

The physicality we shared was rare and we both knew it. But our bond was not just physical: the simple fact was that neither of us could imagine life without each other. I knew Wills hadn't been restless or unfulfilled before the day we met in the laundromat. He told me before then he'd felt settled, satisfied, appreciative, content. *And faithful.* But three weeks after we met for lunch that first time, when we lay beside each other in room 221 of the Brookline Marriott Courtyard, there was no going back. After that day, he was still the same man and he still loved his wife, and he still adored his children, but now a different kind of passion fueled him. I felt the same way. There was no solution. We were destined to be together and we were dealt a hopeless hand.

"When is our next conference?" I asked.

"Next month, the twentieth through the twenty-fourth. For bank executives."

"Oh," I teased, "I'll wear my hair in a bun and my brown tweed suit. And carry a calculator."

"I'll order an ID for you in the next few weeks. You can be a mortgage agent."

"Am I supposed to have math skills?"

"Yes, but no one's asking."

I pulled him to me. "One more time, Wills."

If he was tempted to look at his watch, he didn't. He moved down my body, his mouth kissing me below my stomach until he reached my shaved coarse hairs. He buried his nose and mouth in me.

"Claudia," he whispered afterwards. "I love you so much."

I whispered back. "I love you so much too, Wills."

I watched him close his eyes and I knew he was wishing it could be this simple. In my mind I heard my mother's favorite John Denver song. She quoted from it like it was the most important life lesson of all:

"If I should live forever
And all my dreams come true
My memory of love will be of you."

PART 5

Loss

55

Cole

Barely a month after Emily's wedding, I was mugged. I ended up in the ICU overnight and then transferred to the fifth floor of Saint Vincent's Hospital in Greenwich Village. A nurse propped a pillow under my right arm so I could almost sit up, and she held the phone for me while I called my brother-in-law.

"Brett, I got jumped last night," I told him. "My collarbone's broken and I tore my ACL. They won't let me out of the hospital without a discharge plan and I need someone to sign for me."

"Holy shit, Cole, are you okay?"

"Not really. I'm pretty messed up. My right eye is swollen shut and I think my nose is broken; I have a lot of pain. They're pumping me with morphine."

"I can be there by six tonight," Brett said. "I'll catch a quick flight." He didn't ask for details.

"Could you drive? So I can go home with you?"

"Sure, Cole, sure. I'm on my way."

"What will you tell Em?"

"What do you want me to tell her?"

"Not that I got jumped. Not yet. And I definitely don't want Mom to know. Not until she can see I'm okay."

"I'll come up with something, Cole, don't worry on that."

56

"You look like hell, Mr. Macabee," the cop said. "And you also look like a guy who never saw it coming."

I tried to smile. "That's about right."

"You're the Cole Macabee on the nightly news, right?"

"Yes," I said.

"I like the way you cover the Mets. Not so much the Yankees. You're a Boston guy, aren't you?" He nodded with a grin. I tried to nod too.

"Mr. Macabee, I need a statement from you. Are you up for that?"

The facts were easy. I'd been the lead sportscaster for the New York FOX affiliate for the last three years. I was attacked by three guys outside of The Vault, a gay bar in the village. I was at the bar making small talk with a twenty-something actuary and everything seemed normal. There was an overweight muscle guy wearing a ratty motorcycle jacket at the bar, and he cornered me outside ten minutes later and punched me with closed fists while two of his asshole friends held my arms behind my back. They flung me onto the cement sidewalk and the motorcycle guy kicked my ribs and legs and the side of my head. In all, the assault probably lasted one minute, but I was lucid and terrified and I wondered if he was going to kill me or if I would end up with brain damage. I never lost consciousness but I was close by the time the cops arrived. The EMTs took me by ambulance to Saint Vincent's.

"This happens more often than you'd think," the cop said. "These guys frequent gay bars as far out as the Jersey Shore. They beat up on gay men randomly. We've booked them before."

"Jesus," I said.

"We've already picked up two of the guys and arresting the third is just a matter of time. We'll need you to ID them, once you're up to it."

I was lucky to have a good cop. "Officer, this is not something I want on the news."

"I can buy you a few hours if that helps," he said, "but assaults are public information. And you're a public figure."

"I don't want anyone to see me like this."

"Mr. Macabee, I've seen a lot worse, believe me. Looks like no dental work needed; that's a blessing. And besides, we don't release photos." He hesitated before continuing. "But as you know, the press will be all around you minutes after I file."

"I could lose my job, officer."

I sounded pathetic, but my concern was real. Not much had changed in the two decades since AIDS made being gay a public health threat. It also didn't help that *The Diagnostic and Statistical Manual of Psychiatric Disorders* book still classified homosexuality as a mental disorder: even in 2003 it still wasn't entirely safe to be gay. And I, a big city sports reporter who interviewed male athletes in various stages of undress in their locker room, would be crucified.

The officer assured me that justice would be done. But lying in that hospital room, black and blue and sore as hell, I had one thought only: *My career is over.*

<h1 style="text-align:center">57</h1>

After Brett met with the hospital doc and the social worker, I headed back to Boston against medical advice. My blood pressure was all over the map but I was gone before the press could snap their cameras at me.

Brett was nonplussed. "You can stay with Em and me until you're on your feet. We have a family doctor who I'm sure will see you. The hospital said you need an orthopedic surgeon for your knee and a visiting nurse at our place for a week or two."

I nodded. "I have to call the station; I called in sick this morning. I told my boss what happened but I underplayed it. This will go public any minute and the doc told me it could be weeks before my face settles down. I might not have a job by then, but I want to be sure they've made arrangements. Shit."

A few months earlier, Brett had told me how his car had side-swiped and killed a dog on his way to work. His voice had the same even tone now as it did then. "Aw Cole," he said, "you're too good looking to get kicked off the air. But if you have to, we'll hire an attorney. You must have employment rights. Let's wait to worry on that one."

Every bump and stop and start in the back seat of Brett's SUV just about killed me. The codeine the hospital gave me made me groggy enough to sleep on and off, and Brett just kept talking. He told me about Emily's promotion and about my mother's first ever speeding ticket and how Aunt Louise barged her way into the mayor's office to complain about the inconsistent garbage pickup on her street.

He didn't give me space to wallow. We both knew I was in for a mess.

58

Emily

My brother stayed with us for almost a month. His arrival brought an avalanche of family support: even Aunt Louise put aside her homophobic leanings and agreed that he had been horribly wronged. It took the New York press just a day before word of Cole's assault hit the *New York Daily News*. The headline read: 'FOX Sports Anchor Assaulted Outside Gay Bar.' In short succession, he emerged with broken bones and a tattered reputation.

Cole's ACL was surgically repaired at the New England Baptist Hospital and he was still drugged when they wheeled him out of the recovery unit. He greeted Brett and me with a slurred enthusiasm. "Hey, hi ya, you two," he gushed. "You're both so nice. So, so nice."

He looked at his bandaged leg, hanging above his body on a pulley type contraption that he was instructed to pull every hour. "Oh, I still have my leg," he said, surprised. "I'd rather have a leg than a job. Wouldn't you, Brett? Oh wait, what about a tuna fish sandwich? Can I have a sandwich? Do you want one too?"

And so it went. Mom, Aunt Louise, and Claudia all came and we crowded around his bed, to the silent irritation of the older man in the other bed, who pulled his curtain shut and turned up the volume on his television. Every thirty minutes a male nurse named Anthony came to check Cole's vitals, reminded him to pull his leg pulley, and brought him graham crackers, apple juice, and a cherry lollipop to suck on.

"I want coffee and tuna fish," Cole insisted.

Anthony just smiled. "Not yet, Cole. Not until you burp and BM."

Later, at the nurse's station, Anthony approached Brett. "He's the sports reporter in New York? He is, right?"

"Yes," said Brett. "Have you seen him on TV?"

"Yes, and I remember him from Providence. I went to nursing school there, a couple of years behind him. I remember when he left Channel 12 for New York. My cousin lives in Brooklyn and when I visit him, I've watched Cole on FOX. He does a good job."

"He's had a rough go of it," Brett said.

"I know," Anthony said. "I've followed it. Disgusting." He flinched.

"I think nurse Anthony is gay," Brett told me.

"Because...?"

"Because he knows all about Cole. And he seemed to take it personally."

Cole wasn't discharged the next day. As soon as he ate his tuna sandwich and guzzled down a cup of Dunkin's coffee, he vomited. And he had troubles at the other end as well.

"Not just a burp," Anthony told him. "You need a BM before we can discharge you. You know what that is, right?"

Cole smiled. It was the first time I saw him smile since the beating. Although Anthony was no exception to the quality care my brother received at New England Baptist, he seemed special.

"Work your ass off, Mr. Macabee, if you want out of here," he advised with a grin.

"Yeah, yeah, yeah," Cole grinned back.

A physical therapist insisted that Cole get up and with his crutches walk the corridor with her every four hours. My athlete brother willed himself forward and did what he was told. He was too vulnerable to be his sweet confident funny self, but he was coming along. We were relieved.

Anthony was on duty when Brett arrived to bring Cole back to our house.

"Here's how to reach me," Brett heard him say, handing Cole a folded piece of paper. Cole extended his hand.

"Thanks a lot, Anthony. You've been great. I'll call you on the other side of this."

Cole was discharged after three days and set up for four weeks of physical therapy at our house. But our relief was short lived.

59

Cole drank. He wasn't unpleasant but he was absent and dull. For the first two weeks a physical therapist named Greta came to the house every day. She encouraged him and walked beside him inside and outside the house, each day pushing him to go a little further. For the first week, she came at three o'clock, and she scheduled that time for the following week too. But then she changed that, coming mornings instead, at 9:30. One day, after she and Cole finished up and he had returned to his bedroom, she stopped and made small talk with Brett, who happened to be home. She was hesitant, as if something was bothering her.

"What's up? Is Cole okay?" Brett asked.

"I'm concerned about him falling," she said.

"How come?"

Greta shifted her weight. She was unsure what to say, but Brett caught on. "Is that why you changed his time from afternoons to mornings?"

"Yes."

"You noticed."

"Yes."

"Thank you, Greta. I get it."

"He needs to be safe."

"I know. We know that."

That night at dinner, Brett and I confronted Cole.

"You're drinking," Brett said. "It's a problem, Cole. Even Greta noticed."

"Nah," Cole said. He glared at us. We were surprised by how angry he was. *What did we expect?* he demanded. *What would we do if we were in this position?*

"This is about getting by," he spewed, "and if drinking helps me do that, that's what I'm going to do."

Brett pushed back. "You're unsteady on your feet. That's all you need, if you fell. You drink at lunch, and you don't stop. You have a minibar in your bedroom Cole, for Christ sakes."

Cole's body tightened. His face ballooned. His teeth clenched.

"Fuck you, Brett. I don't need this."

He pushed his chair away from the table, grabbed his crutch, and furiously hobbled back to his room. He didn't come out for the rest of the night, and he barely said good morning the next day. When Brett and I got home from work at quarter to six that night, he was gone.

60

Christine

When Emily told me what happened in New York, I was shocked, worried, heartbroken, and I blamed Jimmy. And when Cole stormed out and disappeared after Emily and Brett confronted him about drinking, I understood even more how badly his father had failed him. And for the first time, I wondered if I had failed him too.

For several days afterwards, my son either avoided my phone calls or responded in short crisp sentences. He refused to talk about himself and communicated with me only superficially, unless I cried. When he realized my tears confirmed how distressed I felt, he softened and tried to sound like his old self. But my Cole had had a terrible thing happen to him—a crisis that threatened everything he had hoped and worked for. If there would be any relief and consolation, it wouldn't come from me. That was hard to accept. I had raised this boy from day one. I'd always been sure I knew more about my famous son than anyone else on the planet. I was sure his father's drinking and criticisms had hurt him, but only now did I realize that Jimmy might have left him with wounds that might not heal. Maybe the damage inside our family was too large and too grave to heal. But God forbid, maybe it wasn't just because of Jimmy. Maybe, the damage had come from me too.

61

Cole

Nine weeks after my assault I was back in New York facing my legal problems. I knew I was drinking too much and I knew it affected my decisions. I waffled on whether to accept a work severance, knowing it would end my historic rise and fall with FOX News.

My facial bruises had pretty much cleared up by the time I met with Julian Edwards, the station manager for the New York affiliate. Julian was a good guy and had worked as a seasoned reporter for twenty years before taking over the news division, inching his way up through the ranks of network TV. He had a degree in communications from Boston University and had been a minor league baseball player for the Iowa Cubs, the same minor league team that tried to recruit me. He knew the ropes.

"Good to see you, Cole," he greeted me, extending his hand and motioning me toward a chair across from his desk. "Nah," he said, "on second thought, let's sit on the couch; less formal."

I got right to the point. "I'm ready to get back on-air, Julian." I'd practiced this sentence and I said it without emotion.

"I can't let you do that, Cole. It's been taken out of my hands. The board's involved, and attorneys too. There's been backlash."

"Because I'm gay, Julian?" My preparation for this meeting vanished. My cool was gone. In its place I reacted with disgust. Julian pretended not to notice.

"It's complicated, buddy. I wish I could say more. I have the authority to offer you a one-year severance package. Your salary and full benefits. I think it's a good offer. Otherwise, we'll put you on the weekend beat." We both knew that assignment would suffocate my career.

"A good offer because I'm gay?"

Julian leaned back and locked his fingers behind his head. "I think the world of you, Cole."

"It sucks, Julian."

He weighed his words carefully. "It's not just an issue at our station. And not just about ratings or public opinion."

My spine was on fire. "No Julian, it's about fucking homophobic athletes who liked me just fine in their locker rooms until they started thinking I'm scoping out their dicks. Is Jeter involved in this?"

"I'm not authorized, Cole."

"It's disgusting, Julian. I've worked my ass off at this station. I've won awards and been cited for my professionalism. Some maniac attacks me outside a bar and I lose my job? That's so wrong."

Julian squirmed. He'd obviously been coached about what he could and couldn't say. I knew if it had been left to him, he would have defended me. Still, despite the legalities and business side of it all, I was hurt that he didn't take a stand, even if it meant him going down with me. Actually, I was unrealistically surprised at how little professional support I got from anyone in the media. So much for gay men in professional sports. When gay rights were pushing forward and even military service for gays was inching closer, I was victimized a second time.

I consulted a lawyer before deciding to take the severance. I had no doubt that a dispute would be covered by the national press. Even if I won, I would effectively be known as 'the gay sports reporter,' and one way or another this would be the kiss of death. The lawyer felt it was better if I just let things quiet down and look for a reporting job in a small market in a liberal state like Connecticut or Vermont. That opportunity actually happened, but not as planned: I was drinking so heavily that when I got the chance to work on-air again, I almost lost it in the short end of four months.

<h1 style="text-align:center">62</h1>

Charges were brought against the three men who assaulted me and I was the prosecution's star witness. The trial lasted two days and was of course covered by the full press. I looked presentable, at least I thought so, but by then my broadcasting job was toast. I'd returned to Manhattan bitter and exposed. The *New York Daily News* had a field day with my sexual orientation, and several well-known athletes who didn't know me very well made it known they didn't want me in their locker rooms. (For the record, not Derek Jeter. He quietly let me know he was okay with who I was.) My reputation and career were debated and dissected in the media and on the New York talk shows and everything I had hoped to avoid came roaring out. Even worse, I had to face the bastard guy who plummeted me with his fists and feet.

His name was George Pazucki. His court-appointed attorney probably tried to dress him up but he showed up in court wearing a faded brown tweed sports jacket a size too big, the kind with outdated oval suede patches sewn on each elbow, and a wrinkled denim shirt, buttoned at the top and too tight around his neck. His jeans were new but that made the rest of him look even worse. He was about five-foot-five and overweight by at least forty pounds. His stomach protruded like a volleyball.

Pazucki headed to the witness stand with the same swagger I saw that night at The Vault, and he proceeded to lie through his teeth. Under questioning he said I started the altercation by forcefully coming on to him. I was facing his bullshit while Pat Robertson and Jerry Falwell were nationally spewing their version of God's wrath toward homosexuals.

I was cross-examined by a bone-thin, wiry-haired attorney named Custer A. Carson. He spoke with a deviously slow southern drawl, as if he planned to pounce at just the right moment.

"Mr. Macabee, have you ever been involved in an altercation because of your sexual orientation?"

"Before this one, no."

"No, Mr. Macabee?" Mr. Carson stared at the jury and then fired back at me. "Didn't an individual named Louis Summa call the police on the night of September 3, 1995 with a report that you were threatening him with a weapon?"

I was stunned. What the hell was he talking about?

"Objection!" the state attorney said. "Irrelevant."

"No, it is not, your honor. The record will show that this is not the first time Mr. Macabee has been involved in an altercation with another man based on his sexual orientation."

"Objection overruled," the judge said. "You may answer the question."

I said nothing.

"Shall I repeat the question, Mr. Macabee?"

"I don't know what you're asking me."

"Let me refresh your memory, sir. On the night of September 3, 1995, did an individual named Louis Summa call the police because you were threatening him?"

"What?"

My mind spun. I barely remembered Louis. He and I hooked up for maybe a month until we had a ridiculous argument at my apartment. I was cooking spaghetti at the time.

"Did you hurl an object at him with the intent of causing him bodily harm?"

"No, absolutely not. Wait. Do you mean the colander?" I asked incredulously. "I threw a plastic colander at him."

"So you did throw an object at Mr. Summa?"

"Yes, a plastic colander."

"Do you have a temper, Mr. Macabee?"

"No."

I knew not to fidget or in any way reveal my desire to strangle this mealy attorney. I kept my hands in my lap.

"Were you already angry when Mr. Pazucki approached you outside The Vault?"

"No, sir. I had no reason to be. And I had no time."

"Objection."

"Sustained."

"Were you angry when you approached Mr. Pazucki and he called you a fag?"

"No. I never approached him and he never said anything."

"Isn't it a fact that he insulted you and you hit him?"

"No sir, absolutely not."

Mr. Carson pivoted. "What happened the night of February 17, 2001 in Cleveland, Mr. Macabee? Were you involved with the police on that night?"

"Objection! The defense attorney is trying to defame the character of the victim."

Mr. Carson shook his head. "The question speaks to Mr. Macabee's frame of mind."

"Overruled," the judge said, "but be careful, Mr. Carson. You are on a narrow path here."

Mr. Carson stared through me. "Were you arrested?"

"Yes, along with thirty other people."

"Is it a fact that the police report said you were the ringleader?"

"What are you talking about? There was a fight inside a bar and the police cruised in and arrested everyone in sight. Rights were violated."

My hands were no longer in my lap. My hands were punching the air in front of me.

I was not prepared for a character assassination. Toothless Mr. Pazucki was presented as a zealous religious man who opposed homosexuality and attacked me outside after I tried to pick him up. Thankfully the DA never lost his cool: he straightened out that picture on cross examination and thereafter, he factually proved that Mr. Pazucki's hostile criminal behavior was far weightier than my brief aggression with a plastic colander. The trial lasted two days and Mr. Pazucki was found guilty of assault and battery.

Unfortunately, my reputation suffered the same fate.

63

Claudia

After the trial, we didn't hear from Cole. My mother was out of her mind, and Emily and Brett felt responsible, feeling they pushed him too hard when he was vulnerable. We at least knew he was still in Manhattan, in his apartment, but he wouldn't answer the phone. I managed to track down his old buddy Shawn Mullins, who lived across the bridge in Brooklyn Heights, and he agreed to go to Cole's place and fill us in. He called me a day later with dire news. When no one answered the door, Shawn checked the mailbox to see if mail was being picked up—it was; and then he knocked on the apartment door directly across from Cole's.

A glitzy thirty-four floor high-rise one block from Trump Plaza, Cole's building was the opposite of our home in Waltham. When he got the job at FOX, he moved into a one-bedroom corner unit on the twenty-third floor, complete with concierge service and access to a full workout gym. The tenant across the hall was a middle-aged stockbroker for Morgan Stanley. Shawn had met him once. The stockbroker opened the door cautiously. Shawn said he looked irritated.

"What do you want?"

"I'm Shawn, Cole Macabee's friend. I'm sorry to bother you. I'm looking for Cole. Have you seen him?"

The stockbroker nodded. "It's a good thing somebody's looking for him. That guy's a mess. I've seen him a couple of times when food or booze gets delivered. He opens his door just a crack and from what I can tell he can hardly stand up. I didn't know he did drugs. He looks pretty messed up." Then, seeing the look on Shawn's face, "Does he have a family? Maybe you should call somebody."

"Listen," Shawn said, "can I give you my phone number and email? If it gets any worse, you could call me?"

"Buddy, it's worse already. He answers the door like an addict, but as you've found out, most of the time he doesn't answer the door. You're not the first friend to show up knocking. But okay, give me your info and I'll let you know if I think he's dead."

Three hours after I heard from Shawn, Emily got a surprise phone call from Anthony, the nurse from New England Baptist Hospital, where Cole had had his surgery.

"He's with Cole now," Emily said. "Anthony was in the city and Cole was incoherent when he called him. So Anthony went to his apartment and ended up contacting the police. He said it's bad. He wants to call an ambulance. I told him yes, please. He'll get back to me when they get to the hospital. Anthony's pretty sure they'll do an involuntary admission. He said he'll stay with him until Brett and I get there."

"Oh my God, Em," I said. "What should we tell Mom?"

"I think we should wait. Does she know you heard from Shawn?"

"No."

"Then let's wait until I get there. That way we can give her some reassurance that we have a handle on this." Emily paused. "That damned booze. We'll bring him home, Claudia. But he can't stay with us again. We can't handle it. He needs a program." She hesitated. "Do you want to come with us, Claudia? We could pick you up."

I hesitated too. "I can't, Em. My boyfriend's coming tonight."

I didn't bother waiting for Emily's reaction. I knew my excuse was pathetic.

64

Cole

Thanks to Anthony Lopez, on a day when I could have just as well died, I was taken to Mt. Sinai Hospital by ambulance, drunk and drugged out of my mind, and held there for seventy-two hours on an involuntary admission. Brett and Emily got me back to Boston and into detox at Newton-Wellesley Hospital and two weeks later, I teetered between potential and the gutter. That's when I heard about the Vermont job.

A word about Anthony from the Baptist Hospital: it was obvious he was interested in me and had followed my career and my assault close enough to know we belonged on the same team. It was solely because of him calling the cops and pushing his way into my apartment that day that I ended up in the ER and detox. But nurse Anthony Lopez was in no way my type. Barely five foot five, dark skinned and Hispanic, slight and thin with thick eyebrows and black curly hair that he used product on, he was the opposite of the tall professional-looking athletic men that I found most attractive.

I applied for the sports job at WCAX in Burlington, Vermont three weeks after my detox. Anthony was with me when I called the station manager to check on my application. The receptionist took my name and put me on hold. In less than a minute, Harry Hennessy came on the line.

"Mr. Macabee," he said, "I'm Hennessy, the station manager. I understand you might be in the market for an on-air job."

It was clear he knew who I was.

"Yes, sir."

"Are you in town now?"

"No sir, but I would be happy to schedule something this week."

"Tomorrow?" he asked.

I couldn't do it. "Ah, would Thursday work?"

"Sure. Three o'clock."

"Great."

I had two days to pull myself together. Anthony offered to drive me to Burlington. I still used at least one crutch for normal walking, but I could certainly manage the trip. I'd lost weight so I shopped for new clothes the night before we left.

"I'll pay for gas and buy you dinner," I told Anthony. I neglected to tell him I'd also be drinking again as soon as my interview finished. The drive back to Boston was punctuated by the rustling of my paper bag every time I took a swig of whisky, which I did about twenty times while Anthony fumed.

"Hey, I didn't buy into that, bro. That's really stupid of you."

"Yeah, it probably is, but it's only for today. Tomorrow I'll be back at AA."

"Ya, right," Anthony said.

I managed to look the part for the interview. I wore a pair of dark brown cords, a pastel green button-down collared shirt and a dark brown tie, certainly appropriate attire in the world of Vermont athletics. I still had some bruising under my left eye and I moved slowly, but I was sure that Mr. Hennessy knew all about that; otherwise, he wouldn't have taken my call so quickly. I figured he probably saw me as a once-rising star in a major U.S. market, and I had some modicum of face and name recognition. If I was healthy, maybe he thought I'd be at least a novelty in Vermont and at best, I could help with ratings.

Burlington is just off US Route 89. The station was tucked into a strip mall, its entrance manned by a weaponless security guard. I signed in, the receptionist called Mr. Hennessy, and I took a seat in a spacious lobby with a fifteen-foot ceiling and several skylights that let the sun shine directly inside. Oak furniture and three giant ferns in giant planters were scattered throughout the area. Once I heard irregular footsteps approaching from behind, I stood up and faced a man, probably in his sixties, who extended his hand to me.

"Hello, I'm Hennessy."

I leaned forward on my crutch and shook his hand. "Hello, sir. Thank you for meeting with me."

"Difficult ride?" he asked.

"Not at all," I lied.

65

"Let's head to my office, Mr. Macabee."

Harry Hennessy's handshake was solid. He made eye contact with me and he had an informality that immediately put me at ease. Dressed in a white cotton shirt with the top button open at the neck and green khakis, he had probably shaved that morning but he still had a slight stubble. His hair was gray and wavy; I couldn't tell if he had combed it or not. I learned quickly that the dress code in Vermont could not be further from the fashionistas of New York. I noticed he walked with a slight limp, and with my one crutch I followed behind him.

We walked along a dropped ceiling corridor to a tidy reception area where a young woman was on the phone and typing at the same time. Mr. Hennessy pointed at me and she looked up and waved. The walls behind her were painted firebrick red and covered with poster-size photos of Vermont and the Green Mountains, one photo for each season. At first glance, Mr. Hennessy's office looked like a construction site: stacks of books and magazines and papers were strewn everywhere. In contrast his desk was neat as a pin, only three small stacks of papers arranged side by side.

"I'm a former newspaper guy," he smiled. "We work better in messes, but I make sure I can find things on my desk."

He cleared a path and directed me to a mahogany chair with a red leather padded seat and arms. The gold-plated Harvard seal on the back of the chair caught my eye and he noticed.

"Yup, I'm a Harvard guy," he smiled again, "and now I'm a Vermont guy."

I sat down and he made his way around to his desk and he sat down too, rocking back on his swivel chair and balancing himself to face me.

"I know who you are," he said. "For the record, I think you got a raw deal."

"Thank you," I said.

"So do you have an interest working in this market?"

"I do, yes." I cleared my throat. "Mr. Hennessy, I need to be away from being the story instead of telling the story." I knew he would understand that.

"How much were you making at FOX?" He was direct. I liked that.

"Ninety-five thousand, plus profit sharing."

He showed no expression. "The best I can do is sixty-five nine. And a car allowance."

I winced. He probably thought it was in response to the salary, but it wasn't that at all. I was angry and dysfunctional, certainly, but until now I hadn't faced how far down I'd fallen.

"Could you make it seventy-five, Mr. Hennessy?"

"Probably."

He was a straight shooter. I thought I'd like working with him.

"Any problems I should know about?"

"No," I lied. When he didn't respond, I asked, "What will I be covering?"

"College varsities. The Red Sox. Winter sports. Do you ski, Mr. Macabee?"

"Yes."

"Do you skate?"

"No, not since high school."

"We have a class-one high school hockey team in Montpelier. And an Olympic coach based in Burlington. It's a small state but you'll cover all of it."

"What time slot?"

For the first time he looked surprised. "Why, six and eleven weekdays, Mr. Macabee. You'll be our senior guy."

"Mr. Hennessy—"

"Call me Harry."

"Yes, sir. Call me Cole."

"Okay, Cole. That's one down. Look, do you want the job? I need to check the salary bump with my board; I can't promise that. But I can promise you'll learn a hell of a lot here. And it's a nice place; a nice place to regain your footing."

Harry was right. News of my hiring appeared on page three of the *Burlington Free Press* and page two of the *Montpelier Weekly Press*. Both included the same three paragraphs; my biography, my new assignment, and a brief synopsis of my assault and trial. But they don't call Vermont the most liberal state in America for no reason. My sexual preference was a non-issue, even though the 2003 state law recognizing civil unions was controversial. Still, I was no longer dealing with overriding homophobia or ballplayers making two million dollars a year.

Mostly for privacy, I decided to live in Montpelier and not Burlington proper. I found a two-bedroom apartment on the second floor of a two-family white clapboard house, complete with a full length wraparound white porch. It was thirty miles from Burlington, but I didn't mind. Two miles from downtown, the house sat on three acres right on US Highway 302. This was rural America, where high density traffic was non-existent. The whole scene was calm and the air was fresh and, if I'd had my act together, I would have been a newly planted success story from day one.

Needless to say, I was not.

66

The chill hits Vermont by late August and by late September, fields were plowed, firewood was stacked, and wood stoves were ready for the months ahead. I liked it here: the station had Harry's fingerprints all over it: old school friendly and progressively relevant. There were twenty employees in all, including four news reporters, two weather people, myself, a weekend back-up, and a UV intern who sometimes did the weekend on-airs and handled most of the high school interviews. The secretaries, the camera crew and the sales staff were all earnest and likable. My work schedule started around two o'clock each afternoon, Monday through Friday. I was on-air for the six o'clock news and then I prepared and edited for the eleven slot. Most days I shot a local interview or two, spent a couple of hours checking the news ticker, and wrote my stories. Except for one playoff game at Fenway Park, I stayed local: the big news here was Vermont's high school and college teams.

There was one gay club in Montpelier. I'd been to it a few times, but once I became recognized as a local sportscaster, I pulled back. It was a whole lot different here than New York and I had no interest in exposure. I was still drinking and that was not a scene I wanted circulated. Anthony had come up for the weekend twice: he was a sweet guy who hoped for more than I did. I wasn't totally closed, but he disapproved of my drinking, and for me that was a non-starter.

My face and ribs had healed; my knee was just about back to normal. But I was still pissed. Anger swelled up in me. I kept it to myself and it was probably the reason I hadn't made any real friends. I found myself reliving the beating and the trial more often than was good for me. I worked so goddamn hard to get that plum New York job. I did nothing to lose it and the bottom line was it sucked to be swallowed up by such unfairness. I found myself air-punching my father, who I also blamed. The best thing for me was to keep myself in check and keep up with my work.

The birds were already heading south when I had my first performance review with Harry. It wasn't scheduled and I didn't know about it beforehand, but I'd been on the air for four months when he called me in.

"How are you doing, Cole?"

"Good."

"I don't think so," he said. He cocked his head and his eyes locked in on me.

"What?"

"Your drinking, it shows. I hope it's not drugs too. Is it?"

I was caught off guard. "No," I told him.

"Look, I know what you're capable of. I'm a newspaper guy, remember. I know how to research a story. Before you came up that day, I watched five hours of you on-air. I watched your promo. I talked to Julian Edwards at FOX. What I saw and what I heard about you is not what I see and hear today."

I was speechless. I didn't dare move for fear my anxiety would show. Harry leaned forward and his face was stern and no nonsense. "You slide too far, son, and you won't get back. I'm going to make you the best offer of your life. You can take it or leave it. I want you to take a leave of absence. Posthaste, you will voluntarily admit yourself to an inpatient alcohol treatment program. You will finish that program and you will come back to the station sober. You will then agree to attend AA and have a sponsor for the next twelve months. In exchange, I won't fire you and you might just get yourself another fancy big market contract someday, if that's what you want." He shook off my stunned reaction. "One more thing. Don't bother arguing with me about if I'm wrong or right. I don't want to hear it. I lost my son to drugs, Mr. Macabee, and I know what self-destruction looks like."

I had no clue that my daily beer and hard liquor intake showed and I was caught off guard and scared. Harry left no room for discourse.

"What do you want me to do, Harry?"

"I'm giving you two choices; either one's fine with me. You can decide right this minute, do your broadcast tonight, and we'll get you into the Brattleboro Retreat Center tomorrow morning. Or, if you prefer to drink your guts out tonight you can give me your answer tomorrow by noon. Actually, you have a third or fourth choice, you can bolt and I can fire you. Or you can quit. But what you cannot do is stay on the air here as a drunk. I won't have it."

I did the broadcast that night and went home and got sloshed. I finished off a bottle of whisky with some beer chasers in between. How dare he threaten me like that? I hadn't missed work and my on-air reviews were good. Still, just after midnight, crawling to the toilet and vomiting until my guts flushed out, I knew Harry was serious. If I didn't agree with his plan, I would lose my job. Yet another job. That was a hopeless resume to carry forward. I tried to envision what I would do then; how horrible for my goals and efforts to go to hell just like that. That was bad enough, but even that was pushed aside when I thought about my poor mother. My biggest fan. I would break her heart again.

I called Harry at the station the next morning at 7:40. He answered the phone himself and he was quiet, patiently letting me muddle through words that had to be mine.

"Okay," I said. "I'll do it. Is tomorrow morning okay?"

"No," he said. "It has to be today. I told you that already."

Harry picked me up in his beat-up Ford truck and we drove the two-hour ride on Routes 89 and 91 to Brattleboro. Defiantly, I'd packed only enough clothes for three days, plus my shaving kit and hair cream, my laptop, and a hardback copy of Yeats; all this in my black Italian leather carry-on bag. Harry watched me fling the bag into his way back and said nothing. Midway, when we stopped at a rest area for coffee, he said, "You should call your family. They may not let you make calls once you're admitted."

He proceeded to tell me that a detox bed was reserved for me; that he'd cleared it with my health insurance, and he'd arranged for my temporary replacement through the coverage pool, starting that night.

"How will you explain this?" I asked him.

"We'll say that you're on medical leave and we expect you back on air in a month or two. This isn't New York. It won't be front page news." He paused and turned his head to me. "Cole, if it takes a full sixty days, we can handle that."

I wish he were my father. I wish my father had looked at me like this.

67

Claudia

During our weekly dinner routine, Mom scraped the dishes and handed them to me to put in the dishwasher. "I'm heartbroken," she said. "He's still drinking? After seeing what it did to your father? What's happened to Cole, Claudia?"

"I don't really know, Mom. He obviously fell apart when he lost his New York job, and from the sound of it, he's in trouble in Vermont."

"When can we see him at that rehab place? He called Emily, you know. He hasn't called me. That's bad. I'm his mother and he's avoiding me."

"He was probably allowed just one call. He has to get detoxed and into their routine before his family gets involved. I can understand why it would be hard for him to tell you all this. It's a good program, Mom. I read about it."

My mother's voice weakened. "Will you drive to Vermont with me, Claudia? Next week? We could make a day of it and maybe meet with that Mr. Hennessy and find out what really happened. That would help me."

I swallowed. This was not the way I planned to tell her about my trip. "I'm taking a vacation next week, Mom."

"To where?"

"Virgin Gorda," I said. "It's a tropical island in the West Indies."

My mother was surprised, but she tried to hide it. "Oh, I didn't know that."

I hesitated, and then I lied. "I decided kind of out of the blue. I leave next Monday and I'll be gone for five days. I'll leave you an emergency number. Mom, I have this chance to go, to soak up some sun. Maybe even snorkel. I'm looking forward to it. Cole will be okay, Mom, he's in a program. He's safe. Nothing can happen before I get back. I want you to be okay with me going."

She didn't question me. She knew who I was going with and she disapproved, but she forced herself to sound cheerful. Her face was tight but she kissed me.

"That sounds nice, honey. It's okay. You deserve the time. Nice and warm."

I kept my guilt under wraps. "Mom, if anything happens with Cole, you can reach me and I'll come back. But honestly, I don't think we'll know anything for a couple of weeks. This is something he has to deal with on his own."

"I know," Mom replied. "I know that only too well."

68

The trip had been planned for months. Wills would fly to Saint Thomas, hop on an eight-seater plane, and fly over the Caribbean Sea to the small island of Virgin Gorda. Once there he'd taxi to the Jeep rental place, drive to the hexagon cottage rental where we'd stay for five days and four nights, and ready the place for my arrival.

He had the option of staying at the upscale Little Dix Resort on the North Sound, with its grand restaurant and where he would meet his clients, but instead, he chose the Guavaberry cottages, nestled in the middle of the Baths National Park, because they offered us almost total privacy. Plus, his clients were Japanese businessmen who didn't ask or expect anything except full days of uninterrupted work. And because this would likely be a one-time consult (although I did bring a back-up costume, this time as Nelly Pickler, an accountant,) Wills and I could enjoy ourselves openly.

When I arrived the next day with a red hibiscus in my hair, compliments of the boat captain who ferried me over, Wills was waiting for me outside the Leverick Bay restaurant. He looked every bit like an islander himself, so handsome in a light tan suit, tieless with an open-collar white pressed cotton shirt. I paid the taxi driver and ran toward him. He wrapped his arms around me and lifted me off the ground.

"Oh my God," I shouted, "I cannot believe this. *I cannot believe this.*"

He smiled. "Wait until you see our place. And guess what? They told me today I can plan on a noon wrap-up on Thursday. We'll have a whole afternoon to snorkel."

"Ha, time to snorkel if we make it out of bed! Actually, okay, I'll snorkel. I wonder what we can do underwater!"

Wills tossed his head back and smiled again. "I'm picturing that. Would snorkeling defy gravity?"

I laughed. "That, and if you're weightless, can you still moan?"

The restaurant was classic Caribbean: floor to ceiling white shutters along all the walls, wicker chairs with bright floral cushions, palms, hibiscus plants and ceiling fans all along the interior. We sat side-by-side at a corner table and pressed against each other, our legs and hips locked together.

"A bottle of Trimbach Cuvee Frederic Emile Riesling, please?" Wills told the waiter. My favorite. "Aw, Wills, you remembered. That's so sweet of you."

"Claudia Macabee, nothing but the best." He grinned.

I had no doubts. For years now I watched this man wrestle with his love for me and his love for his family. Sometimes I could see guilt carved into his brow and in the creases around his eyes. I tried to make things easy for him: he loved Natalie and he loved me too. It was just that simple. I was happiest when it was just that simple.

We walked hand-in-hand along a three-foot-wide sand path bordered by red ground flowers and huge ferns until we reached our cottage.

"Holy good God," I squealed. The place was heaven. Two separate hexagon buildings were attached to each other by a small breezeway. Inside, one hexagon was a combination living area and kitchen, and the other a spacious bedroom and bathroom. Both had fourteen-foot- high ceilings with eight-inch-thick wood beams that spread out from a central peak, forming an overhead star. The beams stopped just above floor-to-ceiling open-air shutters that covered every wall. Wills had no sooner put my suitcase down when I pushed him backwards onto the king-sized bed and I fell on top of him. Within seconds our clothes were off. A tropical breeze against our bodies added a new element to making love.

"I'm so in love with you, Claudia," Wills whispered. "That will never change. I want you to always know that."

"I know, Wills. My mother talks about devotion like it's a sacrament. We have that." I snuggled close to him and he wrapped his arms around me. "I'll always love you."

"I know, honey," he said. "I wish sometimes it didn't make me so sad."

Our lovemaking that night was slow and deliberate, as if we could slow down time. We'd both had plenty of sexual partners but this was a fusion we experienced only with each other. The ceiling fan quietly hummed above us. I pressed my face to Wills' ear. I whispered, "You are such a good man."

In these moments he needed reassurance. No matter how hard he tried to cover it, his infidelity punctured the sanctity of our relationship. Circumstance had not been kind to us, but what we did have was irreplaceable. *Imagine if we had never found each other.* We often reminded ourselves of that, as if to justify the other messy details.

Wills' arms were still wrapped around me. "It's not fair to you, Claudia. You should be with a guy who can cherish you every moment, and instead you wait for me, and accept the little I can give you. I'm so sorry, honey."

He'd said this before. I always responded in the same way.

"It's okay, Wills, really. It's enough. You make me happy. You're an honorable man. I'm so sorry it has to be like this. I wish polygamy was acceptable. I even wish we could all be a family; that Natalie would know that our love for one another is not a take-away from her."

I looked at his face as if I were studying a painting. "I wish you could be at my family's Christmas dinner. I wish I could buy your kids birthday presents. I wish you knew my mother."

"I wish all that too, honey."

Sometimes he cried when we talked about our circumstance. He was cheating on his wife and he'd been cheating for years now. He couldn't grasp how it was even possible to love two women as deeply as he did. He never hesitated to tell me that Natalie was loyal, loving, kind, spontaneous, generous, intelligent. Their children could not have a better mother or a better home. And he and she were compatible in almost every way; once when we were both drinking, he unthinkingly admitted that their lovemaking was good and satisfying. But he quickly added that since that first day in the laundromat, he had a dull pain in his chest that never went away. Sometimes he talked about his discomfort, and once or twice he grimaced and clutched at his heart. He told me the worst was that he wasn't able to give a hundred percent of his emotional and physical presence to either one of us. When he was home, he longed for me. When he was with me, he worried about Natalie and the kids.

It was around four o'clock in the morning and pitch-black outside when I heard Wills slip out of bed and push open the patio screen door. I could see his silhouette, naked, his hands out of sight, praying, he told me afterwards. He'd call Natalie after breakfast and tell her about the coconut shrimp and mango salad he had for dinner and about his clients. He'd describe the architecture and flowers on the island and tell her about this very patio; ask her if Petunia's cold was any better, and how Ryan had fared on his writing assignment. He'd say, 'I love you, Nat' and mean it, and he'd hang up, temporarily relieved.

Most of my friends, and sometimes even Emily, called him a cad, cheating on his wife and stringing me along, but I knew better. I wondered how many other people ended up in a hopeless situation like this, just because destiny showed up unexpectedly and couldn't be undone.

The next morning, he told me what he prayed for. "I prayed that you and Natalie will always be loved and cared for, the way you deserve."

He looked at me so softly, with an unsteadiness in his voice.

"Wills, I think we're both already loved and cared for, the best you can. Nothing has to change, at least not with me."

He smiled. "Thank you, honey."

For the next three days, when his workday was done, Wills and I dined, lay in the sun, chilled on the patio, and made love with a freedom that was light-years away from a ticking clock. We grilled ribs and steaks and island vegetables, held hands on the beach at dusk, and looked up at the black night sky and bright stars. It was the most relaxed we'd ever been together. Our bodies, butt-naked or scantily clothed in bathing suits or shorts and tees, pushed together in the warm crosswinds.

When we flew back to Miami and on to Boston, it only took a nanosecond standing at the luggage carousel before reality returned. Wills and I were together, and then we would walk in separate directions, each step widening the distance between us. That night, I cried myself to sleep, and I wondered if he did too.

There was a letter from Cole waiting for me when I got home. He had written it when he first arrived at the rehab program. I didn't know how he was faring now, but I was glad for this diversion. On this sad night, home alone, I had to think about my family instead of the huge hole in my heart.

Dear Claudia,

Just a short note to ask you to tell Mom that I'm okay. I know she's probably crazy with worry, but I couldn't bring myself to talk to her so I called Emily instead. I'm in a drug and alcohol program and I hate it, but I have some shit to deal with and figure out. Please tell Mom I'll be fine. Take care of yourself! I hope your boyfriend's treating you well. Love Cole

PART 6

Hope

69

Cole

The Brattleboro Retreat Center sits on a thousand acres of Vermont's rolling hills, peppered with mature trees that tower over several nineteenth century three-and four-story brick buildings. The place reeks of history. Harry pulled up to the admissions building, a grand structure with forty- foot columns, got out of his truck and, staring straight ahead, waited for me to get out of the truck too.

"Listen Harry, I'm not going to bolt. You can leave."

"No, no," he said. "I'll wait until I know you're in good hands." His voice dropped. "I've done this before, son. No fooling around."

We walked up a dozen brick steps and I pushed open a ten-foot-high solid oak door that spilled us into a lobby decorated like a Victorian living room. I approached the front desk and told the perky girl looking up at me my name.

"Welcome, Mr. Macabee," she said, as if I were checking into a four-star hotel. She handed me a packet of forms. "Have a seat. You have to fill these out. Bring them back here when you're done. And you probably know already, but here's a brochure about our program."

Harry had made himself comfortable, sitting in a padded mahogany chair with worn wooden arms, not unlike the one in his office. I took a seat near but not beside him, and I read over the packet. Most of the information was standard but one part instantly irritated me: *You will meet with a Licensed Independent Practitioner (usually a physician's assistant, nurse practitioner, or social worker) to discuss your history of mental health/substance abuse treatment and current needs.*

Oh great, I thought. *They want into my head.*

Then a light bulb went off: I wouldn't be drinking today or tonight or tomorrow. Instead, some mental health types would try their best to psych me out. *Nope, I'm not going to let that happen.*

"I'll hold your job for you, Cole." The voice came at me like a ghost and it took me a moment to process that it was Harry. "As long as you complete the program and come back and stay sober." He said this in a low voice and nodded for emphasis. I nodded back even though I wasn't sure this was what I wanted or what I would do. So what if I drank on my own time? It didn't interfere: I was reliable, I was showered and clean-cut, I wasn't mean, I went to the gym, I paid my bills—not exactly the profile of an out-of-control drunk like my father. I wondered if Harry was projecting his son's problems onto me.

Harry's toughness reminded me of my mother. Twice in high school she grounded me for drinking. The first time the guys and I downed three six-packs in my friend's basement, and she knew the second I walked in the door. "Supper's delayed for fifteen minutes," she announced to everyone. "Cole, meet me in the living room."

"What happened?" she confronted me and she insisted I answer.

"We were screwing around in Jeff's cellar and there was beer in the mini fridge." I looked at her earnestly. "It was just for fun. I wanted to try."

"Free pass this time," she said. "But not again."

I nodded. "Okay."

The second time, I came home from a school dance two hours past my 11:30 curfew and my mother was waiting for me in the kitchen. She stared me down, said nothing, turned around, and headed for bed. The next morning, she informed me there would be no football practice for two weeks. I was the back-up quarterback and the team had a chance to make the state semifinals. My coach begged her to loosen up but she wouldn't.

"I spent too many years making excuses for my husband, gentlemen," she told the coach, the guidance counselor, and me at a school meeting, "and there is no way I'm going to condone or excuse my son drinking."

Our team went on to lose two of the remaining four games.

70

A woman younger than me took notes on a lined legal pad. She had brown hair that curled to her shoulders, a round cheerleader-like face, white teeth, healthy cheeks, and serious looking green eyes.

"I'm Cheryl," she said. "I'm your counselor. So how are ya?"

"Not good," I said.

"You look excited to be here." She smiled.

"Right." I scowled.

"Do you have a therapist on the outside?"

"No," I said. "I'm here because it's a condition of keeping my job. I've never been in therapy. I'm willing to stop drinking, but I don't want my head shrunk. I'm not in need of that."

Cheryl nodded. "First thing you should know, Mr. Macabee…"

"Please, call me Cole."

"Sure, Cole. So, everything here is a hundred percent confidential. We have an extra challenge because you're a public figure, but we're very good at protecting privacy." She paused. "Full disclosure: my brother plays varsity baseball in Rutland and you did a TV interview with him a while back. It meant the world to him."

"Thanks," I said.

"So, what do you know about our program?"

"I know everything. All I don't know is how long."

Cheryl put down her pen. "Detox comes first. You're scheduled for a physical exam this afternoon. We want to make sure you don't have any underlying conditions that could get in the way."

"How long is detox?" I asked.

"Just a guess—five to seven days. Maybe three or four, depending."

"Oh great," I said.

"The first few days can be challenging," Cheryl continued. "It will probably tax your resolve and then your patience. Withdrawal symptoms are no fun. You know that, right?"

"Yup," I said. "Anxiety, agitation, panic, shakes, nausea, chills. I know the drill."

Cheryl added, "And muscle aches, trouble sleeping, cramping, sometimes trouble breathing and a racing heart. We have medication to help you through it."

"And then what?"

Cheryl looked at me kindly. "Well, first let me ask you a few questions. I've read your hospital records. You started drinking heavily after you were attacked?"

"More or less," I said.

"History of alcohol or drug abuse in your family?"

"Yes, my father was an alcoholic and so were my mother's parents."

"Did your father drink when you were a kid?"

I scoffed. "The question should be do I remember him sober."

"That bad?"

"Yes. My mother protected us."

"Who is us?"

"I have two sisters."

"It's rougher than most people realize," Cheryl said, "growing up with an alcoholic parent. It affects the whole family and it affects kids in a way they don't even know until it comes sneaking out in one way or another."

She was right about that. "I pissed him off. But my sisters and I had good childhoods," I told her. "My mother made sure we were all right."

"How did she do that?" Cheryl asked.

I laughed. "She just did. She's an expert at insisting on happy families."

"Does she know you're here?"

"No, not yet."

"Do you plan on telling her?"

The question felt intrusive. "I called my sister. She'll take care of it."

Cheryl picked up her pen again. "Okay, so to answer your question: after detox you'll move into Riley House with other residents and you'll follow a daily schedule we arrange for you. That includes AA and therapy sessions. We use a cognitive and behavioral approach, so you learn what triggers you to drink. And you'll take part in everybody's favorite: group therapy, facilitated by me."

"I hate that already."

"That's okay, join the crowd," Cheryl grinned. "We hope you'll share what got you here: that helps you but it also helps everyone else in the group. We'll also want your family and significant others to be part of your treatment plan. They need to know how to help you stay sober."

I pictured my mother and felt a sharp pain in my chest. I abruptly brought my hand to my heart, trying to stop it.

"What just happened, Cole?" Cheryl was still calm.

"I won't put my mother through this."

Her expression softened. "Not to be obnoxious, but you probably already have. Listen, I see pain right now. You don't want to hurt her; I get that." She put her pen down for the third time. "There will be a family meeting at some point, and it will be important for all of you, but no worries: it's not even a decision you make now."

Jesus, I thought. "Cheryl, how long will I be here?"

"That depends. Our most optimal program lasts ninety days."

"No way," I said.

"Take it day by day, Cole. We're here to help you. There's one important thing you should know: this is a voluntary program. Drink or drug and we'll ask you to leave. You have to want sobriety more than you don't. We'll support you and we know what we're doing, but we don't coddle."

I wanted to hate Cheryl but I didn't.

"Relax," she smiled at me. "It's all individual. Let's get you started."

71

They detected alcohol in my system at a level of .05. This revealed my first lie.

The doctor was matter-of-fact about it. "Mr. Macabee, we're starting you on Acamprosate. You can expect that unpleasant symptoms might begin this afternoon and maybe sooner. You're in detox voluntarily, but if we determine you're a danger to yourself or others, if we have to pursue a court order for an involuntary admission, we will do so, so it's in your interest to work with us."

This was a threat. *Fuck you.*

Chuck-the-roommate introduced himself as a forty-two-year-old boat mechanic from New Jersey. He was in the program because two nights ago during a visit with his New England grandmother, she poured his backpack of booze down the toilet and when he found out, he just about ripped her house apart. She called the police and arranged for his admission to Brattleboro, even before insurance okayed his claim. Chuck recognized me from FOX but didn't say anything more than that. I watched him size me up as a pretty boy; even my skin contrasted with his stubby beard and rough oversized hands. Surprisingly, his jeans had ironed creases down the front of each leg. Not many men ironed their jeans, but I did that too.

"Welcome to the circus, buddy," he said, extending his hand. "If I'm any example you're in for a rough ride. And after the physical shit, they expect us to talk. Bullshit to that. But beware: Cheryl is clever. She knows how to get to you."

Chuck and I were going to do just fine together.

Four days into detox, after vomiting for thirty-six hours and curling up in a fleece blanket, trying to stop the chills and stomach cramps, and then telling a group therapist (not Cheryl) to go to hell (I apologized), I called Emily. Brett answered the phone.

"Bro, they want me to think about people for a family meeting, probably in a few weeks. Will you or Emily come?"

"Sure, Cole. We'll come. And Christine?"

"Definitely not. I'm not ready for that. I hope she doesn't think this is her fault. How is she?"

"She's totally worried about you. She's chomping at the bit to see you."

"Make something up, Brett. Tell her parents aren't allowed. I can have three people, and I thought you or Emily, Claudia, and maybe Anthony."

"Anthony from the Baptist Hospital? What's with that?" Brett asked.

"He's come to Vermont a few times," I answered. "I guess we're kind of dating." I hesitated. "But it's no big deal. He's just a good influence because he's straightlaced and doesn't drink."

"And you have us too," Brett said.

"Yes, of course—my family."

Why do I drink? Is it hereditary? Am I weak? Yesterday in group, it was clear I'm luckier than most of the people here. Hell, only five of us are employed.

"One of us will be there," Brett said. "Tell Anthony he can drive up with us if he wants." He asked me a second time: "But what about your mom? I think I should tell her you called me."

"Okay, tell her this program is killing me but I'm hanging in. Tell her I love her and she'll have a sober son this Christmas. And tell her this is absolutely not her fault."

The treatment program was worse than I thought possible. I was up at six each morning, with daily in-your-face confrontations and painful admissions. I still longed for the antiseptic numbing liquor provided me. I would leave Brattleboro sober and determined, but not before I faced my father.

72

"What did your mother say when he attacked you?" Cheryl asked.

"She said no one had a right to hurt me. Or something like that."

"Did you ever talk to her about how your father made you feel?"

"No," I said. "No."

"Why not?"

"She didn't need to hear that. She tried hard enough already."

"Why do you think she stayed with him?"

"Honestly, I don't know."

My father's physical attack was small change compared to the insults he threw at me. One time, when my mother and the girls were out with Aunt Louise, I was at the table doing homework when he came home and he was on me right away.

"Why do you look like that? Why can't you look like a god-damn boy?"

I was in sixth grade and co-captain of our neighborhood baseball team. I had friends and I had good grades. But my father couldn't stand that I used hair gel and let my hair grow halfway over my ears, even though lots of pre-teen kids my age did the same thing. But that wasn't what bugged him the most: I knew it wasn't just my appearance. It was my *delicacy.*

"And you cook," he shook his fist at me. "Boys don't cook. And they don't wear aprons either."

I tried to calm him down. I said something like, "Dad, why don't you take a shower?"

That really pissed him off. "Why don't you act like a boy instead of a flying fag?"

I slammed my fist on the table. I surprised myself: I'd had enough. "Oh yeah? Screw you, Dad," I screamed back. "I don't care what you think."

This must have startled him because he kind of backed off, but he was still disgusted.

"I have a faggot for a son." He held on to the wall and then the sink, until he finally staggered upstairs.

"Who did you tell about this?" Cheryl asked.

"No one," I said, "but I definitely got the message."

"Wow," Cheryl said, "I can't imagine how you felt when he died."

"That's for sure. When Mom told us he'd been killed, at first, I thought he must have pissed someone off the way he had me. The news was a sucker punch for me, probably because I'd thought once or twice about killing him myself."

I didn't want Cheryl to know, but I was a mess when my mother told us. My first thought was *It was my fault.* I winced. Cheryl noticed. "What? Tell me, Cole. It's important."

"I remember that day," I said. "I remember how my mother stretched her arms straight in front of her, wide on the table, and she spread her fingers wide too, in all directions They looked like branches. It's funny that I remember her doing that more than her words."

"That makes me think of branches all coming from the same tree," Cheryl said. "Kind of like the way your mother stressed unity to you and your sisters."

"Devotion…"

"What?"

"She called it *devotion*. It was part of her formula: poems, food, and devotion."

Cheryl nodded. "Did it work?"

I laughed. "It kind of did…I liked it."

For a long time after my father died, I had these pockets of anger that I didn't know what to do with. My way of dealing with it was to shut down. My mother told me to write about my feelings, so for a while I wrote one poem after another, until my worst emotions spilled from my head onto my journal. I burned that journal the day I started college. I only remember one verse from all those poems I wrote about him:

> "Dad I'm sorry I didn't go
> With you that day to the fishing show
> I was tired and I slept instead
> Never thinking you'd soon be dead.
> You taught me life is hard, to use my head.
> And one time when you let me drive
> You said only the tough survive.
> You wanted me to be a man
> But you yelled too much to understand.
> I was sure I was not a favorite son
> But I tried to love you Dad,
> Now your life is done."

Cheryl nodded. "You have to deal with this. It won't go away if you don't."

I wanted to scream *No!* but instead, I just shrugged.

73

Claudia

Brett's call to Mom temporarily calmed her down. She was hurt and upset that she hadn't heard from Cole directly, but at least she knew where he was and he was safe. I reacted in the same way: with a clearer conscience, I resumed my Tuesday nights and catch-as-you-can weekend schedule with Wills. But a new opportunity had surfaced: our spillover from Virgin Gorda was still apparent when he picked me up at my apartment at nine-thirty on Saturday morning and we drove to his house. I was going to meet Natalie. He'd told her I was a work-friend who volunteered to help them pack boxes of giveaways for a giant annual Goodwill yard sale the next day. I bought lobster rolls for lunch and Natalie had the coffee and wine ready. The kids were at their aunt's house.

I wore a white gingham blouse with a frill covering the buttons and tucked into my favorite fitted jeans, a faded denim with shamrock stitching on both back pockets. I pulled my hair back in a ponytail and wore my running sneakers. Wills and I had talked about this plan for a couple of weeks. Natalie and I would finally meet. It was my idea, and he was nervous about it. The pretense wasn't honest, but I prayed things might go well enough that a fledging friendship, even a distant one, might take root. I knew it was ridiculous and unlikely, but I really hoped. *Maybe if Natalie knew me.* On this day I'd meet her, and maybe on another day I could meet the kids. Maybe I could take them candlepin bowling.

Natalie was at the front door when we arrived. She extended her hand to me, backed up with a genuine smile. "Thanks so much for coming to help us," she said. "And for bringing lunch. Will tells me you're the best."

The house was just as I envisioned: a two-story Colonial with a huge living room, a stone fireplace built into the back wall, dark brown leather couches, and dozens of framed family photos scattered on every surface. I skimmed the room quickly, trying to avoid that last part.

"And you brought lobster rolls," Natalie said. "That's a heck of a treat."

"My pleasure. I'm very glad to meet you, Natalie," I said.

"Me too. Let's eat lunch on the porch and then we can pack the ridiculous amount of stuff Will and I and the kids are donating. I made a salad and Will bought a watermelon. The big question of the day is 'Coffee or wine?'"

"For me, coffee," I said. I knew better than to risk a loose tongue.

Our conversation flowed easily. *Where do you live? Where are you from? Your brother's on TV? That's great.* And I reciprocated: *How old are the kids? Wills told me about Ryan's award. How is Petunia's asthma? Have you seen Meg Ryan's new movie? Oh, I love Talbot's clothes too.*

"Thanks so much for helping us, Claudia. We might as well start in the kitchen while Will takes Petunia's bunk bed apart. We're remodeling our kitchen next spring, plus I'm a bit of a packrat. We have lots to give away. I'm finally willing."

"I'm a good packer," I said.

"That's perfect," Natalie said. "I supply. You pack. Teamwork." She smiled. She pulled the old microwave to the edge of the counter, cradling it in both arms and picked it up. Its weight surprised her and she dropped it down forcefully.

"Here, let me take that," I said.

"No, it's okay, I've got it."

"But let me help. I know that crazy slip off the bed hurt your back."

Natalie froze in mid-motion. She took her hands off the microwave, turned around, and fell back on the counter, as if she'd been pushed. Her expression was no longer welcoming.

"What did you say?" she demanded.

I knew instantly I'd made a huge mistake. "Err, Wills mentioned you hurt your back some time ago."

Natalie snapped. Everything about her was different. "Why would you know that? Why would he ever have mentioned that to you?" She shook. "I thought something about this was off. It was so important to him that you come today. But it's more than friendship, isn't it? It's *you*. It's *you*, isn't it?" Her voice was shrill. I wanted to respond, to offer some explanation, but I just stood there.

She hissed, "You have one hell of a nerve. Get out! Now!" Her anger ricocheted through the living room and to the back room where Wills was. I heard metal slam on the floor—a wrench? Natalie had stormed past me and must have cornered him in their daughter's bedroom. I heard rage laced into her words. "Get her out of here. Get her out now."

Wills stood at the entrance to the living room while I fumbled to open the front door. I didn't look at him. I heard him say something and he took a step toward me.

"Don't," I ordered. I turned around and raised my fist to his face. "*Don't.*"

I shut the door behind me, steadying myself on the porch railing, trying to keep my body erect, as if the slightest loosening of any muscle would disable my ability to move at all. The day was calm and there was no wind, but my hip-length coat shook from side to side with each horrid step I took. Wills was standing at his front door when I slammed my fist onto the hood of his BMW. I ran toward the street as though the last ten minutes never existed.

This is what he told me afterwards. He sounded as though he memorized it: "I heard Natalie yell at you. She walked into the bedroom and I'd never seen her so upset. After you left, I tried to calm her down. She just kept saying, 'I never thought you would disrespect me in this way. I should have known. How dare you bring her here?'"

I didn't want to hear any of this, but Wills was desperate to explain.

"Claudia, Natalie cried when she said all this. I pleaded with her to tell me what happened. Finally, she said, 'You told her private things about me. I know you wouldn't have told anyone at work about me falling off the bed. And you set this up so your wife and your mistress could have a dandy little day together. This is sick. And I'm done.'"

Wills stopped and took a deep breath. "She told me you knew about her fall. Something clicked for her, Claudia. She couldn't stop. It isn't like her to lose control like that. There was nothing I could do. I should have known better, honey. It was a mistake. I should have known. I had the same hope you did; that somehow things would work themselves out. I was wrong. It's my fault."

I listened, but none of the words mattered. Natalie knew, and she'd been harmed.

74

In the middle of all this, I called my mother and told her I couldn't make Cole's rehab meeting in Vermont.

"You have to come," she said.

"Something's come up, Mom. I'm sure Emily can go instead."

"No, Claudia." Mom's voice was stern. "This time I'm not asking. You know more about Cole and what happened as kids than anyone else, and your brother needs you. And I need you. I've let you off the hook enough already. You have to come."

So, despite the agony and uncertainty that Wills and I might be finished, it was decided: Mom, Brett and I would go. Cole was the priority. I was in no shape, but my mother was right: I had no choice.

<h1 style="text-align:center">75</h1>

Cole

I was in the fourth week of the program when my family meeting took place. Mom had left me, and then Cheryl, a phone message insisting that she be included. She was adamant. As hard as it was to agree to this, as soon as I saw her, I knew she was right.

Claudia looked like hell and I didn't know why. She kept her eyes open and she managed to listen, but it was clear that something was wrong.

I expected the meeting to be a rally for my recovery and a sobriety plan for the future. Cheryl began softly. "Cole, it's important that your family understands why you drink. And what you need not to drink." She kept her eyes on me with a look and message I recognized: *'Take all the time you need, but don't think I'll get so uncomfortable that I'll answer for you.'*

I'd thought about this for days. At all costs, I was not going to upset my mother. I looked at her now, sitting at this giant conference table, her hands politely resting in front of her, her frizzy red hair pulled back behind her ears. She sat across from me, here to help her grown son grow up.

"Well," I began, "My life gets out of control when I drink. I have a lot going for me and I don't want to hurt myself or anyone else."

Cheryl nodded. She was kind enough to accept my platitude answer. Then she looked at Mom and Claudia. "Why do you think Cole became dependent on alcohol?"

Mom didn't hesitate. "There was no problem until he got beaten up and lost his job. None of that was his fault, not one bit. But it also runs in our family. Cole's father was an alcoholic and so were both of my parents."

"So, you and Cole and the family were all exposed to the unpredictability of that for many years. How did you deal with it?"

Claudia and I knew instinctively that Cheryl was fishing. My sister, with black rings under her eyes and an unmistakable tiredness, leaned into my mother's shoulder, already in protective mode.

"Well, that's a good question," my mother began. "My own childhood, I turned to my sister and to poetry books. I stayed out of my parents' way. With my kids, I made it clear to Cole's father that if he laid a hand of any of the kids, he'd be gone. He knew I meant it. And I made sure that whatever their father couldn't give them, I did. I tried really hard. And my sister Louise tried too."

"Is that how you remember it, Cole?" Cheryl asked. She was such a sneak, the way she set me up.

"Yes. My mother is a saint. That's what I remember."

"And your father...?"

I swallowed. I looked at my mother and I felt my forehead stiffen. My lips quivered and she noticed. "Cole," she said, "we're here to help you. For God's sake, stop worrying about me."

"My father didn't care," I finally said. "Even when he was sober, he criticized everything I did. My mother tried to make up for him, but I knew he couldn't stand me."

Almost in sync, Claudia's head snapped back, so did my mother's, like two side-by-side bobble dolls. I don't think either had ever heard me say this out loud.

"Go on," Cheryl said.

"There's nothing more to say. He hated me. We probably hated each other."

"Did you know this, Mrs. Macabee?"

"No. Not to this extent."

"Did you, Claudia?"

"No."

"You probably understand in some way?" Cheryl directed this to my mother.

"No, I don't, actually." Mom spoke emphatically. "In my own upbringing, I didn't have a mother to protect me. My mother was worse than my father. Cole was a wonderful child. There was never a day I wasn't as proud of him as a parent could be. I think in some way you're asking me how I could have missed the true effect Cole's father had on him. And that his father was this awful to him. There were a few times I stepped in, but the answer is I didn't see it to this extent."

Claudia made a soft sound and started to cry. I didn't know why she was so vulnerable, but she was also in protection mode. "Listen," she said, "if this is about blaming my mother—"

"Stop, Claudia!" The rise in my mother's voice shut down all dialogue. She slammed her hand on the table. "If there is some-thing I could have done or can do now to help Cole, I'm ready for it." She looked at me forcefully; I'd never seen this look before.

"What do you wish your mother had done, Cole?" Cheryl asked.

I was dumbfounded that I was being asked about a feeling I'd carried with me probably since the first time I used a fork. "I wish she had left him. Right away. We would have all been better off."

My mother folded her hands again and she didn't move. It was a long moment before she spoke. "Son, I thought about doing that every day your father was alive. And I've thought about it for the twenty-one years since your father died. I made a judgement. At the time it was the best I could do with the resources and information I had. I sought advice from a priest. I met with your school's guidance counselor. I read books. I listened to your Aunt Louise nag me every which way. I decided that it was best that I make it work with your father, and that we not add financial struggles to the problems we already had. I figured your father was insignificant in our daily lives and I thought I could keep it that way. He was a good man at one time, Cole, I want you to know that. But by the time you were born I'd already decided I would build a safe space for my children, and whatever you kids lacked from him, I would do my damnedest to fill in."

Hearing this, and seeing my sister in such tough shape, I needed to shut it down. I was determined not to cry and I stiffened my shoulders so they wouldn't shake.

"Stop," I said. "Please. I know, Mom. It was okay. Really it was. None of that is why I drink."

Sitting in that conference room with my family, I felt heartbroken, not because my mother's efforts hadn't been enough, but because all this time she thought they were. I was stunned by how naive she'd been to think she could make up for my father's absence and anger. But maybe I was naive too, blaming him all these years. My mother had been determined to not to let him destroy us. And maybe he hadn't. My whole childhood, my mother resisted that outcome with every bone in her body.

"Mrs. Macabee," Cheryl said, "I can see where Cole's strength comes from. And how difficult this was."

It was Mom's turn to stiffen. "No, Cheryl, I have to correct you again. It actually wasn't difficult. I had my children and our house and my sister and we all had each other. Certainly, I wished I had a good husband and the kids had a good father, but that was one missing card we had to accept. But we had our health, we had each other, we had family meals and vacations, we had poetry, we even had my hero, John Denver." She stopped and grinned at me. It was the perfect levity. We all laughed, even Cheryl.

"Why John Denver?" she asked.

"My fantasy husband," my mother said, still grinning. "He kept ME from drinking. I was president of his fan club."

Cheryl smiled, but only for a second. She had an agenda. "It's so difficult to shelter children from a parent's alcoholism. It sounds like you did a remarkable job of it, Mrs. Macabee." Then she turned to me. "Any thoughts on how else your mother could have protected you?"

My voice cracked. "She did protect me." I'd heard enough. I cupped my face in my hands and shook. My mother pushed her chair back and flew across the room so fast she was beside me before I could even look up. She put both her hands around my head and pulled me to her. For the first time in over twenty years, I sobbed.

76

Claudia

I was ready for a mental hospital. Not only did I not have Wills, I had to hear my mother and brother talk about our family in the rawest way. The scene at the Brattleboro Retreat Center forced me to look at my own childhood, and the gaps in my memory confirmed how much I'd blocked out. That made my own problems worse. Heartache has its own physiology: a hollow stomach, a tight chest, loss of appetite, exhaustion, insomnia, intestinal disorders. I had all of these. I hadn't slept, and I couldn't keep food down. The hole in my stomach was the worst. I made it through Cole's meeting, but barely. I was glad for the meeting, glad for Cole and my mother, but my own pain was too deep to escape.

Over the first five days that followed the blowup with Natalie, Wills had left me dozens of phone messages and emails, but I couldn't bring myself to respond. I couldn't stop crying. When I walked out of his house that day and flagged down a cab, the driver asked if I needed to go to the hospital emergency room. "No, no," I sobbed. "It's about a guy."

"Oh," the cabbie nodded, "that sucks."

"It's like I've been shot," I told my sister. "I've called into work sick for a week now. No matter how hard I try to push myself, I just can't."

"I wish I could encourage you." Emily sat across from me at Casa Mexico, nibbling on chips and guacamole while I aimlessly stirred my pina colada. "But all I can say is give it time. Pain really does lessen in time."

I shook my head. "I'll never be the same, Em. He says he can't live without me and I can't live without him either. Maybe I could believe he'd be happy with me if he didn't have kids. But I don't see him ever being okay if he left them. And we've really hurt his wife."

"People do get divorced, Claudia, and non-custodial parents do find a way to be in their children's lives." Emily paused. "But you don't see it that way, do you?"

The question was gently confrontational, reflecting not inquisitiveness but truth.

"No, I don't. He couldn't leave his kids. I'm not sure he could even leave his marriage. I ache for him, Em. And he's the one person in the world who could comfort me through this; that's so ironic."

"But understandable."

"He wants to see me. Do you think I should?"

Emily shook her head. "Claudia, I don't. Actually, I want to tell you a resounding no, but I don't really know the answer. Truly I don't. But sooner or later, you need to know what's happened between him and his wife."

"It was so horrible," I said. "I thought it could be a step in maybe functioning like an extended family: maybe I could get to know his wife and the kids later on, and it could be nice; maybe we could even spend some time together, you know, take it slow; nobody had to know the extent of Wills and me. It blew apart,

Em. I said the wrong thing. I should have known because of the way she fell. I knew that was a private deal. And why would he be telling me something so personal? I knew that was a private deal. I made a big mistake."

Emily wanted to sympathize, but I could tell it was hard for her to overlook my role in this mess. "Don't take his calls, Claudia," she advised me. "Give yourself time. You can't win."

When I got home that night, Wills had left me another message. "Claudia, for God's sake," Wills begged, "Please pick up the phone. I need to talk to you, Claudia. Please, I'm worried about you."

When I finally answered, he told me he was staying in a rented room in a Victorian bed and breakfast across from Boston City Hospital and that he and Natalie had met once, at a pizza place on Boylston Street. He said they talked about a trial separation, and if they decided to stay together, she would insist that he end his affair with me. Either way, even if they separated for good, she promised to never withhold the kids from him.

"I tried to explain, Claudia, I wanted her to know how much I love her and the kids, that I didn't mean for this to happen. But that I love you too."

I knew Natalie could never accept his affair with me. In her shoes, I would have done the same thing. *Take your time,* Wills said she told him, *because this can't happen ever again. You would defame me and I would despise you.*

There was no solution. Wills suffered away from his children. And probably away from Natalie too. I felt sympathy for all of us. I know it's hollow to say, but it was never my intention that he would have to choose.

He pleaded. "Please Claudia, please let me see you. I'm so sorry this happened. I'm so sorry, honey. We need to talk."

I finally agreed to meet him after work. I told him what Emily told me: "No holding hands; nothing like that."

"Yes, okay," Wills said. I suggested the arboretum in Brookline. There was a certain bench tucked behind a giant maple tree, so we'd have privacy. It was almost dusk when I arrived. As I approached, his back was to me. When he turned around, he put his hands in his coat pockets and waited. I walked toward him but I held back. I'd been embarrassed and humiliated by the unsavory scene with Natalie, and I was pretty sure he would return to his wife. I knew when that happened there was no way for me to fit into any of it. I wondered if he planned to lie to me. Natalie would never accept an open marriage. I was sure there was no solution. Our affair had to end.

Wills had dark rings under both eyes, almost raccoon-like. He stood about three yards from me and I pointed to the nearby bench. We sat facing each other. I was careful not to touch him. "How are you?" I asked.

"Been better."

"You look like hell."

"I know."

"Have you gone home?"

"No." He shook his head. "What have I done, Claudia?"

"You and thirty million married men," I said. "And the thirty million women who love them."

He forced a smile. "Claudia, I can't be apart from you. I can't stand it."

"But we're apart most of the time anyway, Wills."

"I will leave Natalie. I can't lose you." He twisted his hands into a ball and his fingers moved his college ring up and down.

"Wills..." I stopped, trying to find the right words. "We've had this hope that someday I could fit into your life, maybe even into your family, and because of how much we love each other, we've tried to make it be okay." I insisted he look at me. "That's not going to happen. Even if I were able to go back to the way it's been, you couldn't. We both know that."

He tried to breathe normally, but he kept swallowing. "Claudia, I can't lose you. I'll make it work. You have to trust me."

"What if you lose custody of your kids and Natalie moves back to Chicago? Are you prepared for that? Because it could happen."

His head snapped back, as if I struck him. "I can't think like that, honey. I just know I love you. I can't let you go." He spoke with great pain. He reached for my hand and I let his fingers lock into mine. He pulled me to him, wrapped both arms around me and pressed his head into my shoulder. Finally, I spoke. "What's happened with Natalie, Wills?"

His body tightened. "I don't want to talk about that."

"You have to," I said. "Or I can't continue."

"We're talking."

I nodded. "And?"

"Talking about therapy together, that maybe I'll see the kids and stay for dinner this Saturday."

"Did you promise to stop seeing me?"

"No, stop, Claudia." He pulled away and looked at me. "You have to trust me to sort this out. I can't discuss this with you. I owe Natalie that much. She asked me to promise that much. But I'm here to tell you that I love you and I will do what I have to for us to be together."

I wanted so much to believe him. I knew what my mother would say; what Emily had already advised me: *Don't, Don't.* But they didn't know him, and they didn't know me with him. They didn't know the good of it. Finally, I responded. "Okay Wills, okay for now. Take your time. It's not just about you and me. We can't go back to the way it was. I agree with Natalie that you take your time. Please."

Wills brought my hand to his lap and I felt him. His head fell onto my chest and we both cried.

77

Cole

I had a choice about who would pick me up at the end of my treatment program, and I chose Harry. He arrived twenty minutes early, dressed in his jeans, a red and black checkered flannel shirt, and a red tie. He was waiting for me in the reception area and extended his hand to greet me, making a firm nod of his head. We said very little for the first thirty minutes of the ride back to Montpelier. I think he was waiting for me to own up. Finally, I spoke. "Harry, I know what you've done for me. Thank you."

He took his eyes off the road and looked sideways at me. "Success?" he asked.

"Yes."

"That's all I need to hear. Are you ready to be back on-air?"

"Yes. Definitely."

"All set up with AA?"

"Yes."

"Then you start tomorrow night." He didn't look at me this time, but he nodded again. "Nice to have you back."

"I won't let you down, Harry."

"Jesus, I hope not. That would be a damn waste, wouldn't it?"

A fucking damn waste, I thought. *But not this time.*

78

Claudia

After the arboretum Wills and I met again twice, once at Durgin-Park for lunch, and once outside the Boston Museum of Fine Art. Both times were so painful that we agreed to a month without contact. But a week later he called me at ten o'clock on a Monday night. I had just settled into bed.

"Hello." I spoke haltingly.

"Hi honey. How are you?"

"Wills, is something wrong?"

"I can't do this, honey. I miss you. I was wondering how you'd feel about coming to the B & B tonight?"

"No," I replied. "I won't spend time there. You know that."

"Can I come to your place?"

"No."

"Then tomorrow after work? Or during the day? At your apartment?" He pleaded.

"Wills, why are you asking me this? Has anything changed? I need to know what's going on with you and Natalie. I can't go back to the way it was."

"Can we talk in person, Claudia? I promise I'll be straight with you."

The next day at my apartment, I was determined to talk and listen. Just that. But Wills looked so pained, I put my arms around him and within minutes, we were making love. We clung to each another. Afterwards, we pulled the covers over our heads as if we were back in Virgin Gorda. Then we talked.

"Natalie and I have come to an agreement," he said. "We will separate. I'll go home on weekends and we'll function as a family with the kids, but I'll stay at the B & B, and in time I'll probably rent a small apartment. We won't be intimate, Claudia. She understands I can't leave you. That's all I can say for now."

For the next three weeks, Wills stayed with me during the week and slept at the B & B on Saturday and Sunday nights, spending both days with Natalie and his family. Neither of us talked about the future. This made being together easier, but it also created a joint desperation, and for me, a no-win depression when we were apart. But at least we were able to function and work. We leaned on our new routine: Wills arrived at my place around six each night and I cooked a simple meal or he brought us a take-out dinner: meatball subs or a roasted chicken, wine. Every so often I went all out: my mother's roast beef and roasted potatoes, green beans, butternut squash, chocolate cake. The comfort of food was embedded in me, and I used it to the hilt.

On the fourth week of our new arrangement, on an otherwise nondescript Thursday night, I decided to surprise Wills with my special filet mignon, slathered with my caramelized onions and sautéed mushrooms. I added garlic mashed potatoes and my oven-roasted Brussels sprouts, making sure the plates looked perfect. We usually ate around six thirty. When he hadn't arrived by ten minutes to seven, I transferred everything to the warming oven. At seven fifteen, I shut off the oven and left the empty plates on the counter.

I didn't hear from him that night. Anger got me through hours of sleeplessness, but by the next afternoon, I panicked and left him three phone messages, with no response. I kept calling and emailing him over the next two days and nothing. Finally, I called his secretary directly and she told me he was out sick. My best guess was something had happened with Natalie, and cornered, Wills chose his family. I told myself that this was it: I wrote a letter as much to myself as to him, filled with declarations that I would not allow this to happen again, not ever. I left him one more phone message. Surely I deserved better than silence; I told him I'd had enough.

Three agonizing days later, he called me mid-afternoon at work.

"Claudia?" His voice was weak and tentative. Because my company had installed wall-less work pods in the last year, this was not a place I could talk. I swallowed and cleared my throat. I tried to call up my professional voice.

"Yes," I said.

"Claudia, I'm so, so sorry, honey. I've been sick. I've been in bed. This is the first chance I've had..."

"I'm not interested, thank you," I said. I was determined not to cry, not to sound weak.

"Honey, I know you're at work. I'll be there tonight. Is that okay, I'll come?"

Later I wondered what I would have said if I'd been alone at home.

"I don't think so."

"Please, Claudia. I can explain..."

"I'm not interested. Thank you."

"Claudia, please. Please."

"Okay then, that will be fine." My tone was tight and formal.

At three thirty I gave up trying to work and called Emily. "Can you meet me at Casa Mexico?"

"Now?"

"Yeah, it's important. For even a half hour?"

Emily knew this was not a casual invitation. She was at the bar waiting for me, patiently stirring her pina colada. She spotted me and waved.

"Let's move to our table." She eyed me, looking for clues. The subject matter was obvious. We sat in the darkest part of the restaurant, a corner table with dim light.

"What happened?" she asked.

"He stood me up for dinner and he didn't call me. I couldn't reach him. Not for three days. Not a word. That's the first time. It's never been that long in all our time together. I didn't know what to think, Em. I almost went crazy. I was too embarrassed to even tell you. He called me an hour ago and said he's been sick."

"Keep going."

I started to cry. "What am I doing, Em?"

"Don't ask me that question, Claudia. It's no longer that simple." Emily slid her hands across the table and reached for mine. "I know you love him," she said softly. "But there's no way." That made me cry harder.

"I believed him. I kept telling myself, *Who says you only love one person?* But he's not mine, Em. I know that. If he was sick, he should have been sick with me. For him not to have called me, he must have gone home. And for me not to even know."

"Is it time, Claudia?"

"Time?"

"To end it?"

I froze. I looked up at the yellow and red piñata hanging over the bar. My life was in that piñata: if I slammed hard enough, every precious accumulation and memory would spill out and be lost to me forever. I shook my head side to side, almost violently. I pushed out my words. "I can't."

Emily tightened her hold on my hands. "It's okay, Claudia. Tell me what he said."

"He's coming tonight."

"And?"

"I can't end it, Em. I try so hard. He's a decent man, a good man. You don't know him; how good his heart is. He would never hurt me on purpose. This can't be easy for him either."

It was Emily's turn to shake her head. "But you take his side every time. You have a side too. You try so hard. You're not the first person to have an affair. I don't say that to sound heartless, but sooner or later, all those missed holidays and all those big and little disappointments add up. I hate to see you like this, Claudia. If you were free of him, maybe in time you could be open..."

My right hand shot up just inches in front of Emily's face. "Stop, Emily, stop. I love this man. I could never be free of him. I know that."

"People do recover," Emily said.

"Not me."

"So that means what?"

"What would you do? Honestly. Could you see yourself without Brett?"

"Claudia, I'm not you, and it's not the same. I *have* Brett. I truly can't say. But since you're asking me, I hope I would break it off. Maybe not forever, but maybe go a full month, maybe two or three, without contact. Get some distance to figure things out. Maybe he needs to make some decisions. This is not devotion, Claudia. This is slow suicide."

"I have to see him, Em."

Emily sighed. "I know."

79

My phone was ringing when I got home and it was Cole telling me he was back at work. I swallowed and hoped my voice sounded better than I felt.

"Congratulations, Cole. That's great. Does Mom know?"

"I'm calling her next. Claudia, I want to thank you for coming to that meeting. It helped me." He paused before continuing, "What was going on with you? Are you okay? Emily told me you're in a dicey situation with your boyfriend."

"I'm still hopeful," I lied. "We're working on solutions." I tried to sound normal, but my voice cracked.

"Do you want to talk about it?" Cole asked.

"No," I said, "Not now. I can't."

He didn't pry. "I know you love the guy. I hope it works out. You know I'm here, Claudia. I could meet the two of you for dinner. I should have done that already."

I knew Emily had told Cole more than he was letting on. He was trying to soften the reality that no one in our family knew Wills. After all this time. And now, an offer comes, when I'm hanging by a thread.

"Thanks, Cole. I appreciate that. I just need some time."

"Sure," he said. "I'm here, Claudia." There was an awkward moment before he changed the subject. "Did you hear about Mom and Aunt Louise visiting me in Vermont?"

Normally I would have laughed at the thought of that. I welcomed the change of topic.

"Why? And when?" I asked.

"Yup," Cole chuckled. "Next weekend. Aunt Louise set it up. Her motive is suspicious, but I have no doubt the truth will reveal itself."

If anything could distract me from my own situation, it was the wild thought of my Aunt Louise and my brother together for a weekend. And my mother sandwiched in between.

I couldn't imagine.

80

Cole
2004

Barely a month after I'd returned to work, I woke up to three phone messages in rapid succession. The first was from Emily, asking me to call her later to talk about Claudia. The other two, in the span of five minutes, were from my Aunt Louise. When the phone rang yet again, I reached for the receiver and had no time to even say hello.

"Cole!" Aunt Louise shouted, "Wake up! It's your aunt. Your mother and I are coming to Vermont. For a weekend visit. I'm already packed."

Aunt Louise and Mom arrived at the Greyhound Bus Station in Burlington the following Friday afternoon and stood at the exit door, looking lost, in search of me. The first thing I saw was my mother's red and white polka dot dress blowing upward, followed by Aunt Louise's neurotic hands waving in all directions.

"Here, Cole! Here we are!" Aunt Louise's wild waves almost whacked the nose of a guy in a business suit and startled him to attention. Typically, she didn't notice. I chuckled as he took a dozen or so steps backwards, far from her swinging range.

I pulled my car to the curb and jumped out, willingly falling into the chaos of their flapping arms and wet kisses. Then I crunched four regular sized suitcases into my trunk.

"Four suitcases for two overnights?" I politely asked.

"Oh, don't be silly," Aunt Louise replied. "One is a care package for you; even the Asian Grill's homemade egg rolls are stuffed in there. On ice. And three loaves of your mother's pumpkin bread."

Mom added, "And the other one is our family poems and photo albums. In case we get bored..."

I chuckled. "Oh, I don't think we'll get bored."

My pal Andy was at my apartment when we arrived. He was wearing my zebra-striped, knee length apron, trimmed with pink fabric and tied with a pink bow in the back. He had already sliced green peppers, stuffed my mushroom caps, and was tending to the cream of broccoli soup I'd partially made. With opera music not so quietly playing in the background, my mother greeted Andy's over-the-top accessible grin with equal enthusiasm. She walked right up to him and kissed him on the lips. He flung his right arm around her waist and pushed her backwards, Fred Astaire and Ginger Rogers-style.

"I am Cole's friend Andy," he announced with fanfare. "And you must be the world- famous Mrs. Macabee." He swung his free arm upward and bellowed:

"O Captain! my Captain! Our fearful trip is done,
The ship has weather'd every rack,
the prize we sought is won."

Andy bowed. "Or should I sing..."

"All of her nights have gone sad and shady
She's getting ready to fly."

John Denver. My mother made a sound that sounded a lot like a young bird.

"Oh God, Mrs. Macabee, Did I hurt you? I'm so sorry."

"No, no, don't be silly," she sputtered. "That's how I sound when I'm flabbergasted." She flung her hand in front of him and waved it back and forth, like a windshield wiper wiping away frost. "Oh my, Andy, you just about gave me a hot flash!"

Andy, You suck-up phony, I thought to myself.

During this exchange, my Aunt Louise ran her finger along my end tables, lifted her hand to her mouth, pursed her lips, and blew. Little particles of dust flew upward. No mention was made, but I was sure my apartment was going to be spotless by the end of the weekend.

Aunt Louise approached Andy very differently. She extended her hand to him and bowed slightly. "Not everyone is so emotional in our family," she said. "Some of us greet strange men without locking lips or gushing forth. I am Cole's Aunt Louise. Has he told you about me?"

Andy looked at me for guidance.

"Of course I have, Aunt Louise," I said. "I tell people that there's no problem in the universe my aunt can't solve."

Aunt Louise nodded. "That's right!" And then for good measure, "But I'm also a devout Catholic, and you may or may not know that I myself was trained as a Sister of Mercy in my coming-of-age years."

"Andy," I interjected, "she's warning us that she may not approve of non-traditional lifestyles."

Aunt Louise ignored me. "I follow the Lord, Andy, and I am convinced we wouldn't have half the problems in the world if more people did the same."

My mother shot a disapproving look at her.

"Oh, don't worry, Christine, I wouldn't be here if I didn't think Cole must know something I don't. I'm here to see for myself, that's all."

Time for a pivot. "As you can see," I said, "Andy is fixing us dinner."

Andy had brought his grandmother's china with him and had set quite a classy Victorian dinner table, complete with starched white linen napkins and three short and spaced-out vases of miniature pink roses. We ate supper like royalty: my broccoli soup, stuffed mushrooms, chateaubriand with Mornay sauce, roasted root vegetables, grilled tomatoes, and Andy's famous key lime pie for dessert. He offered my mother and Aunt Louise hot apple cider and Fudgsicle smoothies, and we finished up with cappuccinos, all so seamlessly that no one seemed to notice the absence of wine or liquor.

"I made plans for breakfast," I announced during dessert. "There's a buffet breakfast at the Club Café. By some stroke of luck, Eartha Kitt is performing. You both like her, right?"

"That sounds lovely," my mother said.

Aunt Louise beamed, "I love Eartha Kitt."

"One thing," I said, "There will be a lot of gay men and women there because it's a gay club. Not everyone will be gay, but I wouldn't want either of you or anyone there to be uncomfortable."

"What is the dress code?" Aunt Louise asked.

"Casual," I said.

"Will body parts be covered?"

"Probably." I rolled my eyes.

"Okay," said Aunt Louise.

"Fine," said my mother.

"I wouldn't miss it for anything," smirked Andy.

I had to beg for reservations. Normally brunch is first come first served, but I couldn't have my mother and aunt sardined in the

bar area among a standing room only crowd. Jamie the maître d'
seated us almost immediately in the main dining room, winking
at me as he pulled a chair out for my aunt.

"Seems like a well-mannered young man," Aunt Louise said.
"Is he...?"

"Yes," I answered. "He is."

A waitress who looked like the actress Sissy Spacek took
our orders and within seconds she was back with a pot of coffee.
When she turned to attend to another table, my aunt asked again.
"Is she...?"

It was almost comical. "Yes," I said. "I believe she is."

"Shhh, not so loud," Aunt Louise whispered. "There is no
need to make a federal case of an innocent question."

And so it went. Aunt Louise pointed out four more people
and three times I nodded yes. With Andy and I adding extras
from the buffet table, we had a lovely breakfast. Jamie brought
us hot buttermilk biscuits on the house and everyone but me had
Bloody Marys. Two friends from the gym stopped by to say hello.
As they walked away, I looked at my aunt and just nodded. She
raised her chin slightly upward.

Overlooking the Old Mill River and modeled after its sister in
Boston, Club Café could have been any upscale restaurant in
any city. With fourteen-foot-high ceilings and sand-colored plas-
ter walls, the converted 1910 bank building had made itself a
fine adjustment. When we finished breakfast, we walked down
a hallway to a room with dark purple velvet drapes and twenty-five or so three-foot-wide circular tables, each with the padded equivalent of card-playing metal folding chairs. This is where
Eartha Kitt would perform. We were escorted to our seats by
a transgender male-to-female waitress named Tiffany. She stood
out with short spiked black hair, three-inch-wide hooped earrings,

a silky black see-through blouse with a black bra underneath, and very tight black slacks that extended just above her fake four-inch Italian heels.

"Louise, don't ask. Wow," my mother said.

"That's Tiffany," Andy said. "She's very sweet. She's been beaten up I don't know how many times for the way she looks."

"What does she do to be beaten up?" Aunt Louise asked.

"Nothing, absolutely nothing," I answered. "Except maybe refuse to tone it down because when he was Thomas, he spent too many years already pretending to be normal."

Aunt Louise's mouth dropped. "He? She's a he?"

"No, she's a she now," I answered. "She would be a total she if she had the money for sex change surgery, but that's another story."

Aunt Louise frowned. "Let's have another Bloody Mary, Christine."

My mother nodded. "Yes, Louise, that's a fine idea."

81

Eartha Kitt was smaller and more vulnerable than her photo shoots would lead anyone to believe. She entered the equally tiny stage wearing a royal blue sequined gown and was finishing her first song, "Snuff Out the Light," just as Tiffany delivered our drinks. Aunt Louise was ready with a twenty-dollar bill and her surprise was obvious when Tiffany politely said, "Thirty-five dollars will do it."

"I have this," I said, pushing Aunt Louise's money away. "I'm so glad you've both come to visit me."

"Tiffany," Aunt Louise whispered, "May I call you Tiffany?"

"Of course." This reply was couched with genuine surprise that a strange elderly lady was in the house at all, not to mention calling Tiffany by her name.

"Thank you very much for your excellent service, Tiffany. I believe we have the same color nail polish." And with that, Aunt Louise held out her fingers as if showing off a new diamond ring and slipped the twenty-dollar bill onto Tiffany's tray.

"Thank you very much, ma'am," she said.

"The pleasure is mine, Tiffany. Thank you."

This exchange took place while Eartha belted out "Mambo De Paree." When she finished, she bowed to enthusiastic applause and leaned into the microphone in front of her. "I happen to have a great appreciation for the gay audiences," she began, highlighting her smoky voice. "When I was in trouble with the government, and Lady Bird Johnson blacklisted me at the White House for voicing my opposition to the Vietnam War, it was the gay guys who kept my name alive, because they kept looking for my records and they were imitating me. I'm very grateful for that. I feel very close to the gay crowd because we know what it feels like to be rejected."

This was too much for my aunt. "Oh, dear God," she whispered, "Eartha Kitt is gay too?"

"No, I don't think so," I whispered back. "She just knows what she's taking about."

For the next fifty minutes, with a tape recorder providing the orchestra section, Eartha sang her heart out: "Mack the Knife," "Moon River," "My Funny Valentine," and "Little White Lies." When she purred the lyrics to "Santa Baby," the crowd went wild. Dollar bills flew onto the stage and without missing a beat, Eartha leaned down, scooped up the bills, and stuffed them into her cleavage. When the song ended, she held the microphone an inch from her mouth and purred:

"I am so glad to be at the Club Café. I know what it's like to be orphaned, you know, to have no family or to have your family reject you. Don't let anyone put you down because of who you are and who you love. It's all about falling in love with *yourself* and sharing that love with someone who appreciates you, rather than looking for love to compensate for a self-love deficit."

Aunt Louise clapped. After a second round of drinks, she and my mother were clearly feeling good. When Tiffany brought the check, I had my credit card ready. I watched Aunt Louise search through her pocketbook while Eartha was singing "Moon River," but I insisted on paying, especially because I cringed thinking about her leaving a puny tip. I was not prepared for what happened next.

"Tiffany," Aunt Louise said, "where are you from? Where is your family?"

"I'm from Maine, ma'am, and I don't really have a family. Not like you do, anyway."

"Do you have a religion?" Aunt Louise asked.

"Oh yes ma'am. Presbyterian. I believe in God."

Aunt Louise reached for Tiffany's hand. "I want you to have these," she said. I knew from the string of sparkles what she was handing over.

"These are my rosary beads, Tiffany. They were blessed by Pope John Paul II himself. I think they will bring you the blessings of the Lord. I can see your goodness, Tiffany. These rosary beads will protect you from stupid people."

Tiffany stared at the beads in her hand and I could see her trying to process what was being said. "Do I know you?" she asked.

The answer came complete with a full set of balls, "You do now! I'm Aunt Louise!"

What happens when good intention is infused from one person to another? It's not language that does that. I could only guess those rosary beads were a symbol of something bigger, and not easily understood, except Tiffany and my aunt both seemed to recognize the power of it.

"Ah, okay, Aunt Louise. Thank you very much. Once I had an Aunt Helen but I think Aunt Louise is better."

Tiffany leaned down and planted a kiss on her new aunt's heavily powdered cheek.

"We need adoption papers, Aunt Louise."

Not to be outdone, my aunt had figured that out already.

"Write down your address, Tiffany; I'll send you a Christmas card."

82

Claudia

I tried to distract myself by thinking about the weirdness of Mom and Aunt Louise visiting Cole, but I couldn't shake my growing panic about seeing Wills. When he arrived, even though he had a key, he waited until I buzzed him in, and when I opened the door, he didn't reach for me. Instead, he stood in place with his shoulders slumped.

"Claudia, I'm so sorry."

I stepped aside to let him pass me. "This one killed me, Wills. I can't take much more."

"I was too sick to call, honey. I called as soon as I could."

"Were you at the B & B?"

He hesitated. "No, I went back home. I got sick at work and they called Natalie. I was hospitalized for a couple of days and then I stayed in bed until I could function. I called you as soon as I could."

"Hospitalized? And you didn't tell me? And you never thought to come here?"

"Honey, it's complicated. It's complicated."

"What, Wills? Why?"

"I was flat on my back, honey. I didn't have time to think things through."

"What was wrong? Are you okay?"

"Yes, yes," he said. "Now I am. I was exhausted and dehydrated. They had to monitor my vitals and give me fluids. But I'm okay now."

"Your vitals? Wills? What does that mean?"

"My heart raced. But it was just a scare, honey. But I'm okay. Honest."

I felt relief and sadness at the same time. "Do you ever think it should be me taking care of you? Or what if I get sick and need you? Does any of this really work for you, Wills? Because it's killing me."

"I'm here now, Claudia. I understand what you're saying. I know this can't happen again. I promise. I can move in now if you want. Or we can get a place together."

I'd waited years to hear these words. But I couldn't accept them. "What, and wonder what that means between you and your wife? I left work early today after your call; I'm a basket case. I love you, Wills, I will always love you. But what the hell are we doing?"

"Claudia, I'm sorry. I was sick."

For the only time in all these years, I wondered if he was lying.

"Please forgive me, I couldn't, Claudia." There was panic in his voice. I reached for my own resilience and there was none. There was no way I could banish him. Absolutely no way.

"Okay Wills. Let's calm down."

His relief was apparent. I put my arms around him. "Can you stay tonight?"

"Yes," he said.

"Take off your coat," I said. "Let's just take it easy. Let's relax. Then I'll fix us dinner."

We had a fitful night, locked in each other's arms. We made love, but Wills lacked his normal strength. He held me with a desperate neediness. The next morning, we were up at sunrise, showered together, and for a time we sat on the couch, just holding each other. When he dropped me off at the Harvard Square Red Line, he kissed me openly. We both knew it was decision time.

"Honey," he said, "I'm asking you again to trust me. Maybe that's too much to ask. But I believe we'll get through this. I love you, Claudia. Think about what I said last night, about living together, because I'm ready."

"I'll see you tonight, Wills."

"Yes, Claudia. You bet, honey. I'll see you tonight."

I stopped abruptly at the stairway leading to the subway line. I needed to go back home. Wills was promising me fidelity, availability, commitment. I wasn't sure he could deliver. And if he couldn't, I was afraid I would once and for all sink too deep to be able to rescue myself.

I called in sick to work. He had proposed that we live together. I knew he was afraid of losing me, but I had to be sure that offer didn't come from fear. It was all so complicated. I couldn't bear it if we took this step and things turned out worse than they already were. I saw my mother's face. I never viewed my affair with Wills beyond the two of us, but envisioning my mother's reaction if anything happened to me jarred me into unimaginable guilt and sorrow. I undressed and went back to bed. I slept until eleven, then turned on the morning game shows, something that reminded me of my father, the way he stretched out on the couch watching television. I called Emily at work and left a message, "Nothing urgent; I'm home, call whenever." When she called me back, I told her I was okay, that I had some thinking to do and I'd call her after dinner. She asked about Wills and I put her off, answering vaguely that we were talking. At two o-clock, I showered, finally got dressed, and went back to bed again, burying my head in Wills' pillow. That's where I was at 4:30 when my doorbell rang. I had a mind not to answer it, but I pushed myself up and pushed the intercom button.

"Yes, who is this?"

It's Natalie Brimfield. I need to see you."

83

I felt immediate terror. I buzzed Natalie in, but I barely opened my door. Why was she here? What had Wills told her? I braced myself, hoping I could react quickly if things got out of hand. When we finally faced one another, neither of us spoke. Natalie's eyes were red and swollen. I winced at the thought of what might have happened between them.

"Please let me in," Natalie said. "I'm here because Will asked me to come."

This made no sense. Wills would never do that. I nodded and stepped aside so she could enter my apartment. She took a deep breath, a heave really. There was a weariness to it.

"Please," she said again. "I need to talk to you."

She followed me through my small hallway into the living room. I didn't want to do this at all, not after the kitchen fiasco, not ever. I didn't want to hear one word that she had to say, but I forced myself to point to the couch, and I motioned for her to sit down. Then I sat across from her.

Natalie sat on the edge of the cushion and folded her hands in her lap. She took another deep breath and released it so slowly I could see her chest contract. Neither of us made eye contact. Finally, she looked at me and cleared her throat.

"Claudia, I'm here because Will collapsed this morning at work." She took several rapid breaths. "He wanted you to know." She gripped her hands together and her face tightened. She took another deep breath. "His heart gave out."

"Oh my God." I felt my heart begin to race and I brought my hands to my face. "Is he okay?" I turned my head away before Natalie could answer. Why did I ask? When I looked back at her, I already knew the answer.

"No," Natalie said.

"No?"

"No, he's not okay." Natalie struggled. She was trying to arrange her words. Her shoulders dropped. "Will died. Late this morning."

In that instant, she and I were alone and together, in the same room, in the same moment. We stared at each other in mutual stunned horror.

"Oh my God, no. Please, no, please." I covered my face with both hands and shook my head from side to side as if I were having a seizure. Natalie sat motionless. She waited until I caught my breath, and in a forced and measured voice, she spoke again.

"Will was taken by ambulance to Mass. General but it was too late. He never regained consciousness. He wasn't alone. I got there in time. I believe he knew I was there. The nurses even said so. And his brother talked to him on the phone too. I was with him." Natalie repeated, "He wasn't alone."

Forced to witness my short plaintive moans, Natalie began to cry too. I tried to muffle a sound that came from so deep in my chest; a moan bracketed by little squeaks—squeaks like a puppy would make. I folded my body in half, clasped my hands around my knees, and sobbed. I shook like I was sitting on an earthquake. Natalie watched me with what looked to me like sympathy. She steadied herself and used both fists to push herself to a standing position.

"Look, I can't help you, but I do understand that you matter; that you mattered to Will. He wanted you to know." And then, as if she were talking to herself, "And I don't know what to do about that."

I stood too. My eyes scanned the photos of Wills and me on my fireplace mantle and on the shelves of my bookcases, and I panicked. I especially didn't want Natalie to see the picture of us at Loon Mountain last winter, with our skis and scarfs and down parkas, our arms around one another, grinning, both of us tucked into the misshaped hats I had knitted for us the winter before. If she noticed, she didn't let on. She sat down again and leaned forward, also wrapping her arms around both knees.

"There will be a wake and a funeral," she said. "If you come, you cannot reveal the nature of your relationship with Will." She must have rehearsed this: she spoke in a different tone of voice; her permission wrapped in both acknowledgement and warning.

"Oh no, Natalie. I don't think Wills…" I struggled to speak. I wondered what it took for her to face me in this way. I didn't deserve the consideration she was giving me.

She quickly interrupted me. "Listen," she said. "I knew you—someone—existed long before that day in my kitchen." She spoke softly. "Until he met you, Will was never unfaithful, I'm sure you know that. I'm not sure I will ever understand. I didn't know your affair had continued, and I didn't know who you were until he brought you to our house. He changed so much and so fast after he met you. I had him, and we had each other and our family, and then we didn't. He became someone else because of you." Her face tightened and her eyes closed. It had pained her to say this.

"Natalie, I'm so sorry. I'm so very sorry."

I thought I might lose my mind. I pushed out my breaths, trying to hear her. Natalie's voice changed again. This time she was matter-of-fact. "Claudia, Will and I had decided we would stay together, at least until Petunia finished high school. We had that arrangement and we kept our focus on our family. But after you came to our house, we had to try all over again to figure out what to do. You may not know this, but we love, we loved one another." Natalie stumbled over the proper tense. It was the line between life and death—present tense, past tense. "We have always loved each other."

I nodded. "I know that," I said. "I've always known that. He loves you dearly. I know that. But he didn't tell me..."

"That I was aware of the affair?" Natalie shook her head. "No, I thank God for that. That was part of our agreement. That was between us. It was the least he could do for me. You know, can you understand that?"

I nodded again. I tried to control myself, to speak rationally, but I was stunned and frozen. I straightened my posture, hoping it might improve my ability to speak. I sat down again and forced out my words. "I'm so sorry, Natalie. I know it was wrong. I didn't set out to fall in love with him. He is such a good man; you know he's not the kind of man to cheat on his wife."

The irony of this statement snapped Natalie's head back. She blinked several times and stood up again, this time abruptly. "Don't go there, Claudia. He did cheat. I've tried to understand but I never really could. He told me the two of you had some connection he couldn't explain. I didn't understand. I don't. I don't want to. You were Will's mistress and that is despicable. He obviously got something from you that kept him coming back. I don't want to know." She looked hard at me. "If I had pushed him, he would have left us. The kids would have suffered. And I couldn't bear that. I don't think he could have either. I couldn't let that happen. So, I compromised."

We faced each other directly. "I was never sure that his affair had ended," Natalie said, "but we never talked about it again until you came to the house. What balls the two of you had to do that to me. I'm not here to reassure or forgive you. I'm here because he asked me to understand that you would be affected. He asked me to come here if it came to that."

"Affected? Came to that? What does that mean, Natalie? You say that as if he knew."

Natalie looked surprised. "That first heart attack scared the hell out of us. It left him vulnerable."

"What first heart attack?" My voice cracked. How could I not know about a first heart attack? "What? When?" I asked. And suddenly I knew the answer: that was why Wills had disappeared for three days. He told me he was sick. But a heart attack? *Oh my God.*

"Claudia," Natalie responded, "I can't get into this with you. I can't. Maybe someday. I have to get back to the kids. I have to plan." She shook her head. Her tears were gone. She finished what she came to say. "I can't have you coming to Will's wake and funeral and causing a scene. No one knows about you. It would kill the kids."

"Natalie, I don't expect..."

She put her hand up to stop me. "Wait, let me finish." Her voice shook and her body swayed, but she continued, "If there's a way for you to come, I'm not closed to that. But you can't make a scene, Claudia. No one would understand." She looked at her watch. "I have to go. The kids are with my sister. They're waiting for me. They need me. Do you have our home phone number?"

Such an admission would have been implausible twenty minutes ago.

"Yes," I whispered, "Yes I do."

"Think about what I'm asking you, if you can do it. The wake is Tuesday and the funeral will be Wednesday, at the O'Hara Funeral Parlor in Arlington. The obituary will be in the *Boston Globe* tomorrow."

Natalie stood, buttoned her coat and walked toward the door. I pushed myself to follow her. I wanted to touch her shoulder, to comfort her, to say something more, but I couldn't. I knew all along that Wills would never have married anyone unworthy, and Natalie had just confirmed that in spades. My Wills was a good man. He cheated, I cheated, but we meant no harm. Asking us to give up on one another was like asking an ocean liner to stay in the harbor, or a high-speed train to crawl through a mountain pass. We weren't made that way. We couldn't help ourselves. If Wills hadn't been married already, we would have been together for a lifetime. I thought about all this as Natalie made her way to the hall and reached to open the door. She turned the doorknob halfway and turned around.

"I'm sorry."

"Thank you," I struggled to breathe. "Thank you, Natalie. I'll pray for you and the kids."

"I hope you have support."

"I have a close family," I said. "I hope you and the kids have support too."

She nodded.

I watched her descend the stairs. I closed my door and pushed myself to my bedroom. I thought I heard Natalie's car door close. I imagined her driving away. I stood motionless for probably fifteen minutes, until I fell onto the bed, wrapping my head with my hands, like a tourniquet. I pushed my knees up to my stomach and buckled my body in two. I cried until all I had left was the scent of Wills' pillow.

84

Wills was dead? But I was fixing dinner for us tonight, wasn't I, in less than two hours? I tore at the spread and brought his pillow to my face. Thank God, his scent was still fresh—his Aveda hair gel and his Old Spice, and the sweat of his body, the sweat of our lovemaking.

Oh Wills. Oh Wills. Oh Wills. I reached for the picture of us in Virgin Gorda and I brought it to my heart. I tried to stand, but the room spun. I fell back on the bed and pushed his pillow into my stomach; it buffered my fall onto the floor. I must have stayed in a fetal position for several hours because it was after nine o'clock when I finally tried to move again. I didn't turn the light on, and I didn't answer the phone when my mother called. I just blinked and stared.

Oh Wills, my beloved boy. Oh Wills. Oh Wills.

85

I wore the black dress I'd bought for the Bankers' Convention. It was one of Wills' favorites—he said the scooped neckline gave a tease of my breasts. At the last minute I gave up on pinning my hair up and instead let it fall to my shoulders. He loved my hair: how often he ran his fingers through it and breathed in my scent.

These years of loving him: maybe that love carried less weight than his twelve-year marriage to Natalie, than his devotion to his wife and his children, but he was my north star for one thousand, two hundred, and sixty-nine days. *That mattered.*

My life was over. *I have a close family,* I told Natalie. But they couldn't help me with this. Grief would shadow me. Thank God Emily came to the wake with me. I wished my mother could have come. *"I'm sorry he's not welcome at the dinner table,"* she had explained, the few times I inquired. *"Not as long as he's married. Separated, maybe."*

I hated that my mother would never know him.

After years of disguises, who the hell should I be today? Natalie made it clear I could mourn in public—how could I not mourn? But I can't stand out; decorum would be important. I settled on the identity of an old friend from college, someone who had lived in his building. I'll say I met him freshman year, and even though

I transferred my junior year, I'll say he was always special to me. I'll say I just moved back to Boston, if anyone asks. I know there are risks, no matter what I say. People are connected by threads that bind them to others; but affairs don't allow that. Wills and I were a universe of two; our wishes and plans were unlimited as long as we didn't step into real life. Yes, I'll be an old college friend. And if I need to, if I can't control my grief, I'll come across as an unstable person; as if I'm an unstable person in general, not just because it's Wills' wake.

When Emily and I walked into the funeral parlor, an older man with gray hair, a trim body, and a black suit approached and extended his hand.

"The family thanks you for coming," he said. He placed his hand on the small of my back and guided us to the sign-in book. Six pages of signatures and condolences already. *This is Wills' normal life.* Emily held on to my elbow while I turned the pages. On the top of page four, there was a small heart, colored in with a pink crayon. Beside the heart, meticulously scrawled in big girl letters, *Daddy*. Emily wrapped her arm around my waist.

Coming was a bad idea. I can't do this. Emily kept her arm firmly around me.

"You can do this. You can do this," she said, as if she read my mind. I swallowed and looked at the book again. *Don't mess this up, I can't sign my real name, can I?*

"Em, what do I write here?" I whispered.

"Write your name," she whispered back. "And I'll write mine. It's not the person you're covering up, just the circumstance."

A small black sign with *Brimfield* in white plastic letters pointed to a large room already packed with people standing and sitting, from front to back. I saw Wills up front, lying in a white satin-lined mahogany casket. I knew this side view of him so well from watching him sleep. *But that can't be Wills. That can't be him.*

As we approached the casket, Emily whispered, "Let's make this one quick. You can come back again before we leave. But this time, let's be quick."

Wills was surrounded by dozens of flower arrangements. Only the top half of him was visible, his hands folded at his waist. A huge bouquet of red roses had been placed just below his hands, draped with a purple satin banner that read "BELOVED HUS-BAND AND FATHER."

I don't belong here. This is not my Wills. This is a family man with a wife and children. It was all I could do not to touch him. He had an odd expression, like he was politely bored and couldn't keep his eyes open. His face was shiny and polished and his lips were too red. *Oh my God Wills.* I stared at his light gray silk shirt and his favorite dark paisley tie. His wedding ring was prominent. He looked oddly peaceful, but this was not the Wills I knew. Except it was. *I love you, honey, wait for me, Wills. Am I moving my lips? Am I in shock?* I felt Emily's hand on my back and we both stood up. I gently touched his shoulder. I hoped Natalie didn't see.

She was standing with her three children in a receiving line, with an endless string of people waiting to offer their condo-lences. Dressed in a black knee-length dress, black stockings and heels, and a white pearl necklace, Natalie's arms wrapped around little Petunia, who stood in front of her. I knew she'd seen me. *We both know we have to reach for grace when I approach her, but what about the kids? What do I say?*

Emily and I took our place in line. After all these years hear-ing so many stories and seeing so many family photos, I looked at Wills' children for the first time. Four-year-old Petunia wore a light green taffeta dress and black patent leather shoes and folded down white socks. Her eight-year-old brother Ryan, probably in his first suit, stood to the left of his mother, shaking hands and tolerating hugs from family and strangers. And ten-year-old Zoie stood slightly off to the side, tossing her head back, laughing at something one of her friends said. She laughed just like her father.

Wills would be so proud of them. I felt like I knew these kids already: maybe he and I were weird like that, but he didn't hide his family from me and I didn't want him to. There was never a reason to withhold his greatest joys.

"Do we need the bathroom first?" Emily asked.

"No, no." I shook my head. There were several dozen people in line ahead of us and I waited nervously. Even from a distance, Natalie looked exhausted, but she hugged or reached for the hands of each person who greeted her. When she came to Emily and me, standing not more than a foot apart from each other, she made no such gesture. Instead, she straightened her posture and took a slight step back. "Thank you for coming," she said politely.

"This is my sister, Emily," I sputtered.

"I'm so sorry," Emily said.

When I looked at the kids, Natalie noticed immediately.

"These are friends of Daddy's," she told them. Petunia offered her hand to me and wrapped her fingers around my thumb. When I started crying, Emily stepped in decisively.

"Honey, we're so sorry about your daddy," she said, especially to Ryan, the image of Wills. Emily touched his shoulder. "Your dad and mom must be very proud of you," she said. "My sister knew your daddy a long time ago."

I caught my breath. "He was my friend," I said.

"Thank you for coming," Ryan said.

Almost simultaneously Emily and I took a step back and once more I looked at Natalie. "I am so very, very sorry for your loss."

"Thank you," Natalie said. Her eyes pleaded, *Please leave now.*

How deeply she loves him. It's so obvious. Does she know he offered to move in with me? Could that possibly have been only two days ago?

86

The next morning, Emily and I slipped into the back row of the Saint Augustus church, just before Wills' brother, his best friend, and his eight-year-old son solemnly wheeled his casket to the front of the church. I prayed so hard that he could feel me, and I told him how kind Natalie had been to me.

The church was filled to capacity. When the organist began playing "Amazing Grace," I cried with no caution, because everyone around me was crying too. I recognized Wills' brother from photos, and from a distance I could see his mother and stepfather sitting with Natalie and the kids in the first row of pews. When the pallbearers reached Natalie, she reached out and rested her hand on Wills' casket.

It was so unreal.

The priest raised a holy wafer above his head. "Heavenly Father, we are here today to celebrate the life of William Alexander Brimfield, beloved husband to his wife Natalie; loving father to his children Zoie, Ryan, and Petunia; doting son to his parents Phillip and Janelle; faithful brother to Charles; and loyal friend and colleague to many. We welcome William's family and friends as we pray for his holy arrival into the arms of God our Savior."

There was a scorching reality with the omission of my name and it burned into me. *I don't belong here. There is no place for me*. I motioned to Emily, who at first looked confused, and we quietly stood and exited the church. Once outside, I fell into her arms, and I cried so hard I thought I might never stop. I knew I wouldn't be able to go to the cemetery, but Emily and I waited in her car until the funeral procession left the church. I saw Natalie and the kids get into the first limousine, and I cried and prayed for each of them.

87

Christine

I racked my brain about how to help Claudia. I was afraid she was close to a nervous breakdown. I'd never seen her so upset, as if strength had been drained right out of her. Thank God Emily went with her to the wake. The fact that I didn't know this man and I never approved of him made things harder. When Jimmy died, I was able to publicly mourn, I got support, I had other people around who shared my memories. But Claudia had none of that: she was the 'other woman,' the product of an illicit love affair, in a relationship her family had never acknowledged. Had I done her a disservice by not meeting this man?

I wasn't sure what my Claudia needed from me, and I questioned if I had let her down: all my talk about devotion and loyalty—what part did that play in her decisions about men and about this man?

First Cole, now Claudia. I tried to be a perfect mother. But I had to face the fact I might have had it all wrong. And, if that was true, I didn't know what to do next.

88

Claudia

In the weeks that followed, I lost twenty-four pounds, and I arranged a two-month leave of absence from work. I thought maybe I'd check into the Kripalu Retreat Center for a week of prayer and solitude, but no matter what I did or how hard I tried to be okay, all I thought about was Wills, and what would never be. Most days, I forced myself to take a morning shower, but I stayed in my pajamas. My family doctor referred me to a psychiatrist who prescribed Prozac for my depression, and I signed up with a therapist who kindly let me sob in her office every week for eight weeks. My mother called me every day, and when I didn't answer the phone, she left encouraging messages. Both she and Emily regularly came by with food and tried to push me into small talk. They told me about Cole's nomination for Best New England Sportscaster and they prodded me to return Mom's calls more often, stopping short of guilting me, but making it clear that my family was grieving too.

My feelings were all over the place. When I thought about Natalie, I often felt the guilt of resentment. She was legitimately comforted in a way that would never be accessible to me. I never imagined any loss could be so painful. I spent most days rereading

Wills' letters and cards, staring at his gifts and photos, clinging to his pillow. I listened to his phone messages over and over, and I played the Swiss music box he surprised me with for my thirty-fifth birthday, over and over. I turned to him for comfort, always with despair. And there was also the fact that Natalie had treated me with a kindness I didn't deserve. What was I supposed to do about that?

I couldn't talk to my mother about this: my relationship with my family was surely compromised. I was obsessed that Mom had never even met Wills, and she could never grasp the sanctity of our relationship. However difficult it had been for me to keep my joy private when Wills was alive, keeping my grief private was excruciating. Cole called me about once a week and tried to help, but he was in Vermont and besides, what could he do? He kept saying grief gets smaller in time. I didn't believe him.

My mother waited me out. She called and visited but she didn't confront me. Initially her messages were light, *Claudia, please don't tell me I have to rely on Aunt Louise to make the turkey stuffing and the pies...Claudia, honey, can you help me balance the checkbook?... Sweetie, how about I get us tickets for the Boston Pops this year?* She persisted: invitations to supper, movies, cooking lessons.

Always, I declined. "Mom, I'm sorry, I can't."

Finally, after two months, she left me an authoritarian phone message. "Claudia, you must call me back. It's about me and it's very important."

It took all I had but I dialed her number. I was afraid she was sick. If not, I was prepared to tell her I just couldn't help.

"Oh, Claudia honey," she began, "I opened my mail this morning and there's a letter from the IRS. They say I owe twelve thousand dollars. I'm shaking in my boots. I need help. Can you come today? I'm hyperventilating."

"Mom, I'm sorry. I can't."

"Claudia, please, I need you."

"Ask Aunt Louise, Mom."

"I can't, honey. Because it must have to do with your father. After all these years. Please honey. Will you come this one time? Or for lunch tomorrow? Just this one time?"

The next morning, disheveled and disengaged, I arrived at my mother's house. I'd showered and my clothes were clean, but my shoulder length hair that I took so much pride in was uncut and snarled. I kissed my mother, expecting her to push the letter toward me. Instead, she said, "I made coffee. And your favorite biscuits."

I followed her to the dining room table and sat there as I had a zillion times, but this time I was hollow. "Where's the letter, Mom?"

She put the biscuits in front of me and sat down. She sighed. "There is no letter, Claudia. I lied to you because I'm so worried about you and I can't stand to see you like this. I know grief has its own timetable but honey, you can't shut me out like this. And you have to live." I think she expected me to push her away but instead my head free-fell onto the table and I began to cry.

"I'm sick, Mom. I'm so sick."

"Sick? What do you mean, sick?"

All I could do was shake my head and cry.

"Tell me, Claudia. Talk to me." My mother wrapped both her arms around me and cradled my head. I made a primitive sound, a wail really. I had this image of an ancient steamship engine trying and failing to start up again, after years of neglect.

"What is it, Claudia? How sick are you?"

"I can't live without him."

"Let's move to the couch," Mom said. "I want you to tell me about him." She propped several pillows around us and, in my mother's arms, all the details spilled out, my agony encased in memories unique to only Wills and me. For the next two hours I told her how Wills and I met, I described my disguises, I talked about his children, about our trips, about our love and about the pain; about his heart, and how Natalie came to my apartment that day. My mother listened and she nodded at the hardest parts. When I said I wished I was dead too, she tightened her grip around me, rocked me in her arms and waited.

"There's nothing I can do, Mom."

"What do you want to do, honey?"

"I want to die."

She was ready. "Claudia, when your father died, I tried to make it look easy, but it wasn't. I cursed him for a few months because of his drinking, but I do know a little about what it's like to lose someone you love, because there was a time when I loved him. Plus, he was your father. That fact alone meant his memory should be honored. I made a promise to myself that I would be the best mother on the planet and I've tried to keep that promise. There's nothing you kids could do, even if you murdered someone, that would ever change anything for me, because besides for how much I love you, it was a way for me to honor your father. I know you understand devotion; but I learned the hard way that it helps to have a way to honor it."

"I don't have that option, Mom. I'm a persona non grata."

"Does it still need to be that way?" Without looking at me, I knew she was trying to make a point. I countered before she could even speak.

"How could it be otherwise? I'm the other woman. I have no role, no place. Nothing."

Oddly, my mother laughed. "Claudia, honey, there is no other woman when the other man is deceased. No offense to your Mr. Wills. Surely you can think of some way to honor him in your life. Devotion doesn't die when the person does."

I pulled my tears back. I was clearly in pain, but I asked her to explain. "What are you saying, Mom?"

She thought for a moment. She closed her fist and tucked it under her chin. "I might phone up his wife. In time. Through her kindness she opened a door for you, maybe. Ask how the kids are doing. Gently ask her out for coffee. And if that goes anywhere, I might try on being Aunt Claudia. So-to-speak."

"You've got to be kidding."

"I'm not."

My mother...

I waited two weeks before I called Natalie. I left a message and she called me back.

89

I was seated in a corner booth facing the door at the Marigold Cafe in Somerville when Natalie arrived. I waved and stood up as she walked toward me.

"Thank you for coming," I said.

"It's odd," she responded.

"Yes, I know. My mother suggested that I call you. She did that for my benefit, but she hinted it might help you in some way too."

"I can't imagine..." Natalie said.

We looked at the menu and we each ordered coffee, a side of fruit, and an English muffin.

"How are the kids?" I asked.

"It's tough," she replied, "but we're doing okay."

I knew what must be said. "I never meant to hurt you, Natalie."

"You broke up my family. I lost my husband. How could you ever justify that?"

"I can't. I don't. I loved him too; that's all I can say to justify what happened. I knew it was wrong on every level. I want you to know he never hid how much he loved you. We just couldn't seem to end it. I know that's no excuse."

Natalie straightened her body; she looked determined. "Once when I was in high school two boys pursued me, and I liked them both. I chose one for my senior prom and the other boy came to my house and begged me to reconsider. He cried his heart out. I'll never forget how it felt to hurt someone like that, only because someone else mattered even a small bit more. I remember that feeling when I try to understand what happened with Will, how it must have felt for him, but I always end up wondering why the hell it wasn't me who came first."

"But you did come first, Natalie. He couldn't leave you for me and not just because of the kids. He loved you. Surely you know that. I think it came down that he couldn't live without either of us. It was an impossible situation."

"And then he died," Natalie said. There was a bitter finality in her words.

"Yes."

"So now what, Claudia? What did your mother have in mind?"

I cleared my throat. "Do you think we could ever be friends? Or I could help you with the kids? In time, maybe?"

"Are you fricking kidding me?"

"No."

Natalie took a deep breath and fell back onto the padded booth. "Oh my God! You and me?! I don't think so. How exactly would that even look?"

I had braced for this reaction. "I don't know. Maybe in time I could get to know you and the kids, you know, someday; or maybe help you sometimes. Maybe we could find a peace from how much we both cared..."

Natalie looked confused. "I can't imagine. Mostly I hate you. I have to think if I want to give that up."

When Natalie called me two months later, I was ready.

"Coffee again?" she asked.

"Sure. Yes. Great," I said.

We met again at the Marigold Cafe and this time we shook hands. She told me that Wills' gravestone had been installed, and I took that to mean I had her permission to visit the gravesite, something I hadn't dared do.

"I've been thinking, and processing," Natalie began, "I have a counselor I discussed this with. It does me no good to stay bitter. It hurts me to know that you're a decent person; I wanted you to be horrible. But I also know that Will wouldn't have sacrificed what he did for someone horrible. It must have been awful for him. It's hard for me to look at it that way, but it's a step forward for me."

I hoped my face communicated how I felt hearing her because I wasn't sure I had the right words to respond. "Natalie, I really don't know what to say. My mother refused to meet him because the whole thing was so wrong. That part was so awful, having everything be secret and wrong. I envied that he rightfully belonged with you; I envied you for that. All I can say is I am so sorry. I am so sorry what I did to hurt you and your family."

Natalie stiffened. "I accept your apology," she said. There was a sincerity in her tone that made me cry.

"Please don't cry," she said. "We've had enough tears. Let's have lunch and I'll tell you about Petunia's birthday party. She's turning the big five. This might be a first step. I'm inviting you if you want to come."

Later, when I told Emily, she couldn't stop laughing. "You're going his daughter's birthday party? This should be on *Oprah*!"

"It was Mom's idea."

"The party?"

"No, not the party. Reaching out to Natalie."

"Mom told you to do that?"

"She did. And I listened to her for a change."

I stayed at Petunia's party for an hour. There were thirteen girls from school and the atmosphere was controlled chaos. I assumed the role of grown-up assistant: I wore a Mickey Mouse hat, twirled a noisemaker, and cut and distributed the cake. The Birthday Girl barely noticed me and Natalie was too busy to chat or connect, but the very fact that I was at Wills' house, with his wife and children, feeling his energy: somehow, in that hour, my heart started to open again. It was the first time since Wills' death that I felt anything even close to peace. When I told my therapist, she said it was a transformative step in healing. I couldn't look to Natalie or Wills' children for absolution, but maybe through them, Wills could have a place in my life after all.

90

Christine
2005

Claudia was back and we were cooking together again. I still worried about my kids, of course, but with Claudia finally okay, and Emily with her gem of a husband, that left Cole. He called me about once a week, and I was pretty sure his life was safely back together, but I needed to be sure. I waited a few months until I asked him to make a trip home. I made some corny joke of it, but he knew I was serious. He walked in the door the first weekend after my call.

We had lunch and caught up on niceties. Then, never one to beat around the bush, Cole looked at me and shrugged. "So, what's up, Mom?"

It was just the two of us sitting in the living room, facing one another on the same couch he grew up with. His legs were tucked under him and the grandmother clock as usual ticked extra loud from the dining room.

"I made your favorite roast beef for supper."

Cole shook his head. "Mom, I know I'm here for more than roast beef. Are you okay? Is something wrong?"

"How are you doing, honey?"

"I'm good—fine, actually. The job's good, it's great living in Vermont, and in case you're wondering, I still go to AA every day. I'm also as relieved as you must be that Claudia's back to herself."

My next words just spilled out. "I didn't know you wanted me to leave your father."

Cole looked puzzled. "Is that why you asked me to come?"

"Partially. I've been thinking about it ever since your family meeting. It eats at me."

"Mom, I'm fine. We're fine."

He waited for me to say something. "Son, I told you why I stayed with your father but I didn't realize until that meeting how much I missed the mark by believing I could protect you. I've done a lot of thinking, and I've faced something important, Cole. It may not seem like much to you, but it's important, and I have to tell you."

He still looked puzzled. "What, Mom?"

"I hope I can say this the right way. We've been through a lot in this family. We've overcome my bad childhood, your father's drinking, his accident, your assault and trial, and your own drinking, and Claudia's breakdown. We've survived everything thrown at us. I'm not always as strong as I look, you probably know that already, but I decided a long time ago that I would have enough strength for my family."

"Definitely," Cole nodded.

He waited for me to get to the point. I knew what I wanted to say. "Probably based on my own childhood—I wouldn't have made it this far without Aunt Louise; then seeing how your father drank, and then his dying like he did, I knew we could end up with serious problems. The day after your father's funeral; do you remember? Emily was crying at the table, but you just stared ahead, like you were a statue. It scared me to see you shut down like that, but I also saw strength in you that day. I knew so much about alcohol and what it can do to a family, and I was determined to protect you kids. That's why I was so strict about everyone being home for supper. I kept us close, as a family, kept us learning from the great poets and I made sure we had ways to share our feelings."

"Mom, you did a great job. Really. Are you questioning that, is what you're saying?"

I took in a deep breath. "I'm saying that if you drink again your alcoholism could blow our family apart, and we may not be able to survive the damage."

I said this so bluntly and forcefully that Cole looked like I punched him. "I'm saying that our family cannot overcome losing you because that's not how we're built. Our foundation depends on one another, Cole, and any break in that foundation and we're all goners."

"Whoa, Mom, that's a lot of pressure. That's a lot to lay on me."

"I know it is. But you have to stay sober and live a sober life or it won't just be you going down the tubes. It's the same with Claudia: she can't check out either. I've told her too. We cannot afford any empty seats at this table, Cole; our family wasn't built that way. I understand this is a burden for you, but caring for the welfare of the rest of us is essential. We're all connected and you have to know that."

"But it can't be all about what I do or don't do."

"*But it is.*" My tone bordered on shrill. I took a breath in to calm down. "Of course we all tumble and stumble. Of course we have messy lives. But we need to count on one another to get us back on our feet. I'm so glad you're sober, son, and I believe you're serious about it. But I have to be sure you understand how high the stakes are. Every one of us can only be as healthy and happy as you are. That's just how it is."

"Mom, I don't plan to drink again. But I could slip. That could happen."

"And if you slip, we'll be here to help you get up again. A slip is not fatal. You know that, Cole. That's my point. We're all on your side. Aunt Louise too. It's important that you understand the strength of that. Long after I'm gone, you'll still have that strength and support, and if we play our cards right, so will the people who come after us. Look at how the new folks have fit into our family. We've expanded without losing any oxygen for ourselves. It's because we're a family."

I stared at my son really hard. "Tell me you understand. That's what I need from you."

Cole folded his hands in front of him and pushed his thumbs together. He let out a deep breath of his own. "I understand. I hear you, Mom."

I leaned over and hugged him. He cleared his throat. "I don't think I'll drink again. It's a day at a time in AA, but I know the stakes. But Mom, there's something I have to tell you. It's about Daddy."

I took a deep breath. *Was it worse even than I knew?*

"Tell me."

"The day he died; remember I stopped home that day? I was home before you because I needed my glove for practice. The phone rang and it was Daddy. I knew right away he was drunk. He mumbled something about being late for supper. I just rushed him off the phone so I wouldn't be late."

Jimmy called home? "What time was that, Cole?"

"It must have been a little before four o'clock. Because I was almost late for practice." Cole shook his head. "Mom, I could have prevented that accident, if I took the time to even care. I just let him go off drunk and he was dead an hour later."

This was a lot to take in. I was surprised and shocked. But I knew what this meant.

"You blame yourself?"

"I could have done something."

"No, no, Cole. Oh my God, no. Even if I myself had answered that phone call it wouldn't have made a difference. Once your father started drinking there was no helping him." I stopped for a moment. He had carried this guilt for a long time. "Why didn't you tell me, son?"

"I couldn't. When I left, I didn't think much of it, and I forgot to leave you a note about him being late for supper, and then after the accident..."

I stopped him. "Cole, your father chose to drink and he chose to die. You know enough about alcoholism to understand that, as an adult, don't you?"

Cole's face relaxed. "I swore I'd never tell you."

I stared back at him with nothing but love. "I'm glad you did. I'm glad you did. Honey, you have to let this go."

"I'm working on it."

"He threw his life away, Cole. You can see that. And the people who loved him ended up blaming themselves for it. That's the worst part."

Cole nodded. "I know. I understand that."

"So, no more drinking? I can count on you?"

"Yes," Cole answered. "I'm pretty sure you can count on me. You sound like Anthony. He can be your second set of eyes."

"Okay Mister TV Star, I'm making us roast beef and mashed potatoes. Let's you and I have a mom and son candlelight supper. And after we eat, I have a new poem to show you. It's by a woman from the Cape named Mary Oliver. It's about geese flying high in the sky and heading home again, to take their place in their family. The poem is called "Wild Geese" and pretty much about us."

PART 7

The Later Years

91

Christine

Five days after Cole went back to Vermont, Louise found me spread out like a dead bug on my kitchen floor.

I was at the stove stirring love into my spaghetti sauce. I don't remember falling, but lying there on the floor, I knew I couldn't feel my right arm or leg. I was startled by Louise's blood-curdling screams. When the ambulance arrived, two EMTs carefully slid me off the floor onto a stretcher. They secured my neck and asked me to smile and move my arms and legs, which I could do on my left side but not my right. They asked me what month it was, and who the president was, and according to Louise all I could say was "Kennedy." I was in some zoned-out state and I couldn't focus. They let Louise come with me in the ambulance. She was white as chalk.

"Loooise, I okay?"

She looked down at me, stroked my forehead with one hand and held my good hand with her other. "Be quiet, Christine," she ordered. "Don't move and don't talk."

"I cannant move," I said. "Why why?"

"You fell, Christine. We're on our way to the hospital and you'll be fine. But be still."

"Nooooo, Loooise. I die?"

"Shush!" Louise snapped. I'd made her mad. But then she leaned over and put her face right next to my ear. "I'm here, Pip. Don't worry. You know I take care of things. You're not going to die."

"K, won't die," I mumbled.

I closed my eyes. I didn't want to upset Louise any further. From a deep place in my mind, I heard a familiar voice. *Chrissy, it's me, Sabrina. I'm here, Chrissy. Don't be afraid. It's okay, Chrissy. No one can hurt us.*

"K Sabrina."

"Sabrina?" Louise raised her voice. "No Christine. No! It's me, Louise."

"K," I mumbled.

The tiny ambulance space began to spin and I passed out.

92

A huge white cylinder tank just about took up the whole room. They told me I had to lie perfectly still and they slid me head first into that cylinder. It was so tight inside, there was no way to even scratch my nose. At first, I thought I might be on a train to heaven. My vision was blurry and I didn't know what was happening, but I kept hearing one loud clang after another and a strange voice every few minutes telling me, "This time four minutes…this time two minutes…you're doing great, Christine."

When I was finally pulled out of that claustrophobic tube, a twenty-something-year-old kid in a white medical coat stood over me.

"What happen to you?" I asked him.

"Me?" He looked confused. "Oh, you mean to you. You're at the Waltham Hospital. You had a CAT scan and we just did an MRI of your head."

"Am I dead?"

The young man darted his eyes away from me. "No, no ma'am. Dr. Cares is going to look at your scans and then he'll tell you what you need. Don't worry; he's a good doctor."

"Don't worry? You kidding me?"

For the quickest moment, I imagined my family standing over me. "It's okay, kids," I mumbled. "I here even from heaven."

93

Cole

When I arrived at the hospital, Aunt Louise was frantically praying, Emily was quietly crying, and Claudia was actively taking charge. None of us were prepared for how sheet-white Mom looked and how confused she sounded. Strapped onto a gurney, she reached for my hand and rubbed her fingers along my palm. She motioned for me to lean down so my face was barely an inch from hers.

"Son," she whispered, "trouble. Tell Claudia. Pay my pears." She tried to blow me a kiss, but only half her face moved.

"Mom, don't worry. You're going to be all right, Mom."

"Maybe"…"Stay with Auntie"…"Here…"

"Sure Mom, we're all here."

The scene was unreal. We were cramped in a ten-by-twelve-foot cubby, with all these machines and tubes and urgent beeps and sounds and nurses and techs swooping in and out like ants. I would never forget how subdued Mom was: her eyes kept closing and she looked so helpless. I'd never seen her like that.

When a neurosurgeon came to talk to us, he directed his comments mostly toward Mom.

"Mrs. Macabee, I'm Dr. Cares. You've had a stroke. We've given you medication through a vein in your arm to dissolve the blood clot that caused the stroke. We're also going to do a procedure to remove the clot directly."

Claudia jumped right in. "What exactly?"

"We place a catheter through an artery in your mother's groin and up to the carotid artery in her neck. It sounds worse than it is." He looked at my mother's face and knew she hadn't understood a word he said. "Mrs. Macabee," he said, "your job is to relax and let us take care of you. We'll be taking you to the operating room shortly and you should be in recovery in an hour or two."

"Docor, my vault, my arm..."

"She means her voice," Louise said.

"I understand," he said. "The stroke has caused a loss of function on your right side and that's affected your speech too. It will take time before we know how well your movement and strength comes back. We'll know more in the next seventy-two hours. The good news is you may recover completely and quickly, and in that case, we'll send you home in a week or so with medication and monitoring. If you still have problems, you'll go to rehab from here. Right now, we're concentrating on taking care of the clot."

Aunt Louise had heard enough. "That damn spaghetti sauce," she said to no one in particular. "I thought it was blood splattered all over the kitchen floor. I almost passed out on top of her." She looked hard at Dr. Cares. "Will she be herself, Doctor? Because she's not herself now. She thinks I'm her mother, which is a horrible insult."

He smiled. "It's too early. We'll know more later."

This agitated Aunt Louise even more. She stood up and lunged at him, grabbing the lapels of his medical coat, and she held on like a pit bull. "You cannot let her die, Doctor."

My already tall aunt could look seven feet tall when

circumstances required it, and this was one of those times. She stretched her neck straight up and jutted her chin out, no more than an inch from the doctor's face. Startled, he shifted his balance to defend himself. Finally, Aunt Louise loosened her grip. "Whatever it takes, Doctor," and for good measure, "Please."

Once said, Aunt Louise shrunk back to her normal five-foot-eight perfect posture, which was formidable enough. She let go of the poor man and whimpered, "Please, she's my only sister. And she has children."

Dr. Cares took a protective step back and nodded. "Mrs. Macabee's in good hands, ma'am. Stay calm, and if you're so inclined, some people think prayer helps."

That was right up Aunt Louise's alley. He was barely out of sight before she pulled out rosary beads from her cheap pocketbook.

"Kids, I have extras. We have to pray. This is not the time or place to give God a hard time."

94

"We're heading to the operating room now, Mrs. Macabee."

The nurse looked at all of us and added, "It shouldn't take more than an hour and then she'll go to the ICU recovery. There's a waiting room there and Dr. Cares will come out and talk to you."

The last thing Mom did before they wheeled her away was put her good hand to her lips and try to throw a kiss. "Still me," she said. She lifted her arm slightly in an effort to wave, "Me and poets in heavy."

"Not heavy. She means heaven," Aunt Louise piped in.

The waiting room was the size of a cramped shoe box, with Pepto Bismol-pink walls, framed photos of cheetahs and lions, and one poster demonstrating the proper way to wash hands.

"If I swore, which I don't," Aunt Louise complained, "I'd have plenty to say about this unpleasant room. It makes my nerves even worse."

Claudia asked the nursing station for updates every half hour and she returned with announcements: "She's still in surgery." "She's been moved to recovery."

Forty minutes later, when Dr. Cares appeared at the doorway, he looked relaxed.

"It went well," he said. "We'll monitor her for the next hour and then you can see her. She'll stay in intensive care overnight so try to keep your visits to ten minutes an hour, no more than two of you at a time, but she's made it through the first hurdle."

"What's the second hurdle?" Aunt Louise asked.

"Keeping her still, keeping an eye on vital signs, monitoring her speech and her right-side weakness."

"To see if she comes back to normal? Will she?" Claudia asked him.

"You're correct and we're not sure," Doctor Cares replied. "Her brain has to settle down. She's also at risk for another stroke. And we need to be sure we don't need to consider more surgery. Assuming we don't, she'll stay in the hospital about a week. She needs time. Be patient. She's not out of the woods yet. But so far, so good."

Louise tucked her rosary beads into her purse. "Thank you, Doctor," she purred.

"Ma'am," Dr. Cares grinned, making it obvious he was leaning against a wall, "I'm glad you've calmed down."

95

Christine

There are no hoppy hospitals; relief, maybe, but not ~~hoppy~~ happy. I woke up with a bandage on my ~~grin~~ groin and a pounding head-ache. The room was gray; why do they paint rooms gray? The lights were so bright I had to ~~squat~~ squint and my eyes hurt. I couldn't think straight; I barely knew what happened to me, but there were beeping ~~scents~~ sounds and the ~~scents~~ sounds of some-body pulling those swishing metal ~~curlings~~ curtains. My fingers rubbed on clean sheets, but they were starched and I didn't like that. Hospital sheets. *Oh, that's where I am.* I wiggled my toes. And then a ~~vice~~ voice.

"How are you, Christine?" *This girl is so young.* "I'm Katie, I'm your nurse in recovery. I saw those toes wiggle." She smiled at me. "Very good."

She touched my shoulder. "Stay still and rest for a little while," she said. "How does your head feel?" Her hair was pulled back and netted in a ponytail and she was so petite she looked too young to know anything. But I could see she was ~~kink~~ kind, and when you're in trouble, ~~kink~~ kind counts.

"My sister," I whispered.

"Of course," she said. "Let's let you rest and wake up a little and we'll call her in."

"No, now," I said. "Please you."

Louise was walking extra close to the young nurse, clutching that damn fake ~~licker~~ leather pocketbook. She kept her eyes straight ahead and had no expression. I knew this was not a good sign.

"Here she is, Christine," Katie said, a little too bubbly. She looked at Louise. "It's fine for you to stay here until Mrs. Macabee is moved from recovery. Can I get you some ginger ale?" And then, "We want her to rest quietly for the next hour or so." As if anticipating, she added, "A headache is normal after this procedure."

Katie turned to me. "Keep sipping water, Christine. If you get uncomfortable, I can give you something for it." She took my temperature, checked my blood pressure, and fidgeted with the IV bag.

I nodded. "You're welcome, nurse."

Louise tucked her pocketbook into her stomach and she sat down in the armless vinyl chair beside my bed.

"Come," I told her. The chair screeched when she moved it closer and we both winced. "Come," I said again. I was still whispering but my voice felt stronger. Louise leaned over me and I smelled her damn Shalimar. "You're supposed to rest," she said.

"Sister, listen."

Louise's face had the color flushed right out of it. But her eyes scared me the most. She didn't want to look at me, but I stared at her until she did.

"You have to say. I stay alive?"

"Of course, Christine. Of course you will."

"Sure?"

"Christine..."

I pushed it all out. This could be my only chance. "I have to know...can't leave without. I need."

Louise cleared her throat and stiffened her body. "Listen to me. I'm scared because you're my sister and I love you, but the doctor says everything went fine. You're not dying!"

"Then?"

"A stroke." Louise forced her face to relax. "But it's fixable. I was scared shitless," she added. Then, as if she couldn't wait another minute to tell me: "That damn spaghetti sauce all over you. I thought it was blood, Christine."

I smiled. It was a funny thought. "What chance for me?"

Agitated, Louise wasn't whispering anymore. "Good. All good. Stop it, Christine. You're not dying."

"Oooh ...good...good." With that relief came exhaustion. "I'm very washed," I said. I let my head fall into the pillow. "*Live, live, live,*" I thought. "*Okay kids, okay, okay, okay.*"

96

Still in his sea-blue surgical scrubs, Dr. Cares leaned against the recovery room wall. No way did this man look anything like a doctor. He was ~~sticky~~ stocky and muscular, more like a sumo wrestler.

"The fact that you can move your arms and legs is excellent," he said. "You have some right-sided weakness, so you'll probably need physical and occupational therapy, but there's no evidence that your cognition has been affected. It sounds like you have some word-finding problems and you might have some challenges with your memory, but hopefully that should clear up over time. Your recovery will probably be slow, more months than weeks, but overall, I'm optimistic. I think you'll do well. For now, we're monitoring for complications, but you look good."

"She just told me she saw chickens on the roof," Claudia said.

"Nah," Dr. Cares said. He leaned forward and crossed his heart. "The brain has to settle down. Yes, there are some changes, and we'll have to wait to see, but believe me, this could have been a lot worse."

In fourth grade I couldn't rouse my mother. It took me fifteen minutes of shaking her ~~holes~~ hands and lifting her arms and shouting *'Mommy!'* over and under before she finally opened her eyes. In those fifteen minutes my nine-year-old ~~mike~~ mind wondered where she was if she was dead. Was she still in the living room? And who would be there with her? Would God? I asked Louise that day what she knew about dying and she was totally confident in her answer.

"You go to heaven and live with the Holy Father."

"What holy father?" I asked. "Our holy father?"

"No! Of course not our father. God the Father."

I never really met the God the Holy Father until a doctor who looked like a sumo wrestler said I was going to be okay.

97

Six days later I was transferred to the Spaulding Rehab Hospital in Boston for physical, occupational, and speech therapies every day for four weeks. By the time I headed home I could pretty much walk without a ~~ruler~~ walker or ~~candle~~ cane, but I still didn't talk like my normal self. I kept saying the wrong words and sometimes I slurred. This bothered the kids more than it bothered me. As far as I was concerned, I sounded good enough. My right arm and leg were weak but my strength was coming back.

For another month a physical and a speech therapist came to the ~~hill~~ house twice a week. By July I was cooking again, and by September I still used the wrong words here and there, but I was definitely better. The kids made a game of teasing me.

"Excuse me, Cole, would you pass the um, you know, that white stuff?"

"The cocaine, Mom?"

"No, Cole, the white shaker. Like the pepper shaker."

"Oh, the salt!" Cole exclaimed. "Certainly, Mom."

"Does anyone have an onion for dessert this Sunday?"

"An onion? Do you mean opinion?"

"Yes, of course that's what I mean. What else would I mean? Who in their right mind serves onions for dessert?"

Irreverence kept things light and that's the way I wanted it. But certain parts of my memory were blurry, and some events had become weirdly different: for one thing, I no longer remembered the worst of Jimmy. This drove Louise crazy.

"Um…you forgot about his drinking?"

"Oh yeah," I replied, "I guess so."

"He was bad bad bad," she'd remind me. "Like our parents. But then, if you want to forget all that, Pip, if you prefer to remember a made-up part of Jimmy, be my guest."

"He got me the nest," I said. "And he brought me red ~~razors~~ roses on my birthday. Those are important."

"Not the nest, Christine. The house. *House*," Louise repeated for emphasis. "And not razors. *Roses*. Yes, you did buy a house, and yes, he did bring you roses. What a magnificent atonement for years of alcoholic hell."

I shrugged.

"Christine, I cannot believe you can't remember the hell of it. This must be God's way of repentance. Let him be Saint Jimmy if you want. There's nothing to lose, except the kids and I might throttle you if you carry it too far."

98

On my first day back at Standard-Thomson, the girls arranged a special ~~lap~~ lunch for me, and even the guys from sales and service showed up. I was walking pretty well on my own and most of the time I sounded like the old me. My right hand and arm still moved a little weird, but not enough that I didn't get back to my ~~jab~~ job with the bellows.

In other ways, the stroke had changed my appearance and my movement. The right side of my face drooped a little, and every so often I dropped a bellow, especially near the end of my shift. But I refused to complain about any of it: I was damn lucky I survived.

Three weeks later, Mr. Irving summoned me to his messy office. He fidgeted in his ancient green leather chair with the rusty wheels.

"You've been our number one employee all these years, Christine. But this isn't working."

He leaned back and tried to make eye contact with me, but I kept my focus on the stacks of green file folders piled every-where. He guarded the plant's mechanical drawings like they were the Pentagon Papers. Once Alma Lucas asked him what the heck all those green files contained, and he looked at her like she was crazy.

"Records!" he barked. "How do you think we keep track of your timesheets and vacation days and all our customer invoices?!"

Nobody, not even the managers, wanted to be summoned to Mr. Irving's office because there was a ninety-nine percent chance he'd start by staring you down, and then tell you that something was wrong. Usually, the problem involved ~~soups~~ sales or customers or higher management complaining about something the assembly floor had a part in.

"We have a very grave problem," he usually began, blowing smoke from his unfiltered Camels almost straight at your face. To my knowledge the only person who ever returned from Mr. Irving's office unperturbed was Deloris Costa, who couldn't wait to tell us what happened because her appearance was also the day Mr. Irving's mother died. He was lecturing Deloris about wearing a provocative see-through blouse, and he had just gotten to the part about being ladylike when he took the call that his mother had choked while eating Chinese food at a Chinese buffet. Deloris said he put the phone receiver down and he cried real tears right in front of her. She and I both knew enough about life that a man who cried about his mother had a ~~heave~~ heart in there, even if it was buried on the outside. Most of us warmed up and tolerated Mr. Irving's gruffness a little more after that.

"You're taking too long with the bellows," Mr. Irving told me. I knew I wasn't as fast: I used to do two hundred and forty of the three-inch coils in an hour and now I was only doing...*oh, what the heck is that new number? I could see it: a 1 and a 7 and a 5.*

"What's my hourly count, Mr. Irving?"

"One seventy-five. Slow," he said.

"Yeah, that's slower," I laughed. "But I'm still ~~fatter~~, I mean faster than most of the college kids that come in the summer."

"No, you're not," he said matter-of-factly.

I didn't argue. "That's okay, Mr. Irving. I don't mind."

He twisted his mouth sidewards because he wasn't sure what to do next. He rubbed his nearly bald round ~~heap~~ head with both hands and nervously pulled at the short ~~hips~~ hairs coming out of both his ears. He cleared his throat.

"Everybody loves you, Christine. We hate to lose you, but I have to let you go. You know it's only about the numbers; it's nothing personal. And I'll give you some advice, in general: it might help if you slow down."

"Slow down?" I laughed. "Mr. Irving, you're ~~flinging~~, er, firing me for slowing down." I laughed again.

"I'm not firing you. We're laying you off. You can get unemployment and early retirement. And we're throwing you a retirement party. On Friday, the eighteenth, over lunch. Bring your family. The company is footing the bill."

No more bandaging my fingers because of the hot steam. I was fifty-eight years old and the kids were grown and maybe taking my time would suit me; at my age why should I rush? Maybe the hospital social worker was right that a near death experience changes the way a person decides to live. But a retirement party with a free ~~lunge~~ lunch that included my family? This was unheard of. My first thought was how in the world did Mr. Irving pull that one off?

"Thank you, Mr. Irving," I told him. "I'll be fine. But if you don't mind, I'd like the toasted raviolis from the Chateau at my party." I said this with perfect pronunciation.

Mr. Irving shook his head. "I'll see what I can do," he answered. "I can't promise."

99

My party was held in the company dining room complete with a ~~buckle~~ buffet catered by the Chateau. Alma made sure all my favorites were included—the toasted raviolis, chicken parmesan, spaghetti and meatballs in tomato sauce, Caesar salad, and ice cream with a choice of hot fudge or strawberry sauce. Everyone ~~chirped~~ chipped in to give me a two-hundred-dollar gift certificate to be used anywhere at the Watertown Mall. I could just see Louise and me wheeling and dealing with that double hundred.

While the buffet was being set up, Alma stood in front of a lunch table, clapped her hands over her head and shouted in a very authoritarian voice, "Quiet please!" The hum of voices stopped.

She pointed to me. "We're here to say goodbye to Christine, our friend, our co-worker, one of the few sane women on the assembly line. Standard-Thomson won't be the same without you, Christine. Over the years we've raised our kids together, shared so many raunchy jokes, trapped at least a hundred mice in the locker room, and oh, how we treasure your Christmas cookies. When you lost your husband, we were afraid you'd change but no, you came back and you were still your gutsy self. You have cojones, Christine—pardon me, Mr. Irving and other gentlemen for mentioning testicles in French." Alma paused. "Even Mr. Irving is going to miss you, right Mr. Irving?"

Mr. Irving pulled at his ear hairs and nodded. Alma looked down at her index cards and with the flair of a Shakespearean actor, she began her finale:

"To our dear Christine
Who's never mean
Always a friend
This is not the end.
We love you too much
So keep in touch!"

With that Alma pulled out a handkerchief and wiped her eyes. "We all love you, honey."

Everyone stood up and clapped and ~~humped~~ hooted and blew into those noisemakers you pull out for New Year's Eve. All three of my kids and my sister ~~humped~~ hooted too. The whole thing caught me off guard. It was the same feeling I had when Mrs. Erickson hung up my poem in sixth grade. *I was somebody at that plant.*

Next, Mr. Irving stood up. He held on to the back of his chair and ran his fingers once through his hair. He'd made a special effort to fix his wiry nearly bald head with a wet ~~cat~~ comb and the result was that every line of every one of his hairs was individually visible, plopped there on his head like the coated ~~winds~~ wires we soldered on the circuit boards. He cleared his throat.

"Mrs. Christine Macabee, I speak on behalf of all the employees and management of Standard-Thomson. We will expect to see you at the Christmas party. On behalf of management, we thank you for your service. For almost four decades, you've been an exemplary employee almost the whole time."

The room chuckled. Alma shot me a look questioning whether she should laugh, and I grinned back at her. Mr. Irving ended by waving the gift envelope above his head and he motioned for me to come get it.

I straddled toward him, slightly limping and ~~laughing~~ lean-ing on my left side. I looked at my ninety-six co-workers, many of them still clapping like I was Dolly Parton's cousin. I held tight to the four index cards Claudia helped me write out to make sure I said the right words at the right time. I made a ~~clunky~~ clumsy curtsy.

"Thank you everyone. I will miss all of you. I will miss our ~~coffin~~, er, coffee and lunch breaks. I hope my record of blowing bellows in a ~~shot~~, I mean shift, is never broken and if it is please don't tell me. I like thinking I could end up in the *Guinness Book of Records*."

I curtsied again, this time with better balance. "My stroke screwed up my hand a little and with a ~~nut~~—oops, I mean a nudge from Mr. Irving, it's time for me to take a break. It's a good thing I have a family at home because leaving here feels like I'm leaving my family too. I plan to enjoy myself—I might learn to ~~pant~~, I mean paint and who knows, I might paint Alma chasing the mice away with Jimmy Molini's broom. I might write poems about our ~~lines~~, I mean laughs on the line. I'll spend more ~~tunes~~ time in my kitchen. And all of you know you're invited to our Macabee Christmas party. So, who has a better life than me? All my ~~kinks~~, er I mean my kids are here today. Look at them. Even Cole my famous television star. It's time to say goodbye, but I won't let you forget me. The first week in December, I'll bring you all my Christmas cracks."

"Not cracks, cookies!" a voice shouted from a back table.

"Thank you, Louise. I mean cookies," I said. "Cookies! And myself. I'll bring cookies and I'll bring myself. Thank you."

And then Cole was beside me, his arm locked into mine, escorting me back to my lovely plate of toasted raviolis and chicken parm.

100

2006

My contentment was short lived because I had too much time on my hands. I was taking painting classes at the local community center, and I was cooking up a ~~sweat~~, no, no, a storm, but the kids were gone and Louise was still working. I was bored like I had never been, so when Cole suggested a new and improved poetry slam, I jumped at it.

Claudia designed the invitation and I ~~mauled~~ mailed or hand-delivered seventy-five invites, three weeks in advance, to neighbors, co-workers, friends, and friends of friends. I planned the event for four to seven p.m. on a Saturday afternoon. Claudia and I made all kinds of ~~funger~~ finger foods: deviled eggs, vegetables and dip, stuffed mushrooms, chips and salsa, cheese and crackers, little meatballs, and my special ~~feat~~ foot-high display of strawberries, melons, and orange slices. Louise baked two loaves of bread that, of course, turned out way too doughy, but nobody complained.

Forty-seven people showed up, not counting my family. Even Natalie Brimfield came with all three kids. Cole and his official boyfriend Anthony wore tuxedos, and Louise brought ninety-one-year-old Sister Mary Agnes. My rehabilitation therapists surprised me when they walked through the ~~dark~~ door and, of course, so did all the girls from Standard-Thomson. A little before five o'clock, once the initial food ~~trick~~ train had begun, I stood at the front of my dining room table and pulled out my index ~~eads~~ cards. I was determined not to make any wrong-word mistakes.

"Welcome my family and friends! If you don't know already, poetry is the ~~salt~~, oops, I mean the spice of life. It makes us laugh and cry, reach for the stars, and bury our hammers."

"Hatchets," Louise shouted.

"Yes, hatchets. And not just that. Poetry is a self-help manual. I broke my kids up that way."

"*Brought* my kids up," Louise piped in.

I was already nervous, and making so many mistakes and Louise's corrections didn't help. "Be quiet, Louise, You're making me unconscious."

"Self-conscious," Louise said; this time her tone was a little softer.

"Okay, everyone," I said, "I have to admit I'd be up a ~~crook~~ creek without my sister. She's saved my rump more than once."

"Rear," Louise said.

"What?"

"Rear, not rump."

"Everyone," I announced, "As usual, my sister is trying to help, but you already understand me, right?"

I got applause for that.

"So, shush Louise," I said, "I'm giving this speech whether I trip it or not."

I looked at the index cards Claudia had prepared for me, and began my official speech:

"Invited guests, welcome to "The Second Annual Macabee Potluck Poetry Slam." We have thirteen presenters and room for several more if anyone decides to ~~shuck~~ share a poem at the last moment. Some of the poems you'll hear are old and famous and some are new and made up. I welcome you with the weeds of Shel Silverstein."

"Not weeds! Words!" Louise said. She couldn't help herself. I sighed. "Yes, words. Words."

"If you are a dreamer a wisher a liar
A hoper a pray-er a magic-bean-buyer...
Come in!
Come in!"

I bowed to more applause. Then, for the first time ever, I read a poem I wrote myself.

"Everyone, I'll go first. I wrote this poem on my own. It's called *Family, Friends and How Poetry Saved Me*. It's a little ~~lap~~ long so I hope you don't mind."

I unfolded the sheet of paper Claudia had typed out in over-sized letters, and I cleared my throat. I'd practiced a hundred times and I was sure I could recite this without a mistake:

"Oh to seek a word that's gone
I'm like a car without a horn.
I used to blab without a thought
But now I talk and sometimes not.
I had a stroke but no complaint
I recovered even though my words are faint.
I had to learn to use my arm
And leg and head and still stay calm.
That part I've done but still I mess up
And say saucer when I mean cup.
For someone like me, a fan of words
It's a trick of fate, my words absurd.
But do I care? Not really no,
I'm healthy again and ready to go!
Life gets rough from time to time
But who among us would think to whine
If you have poems and family and good friends
Who have your back right to the end.

So thank you for coming, I like you a lot
And now let's eat, while the food's still hot."

I got huge applause, even from the little kids.

In the two hours that followed, sixteen people read their poems: three originals including mine and thirteen others by the likes of John Keats, Robert Frost, T.S. Elliott, Maya Angelou, and Mary Oliver. When the ~~presents~~ presentations were over, Cole stood up and hugged me.

"My sisters and I are very proud of our mom," he said. "From day one, she's inspired us to keep up with her. Well done, Mom. We can't wait to see what you do next. And we're sorry that John Denver's not around to keep you company."

"My fantasy husband, everyone," I explained. "Until his plane crashed."

Ask me what I took away from this special night, and I'll tell you this: I learned I have a zest for life that can't be ~~smooched~~ smothered; that I've made ~~magnets~~ mistakes but so what? And I learned that anything can succeed as long as there's free food.

101

Cole

A few months after Mom's poetry slam, a strange letter appeared in my mailbox. The envelope had gold embossing on its flap and a return address from Suffolk University. I was sure it was junk mail, probably an offer of a free dinner in exchange for a ninety-minute sales pitch from a retirement planner. I tossed the envelope on the kitchen counter and forgot about it until later that night. I was right and wrong: it was invitation but not a sales pitch.

> You are cordially invited
> to the graduation ceremony
> for the Class of 2006
> May Twentieth, 2006
> Government Center Plaza
> Boston MA
> Reception for the School
> of Arts and Sciences to Follow

At the bottom in scrawly, childlike wide letters: *Hi Cole, I hope you and Aunt Louise can make it. Love Tiffany.*

I called Aunt Louise the next morning. She answered the phone with Loretta Lynn singing in the background. Right away her voice rose three octaves. "Why are you calling me, Cole? What happened? Is it your mother?"

"No, no," I said, "nothing's wrong." I willed my voice to sound lighter than I normally speak. "How are you, Aunt Louise?"

"I'm fine, Cole, but don't mess with me. You never call. There has to be something wrong."

Her wheels were turning. "Oh, how rude of me," she said. "On second thought, are you inviting your mother and me to visit again? By the way, do you still see Andy? Does he still cook?"

"Andy moved to Kansas City, Auntie; he got married and got a new job."

Aunt Louise snapped to attention. "Married? To a woman? No kidding."

"No, not to a woman. *To a man.*" Triple emphasis in my delivery.

"Oh."

"So, Auntie, here's why I'm calling. Did you get an invitation to a graduation at Suffolk?"

"Why yes, dear, from Tiffany."

"Tiffany from the Club Café?"

"Of course. Do you know any other Tiffany?"

"Aunt Louise, I really don't know *this* Tiffany."

"Well, of course you do, Cole. You introduced us!"

"You don't think it's a little strange she's inviting us to her graduation?"

"Speak for yourself, Cole. I've invested in the last two years of Tiffany's college education. I'm excited to see her graduate."

"What?" I was flabbergasted. "You mean you've given her money?"

"No, Cole, I paid for tuition and books directly. Not that it's any of your business."

"Aunt Louise...I'm not sure you know enough about Tiffany." I tried to be delicate.

"Well stop right there, I didn't know a thing about you when I started buying you clothes when you were a month old with a little dinky, and you turned out all right."

It was obvious that I risked walking on my aunt's eggshells so I chose my words carefully. "How can I say this...? Tiffany has a history."

"So? Everyone breathing has a history. Cole Macabee, what makes you think you're so smart? If you took the time, you'd know that Tiffany is a very good and hardworking person. She has no help and she works sixty hours a week and even then, most of it goes to rent. Maybe you're not as smart as you think. Here she's been right under your nose and I know more about her than you do." And for good measure, "I don't see you helping someone who's trying to help themselves."

Aunt Louise was on a roll. I was ready to apologize, but she kept talking. "So now that that's out of the way, will you take me to the graduation?"

"Yes."

"Oh good."

"And I'll buy dinner," I added, mostly from guilt.

"No," my aunt countered, "I'm buying. I'll make reservations at the Parker House and we'll take Tiffany. I'll ask them if we can sit in the seat where John Kennedy proposed to Jackie."

"You're surprising me, Auntie."

"Good. That's good. Your mother likes poems. Myself, I like surprises."

"Aunt Louise, can I ask you something?"

"Yes, of course," she said, her tone now dripping with innocence.

"How often are you in touch with Tiffany?"

"Every week, usually."

"You helped her finish college? And she's landing on her feet?"

"Maybe. All I know is she needed an aunt. And I happened to qualify."

102

A Boston landmark since 1855 and under new ownership, the Parker House changed its name to the Omni Parker House with strong objection from Aunt Louise, who steadfastly refused to acknowledge the corporate sound of it. Just like she said she would, she secured a reservation at John and Jackie Kennedy's engagement table and special-ordered a two-layer vanilla cake with vanilla frosting and a black graduation cap on top and green lettering that read, *Best Wishes Dear Tiffany.*

"The green lettering is for the color of money," she explained. "So Tiffany will be able to earn more than that measly minimum wage."

I didn't correct her that some nights at the Boston-based Club Café, she probably pulled in $200-$300 in tips, nor did I mention the cumulative costs of her funk-filled eclectic wardrobe: jangles and hoop earrings, high-top leather shoes and boots, plaid and swirled miniskirts, and sexy see-through silk blouses with silk camisoles underneath. In my mind, Tiffany didn't suffer to the degree ascertained by Aunt Louise, but it was true that I had assessed her traditional career prospects as dim, and it seemed my bossy aunt was somehow determined to turn that around.

The graduation ceremony was ninety minutes of forgetta-ble speeches punctuated by one slightly inspiring one by Barney

Frank, an openly gay United States congressman who spoke about equal rights but talked too long. When Tiffany's name was called and she crossed the stage for her diploma, Aunt Louise stood up and blew into a one-foot whistle she'd bought for the occasion. The sound was so ear-piercing that people several rows in front and behind us turned toward her, startled, and a few people openly scowled and covered their ears. Aunt Louise flipped off their reactions with her white gloved hand, as if nothing was more important than acknowledging Tiffany's achievement. After all the degrees were presented, a gaggle of graduates tossed their hats high in the air and in their red floor-length gowns, they marched en masse toward the podium. At six foot two, Tiffany towered, and we saw her pump her fist into the air. Aunt Louise blew her whistle again, and the people around us reacted again. My aunt didn't seem to notice. I wanted to sink into my seat, but instead I just smiled and fist-pumped toward the stage.

We'd arranged to meet Tiffany at the Arts and Sciences tent, have a celebratory drink there, and then head to the Parker House. We spotted her near the serve-yourself table.

"Yoo hoo, Tiffany!" my aunt shouted at her. She was talking to a tall and slightly overweight African American man with a closely-trimmed mustache. He wore one of those tropical island straw hats and a light beige suit. They were deep in conversation and the man had his arm on Tiffany's shoulder. When she saw us, she shouted back.

"Here, here we are!" She ran up to Aunt Louise and hugged her. "I did it, Aunt Louise. I did it."

"You certainly did, Tiffany. Cole and I are so proud of you." She elbowed me.

"Yes," I nodded. "We sure are."

Tiffany turned to the man who now stood behind her. "Oh, how rude of me. Aunt Louise and Cole, this is my Uncle Harold.

He drove down from Maine this morning to surprise me for my graduation." She paused before continuing. "Uncle Harold is my only family."

Aunt Louise elbowed me again. If she was surprised, she didn't show it.

"And us too, dear," she said. "We're your adopted family. Hello, Uncle Harold," my aunt added, "we're pleased to make your acquaintance." She held out her hand and insisted he reciprocate. "Will you be joining us for lunch?"

"Oh, thank you, no," he said. "I don't intend to crash the party. I just thought...I wasn't sure anyone else would be here and I thought Tiffany should have family present for this big event."

Tiffany looked sheepish. "I didn't tell him about you, Aunt Louise. Until this morning."

"No matter. You must join us, Uncle Harold. Please." I wondered when my Aunt Louise learned to sound so sincere.

"Well..." Harold hesitated.

"As my guest. I've taken care of all the arrangements. There is no problem adding an extra seat. And if the occasion's not enough, we will be sitting in the same spot where Jack Kennedy proposed to Jacqueline."

Harold grinned and then bowed. He took Aunt Louise's hand and properly kissed it. "In her accolades about you, Louise; may I call you Louise? Tiffany failed to mention your charm. I am pleased to accept your invitation."

Aunt Louise primped like a peacock. She pursed her lips together and straightened her already straight posture.

The Parker House didn't disappoint. We had a grand brunch, five-star buffet style: toasted baguettes, strawberry parfaits, eggs Benedict, German apple pancakes, Canadian bacon, and corned beef hash. Tiffany beamed and Aunt Louise blushed. When we were almost finished, Uncle Harold motioned to Aunt Louise. "Louise, may I have a moment with you?"

"Of course." She waved a finger at Tiffany and me, "Keep talking, you two. Uncle Harold and I will be back in a jiff."

I watched them walk toward the lobby. Harold's hand rested on the small of my aunt's back. When they returned, his hand was on the bend of her elbow, guiding her back to our table. While we enjoyed slices of Tiffany's graduation cake, I noticed that my aunt squared up a bill of a hundred and seventy-six dollars and change. I also noticed that Uncle Harold winked at her when we were all saying goodbye. When she and I drove back to Waltham, we mostly chatted about Tiffany's future. But about ten minutes from her house I brought up the surprise of the day. "Harold seems to like you, Aunt Louise."

"And?" she responded.

"And, do you like him?"

"Perhaps." Then for good measure she added, "I never jump into anything, Cole. You may be sure of that." She fiddled with her hands before clasping them firmly in her lap. She smiled. "He did invite me to accompany him to the horse track."

My eyes widened. A racetrack? Gambling? No way.

"What did you tell him?"

"I said, 'Perhaps.' And I said thank you."

Then, her conniving wheels turning, "Cole, I put up with years of that John Denver. Surely your mother can find it in her schedule to come to a horse race with me."

103

Christine

Three weeks later, Harold Heins, owner, president, and CEO of the American Whoopie Pie Company in Portland, Maine, arrived at my house in a 2005 Bentley limousine, complete with a chauffeur. His wiry black-gray hair was due for a ~~trick~~ trim if not a radical cut but his mustache was neat and he looked slightly dignified. He wore brown corduroy ~~paws~~ pants and an L.L. Bean beige overcoat with a dark brown corduroy collar that had seen better days. His ~~drone~~ dress shoes were scuffed.

Harold and his driver took Louise and me to the Suffolk Downs Racetrack and, despite our objections, he ~~faked~~ funded our losing bets for the better part of a long afternoon.

"You saw something in my nephew I didn't think was possible," Harold told Louise. "I couldn't bring myself to accept Thomas as a woman, even though I personally understand family and societal rejection. My mother was an American Negro and she married my Caucasian father, who happened to be born into the upper-class Heins family. Mother and I fit in only because of her sheer willpower and because my father had financial means. Thomas, who is now Tiffany, is the son, now daughter, of my brother Thaddeus and his wife LaShaya, who, by some twist of

fate, was also a Negro. Thaddeus turned out to be a terrible husband and he divorced LaShaya when Thomas was still a child.
LaShaya died without knowing Thomas had become a woman.
It was something so implausible and unexpected, even to me.
The rest of the family would have nothing to do with Tiffany,
and I must admit she and I kept in touch only through Christmas
cards. But when I received that invitation—a college graduation,
I couldn't let such an occasion pass with her all alone. I wasn't
sure how I'd react at first, but finally, I'm just happy for her."

Harold's eyes twinkled at Louise, who looked at him with
uncharacteristic intrigue.

I just about fell over when I heard what he said next.

"Madam, despite my unworthiness for a woman as cultured
and lovely as you, perhaps you might see something in me as well?"

Even I blushed at that. In all our years, I had never seen
Louise actually look bashful, but it was momentary. She lifted
her eyebrows and coyly brought her right hand to her right cheek.
"Mr. Harold Heins, you certainly know how to compliment an
older woman."

"Older?" Harold said. "Surely you mean elegant. And
majestic."

Louise straightened her posture for the umpteenth time.
"Harold, why don't you come to Christine's for pot roast next
Sunday?"

He looked at me and I nodded. "It would be my pleasure,"
Harold said. "I'll bring wine and flowers. May I bring anything
else?"

"Yes," Louise said. "Bring a few of your shirts. I'll iron them
for you. And bring those shoes. I have polish."

In two short months, Harold became a regular ~~flower~~ fixture in
our family. He fawned over Louise, brought her Whitman's cara-

mel chocolates, sent her ~~flan~~ flowers every week, and even accompanied her to Sunday Mass. They spent Sunday afternoons at my house for dinner. His appearance had improved considerably under my sister's tutelage. They went to the L.L. Bean flagship store in Freeport, Maine and left with a ~~closet~~ wardrobe fit for a debonair sportsman and business executive: cords and khakis, flannel and cotton checked shirts, and several colors of pullover sweaters in solids or a combination of blue, green and red colors.

Louise made sure Harold's shoes were ~~pumped~~ polished and he began sporting a new L.L Bean rain and car coat with the same chocolate-brown corduroy collar. He was smitten with my sister and with her attention to detail. For her part, the features on Louise's face and the angle of her shoulders mysteriously and noticeably softened. She and Harold went bowling, attended concerts, dined at the Pillar House, and without fail, they ~~inverted~~ invited me along. A lot of the time I declined, but the effort increased my affection for Harold. For the first time ever, except for that year at the convent, I was losing my sister, but in another way, with the kids ~~grouched~~ grown, I was becoming untethered; after almost sixty years of reliance on Louise's quirky brand of common sense, I'd be making my own decisions.

Maybe.

104

2007

Driving himself, Harold appeared unannounced at my house at nine o'clock on a bright October Saturday morning. The fall landscape was ~~glued~~ glittered with gold hues. From my dining room window, I watched him walk from the driveway to my back door, shuffling his feet through inches of fallen ~~lilacs~~ leaves, kicking them aside with each step. He knocked and then waved at me through the window. I put down my coffee cup and waved back.

"Come in, Harold. This is a surprise," I said. "Is everything all right?"

"Oh yes, Christine, certainly everything is all right. Am I disturbing you?"

"No, not at all. Coffee?"

"If it's no trouble."

Harold sat down, staring at my mess of paints and brushes scattered all over the table.

"You're painting?"

"Yes, I'm taking a class on Tuesday and Thursday mornings at the community center. I'm trying to paint landscapes that ~~mooch~~ match John Denver's songs."

"I met him a couple of times," Harold said.

"What? Harold, are you kidding me?"

"No, I'm not kidding. I was sponsoring a Wildlife Forum in Colorado many years ago. He was on the board of directors, as was I. I never heard him sing, but he spoke very well."

"Harold, my God, he's my hero. Did you know that?"

"No, I didn't."

"What was he like?"

"He drank a little too much. That's what I remember about him. He was very smart and very committed to our project for endangered eagles, but he looked like someone having a difficult time in life. At the dinner banquet, I sat beside him, and I can say he drank too much."

"What were his hands like?"

"I didn't notice that, Christine. But even drinking, he certainly made a better presentation than me." Harold smiled. I had a feeling he had something important to discuss with me, but he wasn't going to rush it. "I think I have some photographs of him from the conference. I can look for them."

"Oh please, Harold. I would absolutely love that."

"Yes, of course. I certainly will." Harold cleared his throat, squirming and fidgeting like he was taking a final exam.

"What is it, Harold? I got so ~~finished~~ flustered about John Denver I almost forgot. You must be here this morning for some reason."

He pushed his reply out. "Christine, you may have noticed that I am very fond of your dear sister."

"Yes, Harold, I've noticed."

"Well, I wondered if you might approve, um, how you would feel, if I were to ask for her hand in marriage?"

"I would say you're in for a snowstorm of high maintenance."

"What?"

"Oh, I don't mean a snowstorm. Forgive me, since that stroke I have trouble with my words. I'm just saying she's a foot-full." I leaned forward and we both laughed. "Harold, we would be very pleased to have you in our family. You have my blessing, if that's what you're here for."

"If she should give me the honor of acceptance, I should like to plan a honeymoon in Bali. Louise said she used to read about the faraway island of Bali when you were children."

I nodded. "True."

"Would you accompany us, Christine? I know Louise would like that."

"Bali? Heck no. I can't be that far away. But it sounds wonderful, Harold. Just don't be surprised if Louise prefers a weekend in Maine." I smiled. "And if it's Maine, yes, I'll accompany you to Maine." I paused. "But Harold, all these fancy limousines and flowers and now mention of an exotic honeymoon. I don't mean to ~~primp~~ pry, but can you afford all this? I don't want you headed to the ~~outhouse~~ poorhouse because you're smitten."

Harold nodded. "Christine, my American Whoopie Pie Company is the biggest maker of whoopie pies in North America, and I've benefited greatly from the success of my father and grandfather. Money will never be a problem. As a matter of fact, if you decide you want to take painting or poetry lessons full time, I can easily arrange that."

I thought for a moment. "Harold, I'm happy for you. My only complaint is that you didn't show up while John Denver was alive."

"I'll get you photos," he winked.

105

I didn't expect a frantic knock at my door at 9:30 on a chilly night, and I certainly didn't expect the caller to be my soon-to-be married sister, who kept yelling my name and rat-a-tatting at least a dozen frantic knocks.

"Christine! Christine! Open the damn door!"

Thinking the worst, I flew off the couch and there stood Louise, her hair in curlers, her leopard-colored chenille bathrobe dragging beneath her coat. Was the wedding off? Did Harold back out? It was thirty minutes past Louise's standard bedtime, and I knew instantly by looking at her that she was here for a very serious reason.

"My God, Louise, what's happened?"

Maintaining her perfect posture, her eyes darted past me and she shook her head, pushed herself inside, and headed for her favorite chair in my living room.

"I need help," she looked pathetic. "I can't marry Harold until I know what to do."

"Louise, the wedding's in two days. What to do about what?"

Louise lowered her voice, "The marital bed..."

"What?" I was flabbergasted. "Louise, what the heck are you talking about?"

She straightened her posture, keeping her feet perfectly aligned, and looked straight sat me. "I have no experience." Her voice dropped an octave. Except for when I had my stroke, I had never seen my overconfident sister look this scared.

"What is it, Louise? Tell me."

She let out a giant sigh. "Christine, whatever Harold may expect of me on our wedding night, I am skill-less."

"Skill-less?" I had to process that word for a moment. What did it even mean?

Louise's fear turned to impatience. "Christine, I need to know what's expected on my wedding night." And, to be sure I understood, she added, "In the bedroom."

"Oh my God, Louise, are you worried about having sex?"

"Shhh," she commanded, as if there was anyone else around to hear me. "I prefer to call it marital relations," she said. "But yes, I have no idea what to do or how to do it or when to do it or if to do it."

I couldn't stop laughing. Just the image of Louise fumbling around was comical enough. But to turn to me of all people was downright hilarious.

"You're asking me?! Me, who's been celibate for twenty-some years?"

"For God's sake, who else would I ask, Christine? You had a wedding night. Just tell me what you did." Louise paused. "And it might be good to know what you didn't do."

My competent, confident, opinionated sister looked like she might crumble right in front of me. I had to help her, and I knew I had to be very specific.

"Well, for starts, have you ever seen a man's penis?"

She scrunched her nose. "Never! Well, except for Cole, but a baby dinky doesn't count."

"But you've seen pictures, yes?"

"Yes, this morning," she said sheepishly.

"And you know that when Harold is excited, it will be erect?"

"Yes." She squirmed.

I had to think about what next to say. "Okay, Louise, think about it in two parts. Part one: you wrap your fingers around Harold's penis and you move your hand up and down, start gently but then tighten your grip. I'm pretty sure men like that."

Louise made a face. "Then what?"

"Then, if I remember right, he'll be ready to go inside you." Before she could respond, I added, "Oh, I forgot about breasts. He will probably…"

Louise cut me off. "Never mind that part," she insisted. "I know about that." She smiled sneakily. "But be specific about the other part, Christine. What should I be doing at that point?"

"You open your legs and maybe help him to put his penis into your vagina."

"Dear God," Louise moaned. By now her face was pure white.

"You might like it, Louise. You might even love it."

She ignored me. "Then what?"

"Then Harold will thrust his hips back and forth, and maybe you will too. And then, most likely, he'll have an orgasm. With Jimmy, I always made sure there was a box of Kleenex next to the bed, because semen is sticky."

My poor sister. I thought she might faint. "How often will Harold expect this?" she asked.

"I have no idea. He's of a certain age," I shrugged. "Maybe once a week? I suppose it's also possible he may not be interested at all, or might not even be able to have sex. I'm not the one to ask. You'll know soon enough."

At that, Louise's eyes widened, and she clasped her hands together. "Oh, that would be nice," she said. "That possibility never occurred to me."

"Louise, relax. You and Harold are going to stand before God and family and friends and vow to love and honor one another, and we are all going to have a big celebration with wonderful food. Whatever comes next, don't worry about it."

"I can't let him see me naked," Louise said.

"That's fine," I answered. "You can take off your nightgown once you're in bed. And who knows, maybe Harold will wear pajamas to bed. He might be as nervous as you."

"Trust in God but tie up your camel," Louise mumbled to herself.

"Oh my God, Louise, the last time you said that I was married to Norman!"

"Well," she answered, "it's good to plan."

"Not always, Louise. Sometimes it's good to just let things rip. Besides, you know Harold isn't going to spring anything on you that makes you uncomfortable. Maybe you two should have a couple of Manhattans and talk about this before you sleep together."

"Never!" Louise replied. "I would never bring up such a subject."

"Well, then," I replied, "Wait to worry. That's my two cents."

Louise nodded. "Does it hurt?" she asked.

"It might," I said. "I really don't know. You're asking the wrong person. It was years ago for me. But I don't see Harold hurting you under any circumstances."

"At least I can't get pregnant," Louise said.

"Oh Louise, maybe that's why you should trust in God but tie up your camel."

She paused for a second, and we both laughed so hard.

106

Cole

My sixty-four-year-old aunt met with the officiating priest twice before the wedding ceremony and asked for absolution for putting itching powder in Sister Theresa's underwear (she apparently couldn't say the word bra) and for calling her parents offensive names when they drank too much. Father Brennan asked if she had any recent transgressions to absolve, for example, in the past fifty years.

"No," she said emphatically. "I have led an exemplary Christian life."

Apparently, the priest just smiled. "So it will be," he said.

My holier-than-thou aunt described this exchange over Sunday dinner with all seriousness. I tried really hard not to laugh.

The wedding was held on the fourth Saturday of November at the Cathedral of Immaculate Conception in downtown Portland, Maine, a sanctuary church that sheltered more than a thousand Somalian refugees. Because Harold was on the church board and served as a vice president of Catholic Charities, these charitable endeavors and his whoopie pie company made him well regarded in the Portland community. He arranged for our whole family and a number of local guests to stay the weekend at the Black Point Inn in Scarborough, a four-star hotel built in 1878 and over the years host to rail barons, political leaders and one of Maine's most famous native sons, world-renowned artist Winslow Homer. It was barely thirty minutes from downtown Portland and surrounded by beaches on three sides. The view of Maine's rugged coastline was spectacular.

Besides my family and a few local dignitaries, the guest list was a mishmash of characters: Tiffany brought her 'friend' Rodney LaRue, a class B drag queen on the Providence, Rhode Island performance circuit; I brought Anthony Lopez; and Claudia brought all the Brimfields. The Portland mayor and two city council members were in the wedding party, and Aunt Louise had made arrangements for Thelma LaVash and Bertha Budd, her city hall co-workers, to stay the weekend. Bertha was African American, to Harold's delight, and during the reception, she flirted with Harold's best friend and best man, Harry Cooms, a disheveled, retired attorney whose scruffiness and likely alcoholism made him look like the titular character from *The Old Man and the Sea*.

A last minute and very surprise guest was Tiffany's father, Thaddeus, who arrived with a twenty-something girlfriend. Despite Harold's good intention in inviting him, Thaddeus showed no interest or affection toward Tiffany, and after a perfunctory and very awkward hug, he avoided her all together. This was fine with Tiffany, who went out of her way to stick it to her father by drooling over Rodney LaRue. No one gave a thought that my grandfather—my mom's father, who was still drinking his life away, wasn't on the guest list.

Bridesmaids Tiffany, Claudia, and Emily entered the church first, followed by my maid of honor mother. Petunia Brimfield threw rose petals along the red carpet as Aunt Louise and Harold walked arm-in-arm toward the altar while the church organist played Mendelssohn's "Wedding March." There was a slight delay in the exchange of wedding vows while Harry Cooms just about pulled his tux apart before he finally remembered where he'd put the rings, but all in all it was a touching ceremony of happy cheers and happy tears. To my surprise, as the guests headed back to their cars, I found Tiffany crying at the back of the church.

"I wish my mother was here to see this," she said.

Taken aback, I realized how little I knew about her. Even Thaddeus was a surprise.

"What happened to her, Tiffany? I'm sorry I've never asked you."

"She died almost ten years ago. She came upon hard times. After my horrid father divorced her, the Heins family rejected both of us. She died of cancer, two hours before I made it back home to see her. No family except Uncle Harold and me were at her funeral. But it's all turned out good. I don't give a fuck anymore. My life is full."

"Is it weird that your father's here?"

"Nah," Tiffany said. "He can drop dead on top of the wedding cake for all I care."

107

Cole

All weekend at the Black Point Inn, Mom and I kept an eye on one another. I worried about how she'd adjust without Aunt Louise's ever-constant presence, and she worried about me drinking again. Whenever I approached the bar or motioned to the wait staff, she followed me. This was nothing new: if I was going to slip, my mother was going to know it. She had gone so far as to extract a promise from Anthony that he would call her at the first hint of a problem. But her worry was misplaced: I'd been sober for almost four years and I was happy. Anthony and I were at the point of just about living together and that meant a big part of my life was settled. I had mini-celebrity status in Vermont, but it wasn't like Manhattan; there was no need to act highfalutin. A few months back I'd been recruited for a big market on-air job in Philadelphia. It was a logical career move for me and a huge ego boost, but I took one look at Harry Hennessy and it took me less than five minutes to decide to stay put.

Alcohol was no longer in my life. But on the last day of her wedding celebration, Aunt Louise cornered me between the men's room and the buffet table.

"Cole," she said, "I'm so glad you smartened up. Thank God."

I smiled. "Yes, Auntie, I have a laid-back life now, unlike yours."

"Let's not get too laid back," she said, totally missing my humor. "We don't want you to be boring, Cole, but there'll be hell to pay if you drink."

"Why are you telling me this, Auntie? Are you worried?" I probably should have been offended that my family had so little confidence in my sobriety, but I understood.

Aunt Louise straightened her posture, and her expression softened. "I have to know your mother will be happy. Especially now that I'm a married woman. I can't be worried about her."

"Okay, Auntie. Your worry-free status is safe with me."

"Oh, and another thing," she added. "Stay with Anthony. He's good for you."

I nodded. "I'll make a deal with you. You stay with Harold and I'll stay with Anthony."

Aunt Louise took a moment before responding. "Why Cole, there's no question about Harold and me. Divorce is a cardinal sin. I'm wedded for life."

I took this opportunity for an Aunt Louise teaching moment. "I'm not Catholic, Aunt Louise. But if I were, or wanted to be, the church wouldn't recognize Anthony and me as a married couple. It seems gay marriage is also a cardinal sin. Not exactly fair."

My pious, righteous, know-it-all aunt looked at me straight on. "You're right, Cole. That's wrong. The church needs to change."

108

Christine

Louise did her best to accept the wealth that came with Harold, but the two-carat, pear-shaped diamond ring he put on her finger was too much for her. When she saw it for the first time, she looked aghast. I knew what that meant.

"That ring won't see the ~~lamp~~ light of day," I told the kids. I was right: once Louise got back to Waltham, she carefully placed her diamond ring in her ancient jewelry box and she wore it only on Thanksgiving, Christmas, and Easter.

"It's too heavy for my delicate finger," she explained to Harold over Sunday pot roast. I waited for his reaction. He just smiled.

109

Claudia

Walking up the brick walkway with my arms filled with grocery bags and surprises, I looked at the trimmed boxwoods that were now several feet taller than the disastrous day I went to the house with Wills. I was at his front door again, this time visiting his wife and children. I'd met his brother, even his mother; and his children and his wife were now part of my tribe.

Natalie greeted me at the door and I followed her to the kitchen, ready to prep a meal of Chicken Francaise on angel hair pasta, salad, and, for the kids, macaroni and cheese.

"Oh my God, what a wedding that was," she said. "Your Aunt Louise is a hoot. The kids and I had the best time." She touched her heart. "It was very special, Claudia. I hope your family knows it meant a lot to us to be invited."

"Are you kidding? We loved that you came. But you have to appreciate the full history of my prim and proper Aunt Louise finally getting married, at her age no less. Plus, a few martinis may have influenced her, but she just about told my brother that she supports gay marriage. Not something we would have expected in a million years."

"They're a nice couple, Cole and Anthony," Natalie said. "And Harold's a character. He promised Ryan a lifetime supply of whoopie pies. He said he could mail us up to a dozen a week. I immediately intervened. I envisioned my kids and the whole neighborhood bouncing off the walls from all that sugar. If he ever sends that much, I'll politely suggest a change in delivery to once a month." Natalie and I laughed. "He's a fun addition to your family," she added.

I laughed again. "I just found out he's funding my mother's college tuition. I won't be surprised if she matriculates into a degree program. That's just as unbelievable as Aunt Louise getting married." I plopped my bags on the kitchen counter. "I brought that rose wine we like, and I made chocolate cupcakes for dessert."

"I heard that, Claudia!" A squeaky voice came rushing toward me, Petunia's feet barely touching ground. She wrapped her arms around my waist. "What else did you bring? Did you bring my doll clothes?"

"Yes, I did," I said. "I made your little Reesie a nightgown and a school outfit."

"Show me, please, where is it?"

"Wait," Natalie said. "Let Claudia get settled, for crying out loud."

Find a way to honor him, Claudia. That's what my mother told me. All along, she had it right.

The kitchen was clean, the kids were in bed, and Natalie and I were finishing off the bottle of Layer Cake.

"Mom's inviting you and the kids for Thanksgiving," I said.

Natalie looked surprised. "Thanksgiving. That's so sweet. But my sister's coming for a week. Neither of us wants to travel to our parents, and they've already let us know they're staying put."

"Your sister's invited too. If you want to come, it's pretty fun. But honestly, no pressure."

Natalie shook her head. "This is unreal. Emily's right that we should be on *Oprah*. Now we're talking about the kids and me with you and your family for Thanksgiving? How in holy hell has it turned out this way?" And then, with a sigh and sadness, "Do you ever wonder what Will would think of this?"

This was the first time we talked about Wills as a shared experience. It felt both natural and surreal.

"All the time," I said, pausing. "Natalie, I know there will always be some line that neither of us should cross, about what we share and how we feel about him, and I'm never quite sure where that line is. But it's gotten a lot easier. It was my crazy dream to have our families merge. I hope you don't take offense to that. It was a fantasy, but I always knew there was no other way he could ever be at peace, so I had this crazy hope and I held on to it. Except the part about Wills not being a part of it never entered my mind."

Even as I said this, I questioned if we could have made any of this work if Wills were still alive. I was pretty sure Natalie and I could never have ever figured out how to share him. For one thing, he and I were too intense.

Natalie's eyes deepened. "I'm not offended. But if Will was here, I don't think he and I would still be together. I'm just being honest. We had twelve mostly great years. I doubt I could or would have accepted you or anyone else. And back then, my fantasy was to push you down the cellar stairs and not look back."

I let a faint smile emerge. "God has his or her own way of creating bonds," Natalie said. "Polygamy has never been my cup of tea, but if it were, chances are I would have liked you. Maybe if we lived in Utah." She smiled.

I thought about that for a moment. "Natalie, do you think it's strange that neither of us dates?"

"Not for me. Not until the kids are older." She shook her head, "Plus, I'm too busy to be lonely."

I nodded. "My mother never dated after my father died. Not once."

Natalie nodded too. "I think kids benefit from their home life staying the same, even if there's a missing piece in it. Will was devoted to the kids and their memories as a family are good. I want to preserve that for them. But Claudia, I do hope I'll love someone again someday. Don't you?"

I shook my head. "I don't know. I don't think so. Emily keeps asking me. I've dated here and there. But honestly, besides for the sex, I find most men pretty boring. Is it me? My brother isn't boring."

Natalie laughed. "Your brother's gay! Gay men are definitely more interesting."

"That's true," I laughed too. "But do I want a real relationship? I don't even know. I know I should be open. But I'm not ready either."

The honesty of this conversation surprised me. "I can't believe I can even talk to you about this."

"Same here. But we're friends now, Claudia."

Maybe the empty bottle of Layer Cake had something to do with it, but in some crazy, inexplicable way, in this moment, my love for Wills felt complete. My smart mother and some force in the universe made something so wrong as right as it could be.

"Natalie, you and the kids mean a lot to me. And don't think I don't appreciate how gracious and generous you are."

"I'm glad too," Natalie said. "And Thanksgiving, yes, we'd love to come."

110

2009

Emily and I were at our table at Casa Mexico, drinking and nibbling as usual.

"Wills' been gone five years on Saturday, Em. Natalie's having a cookout. Want to come? The kids release helium balloons every year on his anniversary."

Emily thought for a moment. "I can't. I have a baby shower to go to. But I'm so glad how it's worked out for you, Claudia. They're a nice family. And it's nice to have kids around."

I pounced. "Speaking of kids, what's happening with you and Brett?"

"It's not happening, Claudia. We're trying, but apparently there's a problem with Brett's sperm."

"That sucks. Would you adopt? If it came to that?"

Emily looked uncomfortable. "We could, maybe, but we're not ready. It's a touchy subject for us. Mom asked me about it last week and I asked her to hold off questioning us for now. We're stressed about it and we don't want to be."

"I understand. I do. I'll try to behave. Matter of fact, I'll change the subject. Do you ever think about Daddy?"

Emily shrugged. "Not really. Why do you ask?"

"Wills' daughter Zoie was ten when he died. A whole different circumstance than when Daddy died, that's for sure, but it makes me kind of sad that she has such a wonderful memory of her father and we have, what, pretty much nothing..."

Emily looked perplexed. "Do you think Daddy was really, really bad? I remember crying for days when he died, but I'm not sure why, because I hardly remember him."

"Yeah, I think he was really, really bad. I mean, we probably don't know the half of it because Mom kept things pretty normal. He's mostly a blur for me too. Sometimes we watched television with him, do you remember that? But can you say anything we did as a family? And can you even picture him and Mom together? I can't."

"I can't either," Emily answered. "I wonder what she remembers, if she actually has good memories of their marriage. It's sad if Mom never had real love."

I'd asked my mother that very question a few years back.

"Marrying your father should have been everything I ever wanted," she answered, "but for some reason he had trouble growing up, so he drank. There was a time when I loved him a lot. We loved each other, and we had such high hopes for our life together, but over the years, his drinking got too hard, for all of us. I'm sorry about that, Claudia, that you kids missed out on a father. But I'm not sorry I missed out on a husband. I've never felt alone: you kids and your Aunt Louise made sure of that."

Emily shook her head. "I hope she doesn't think she let us down. She created good memories for us, and the older I get, the more I believe that life is as much about memories as it is about living actual moments. But we did get cheated in the father department, and Daddy got cheated in the kid department. I wonder if he ever knew that. Or if he even cared."

"I doubt he cared," I said. "You can see from Cole, how the alcohol grips you and nothing else matters. I'd say the worst of Daddy's drinking is how much it hurt Cole."

"I agree," Emily sighed. "And now here's you and me, enjoying our nachos and margaritas, and Cole's happy as a clam, and all three of us are reasonably well-adjusted adults. We ended up pretty normal."

I laughed, "We're really not that normal. How many kids have fathers who have a car fall on them and die? Or have a brother who's on television? Or a mother who's a John Denver groupie?"

My sister laughed too. "My opinion is that everyone has weird parts of life, and some that aren't easy. But in our case, Mom gave us assurances, and we stupidly or brilliantly believed her. Like her emphasis on poems and the importance of having supper together: we just accepted all that. She kept things very simple and secure for us: I think it cut out a lot of stress. I know it did for me."

"That's a good point," I said. "My therapist pushes me to deal with my childhood, but I'm not interested. I just want to be okay day-to-day. My biggest goals aren't even about me. I don't want Mom to be lonely, I want Cole to stay sober, and I want you and Brett to you-know-what."

Emily ignored that last part. "I think Cole's okay and Mom seems happy. I can't believe she's teaching herself to paint, she goes to the senior center twice a week, and lately she's writing poems that don't even rhyme: they're still corny, but now they're deeper. She has her friends from the plant, and Marla Sacks knocks on her door for coffee just about every day. I don't know what Aunt Louise marrying Harold will mean in the long run, but so far, the only thing that's changed for Mom is her new hobbies. And as for Cole, Anthony's a good influence on him. He's as good for our family as Brett is."

I forced a smile. "Sounds like that just leaves me."

Emily raised her glass. "Yes, it does. Claudia, Brett fell out of the sky for me. I'm not saying you'll ever have what you had with Wills, but life can surprise you. Like it did for me. Don't be closed."

I laughed. "When Mom gets married, I will too."

"Don't count on that! But stay open. Visualize a good guy. It can happen."

I let out a breath. "Don't be mad at me, Em, but I gotta tell you, if there's a happy ending for Mom, and a happy ending for Aunt Louise, and a happy ending for Cole, and you're encouraging me to be open to a happy ending, then please forgive me for hammering home what you told me not to mention, just ten minutes ago. Do us all a favor, and one way or another, have a baby."

111

Christine
2010

It was ~~licking~~ lining up to be a great Thanksgiving. Everyone was coming, even the Brimfields. My kids were all okay. My sister was happily married, and for the first time in my life, I was peacefully left with my poems and my kitchen. I was writing out my dinner-for-thirteen grocery list when the phone rang. I didn't recognize the voice at first.

"Christine? It's Alma. From the plant."

"Alma! How are you? How's everybody?"

"I have bad news."

"What?"

"Mr. Irving. He died last night."

"What? Oh no."

"His daughter called Alan in sales this morning. She asked for your phone number. She wants to know if you'll speak at his service."

"Me?"

"Yup."

The cleaning crew found Mr. Irving slumped face down on his work ~~dump~~ desk, his arms hanging limp by his side, papers and green file folders scattered all around him. He apparently had a heart attack. His daughter Annette told me he left his house to her, and he left his savings and life insurance to the New England Home for Little Wanderers. In his will, he requested that I speak at his funeral on behalf of the company.

None of us had ever met Annette. I imagined her to be an eccentric, bright woman, dignified, and bereft at losing her father. When she greeted me at the synagogue, I recognized her immediately by her ~~nick~~ nose: it looked exactly like Mr. Irving's. But I was genuinely surprised that she was just as frumpy as her father. She was dressed in a musty, olive-green pantsuit—that same awful green, accessorized with a faded navy-blue silk scarf. Her jet-black shoulder length hair needed a cut. And worst of all, her fingernails weren't filed and they still had traces of old pink nail polish. And not just that: she had trouble even maintaining eye contact with me.

"I'm Sol's daughter," she said. "Thank you for agreeing to speak at the service."

"I'm so sorry for your loss, Annette. Your father and I go back a long ~~wick~~ way."

"So I understand," she said.

I thought it was important to Mr. Irving's memory to connect with her, but she didn't seem capable of even small ~~tone~~ talk. I always pictured Annette the accountant—did I even know her name before now?—as an intact adult, able to give Mr. Irving something more than the monotony of his work life. Now, seeing her flat demeanor, her blotchy complexion, and her messy appearance—I wondered if she drank too much, and I wondered how she treated him.

There are no ~~anglers~~ altars in the Jewish religion and no wakes or caskets either. I stood at the front of the Holy Emanuel synagogue and read from notes that Louise helped me prepare. I wanted my speech to be error free. It was the least I could do.

"Hello everyone, my name is Christine Macabee. I worked at the plant with Mr. Irving. He was a good man and a fair boss. He didn't talk about himself but we all knew how much his daughter, Annette, and the plant meant to him. I'm sure he's resting ~~piccalilli~~, sorry, I mean peacefully in heaven or where Jewish people go when they die.

He and I worked together for so many years and he always treated me with respect; even when he had to let me go, he was nice about it. He wore a Santa hat when he gave out our Christmas turkeys and one year, I think it was 1994 because it was the year O.J. Simpson killed his wife, he gave all us girls red razors—I mean roses—for Valentine's Day. Those are things I will always remember about him. I know Standard-Thomson will never be the same without him. I'm sure he's sitting at a desk in heaven. On behalf of the company, we all extend our symphonies to his daughter Annette. May Mr. Irving rest in pieces."

A rabbi spoke after me, but from the sound of it he didn't know Mr. Irving. The whole thing was so anonymous it didn't seem fair. At the end of the service, I looked around at all the Standard-Thomson employees heading toward the front door, and for the first time I wondered who else at the plant might have the kind of loneliness Mr. Irving must have had.

Annette didn't even come close to crying that day. Maybe she was as damaged as Mr. Irving.

"Thank you for the honor of letting me represent Standard-Thomson," I told her after the service. She looked surprised by that.

"My father wasted his life there," she said.

"Oh no," I said. "The company depended on him. We had good jobs. We were able to raise our families and feel secure because of your father."

"Maybe," Annette said. "But for him it was a waste. Thank you for coming. I wish you well." And with that she turned around and walked away.

I cancelled my dinner plans with Louise and Harold that night: I had some reckoning to do with myself. Why didn't I ever invite Mr. Irving to my house for dinner, or to one of our parties, not even once? Why didn't I give him a Christmas present or a ~~curl~~ card on his birthday? A seventy-hour work week in a tattered green suit and lunch all alone day in and day out: these were signs I should have noticed. I wasn't sure what I should or could have done, but the answer wasn't turning a ~~blond~~ blind eye. *We're all just walking each other home:* I read this somewhere and it stuck with me. People weren't made to be alone. Here I'm thinking I'm Mother-of-the-Year and Citizen-of-the-Decade, but I failed to protect my son from his abusive father and I failed to notice a lonely man I saw every day for almost more than half my life.

Mr. Irving probably knew he would die alone. I was still feeling the ~~watch~~ weight of that when Claudia called and mentioned it was the six-year anniversary of William Brimfield's death. Claudia's devotion to him was as strong as ever. She was healthy again, but he was still The One. Here too, I failed to realize that he meant far more to her than an illicit affair. He was her soulmate. I was sorry I never met him. I didn't know if I would have done things differently, but at least I finally understood. And Jimmy: I watched him ~~drown~~ drink himself to death. I watched him disappoint himself, ~~tickle~~ torture my son, and ignore his children. I worked so hard trying to be perfect and trying to make poetry, meals, and devotion into the eleventh commandment. It's taken me all these years to accept my imperfect life.

112

Our family of five around the holiday table had expanded to thirteen, now including two husbands, one partner, one college graduate drag queen, one betrayed wife, and three more fatherless children. Claudia was back from the dead; Cole was sober; Tiffany, Anthony, and the Brimfields had us as their second family; and a very rich African American man who was perfectly willing to let my uppity sister dress him, used some of his stock dividends to ~~funk~~ fund my college education.

Before our big turkey dinner, we traditionally served cocktails for the adults and Shirley Temples for the kids. Normally, we'd go around the table and each of us would say what we were thankful for. But this time, Louise waited until all the drinks were poured until she rat-tat-tat tapped her glass with a ~~spool~~ spoon, and straightened her posture even more than normal.

"Harold and I have thankful news. It's also jarring news."

Claudia's eyes darted to me. Any jarring news from my sister was sure to jar me too. I acknowledged her concern with a grin and a shrug.

"After due consideration," Louise said in her church meeting ~~vice~~ voice, "Harold and I will be moving to Portland, Maine. He has responsibilities there and, as his dutiful wife, I will accompany him."

It was obvious that this was more a bombshell than a jar. After six decades in Waltham, all but one year with me, Louise was leaving. The kids stared at me again, already in protection mode. I tried to look my own version of surprise.

"When?" Emily asked.

"My apartment will go up for rent in four weeks," Aunt Louise said.

"Oh, my goodness. Mom..." Claudia turned to me.

"Mom what?" I said. "Let's take a moment and congratulate Aunt Louise and Harold for ~~fishing~~ finding love and moving to the sea, all in one big splash."

Louise interjected. "I know what you're thinking, Claudia. How could I leave your mother, after all these years, knowing how much she needs me?"

"I don't need you that much, Louise!" I said, chuckling.

Louise talked over me. "It's a legitimate point, children and guests. But perhaps my sister has an announcement of her own."

All eyes turned to me. I shrugged again. "Okay, well, okay: I guess I might be moving to Maine too."

"What the heck?" Emily's eyes widened.

"Kids, everyone, I admit Sunday dinners will probably be affected. But not birthdays or holidays, because I expect each of you to come to Maine on those occasions. Except for Cole, if he has to work. It's barely a two-hour ~~dive~~ drive. Everybody, hear this loud and clear: family dinners are not cancelled. There'll still be pot roast and mashed potatoes every Sunday and you all have an ~~opal~~ open invitation. And Harold is going to help me find a bungalow house of my own, with a perfect kitchen." I nodded toward him. "He's also helping me get the education I put off for a very long time. I'm sixty-three years old and I'm enrolling in college for real."

"You'll be moving close to us," Louise interjected. She looked at Claudia. "Your mother promised: close enough so I can still keep an eye on her."

Tiffany raised her hand. "Well, I guess I should announce that I'm moving to Maine too. To work in the office with Uncle Harold and learn the whoopie pie business."

Harold nodded. "That's right. A trainee in customer service and human resources. I'm delighted, Tiffany."

"My God, this is the end of an era," Emily said.

I'd been afraid this news might make her cry, but instead she beamed. "I'm so happy for you, Mom. And Aunt Louise. And Harold. And you too, Tiffany. Talk about a new start. You all deserve it."

I jumped on that. "It's only a new start geographically. Oh, and because I'll be a college student. But poetry, my cooking, and us loving one another isn't going to change. And because there's more of us now, there's more love to share."

Cole looked around and tapped his glass of cranberry juice and soda water. "I have an announcement too. Anthony and I are officially engaged. He's moving to Vermont full time in January."

"Whoa, Anthony!" Claudia said, "That's worth an official welcome to the family."

Anthony blushed. "Honestly, I can't think of a better family. Thank you."

A still beaming Emily cleared her throat. "So...we have news too."

Claudia squealed. "You got the promotion!"

Emily shook her head. "No, it's even better. Not because Claudia has nagged me to heaven and back, but Brett and I finally decided to adopt a baby. We made an appointment to start the process in mid-December," and then she added, "but we're canceling."

I reacted, "You're canceling?"

Emily shrugged her shoulders and grinned as wide as a person could grin. "We're pregnant!"

"Oh mercy," said Louise. "I'll be a great aunt."

Emily's news was huge. I was surprised, delighted, and chagrined, all in the span of five seconds. It took me even less than that to reconsider my move to Maine. "I have to see the baby regularly. Or I can't move." I was serious.

"Once a week. That's a firm promise," Brett said.

"Okay, whew, good, thank you Brett," I said, "Wow. Is there anything else?"

Harold raised his hand. "With all this news, I have a question. Claudia, would you like to move into your family home? No mortgage or taxes, just upkeep."

"Why, Harold? What made you think of this?"

Harold-the-businessman answered her. "It's a good investment and it keeps the property in the family." Harold-the-family-man added, "And maybe your mother can keep her old bedroom. That way, she can double up visiting you and Emily and the new baby."

Claudia looked interested. "That's a very generous offer, Harold. But I can afford the mortgage and taxes myself."

Harold grinned. "Maybe not if you start taking glorious vacations."

"Let me think about that," Claudia said. She looked at me. I tried not to let my unexpected enthusiasm overtake me, but my new brother-in-law had come up with the absolute best of all ~~words~~ worlds. My kids, Harold, Brett, Anthony, Tiffany, the Brimfields, and a grandchild!—I had it all.

There was yet another announcement: it came from sixteen-year-old Zoie. "I'm applying to the University of Vermont. I want to major in graphic design, like Claudia."

Not to be outdone, Petunia picked up her spoon and clicked the glass in front of her. "I made the honor roll and Mom says we might get a puppy."

Claudia laughed. She looked at Natalie and shook her head. "Yay Zoie and yay Petunia. Yay everyone. My announcement is that I have nothing to announce. Which for me feels lovely."

"Wow," I said. "Anyone else? No? Well then, let me tell each of you how happy I am to share our many blusters together."

"That makes no sense," Louise corrected me for the zillionth time.

"Yes, it does, Louise. We are all blust—, oops, okay, I see, you know darn well I mean our many blessings. We are *blessed*. We're living proof. I love you all. We eat in fifteen minutes and the burlap bag is ready after dinner. Get your poems ready! And let me say again that no one at this table should ever feel alone because you aren't. Look around, family and friends. *We are all what love looks like.*"

113

I was wrong.

Spoon-fed poetry, homemade chicken dinners, and lectures on devotion didn't save my children. I served those up because I wasn't sure what would happen if I didn't, and I didn't know what else to do. I wanted to believe I could shelter the kids from their father and from life, but I certainly didn't help Cole figure things out, and God only knows what led Claudia to fall in love with a married man. But I see things differently now: Cole found strength, Claudia found devotion, and Emily and Louise, of all people, found husbands.

I'm so proud of my children. Maybe I exaggerated the part about poetry and food, but I still think I got the devotion part right. I'm convinced that just one person caring and believing in you from an early age will make a huge difference in how things turn out. If I hadn't had Louise tending to me, I wouldn't have become a strong woman. I was lucky to have her on my side. Jimmy wasn't so lucky.

My family history has a trail of neglect, illness, accidental death, muggings, alcoholism, infidelity, and even abandonment. But all of these experiences, along with Sabrina and John Denver and Robert Frost, and, of course, Louise and my children, have given me a love that's bigger than the universe.

Ask me and I'll tell you that *devotion is the superpower.* Devotion is the way you never end up alone.

Epilogue

2012

These days I live in a five-room bungalow with a full-length wraparound porch and a view of Casco Bay right from my perfect kitchen. As far as I know, I'm the oldest student at the University of Southern Maine, and I have a double major in creative writing and art. My body's stiffer than a tennis racket, but I show up every day; so do my kids, and so does my now-very-rich sister. Cole just moved back to Boston to do the nightly six and eleven o'clock sports news at WBZ-TV—a dream job in his hometown, and he and Anthony are happy, just like any other couple, straight, gay or whatever. He's been pestering Claudia to meet Harry Hennessy, trying to fix them up on a blind date. Claudia has so far resisted because a few months ago, she met a guy who sends her flowers and makes her apple pies from scratch. Last week she told me she just might bring him to dinner one of these days, but not to be outdone, Cole is plotting to beat her to the punch and deliver Mr. Hennessy to our table first. This should be interesting.

Brett and Emily visit Louise and me almost every weekend with their almost-toddler, Christine Louise Butler. She runs to us with her little arms outstretched when she sees her Mimi and her

Auntie Louise. And, on the weekends when the kids don't come to Maine, Louise and I feed everyone at our family home, which is now Claudia's.

My Sunday pot roast is still on the menu, and it's still a family affair, just the way I always imagined.

My Final Exam for Twentieth Century American Poetry 201/ Professor Barnum

FOR MY KIDS
By Christine Macabee

Take both eyes, both hands,
My legs and arms,
Even take the grandmother clock
And every special book.

Take my bank account,
All forty photo albums,
My garden in August
And the miracle April rain.

Take it all if you can promise.
I knew the first moment.
I'm into any burning house,
On to a frigid raft at sea,
I'm ripping the mangled steel with my bare hands.

Anything, anything for these kids.
The edgeless corners of the truest love
And the endless reserve of cavernous protection
Surround these children who live within and without,
These fantabulous kids with crack up wits
And tender expansive hearts.

Take it all, whether you're a thief
or angel,
Whether the cost is temporary or forever,
Take it all to shelter them
Through every molecular motion and moment.

Given the chance to love like this,
The price of my sightless limbless body
And wiped clean barren possessions
Amounts to nothing more than shiny pennies,
Effortless will,
And infinite love.

BOOK CLUB DISCUSSION

1. How would you describe this book?

2. Who is your favorite character? Explain why.

3. Did the book alter your perception in any way?

4. Is there a small moment in the book that you feel could go under-appreciated?

5. What emotions did the book evoke in you?

6. Do you believe that some people are soulmates? Discuss in the context of this story.

7. Is creating an imaginary friend or an imaginary husband a source of strength or a problem that should be addressed?

8. What role does religion play in this family?

9. Does the cover successfully represent the book?

10. Would you recommend this book to others?

I'm happy and often available to participate in your book club meeting. For information, inquiry, or to schedule an appointment, I can be reached at karenjasper@comcast.net

Thanks for reading!

ALSO BY KAREN JASPER

Available through Amazon,
Barnesandnoble.com
Local Bookstores
&
Signed Copies by Special Request

ABOUT THE AUTHOR

I'm a writer, poet, and Master's Level Counselor who likes simple language to describe the common experiences and every day challenges of being human, with encouragement that there can be better days ahead. *An Imperfect Life* is my third book, and the most expansive.

I grew up in Waltham Massachusetts and attended Boston State College, the University of Southern California European Division, and Assumption College in Worcester MA. Many of my observations and stories come from a treasured career as a counselor, psychotherapist, and trainer. I currently live with my irreplaceable partner Janet and our sweet dog Mattie, in the Cape Cod paradise of Provincetown. I'm the mother of a very precious daughter, Jessica; the grandmother of four wonderful grandchildren:—Ryan, Drew, Logan, and Reese—and the mother-in-law of one great son-in-law, Mike.